WRECKING MAN

DOOMSDAY DRIFTER
BOOK 2

MARK DASILVA

CHAPTER ONE

Trusting souls rode patiently as the ferryman escorted them across the bone-chilling river. At times, the ferry drifted at an angle as the current threatened to whisk them away but strong hands by the ferryman's partner kept them on course. The passengers were a mishmash of sorts; old, young, women and men, all staring ahead with some nervously holding their hands in prayer. Others waited patiently for them on the riverbank, waving, and calling out names. When the ferry finally docked, the commuters happily disembarked in a single file passing more travelers that waited their turn to come this way. My objective was to cross the waterway too and I waited for the next sailing.

As I dipped my canteen into the Colorado River, I stared into a pool of water and barely recognized myself. I saw a reflection of a weathered man with small wisps of gray enveloped around a mass of wavy, brown hair. Whiskers on my scraggy beard grew long and shared some of the aging colors. My cheeks were thinner and my eyes looked sad, somewhat sunken, with bags under them like I hadn't slept in years. Sun darkened my skin and wrinkles were more prominent than before. I had aged, that much was clear. Five years of wandering and a lack of skin care products would do that to anyone.

After filling my canteen with my sturdy mountain bike at my side, I stood up and moved along a path to the dock. The bike had been with me for a few weeks, found next to an abandoned house on the outskirts of St. George, Utah. I made my way south from there to the river in an attempt to cross on a ferry, one of the few that operated in the area.

To my right, I could see a small line forming for the ferry crossing that would take me across. I studied both sides of the river and saw no wrongdoings. The task was innocent enough. Get you from point A to point B. There was no hustle there it seemed, no thievery, just an enterprise taking advantage of a much-needed service. The river itself looked somewhat calm, the current slower than other spots. The ferry looked to be about twenty feet long with wood planks serving as the floor and small handrails on either side. Large logs were attached underneath, halfway in the water line. A few passengers were making the trip south where my line formed. More people were going to cross with me.

I tugged on my clothes believing I still looked presentable. My black jacket was thin but kept me warm. I wore a black t-shirt underneath. My blue jeans had holes over the knees. My hiking boots were mismatched. One black, one brown. Not even the same brand. I found what I could and wore it. It wasn't like there were department or clothing stores. No discount racks or mannequins. A dead body was a potential gold mine for outdoor wear, minus the smells and stains.

A large backpack firmly held my trusty crowbar in place by an arrow quiver I stitched there. I still carried it after all these years. The backpack was green, canvas material. Army issue. Inside, essentials like clothes, knives, a small shovel, tape, bandages, water canteen, needle and thread, candles, books, a plate, canned goods, bags of sugar, condiments like salt and pepper, and some loose paper for bathroom breaks were stored. Plus, some plastic for my water-gathering ventures allowed me to capture dew each morning when an obvious water source wasn't available. Attached underneath by a string were my sleeping bag and a hammock, all neatly rolled up. I found the backpack next to a dead man two winters ago, he frozen stiff inside a mountain cave, curled in the fetal position next to a fire long burned out. His ID said he was from Atlanta, Georgia, and stationed at Fort Irwin which was northeast of Barstow, California. He was a long way from home and he wasn't good company, being dead naturally. He also didn't need the backpack anymore.

I was still searching for my family and no progress had been made. My recent jaunt into Utah was to see if my wife traveled to her cousin's house up in Salt Lake City. That wasn't the case; her cousin's family was long gone, no one knew where, and I was just as confused. I was now making my way south but heading eastward a bit to go around the vast Grand Canyon to see an old friend.

The last word I had about my family being alive was from Johnny, my wife's little brother, who admitted that little tidbit of information under duress. He knew their location but he wouldn't tell me their whereabouts no matter how hard I pleaded. Johnny Orr was a former police officer in a beach town just east of Santa Barbara and he had a grudge against me. He believed I cheated on his sister, which wasn't true. Still, the stubborn prick refused to divulge their location when I traveled to see him at his home. That was nearly a year after I last saw my wife and kids and after the gas attacks. So, five years since I saw my family, and four since I ran into my snotty brother-in-law.

I often wondered if he told my family that I came to visit. That I was still alive. I believed he did and that kept me going.

I watched the returning ferry slice through the fast current as I made my way down to the ferry dock, passing a small cabin that served as a waiting depot. Men sat on benches inside, waiting to cross or maybe ready to meet new arrivals. When I got to the dock, I noted that there were six people ahead of me in line, three men out front traveling together that reminded me of the rock group ZZ Top with full-length beards and cowboy hats. A family of three was behind them. Father, mother, daughter. They were dressed shabbily and dirty, the parents possibly in their mid-thirties. The girl was all of about ten.

Next to us but out of line was a man, a farmer type, squatting next to a cow. He held a metal cup in his hands and was squeezing the animal's teat. Milk sprayed into the cup and I had to admit, it looked damn good.

"Milk for sale!" the farmer shouted. "What will y'all give me for a cup of delicious, natural milk? You know you want it! Better than store-bought!"

That line earned a chuckle from me. Ha. *Stores.*

The small family ahead of me looked to the farmer. Their little girl licked her lips and tugged on the mother's arm.

"Please may I?" the little girl asked.

The mother nodded, dug into her pockets, and presented a watch to the farmer. She then asked, "Will you accept this watch for trade?"

"Does it work?" the farmer asked.

"Sure does. See for yourself." She tossed it to him. He studied the watch and shook it. "It's a Timex wind-up," the mother continued.

"Well, that'll do then," he answered and handed the cup to the little girl. The farmer then addressed the rest of us. "See folks? How easy it is? Who else will want delicious milk?"

"Shut up, old man," said a man brushing by who kicked the cup, sending the milk flying. "No one wants your fucking milk." The man was big, had wavy brown hair, dark eyes, a full beard, and wore a leather jacket. He smelled bad; a lingering mix of body odor and alcohol. He reminded me of a Hell's Angel biker. Behind him, another man pushed a motorcycle forward that had a large seat for two and saddle bags. He was thinner, had blond cropped hair atop a flattened face, and wore a white bomber jacket. He stunk like BO as well ut tried to cover it up with bad aftershave. Evil Knievel came to mind. Both men pushed and shoved their way to the front of the line where they were stopped by a chain. The nasty twosome waited there and ignored the groans of ZZ Top behind them. Hell's Angel took out a small jar of moonshine from one of the saddlebags and took a slug. That put me ninth in line and I hoped that would be enough to board.

The farmer, in the meantime, retrieved the cup and refilled it, offering it to the little girl once more. She drank it fully and didn't stop until it was gone.

"Delicious," she said and handed the cup back. "Thank you, sir."

"Got that right," the farmer replied, then went into his spiel once more, although he kept his voice down.

The ferry was operated by two men; an older guy with gray hair, darkened skin, and wearing a white outfit, while the other was a younger, larger man with dark curly hair, a lengthy beard, thin arms, and overalls with no shirt. The ferryman and his partner handled the craft well enough to cross without much give to the current flowing by. The older man sat on a box while his partner manned an oar. A greased, thick rope was tethered to both banks and ran through a metal slot in the raft, keeping it from floating off downriver.

The raft was my only choice to cross. Actually, that wasn't true. This one was just very convenient and I was tired from biking. Up in this part of Northern Arizona, there weren't a lot of places to traverse the cold, rushing water of the Colorado River. Bridges were few, patrolled by armed men, and difficult to cross, especially if you had little to barter. The better bet was these ferries that set up shop along the riverbanks. They were more desperate and willing to negotiate than the trolls that occupied the bridges. However, the ferrymen could be unsavory characters at times though, charging more or less due to tides, current strengths, and just plain whatever they felt like. You had to be careful. That's why I watched it first.

The older ferryman was no doubt the man in charge. After they docked and the travelers disembarked, the older man flung open his gray jacket, revealing a gun in a holster. He stood on his box and announced to us waiting in line.

"Listen up! My name is Captain and my first mate is DuPont! Now, what I say goes! You all must barter your wares to cross and what I deem worthy allows you access to cross! Should you not have anything to offer, or if said items are deemed useless to me, I'd ask you to kindly step aside until you come to me with a proper bill of fare for passage! If anyone dares to rescind their offer while traversing or attempting to rob any of the passengers, you will be shot and DuPont will toss you into the river! And yes, my gun is loaded! Any questions?"

No one spoke up.

"Good. First in line!" Captain stepped down, opened the chain, and eyed those in front. He suddenly grew sullen. A jar of moonshine was thrust hard into his gut. That was accepted right away with no negotiation, but my feeling was, the ferryman knew the men and just wanted it over with. The ruffians stepped up into the raft, hauling their motorcycle with them. DuPont steadied the boat with his oar as the raft's weight shifted.

The ZZ Top trio tried to barter kitchen utensils, which Captain said he had much of. They argued back and forth and finally acquiesced when one man hauled out a bee's honeycomb from his backpack. The slimy, delicious goo drizzled down his arm. It looked fresh, taken recently from a hive somewhere, and that was when I noticed the trader had red bumps on his neck. I hoped the effort was worth the stings he received.

"The honey is yours, Captain. Nature's candy and those medicinal qualities," said one. Captain gleefully took it and waved the threesome forward.

The family stepped up next. "What you got, folks?" Captain asked. He nibbled on part of the honeycomb and hummed his satisfaction. Man, I wanted a bite.

"Not much, I'm afraid," the father said. "But if you take us across, I promise to return with a bucket full of apples."

"Yeah, yeah, not happening. Sorry, got burned too many times before," the ferryman stated and then looked to me and said, "Next."

The woman touched Captain on his hand and said, "Will you take my ring?" She looked at her husband as she said it. "It's my wedding ring. Twenty-four-carat gold."

"Baby, please, not that," the husband said and tried to pull her hand back.

It didn't matter. "Gold's useless these days," Captain stated, shaking his head. "You know that. Now, kindly step aside."

"Hurry the fuck up, ferryman!" the Hell's Angel biker called out. "Ain't got all damn day!" He and his partner propped the motorcycle on its kickstand.

"What about my ring too?" the husband asked, defeated. "It's got silver in it."

"Sorry."

"Please, sir," the mother added. "We have nothing else."

"It's just business," Captain stated. "Had to get a new rope the other day. Cost me nearly all my inventory."

"Madness!" the husband cried out. "We need to cross! Our son lives on a farm south of here! They have great crops and seeds!"

"If you had seed, that would be a different story. Now, what you got, Sir?" Captain asked me, ignoring the husband. I lowered my backpack and opened it.

"Tell you what," I said and reached inside. I pulled up a clear bag of white goodness. "Sugar. For the family here and myself to cross."

Captain's eyes widened. "I'll need to sample first." I opened the bag for him and he licked his finger, plunging into the bag like a child. His finger came out covered in the white goodness and he smeared it over his tongue. "Deal," he mumbled, rolling his eyes. "See that?' he asked the family. "Sugar. Now that's gold!"

After I handed the bag over, the family and myself were allowed to pass. We boarded the raft but I kept them back from the first two ruffians.

"Thank you, Sir," the husband said. "You are very generous."

"Yes, thank you," the mother agreed. "We spoke the truth about our son. They have crops and seed..."

I cut her off by saying, "Keep it down. Certain people do not need to know that." I eyed the Hell's Angel biker guy and his Evil Knievel counterpart who were glaring at us as they passed another jar of moonshine between them.

"You take those men for thieves?" the mother asked me.

"Not sure yet," I said and leaned my bike against the rail. "But they have moonshine and a motorcycle. There's only one group able to travel and drink like that."

"They came from The Digs, didn't they?" the husband asked. "They're slimy Rogues I bet."

"Maybe so," I replied.

Rogues. Pirates of the desert. Steal, murder, and plunder. That was on their resume. While the world was trying to do some good, these monsters were relishing in the bad. They craved anarchy. It kept them powerful. The Digs was their main camp somewhere in Nevada.

I could see the alleged Rogues sizing up the oncoming crowd. I sensed some badness coming from them. Many of us carried backpacks. Moving behind the husband, I whisked out my crowbar and slid it up my sleeve, so only the claw end poked free. I tried to look nonchalant and excused myself from the family, moving slightly closer to the bikers. Just in case.

Captain allowed four more persons aboard, that being four more men who appeared to be quiet, average-looking characters. They talked and joked amongst themselves and didn't appear to raise any red flags. For passage, Captain received what looked like shoes, more knives, a salt block, and an animal trap. After the rest of the passengers were loaded, Captain placed a chain across the dock and jumped back on the raft. DuPont quietly shoved us off the dock with a huge push of his oar. A gush of water cascaded over the sides as the raft dipped, then settled. DuPont stuck the oar into the riverbed and pushed. They got the raft moving. A cold wind started up right away. Staring skyward, I saw gray clouds. That meant another day of rain.

"Where you come from?" Captain suddenly asked me as he dropped the new assortment of wares into the box. I saw a flash of books, shoes, and candles inside.

"North. Utah," I said.

"Salt Lake?" he asked, sitting atop his treasures.

I nodded. "Checked in. Nothing for me there."

"They still under martial law?"

"Afraid so, but portions of it are lifting. Conditions are improving."

"Guess those Mormons got their act together better than anyone else then. Being a tight religious group and all." Captain eyed the clouds forming ahead. "Looks like rain is coming."

I stared up as well and nodded.

"Where you headed then?" Captain asked me.

"Further south," I admitted. "You know a place I can stay in the meantime?"

"Sure. About a mile down the road, a place called Whispering Ranch House. It's a motel of sorts if you want to call it that."

"Good place?" I asked.

"M-eh, but you got little choice. Hardly any shelter around, except trees. The ranch is filled with nefarious characters at times. I had seen enough that cross the river to tell. Most wares look to be stolen. One rough-looking character tried to offer me a set of China. What the hell does a man need fancy plates for in this day and age? Almost got robbed by a few but thankful DuPont here doesn't act kindly to violence. He'll throw unsavory types over the side."

At the midway point of crossing, the two biker guys suddenly flew into action, as predicted. Hell's Angel stormed over to Captain, gripped the older man's gun hand, and placed a knife at his head. Evil Knievel whipped out a machete and leveled it at DuPont.

"Give me the gun, ferryman," Hell's Angel said sternly. "Give it to me or my partner severs the rope."

"You wouldn't," Captain spat.

"Try me."

"You'll kill us all," Captain argued but gave his gun up nevertheless. "There are rapids west of here, you fool! The rocks will rip my ferry in half!"

"Then we'll just have to avoid that situation, won't we?"

I edged closer to the big man and gripped my crowbar. Most of his attention was concerning Captain. Evil Knievel was watching DuPont closely, his machete raised as if he'd chop.

"All of you shitheads, put all your backpack and wares in the middle of the ferry!" Hell's Angel shouted to all of us, waving his new weapon. I crept closer and pretended to struggle with my backpack. "If you don't, you'll be shot and thrown in for a swim!"

"Open them up too!" Evil Knievel yelled. "We want to see what we got!"

Backpacks began to pile in the center of the raft. Some were open, most showing clothes and cooking ware. ZZ Top guys held the most bounty and the largest backpacks. The family huddled together, looking ever more frightened as they had nothing to offer. The four men behind me offered bags of fruit and vegetables. That was a score.

I eyed Captain and nodded at Hell's Angel holding the gun, mouthing "loaded?" Captain shook his head and looked down. The gun wasn't loaded, as he had claimed. I figured as much. Bullets were hard to come by. I walked towards Hell's Angel and held my right arm back.

"Fucking step back or I'll shoot!" he warned me. "Throw your backpack down with the rest." He swayed when he spoke and I could tell he was buzzed from drinking. I went to lower my backpack, but I rose quickly, swiping my right arm out. I caught Hell's Angel in the head, the claw end slicing through his scalp, embedding itself there just behind his ear. He dropped the knife he held and grabbed his head. His other hand pressed the trigger, aiming toward me, but all we heard was a click. When I yanked my crowbar free, I pulled with all my might using both hands and tore flesh from his skull, including his ear. Hell's Angel fell to the ground, squirming in pain. Urine flooded his pants as he rolled around.

With the larger man down and out, Evil Knievel came at me with his machete. I blocked it with my arm, making a loud metallic thunk sound, and that surprised the ruffian. He hadn't seen my crowbar which was still tucked into my sleeve. Slowly, I allowed the crowbar to slip out and I held it for him to see.

Evil Knievel gasped, eyeing both me and his partner who was wailing and bleeding all over the raft. "I don't care who you are," he said and came at me once more.

He threw a barrage of swipes at me, each successfully blocked. We clanged like swordsmen until I ducked under a swing, came up the other side, and walloped him in the back. He arched in pain and dropped the machete, falling to his knees. With the claw end, I snagged the man's collar and hauled him back up. I then kicked the man overboard and he fell into the river with a loud splash. DuPont kicked the machete into the river after him which sank immediately. Seconds later, DuPont rolled a groaning Hell's Angel in as well off the stern side of the raft.

Both men flopped and flailed in the fast-moving river. I heard one man scream, then both, until they vanished under the churning waves.

"Everything's under control," Captain said and motioned for DuPont to continue. As Dupont grasped his oar once more, the others thanked me for interfering and gathered their belongings. I shrugged it off and yanked my backpack back on. The raft drifted to the other dock a minute later where the next set of customers watched me in awe. Captain motioned me over and said, "You can have the motorcycle. I doubt they'll need it in Hell anymore."

I shook my head. "Give it to the family. Maybe their son can use it."

"If that's your wish, then so be it." The motorcycle was handed over to the husband who thanked me and Captain.

"Mighty kind of you. If it doesn't run, I can always sell for parts," the father stated and took the motorbike.

"I wish you'd take something," Captain said to me. "I feel indebted to you."

Truth was, I dodged vehicles of any kind. They made too much noise. Also, it wasn't working earlier. That's why they were pushing it. I guessed the fuel ran dry or a part busted along the way. I wasn't a mechanic. I saw the Rogue backpacks and decided to pilfer those instead. "I'll take whatever is in here," I mentioned. "First dibs."

"Go on then," Captain replied. "I'm grateful." Captain paused for a moment and looked at me weirdly. "Say, are you the one they call Crowbar Man?"

That made me laugh. "Crowbar Man?"

"Passengers tell me about some guy like you. Walks around the west, and carries a crowbar. Dishes out a hell of a lot of damage with it too."

Some of the others paused to listen. "I've never heard that before," I said.

"Well, either way, it was an honor to have you aboard."

A couple jars of moonshine looked good to me inside a backpack, so I took one. There were some clothes, forks, spoons, apples, condoms, cups, and dead rabbits. A complete jumble of stuff with no order. Sounded familiar because my backpack was the same. In the other pack, I found a tent, sleeping bags, tools, and books, which surprised me, because both characters didn't strike me as the kind able to read. The books were about raising crops, making food, mending fences, and other DIY'ers. After only pocketing the jar of booze, I made my way to the ramp.

"Is it true, Mister?" the little girl asked me. "Are you really the Crowbar Man?"

I winked and said, "Must be someone else."

"Shush, honey," the mother said to her, somewhat embarrassed. "He's just a good man who helps others."

The father interjected. "She loves to read comic books."

I smiled at them both and headed off the raft.

Crowbar Man. If that was true, it had a nice ring to it.

CHAPTER TWO

The Whispering Ranch House looked like an old western ruin. It had walls made from red stone that was chipped and loose. Blackened windows faced the front, some of which were broken. A low wooden roof with metal plates affixed sat atop. A large wooden door stood in the center. It was simply a motel but no doubt housed some wicked men within. Bad guys needed shelter too and there was no limit to sleazy characters in the area. Red clay and rock surrounded the place and hills as far as one could see, which was breathtaking and worthy of a mural.

When it was raining and cold, and there was no shelter to be found, such a place was worth the risk. Sleeping in the wet stuff was miserable and I had had enough of it for the last two nights. As raindrops pelted my jacket and backpack, I stared at the road beneath my feet. It led to the house but I couldn't see where it continued beyond that. It was getting late, I was tired from riding, and I coveted food and sleep.

Still, I had to know what I was getting into. I locked my bike next to a tree. Instead of heading to the front door, I chose to make my way to the side I couldn't see. There, I saw a disheveled man with his pants down at his ankles under an eave, his groin thrust into a hole in a barrel. His hair was strings of gray. He was scraggy, small, and covered in red welts. Two green apples sat atop the barrel. He didn't care that I saw him and he merely said to me, "Wait your goddamn turn."

"You can have mine," I mumbled.

The barrel knocked from within. Scraggy Man looked perturbed. "Be done faster if you didn't use your fucking teeth!" he shouted at the hole and dropped an apple inside. "That's two, you fucker! Do me a favor and hold your beard back! I can feel it!" he yelled and slapped the barrel. "Hard to think of women when I can feel your scruff!"

The barrel didn't look all that big. A side door opened slightly and I saw a man's gray boot with the tossed green apple next to it. Whom it belonged to, I didn't know. I didn't want to know. Seeing nothing else that made me suspicious, I headed back to the front door.

Scraggy Man grunted out loud as I rounded the corner.

After I opened the large wooden door, which squeaked loudly, three rooms appeared before me. Once was a large meeting area, with tables and chairs dead center. Men sat and played cards, drank from metal cups, and smoked something that resembled cigarettes. No women were present, as expected. Just like in the old westerns, the men all stopped to take a look once I entered. Off to the right, bunk beds were housed in a smaller room, piled two high. To the left, a door was shut and I guessed that to be the proprietor's sole lodging. I smelled cooked food. Maybe there was a kitchen back there too.

"Guns," a middle-aged man said and approached me. He was clean-cut with dark brown hair, a long mustache, dark brown eyes, and a scar that ran the length of his left cheek. He had a barrel of a chest behind a plaid shirt and a gun tucked into the waistband of his jeans. "Place belongs to me. If you want to stay, you got to give up your firearms. You get them back when you leave. I'm the only one armed and yes, I do have bullets." He produced a handful of what looked like .22s from his pocket to show me, then quickly put them away.

"I don't have any guns," I replied and lifted my arms. The man frisked me, then tapped the crowbar I had tucked into my arrow quiver.

"What about this then?" he asked me.

"That stays," I stated.

"You planning on using it?"

"Not unless I need to."

The owner sized me up further, then nodded. "What you got to trade?"

"Knives," I replied. "Maybe some booze?"

"We got enough utensils," he said. Glancing around, the other men were paying attention to us. I wondered if it was always like that whenever a stranger entered. "Show me the alcohol."

I whipped around my backpack and dug inside. I presented him with the jar of moonshine. "Good enough for a night?" I asked.

The owner looked dubious. "Where'd you get it?"

"Off a guy who doesn't need it anymore."

"That so? Where's he now?"

"Swimming."

The owner paused and then called out, "Sissy, get your ass out here!" A ruckus erupted behind the door on the left. A large woman strolled out, wearing not much besides a stained apron. She had dark curly hair, blue eyes, and big cheeks. She was heavyset, her arms thick with blood. A meat cleaver was in her right hand.

"What's up? This guy giving problems, Harold?" Sissy asked. Her voice was hoarse like a former smoker.

"Nah, it's not that," Harold replied and turned around, showing the jar. "He got moonshine. Wants to know if he can stay."

"Is he a Rogue?" she scoffed, wiping her cleaver on her apron.

The owner turned back around to me. "Well?"

"Nope. I have more than half a brain."

"Fine with me," Sissy said and left.

"How about he take a turn in the barrel?" one man asked from the side. I didn't know who said it but it earned a laugh from the others.

The owner said, "Just so you know, we don't offer any whoring around here. That barrel outside is what you make of it and we don't judge. Matter of fact, that barrel seems to keep the peace so I let these

15

men use it for their purposes. But don't pester the clientele for any other shenanigans. I won't stand for it."

I had to laugh. There weren't that many customers. Whoever was in the barrel would be found out soon enough.

"Something funny?" he asked me.

"It will be when I see a guy with gray soles, smelling of apples."

The owner ignored the comment and stepped aside. "Only got one bunk left. Go on and use it. Just the one night though."

"And a meal," I said.

The owner paused, took a sip from the jar, and then nodded.

"That's all I need," I replied and headed off.

The room was large and held four bunks. One below, one up high, enough for eight. On the left wall, a picture of a sailboat battling high winds was hung. At the furthest wall, a window with opened purple drapes allowed light to permeate. All the bunks had backpacks, boxes, or personal items stashed there. Sleeping bags were either neatly prepped for later or lazily tossed about. The room smelled like smoke and sweat. No doubt I'd be sharing it with men only. No perfume could be detected and I highly doubted a woman would ever want to bunk there.

It had been a while since I shared a room. I preferred to sleep alone. I found the empty one in the furthest corner on the left and dropped my backpack on it. The bunk itself was wood, about five feet high off the floor. Below me, an older black man napped with his eyes open. Grays peppered his beard. He was dressed simply with his arms folded across his chest.

Dinner was lizard skewers and a vegetable soup of some kind. I ate at a table by myself, thinking of the long day ahead tomorrow. It would be a long trek with another couple of nights in the wilderness some-where. I was grateful I had the ranch house for the night at least. The rain was still coming down hard, pelting the roof and creating a water-fall out the front door. Harold came by and tried to make small talk with the customers. When he came to me, I asked him how the ranch house came to be. The owner pulled up a chair.

"Dates back to the late eighteen hundreds when Native Americans and Mormons used the stopover to eat and rest here. It was once uninhabitable, a state historical treasure that prohibited entry, but my wife and I staked its claim since the gas and took residence. We fixed it up inside, built bunks, stabilized the roof with pillars, remodeled the aging outhouse, and opened for business."

"Business has been good?" I asked.

"Better than the B&B we used to own in Sedona. We got kicked out of there years ago by some warlord and stumbled across this place. This one is always full, thanks to the traffic that arrives via Captain's ferry."

Sissy called out from the kitchen. "Oops, got to mosey. See what all the fuss is about." The owner left me to eat the rest of the stew alone.

I watched the other men that were with me. None of them looked nefarious as the ruffians did on the raft. One man with a long beard was playing solitaire a few tables away. His shoes were gray. He was seated close to Scraggy Man who puffed on a pipe. Neither man was talking. I laughed to myself, finished up, took the empty plate to the counter next to the kitchen door, and hustled to the dark room where my bed awaited.

Later that night, while lying in my bunk, a loud groan woke me. It was an unusual sound as if someone was held down and smothered. A sliver of moonlight peeked through the window next to me, so I tried to use that to adjust my eyes in the darkness. The bunks were full of sleeping men and I saw nothing out of the ordinary at first. A man somewhere was snoring and I was surprised I hadn't woken to that. Then I heard what sounded like a thump and a moan.

I lifted my head and saw the outline of a large man hovering over the first row of bunks. I wondered if it was the owner checking up on his customers. He shuffled to one set of bunks and studied the men asleep there. He did something strange with his hands as if he was praying over them. I heard a thump again, then gargling, then quiet. After a few moments, the large man then walked to another bunk opposite and stood over that man at the top. Seconds later, he bent down and looked at the bunk below. He reached in and gripped the man's face. The man there startled briefly but was then quieted after the larger man thrust his right hand forward, held it there, then withdrew. From there, he moved again to the top bunk opposite me and hovered there, studying that man.

He was looking for someone.

The moon betrayed him. I saw a bloody knife in the moonlight. Suddenly, the man's ugly mug came to view and he glared at me. His hair was wet and the left side of his head was mangled and bloodied.

It was Hell's Angel. From the ferry.

"There you are!" he yelled.

His right hand swiped downwards in a stabbing motion. I whisked my crowbar out quickly from my side and stopped his downward thrust. "Fucking kill you!" he spat and he lifted his arm again. I rolled away from the next jab just as his blade had missed me by inches and he stabbed the bunk instead. By then, the rest of the men had awakened and began to holler in confusion. Flashlights lit up and swung in all directions. I scrambled to rise but Hell's Angel caught me by my shirt and yanked me down from the bunk. I tumbled to the floor but lost my tool in the process. I rose quickly enough and searched for my crowbar but realized it was still laying in my bunk. Hell's Angel lunged at me with his knife but I batted away with my left wrist and simultaneously smacked him with my right fist into his chin. Hell's Angel wobbled and staggered against my bunk, dropping the knife when he nearly fell over. He managed to grip the bunk and steady himself. The man who slept below me tried to grab his leg but the Hell's Angel kneed him off.

Just as I went to step in with a follow-up strike, Hell's Angel reached into my bunk and swung at me. I saw a flash of long metal and felt a tremendous wallop on the side of my shoulder. I realized then that he had used my crowbar on me. Although it was a glancing blow, the pain was stunning and I cringed. Now I knew what my adversaries felt.

"How's that, you prick?" he asked me. "Your own fucking weapon on ya?"

Looking for a weapon of my own, I reached into the next bunk and yanked out a blanket. Hell's Angel backhanded my crowbar at me, but I snared it in the blanket, wrapping the tool and his hand with mine. I brought him in close and jabbed him where his ear used to be, plunging my index and middle fingers into his exposed skull for a few good seconds. Hell's Angel wailed and shuddered, releasing my crowbar. He began to sob uncontrollably, so I forced his head down quietly, grabbed his head with both hands and twisted sideways to silence him. We all heard his neck snap. Hell's Angel flopped to the floor in a heap, dead.

A man at the farthest bunk shouted, "My brother's been killed!" And then Scraggy Man yelled, "There's a dead man over here too!" The men searched themselves, looking for wounds. In the end, three men were dead, all due to Hell's Angel's attack.

I couldn't help but notice they all resembled me.

The men were bewildered and afraid to leave the room sensing more killers could be outside. I wasn't about to wait, however, so I unwrapped my crowbar from the blanket. I stormed from the room to search for Evil Knievel or anyone else that came with Hell's Angel.

In the front room, Harold was dead on the floor, stabbed in the chest. There was no one else there; no Evil Knievel, no other alleged Rogues. I quickly ran to the side room where Sissy had emerged before and found the lifeless host halfway under a bed. Stab wounds covered her back. I felt for a pulse and found none.

"What the hell was that asshole doing here?" Scraggy Man shouted to me as he exited the room. "Why would he do such a thing?"

Hell's Angel came there to get revenge on me.

No doubt in my mind.

Before anyone else could make sense of it, I decided to leave.

CHAPTER THREE

Two days later, after leaving the carnage behind at the Whispering Ranch House, I found myself within spitting distance of Matias' cabin. A one-half mile off a small road in the middle of Arizona, south of Highway 40, his abode was not on any maps. Nor was there any mailbox or driveway. You had to trek through thick brush to get to it and that was no easy task. Matias didn't want to be found. Most survivalists didn't.

No sooner had I approached the clearing where the old man and I used to spar, that a lunging Pitbull came at me and I welcomed him with open arms. Matias wasn't far behind and he, too, was welcomed with a hug.

Matias looked the same except for more grays covering his thinning hair. He kept it neat, though, and often spoke of travels to the reservation to meet up with his kinsmen. More than once he also mentioned a woman named Kasey who cut his hair there and I took that to mean there were other motivations in mind for his frequent visits. Matias' wife, Winnie, died years before when gas was released down in Crown Valley. She had been living with Matias' brother, Jack, and the split wasn't amicable.

"Where you been?" he asked me.

I continued to stroke Nuke who demanded attention from me. "All over. Wandered around Central California. Went up through Nevada and crossed over to Utah. No sign of my family."

"Ah, you'll find them soon," Matias said.

"I hope so. It's getting old," I replied and looked away.

Matias sensed my unease. "What is it?"

"Had a little skirmish. Run in with Rogues."

"Casualties?"

"Innocents. The guy was after me," I said.

"Tell me all about it. And where you've been. I want to hear it all."

Matias and I were sitting on the logs outside his cabin. Nothing much had changed since my last visit a few months earlier. The shingles on the roof were peppered with pine needles and the outside kept its rustic charm. He kept it neater than usual, the front porch was always swept. He spoke of making some additions to it though and last I saw, a woman's touch had invaded the single man's domain. For one, a plant sat on the table, watered and healthy. Two, he had new dishtowels. And three, the outhouse door now had a lock. I was waiting for a mass of throw pillows on his bed.

A small fire was lit with a pot of baked beans simmering atop it. They were a honey flavor and simply delicious. Nuke got Matias' leftovers.

In-between bites, I spoke on what had transpired back at the ferry and the Whispering Ranch House. Matias didn't speak until I ended.

"Not your fault," he insisted. "You did right. You saved those people."

"The Hell's Angel guy came after me though."

"You didn't know he would," Matias claimed. "Besides, what makes you think those two morons would have let anyone live on that ferry?"

"I get that," I said and paused. "It's just...the people he killed were innocent."

"And he could have attacked them when he got off the ferry. You don't know what he was up to. He and his Evil Knievel partner. If they tried to rob all of you on the ferry, they probably would have done the same at the motel."

I supposed that was true. Whispering House was only a mile down the road.

Matias continued. "As far as I am concerned, the only good Rogue is a dead Rogue. They are becoming a pest around these parts now. They pester the locals and even scare up the Res."

By Res, he meant Reservation. Matias was a member of the Unikapah Nations Tribe, their reservation not far from his cabin. The members were well-armed but they mostly kept to themselves. The Rogues, on the other hand, ran amok throughout the southwest without regard to borders or territories. They, too, were armed and more heavily so.

Matias finished his bowl and asked, "How about a game of chess?"

A bark gave us away. I had been jogging north on a cloudy morning with Nuke along the small road outside Matias' cabin when the one-eared Pitbull suddenly stopped, skidding in the gravel.

"What is it, boy?" I asked him, trying to catch my breath in the chilly air. I figured it was an animal of some kind, hiding in the trees that hugged the road. Nuke was always one to be on patrol, on guard, on edge. He savored being protective, being a hunter. It gave him a purpose.

A deep guttural growl emitted from his thick throat. He stood rigid, his large shoulder muscles tensing as he eyed the road ahead. Small hairs rose on his back. Poor Nuke lost his left ear when a truck rolled over him four years earlier, protecting me and two others. The cartilage was hardly visible as hair grew over most of it. Matias was responsible for his care and the old man did a great job.

I searched the tree line and stared down the road as well. Leaves and sand reclaimed most of the long stretch but some vehicles had passed by recently. That was a rarity. Gasoline reserves dried out years ago, but the vehicles that traveled nowadays used a different type of fuel. More on that later...

Whatever it was, it was heading south, and then I heard it. An engine. A big one.

"Nuke, come," I told my four-legged friend and then quickly ushered Nuke into the trees. Rogues, it had to be.

It was a dark blue Dodge Charger rolling our way. Newer model, but by newer, I meant made just before the gas attack. No cars had been built since. Anywhere. It was propelled by a V8 engine too, the large motor reverberating throughout the trees.

I gripped Nuke by his collar and held him there behind a tree and thick brush. He was anxious, ready to spring at my command. Even he could tell the occupants were assholes. With the window down, I could make out two bearded men in front of the big car. Two more shadows in the rear although the window there was cramped. They drove uncaringly, almost bored, just cruising. We hadn't been spotted so I merely waited until they passed so we could continue on our morning jog.

And then Nuke barked. The passenger's head turned. I cupped Nuke's snout, whispering "No bark" to him, but the Charger slowed immediately after. The big car stopped, and the red brake lights lit brightly. White reverse lights flashed. The Charger began to roll back.

"Shit, Nuke, now look what you've done," I said quietly and frowned. "We need to go." I tugged on Nuke's collar and we both took off, racing back towards Matias' cabin, hoping to hell the Rogues never saw us.

They did.

We heard the crackle of branches on the forest floor and knew the thugs were getting close. Matias and I stared out the front window of his small cabin, searching for the figures to make an appearance. They were slick, I'll give them that. They hadn't shown themselves.

"There are four of them bastards," Matias said. Beside him, Nuke growled again. The hair on the dog's back lifted but he didn't bark this time. Matias had Nuke trained well over the years and knew the dog would obey his master. Matias, my old friend, was still on top of his game. How he could tell there were four was beyond me.

"Four. That's what I figured," I replied, feeling guilty. I had mere seconds to catch Matias up on what transpired on the road before we were quickly ushered inside. It appeared Matias' secret cabin was about to be exposed.

I felt bad. He always made a bed for me, a rollup foam pad that he kept for such occasions. His own bed was still along the furthest wall. To my right was the kitchen, still organized and neat. Behind me was the table we played chess on, two chairs, a round rug, and a cast iron stove that was used for both cooking and heating.

The new additions were there too; the plant and the new dishtowels.

The chess game sat on the table, waiting to finish. I wondered if we would ever. Matias was up two games to one on this visit. We had stopped playing late last night with no winner. We were supposed to resume today.

"How do you want to play this?" I asked him.

"You stay put," he said. Matias handed me a rifle with a scope that was leaning against the wall. "I'm going gopher," he said and removed his six-inch knife with brass knuckles from his waist. Below his knees, under a rug, was a trapdoor.

"Take a gun, you old fool," I goaded him.

"No need. Keep Nuke in here until it's not okay to be here," he replied.

I nodded and checked the ammo. It was a Remington .30-06 Springfield. Five rounds. Matias had more guns and bullets stashed away so I wasn't worried about running out. Behind me, Matias disappeared. Nuke sniffed the floorboards, whining a bit.

A bullet shattered the window, causing me to jump back.

Game on.

"Hello there!" one man shouted from the trees. "Can we borrow a cup of sugar?"

That earned a laugh from the other Rogues. They were spaced apart.

One of the gunmen seemed somewhat brazen all of a sudden,

straddling a set of trees just outside the campfire ring. He wore a long, beige coat, and dark pants. Long, flowing blonde hair. I believe he was the passenger who first heard Nuke's bark. After I eased the barrel outside the window, I saw more of the men appearing from the thicket. The first Rogue with the flowing blond hair was an easy shot. I lined him up and fired. He went down, flipping over a log with a large hole just off the center of his chest. That woke up the other Rogues who ducked for cover and started firing in all directions. Bullets pinged off the window frame and shot up the inside of the cabin. Nuke wisely hid behind the iron stove. I took root along the wall, squinting from the splinters that showered me as a cavalcade of bullets tried to find me. Suddenly, the firing stopped. I heard clicks, like the sound of triggers being pulled. No more bullets came my way. All that followed was hushed cussing. Were they out of ammo? Was it a ruse?

"Torch the sucker!" a voice then shouted.

"We got it!" another replied.

Whatever happened to, "We got you surrounded! Come out with your hands up?"

Shit. That meant they were going to flame me out. I stared at Nuke, hoping Matias would be able to stop them before they did that. The cabin had meant everything to the old man, including those of us inside. I stared at the wood structure from within knowing it wouldn't take much to light up. I peeked out, leveling the rifle, daring any derelict with a pair of matches to come to view. A head popped out behind a tree to my far right but I saw no gun. I swung towards him, spotted him with the crosshairs in the scope, and shot. The bark above his head ripped free. Although I missed, his head vanished. As I waited for him to take another peek, a man to his left suddenly ran straight for the cabin. Strangely, it looked like his hands were on fire.

He was carrying a Molotov cocktail.

I tried to fire and missed just as he chucked it. The bottle soared through the air and crashed into the wall near the window. Flames instantly rose in front of me, a wall of fire that spread at least five feet across. The Rogue throwing it scampered back behind a tree. I fired once more at him taking a chunk of a branch up high and realized the scope was off. "Damnit!" I yelled. I had to aim lower.

Another fiery cocktail smashed into the cabin, next to the front door. Smoke wafted inside from the first bomb and the second was sending flames under the door. It wouldn't be long before Nuke and I would be smoked out unless the fires were controlled from the outside.

To my right once more, I saw the head peek out. No sooner had that man tried to walk forward when I saw his head jerk back and his neck slice open. Blood cascaded down the guy's shirt. It happened so fast that the man didn't make a sound. The body was then dragged behind the tree. From that same spot, Matias flashed me a sign with his fingers. Two down, two to go.

The smoke was becoming unbearable. Nuke began to whine and scratch at the floor. I coughed and slunk to my knees. We wouldn't last long in there. I grabbed a water bucket that Matias used for drinking and splashed it out the window, hoping to douse the flames outside. It did very little. The heat was growing intensely.

I concentrated on the fire starters. The same man who flung the first bottle made another run for it, carrying yet another bomb in his outstretched hand. I swiveled and fired, aiming lower, striking the bastard in the stomach. He doubled over but kept coming. I squeezed the trigger once more and only heard a click. My five-shooter was out. Through my scope, I could still see the man storming forward, heading towards the door already engulfed in flames.

The man crashed through the door but shattered the bottle against his body. He became consumed with flames from head to toe and his mouth was agape in a stifled scream. He flung his fiery self at me, but I sidestepped right and managed to trip him, causing the flaming dummy to crash into Matias' bed. The man flapped his arms wildly, squirming terribly. A hellish scream erupted from his lungs. Nuke yelped at the flames and drew backward, close to the flaming front door. We were surrounded by fire.

I flipped open a trap door there and Nuke leaped inside the darkness as he was trained to do. I followed soon after, gabbing my backpack and shutting the trap door behind me. Nuke shot off through a dirt-filled tunnel that snaked around a few twisty bends. I was forced to crawl as the tunnel itself was a mere four feet in circumference. The fire's light behind me provided me with some guidance. Daylight streamed from the other end and I could see roots and cobwebs dangling from above. Nuke waited impatiently at another trap door, banging his head against it, trying to get topside. We emerged in the trees out front, with me lifting the trap door that Matias covered with shrub and had used just a minute earlier. I held on to Nuke's collar, just in case.

Matias and the last man were grappling in the brush, rolling over flowers and plants. The other man was larger, seeming to hold his own, before Matias threw his legs over the man's torso, grabbed his arm in an arm bar, and snapped the bone in two instantly. The man began to scream in pain.

I held Nuke by the collar and had a hard time doing so. Seeing the plight of his owner in distress, the Pitbull was more than anxious to join in the fight. And who would I be to not allow that to happen?

Spit and drool cascaded down Nuke's chin. His lips were raised, flashing large, sharp teeth. He barked and tugged. Matias rolled off the man who was trying to grip his flimsy arm. When I released Nuke, he tore off like a rocket. No sooner had the man got to his knees, cradling his busted arm, when Nuke barreled into him, knocking him down, and began tearing at his throat. Matias got to his feet, winded.

"That took a lot out of me," he complained but it was hard to hear him over the man's screams. Matias bent over, trying to catch his breath. His knife was on the forest floor. "I'm losing my touch. The bastard heard me coming," Matias exclaimed.

"He was a big boy," I said.

Behind us, I heard a twig snap. I turned around and spied another man hiding behind a tree further back. Once he saw me, he ran off, heading back to where I assumed the car would be. In his hands, I saw what looked like a sword.

"We got another one, turned rabbit," I said to Matias. "Looks like there were five. Not four."

"You go. I'm too tired," Matias said. Behind us, the old man's cabin was totally on fire. Smoke billowed into the blue sky. We had nothing to put it out with either. "That's a damn shame," he said. "My dear home."

I thought of the car and the fact the fifth man could escape. We could also use the car for ourselves. "I'm gone," I said, grabbed my crowbar, and took off after the guy.

The fifth man stood outside the Dodge Charger holding his sword out. It looked like an old Samurai Sword, complete with a white curved handle and Japanese writing. When he hadn't taken off, I realized he had not been the driver and didn't have the keys. Samurai Man was in his thirties, I guessed. He was thin, and pale, with long dark hair and a beak-like nose. There was something familiar about the guy.

He zeroed in on my crowbar. "I remember you, Mister," he said. "You and that fuckin' tool."

I drew a blank at first and didn't care.

"Coppertown," Samurai Man said.

Coppertown? That caught me off-guard and I hesitated. I had been there many times over the years. The guy's ugly face didn't ring a bell.

"You don't remember me, do you? See, I was one of Bale's men," he said. "We attacked your sorry asses back in the day."

Bale was the leader of the Hellion, a group of drugged thugs who attacked small towns in Arizona just after the gas. While his group was successful on every raid, he was stopped cold by our small forces at Coppertown, an encampment just west. Bale had also severely wounded my friend, Sara. Bale died after we created a cave-in to lock his ugly, raping ass in the mountainside forever.

When the guy mentioned Bale's name, however, it dawned on me. The limp. I smacked a man once with my crowbar on the outside of his leg after I released him.

"Bower." It wasn't a question.

"Yup," he smirked.

He was one of the Hellion we had chained as a prisoner but we released him so he could spread word that we had a jar of the lethal gas that killed millions across the planet. That was true for a time, but we later discovered that the jar had been stolen and used to wipe out the Hellion back in Crown Valley by a pilot named Darcy who sought his vengeance and redemption.

"I left your ugly mug on the side of the road," I reminisced. "You shit your pants on purpose too. Yeah, I remember you. How's the knee?"

Bower pursed his lips. "Payback is a bitch. I've been waiting for this moment. I'll cut you in half and eat your innards." His sword was a long, straight blade and he wielded it nicely, even with one hand, whipping it round and round. He was an expert with it, I'd give him that. Me? I was never trained with a sword. I'd have cut my leg twice by now doing what he was doing.

Bower lifted his sword high and charged, chopping downward. The bear inside me erupted as I conjured up a quick image of Polecat in my mind, the man who raped me years ago and was himself a Hellion. That's all it took. Even after five years, I could summon the bear instantly. That shit never left you.

Thrusting my crowbar up horizontally, I blocked his first strike easily, yet the vibration of metal shook my wrist, the *twang* reverberating in my hands. Withdrawing quickly, Bower shifted and swung sideways but his blade was met again with my tool, blocking the blow. This time, however, I snagged the sword with the claw end, twirled it in a circle, and flung his sword from his grasp. It flipped end over end and landed far off in a bush.

Bower then roared and charged me. I stepped back but slipped on dirt. Bower crashed into me and we both fell to the ground with me losing my crowbar as we rolled. He was plucky, I'd give him that, but I jumped on top of him, using my weight as leverage. I pummeled Bower below me with my fists, each blow finding purchase. Bower spat, growled, and struggled, but my full weight kept him pinned down. His hands flailed for me, slapping my shoulders and head but they were glancing blows and I shrugged them off easily. Dirt and twigs flew in my face during the melee. I kept one hand on his neck, however, and my right pumped up and down like a piston. He was scrappy rather than strong and in those lean times, I probably outweighed him.

Bower tried a desperation bite near my knuckle, but I landed one more heavy punch and I heard bone crack. He went limp under me and I rolled off. Rising to my feet, I found my crowbar lying just feet away. I picked it up and brushed the dirt off.

Bower moaned, holding his cheek, cursing under his breath. Clumps of dirt were tossed at my feet in frustration as he rose to his knees. He staggered like a drunk when he finally stood.

"Do it. Get on with it and kill me," he spat. "Good as dead anyway."

I didn't know what he meant by that and frankly didn't care. I hadn't hurt him that badly. Yet.

Gunshots suddenly erupted behind me. Many of them came from Matias' cabin. It sounded like a warzone back there and I turned back around. Bower used that time to slither under the Dodge Charger.

"Come out from there!" I shouted.

"No!"

I bent down and swung the crowbar under the car, snagging a piece of his clothing. I yanked hard, but fucking Bower held on to the underside of the car and I couldn't haul him out. More gunshots discharged and I was afraid Matias was pinned down. Last I saw, he didn't have a gun.

As much as I wanted Bower, Matias needed my help. Seeing as Bower was going nowhere, not without keys anyway, I decided to hightail it back to help out my old friend after grabbing Bower's sword. I'd get back to Bower soon enough. He wasn't going anywhere or very far. Nuke would find him.

The heat from the fire kept me back about fifty feet. The cabin was fully ablaze, the walls falling inwards, the rooftop teetering. Sparks flew and drifted in the slight wind. I hoped the embers wouldn't start a forest fire. I didn't see any men, however, yet bullets were zinging all over the place. Matias waved to me from the tunnel entrance and yelled, "Get some cover, you fool! You'll be shot!"

I used a tree for shelter. A bullet sheared off a branch near my head. "Who's firing at us? Are there more Rogues?" I asked, ducking. I realized I wasn't armed then either. The rifle I had was left behind in the cabin.

"Afraid not!" he shouted. Nuke's head appeared near his waist. "It's all the ammunition I have! Boxes of them!"

"Oh Jeez!" This all snowballed to hell. With two trees between us, I darted from one to the next, cringing at each crack of a bullet, and ended up diving near the entrance where Matias and Nuke lay in wait. "I'm sorry about the cabin," I said, solemnly. "I'll help you build another."

Suddenly, the roar of a V8 engine drowned out the gunfire. Matias looked at me and all I could say was, "You got to be kidding me!"

"You didn't finish him?" Matias asked.

Dumbfounded, all I could say was, "I'll explain later."

"If he leaves, I don't know if I can ever come back," Matias said quietly.

The smoke was fully black, covering much of the sky ahead. "I don't think you could anyway," I replied. "People will see this for miles."

Matias called Nuke over and looked into his dog's eyes. Their home was destroyed. All because of Nuke and I on a morning run.

"I am so sorry," I told him.

Matias was gathering what he could from the ashes when I returned from the road. There wasn't much for Matias to claim. Just some utensils, mainly. He left the cabin as is, contemplating a return as he righted the iron stove and straightened up a few items. From the ashes at my feet, I plucked the white Queen chess piece I had played. The rest of the board was somewhere under the smoldering rubble. I showed it to him and he waved me off. I pocketed it.

"Maybe they won't find the cabin," I said, hopefully. Gray ash swirled in the wind, floating upward and away. The fire was mostly out, a few embers glowed in burning wood. I added, "Even if they came soon, they won't find anything."

"Was the car gone?" he asked.

I nodded and said, "I didn't think he had the keys. He was pretty banged up." On my left, I saw one of the Rogues we had killed. I walked over and studied the blond man's face. I had shot him in the chest. He was older, in his late forties or fifties. His dark eyes were half open staring at the sky, his mustache bushy and filled with gray, his skin pockmarked with red dots and his gums were bloody and red. Two front teeth were missing. He carried a disease that I guessed to be syphilis. I checked his pockets and found nothing except a buck knife, which I pocketed. Underneath him was a .9mm handgun that had a full clip. I hoisted that up and then wandered to the next victim, the one Matias sliced open with his blade. Although white, that guy had a yellow tinge to his skin. He had shaved recently and smelled like cologne. He may have been good-looking once, probably in his thirties. His weapon of choice was a German Luger of all things. When I checked the clip and chamber, it was empty, so I pocketed it for Matias. Number three was somewhere buried in the ashes while the fourth had been mauled to death by Nuke. I trudged over to number four. He was big-boned, his cheeks carried high, and his eyes were a dark brown. His hair was black, his skin darker, and I guessed Latino. He carried a .25 caliber revolver. A six-shooter, but it was empty too. After checking his pockets, I found razors, jewelry, and fishing lures. Feeling bad for Matias, I offered the goods to him and he declined.

"I'm not touching those," he said. "Don't belong to me. Didn't belong to them assholes either."

I dropped them on the spot.

"Not much left here for me," Matias said.

"I told you I'd help you rebuild it."

Matias sighed. "Maybe it wasn't meant to be."

"This place is hard to find. Bower might not know where to find it again."

Matias turned to me. "Bower? You knew the guy?"

"We crossed paths a long time ago and before you say anything, I was trying to get to him. The bullets had me concerned. I thought you were in trouble."

He seemed to accept it. "I guess a rebuild is possible. I'll think about it. Maybe make it bigger."

"Bigger?"

Nuke stiffened suddenly, cocking his head behind us. Matias caught on quickly and grabbed his knife. We watched the direction Nuke was concentrating and heard twigs snap. Nuke growled and was ready to pounce when Matias grabbed his collar. "Easy, Nuke, I don't think it's bad."

I patted myself down, searching for a weapon and found the .9mm I pilfered earlier and handed Matias the Luger, just for show. Nuke's tail suddenly began to wag and Matias relaxed. He whistled, a high pitch call, and the whistle was answered.

"Friends of yours?" I asked.

"My cavalry," he said with a smile. "A bit late though."

A horse whinnied from the tree line and soon, a brown snout emerged. Another horse, a black one, followed behind that, with a third, slightly gray, trailing it on a rope. There were two riders atop the first two. While they were armed, with rifles slung across their chests, they didn't bother to take them out.

"You trying to start a forest fire, old man?" the first rider said. He was young, had dark hair, dark skin, and a slim face. He wore a t-shirt and jeans.

"Remind me to bring my weenies," the second one responded. He looked smaller, a bit older, with dark hair as well, and a rounder face. Both men eyed the smoldering ashes that were once Matias' cabin.

"I prefer marshmallows," the first one said.

"Fuck them, too chewy," the second one replied.

The first rider eyed a dead body, the man I shot. Then he spied the one with his throat cut and stopped short. Before he could ask, Matias jumped in.

"Clusterfuck," Matias told them.

Nuke was anxious to go at them, tugging at Matias' grip. The first rider dismounted and opened his arms. "Come here, boy!" Matias released Nuke who rocketed to the rider. Instead of attacking, the Pitbull jumped into his arms, licking and nuzzling. Hard to imagine that just minutes earlier, Nuke was ripping the flesh out of a Rogue's throat. The horse was a bit skittish and backed away. "How's my buddy?" the rider continued with Nuke. The second rider stayed on his horse.

"We saw the smoke, old man," the second rider said. "Might as well be the bat signal." The second rider stared at the carnage around us, seeing the dead bodies. He then gawked at me. "Who's this?"

"Verne, allow me to introduce Ted Ratelle," Matias said. Verne didn't offer a handshake and merely nodded to me. However, the other man walked over with his hand extended and Nuke began jumping around him.

"Name's Jordan," the first rider said.

We shook and the tension eased. Matias explained what happened to the two men. Verne then said, "We heard the car. Big block, wasn't it?"

"Dodge Charger," I said.

"Yeah, so the Charger buzzed by our gates but didn't enter the Res," Jordan said. "Rogues we figured. Only ones with any cars on the road."

"Rogues it was," I replied. "This is what's left of them."

"Guns?" Jordan asked.

Matias looked at me and nodded. "Take them," he said. "I don't need them."

"Only one with ammo left is the .9mm," I said.

Matias said to me, "You keep it."

"Mind if we take their clothes?" Verne asked and inspected one of the dead.

I stared at my boots. The fact the bodies were covered with diseases disgusted me but I could have used new shoes. "Take what you want," I decided.

Later, the riders mounted their horses with their new clothes wrapped up. The bodies of the naked dead would be left to the critters. "Verne and I first heard the guns but then saw the smoke. We knew it came from your area," Jordan said as he tied his new clothes to the saddle. "It was my idea to bring another horse, just in case. I figured the old guy would need it."

That meant only three riding out. "Sorry, bud, can't take you," Verne said to me. He never warmed to me like his partner did and I didn't know why.

I had planned to stay a few more days before walking off again on my usual search, but such plans changed. Matias and I spoke quietly after with me mostly apologizing, but my old friend had none of it. "Wasn't your fault. Bound to happen sometime. I'll be at the Res until I sort things out," he said. "What will you do?

"I don't know," I replied. "Try west again. Stop over and see some old friends along the way."

Matias informed the other men. "He's still trying to find his family."

"You're welcome to come to the Res if you want. Stay temporarily," Jordan offered. "But you'd have to hoof it from here."

"No, that's okay," I said. "I got some friends to visit. Thanks, anyway." I hoisted my backpack and shoved the crowbar into the quiver.

Jordan said goodbye and left. Verne just nodded and turned. Only Matias remained. We were quiet for a few moments. Nuke was excited, jumping up on Matias' leg as if he wanted a ride. The horse rocked his head and Matias sensed the animal's discomfort. "We better get going before this horse bucks me."

"I'll see you soon," I said.

Matias did pause though. "This time it seems different. I can feel it."

"It's because the cabin is destroyed," I said. "I'll see you one day at the Res."

"No. It's something else. It won't be easy though. You have a long, busy journey ahead." Matias stared skyward and smiled. "You're close to finding them."

"Is that some wacky Matias prophecy?"

Matias smiled. "Go ahead and scrounge what you want below. You'll need it. Especially the coffee. It's good for your soul."

"Say hello to Kasey," I said and winked. "I'm on to you, old man."

Matias smiled but grew serious. "Beware the trickster." After we shook hands, he turned back around, tugged the reigns, and headed off with Nuke bounding at his feet.

Trickster. Matias meant Ginn.

I wondered whatever happened to the guy.

CHAPTER FOUR

Minutes after Matias left me, I decided to leave the area as well. I passed the smoldering ashes of his former cabin and made my way to the outhouse. Instead of using the outdoor facilities, however, I began a count from the rear corner and walked to a large clearing twenty paces away in a southwest direction. There, I swept my boot back and forth, finding a loose rope I was searching for. I reached down and pulled it up. A trap door revealed itself under some dirt and leaves. Below that was an opening into the dark earth that led into Matias' bunker.

A small ladder descended into dust-covered shelves eight feet below. Canned goods and other supplies would be down there, although I wasn't sure how much was left. The bunker was rectangular, a good twelve feet long by eight feet wide. Not huge, but well-hidden and well-preserved. I removed my backpack and dropped it into the hole where more dust kicked up when it landed and I waited for it to settle.

The ladder creaked under my weight as I dropped in. Most of the supplies were gone. Shelves that were once full, were now mostly barren. A five-year supply doesn't last long, especially with me visiting as much as I did.

A taser sat alone on the shelf. I quickly took that, then scooped up some canned goods and dropped them into my backpack. I found a flashlight, a bag full of Double-A batteries, toothpaste, a toothbrush, and a roll of toilet paper.

"Thank you, Matias!" I shouted happily, juggling the roll.

The toilet paper was welcome. No more leaves or loose paper, at least for a month. As for the toothbrush, I'd toss the old one I carried for the last year which was frayed and flattened. Good timing on that one. Matias gave me dental products each time I swung by so my teeth were still in good shape. I was also fortunate that various pills, ointments, and bandages he supplied went to good use. Smart move for Matias to stock up on those that he scored with good couponing long ago.

I found a coffee can sitting alone on the far shelf. He told me to have some. Good for the soul, he said. I picked it up and something heavy shifted inside.

A Walkman with headphones. Straight out of the eighties. I didn't see any cassettes lying around and nothing else in the can. I opened the door to the cassette player and saw a tape.

Bee Gees. *Stayin' Alive*.

"You did that on purpose, you old bastard," I said.

After I pilfered what I could, I left the bunker and smoldering cabin. I walked my bike through the thick trail planning my day. Once I reached the road, I would head north towards Highway 40 and head west. My stomach was rumbling and I felt bad for Matias and Nuke. We didn't even get to have breakfast. The bounty in my backpack would wait though. I wanted to distance myself from the area first. I could still smell the smoke from the cabin behind me and saw a gray cloud drifting high above.

Not good.

I had almost made it to the road when I heard a sound come from the north, a revolving squeak that could only mean a wheel of some sort. I heard the clopping of what sounded like horse steps and a man's voice egging the animal forward. Debating if I should backpedal into the bushes for safety, I chanced this new encounter more out of curiosity than anything.

Bad guys don't ride horses. Bad guys drove cars.

Still, I hauled out my crowbar and strolled out to the road.

An old man riding a donkey appeared. Behind him, a small two-wheeled cart was tied to his saddle. Instead of fleeing or stopping, he clicked his tongue and kept coming, even after spotting me. He wore a black tuxedo, hat, and sneakers. Gray hair poked out from the bottom of the hat. His eyes were dark, his cheeks plump, his nose prominent, and he sported a thick, curly mustache. Come to think of it, he was the worse-dressed version of the Monopoly Man.

Slowing only when he saw my crowbar, he lifted his chin, then smiled. He yanked his reigns and ordered the donkey to come to a halt next to me. The animal complied and snorted. Its black eyes blinked.

THE SHOEMAN was painted on the side of the cart.

"Hello, friend," he said to me, dipping his hat.

"Hello, friend," I replied. I was weary of the old-timer. You didn't see those types alone normally, especially with a donkey and cart. Rogues commanded the roads. Either he was in cahoots with the bastards or incredibly lucky thus far.

No weapons were visible. I knew I had the upper hand with my crowbar at the very least, yet I remained cautious, if not guarded.

"Might you know the source of the smoke?" he asked me, sniffing the air. "I figure good customers could be in need of some shoes. I have not seen many and man usually makes smoke."

"Nothing there," I said. "Just my campfire."

Somewhat disappointed, he then pitched me. "Might you require new shoes then?" he inquired. I looked at his cart. Shoes, sneakers, boots, high-tops, sandals, and loafers, some of which were tied together by the laces. Some with dried blood.

I glanced up at him with suspicion. "The Shoeman, huh?"

"Indeed. I travel far and wide, ready to trade," he said, sweeping his hand. "If there is one important thing we all miss from the past, well, that would be a good pair of shoes. Take a gander. Touch them if you like. Try them on."

"Where did you get them all?" I asked.

He lifted his head high. "Roadkill, of course."

"What?"

"The dead," he said matter of fact. "Many a person that no longer has the need, I simply take. Keeps the cost of goods sold down to a wee penny. Trust me, they don't mind. None have argued. Nary a complaint."

I was always skeptical of any trader. They often stole when they said found, alive when they meant dead. "I won't wear a dead man's shoes," I said.

"To each their own," he remarked, then nodded toward my backpack. "Might you have some food to spare?"

This was the point where things could get rocky and I tensed, ready for anything. His hands were still visible. I looked behind him, in case this was a trick.

"We haven't traded," I said to him.

"You don't want my shoes."

Regarding the direction he came, I then asked, "You've traveled far, Shoeman?"

"From Mexico way," he replied. "The Sea of Cortez is lovely this time of year. Whales are breeching, kissing the beautiful, salty air. A most precious sight seen from the shore. The locals say that brings much luck, to witness such a spectacle. Why, once you've seen the ocean, you've seen home."

"You came straight up from there?" I asked. "Through the Mojave?"

"No sir," he said and patted his donkey. "Headed west to Tucson. Then straight on up to Pinecrest. Just left there days ago."

"Pinecrest? There's people there?"

"A few. Good customers, mostly nice."

"What about Crown Valley?"

"Pfft. I avoided that graveyard," he said with disgust. "There is no business in that hellhole. It's like the plague had hit there."

I thought back to when Darcy crashed his SkyBlue jet into Crown Valley and wiped out the rest of Bale's men with the Super Gas he stole. The very gas that wiped out normal times and carried that moniker. I hadn't been back there since I discovered Darcy's act of restitution.

I wondered if Chuck was still alive. He was one of Bale's men that attacked Coppertown whom we released along with Bower to tell a lie. A lie that we still had the gas, despite Darcy's taking of it. Luke, the mayor of Coppertown, called it a deterrent.

One look at Crown Valley could dispel that lie.

The Shoeman continued. "So, I was heading to Kingman next when I spotted the smoke from the 40 Freeway. Made my way down here."

"There's nothing this way."

The Shoeman paused. "Very well. Anyway, I suppose I'll make my way over to Barstow, then back down to the Sea of Cortez once again. Go full circle. Can't stay in one spot, bad for business. This old ass has weathered many a storm and crisscrossed many a tangle. The donkey hasn't done too badly either." He laughed.

The Mojave was where I was headed. "A woman and two boys?" I asked. All too often, the response was negative.

"Yours, perhaps?"

"Yes."

"None that I seen."

"What about Rogues?" I asked.

"None that I seen."

While I kept my eye on him, I reached into my backpack and tossed him a can of corn. It fell into the horde of shoes but he didn't seem to mind. He tipped his hat again and thanked me.

"You're lying about not wearing a dead man's shoes, by the way," he proclaimed as he moved turned his donkey and cart around. "Your boots, although mismatched, look too fine to dance on this sandy floor five years on."

"I can't sing either," I yelled back to him.

He giggled and clicked his tongue. The donkey slowly trudged forward. The Shoeman's back was to me and that implied trust. That was rare.

Staring down at my boots, I thought about reconsidering as I wiggled my toes inside them. My left one, black in color, a smaller boot, was showing some wear with a hole in the side. The right, tan in color, was newer and more comfortable, hiking up my leg almost to my shin. Walking on the desert floor ruins them fast. I had been through so many. I was tempted to shout to him to stop, and maybe inquire about a new pair, but at that moment, I heard the distinct sound of an engine. That meant Rogues.

Birds scattered from trees down the road from the direction I was headed. The donkey sensed something too coming towards it, head-on. It reared and bucked, the cart spilling some shoes. The Shoeman tried to regain control with clicks and *whoas,* but the swirl of dust rising from the trees and the throaty rumble of an exhaust meant a vehicle was coming fast. It sounded like a truck. That meant bad news as I was sure the Shoeman was aware. Panicked, he was trying to dismount and his foot seemed caught in a stirrup. Although I was further down the road, I did not want to be seen and quickly ducked into the bushes next to me with my bike, hiding behind thick growth.

The Shoeman was doomed. There was nowhere to hide. Even if he ran into the woods, the donkey and cart were dead giveaways that someone was close by and he'd be hunted down. Excited voices filled the air and then I saw it, a white Toyota truck, and it was barreling towards The Shoeman. Two armed men were standing in the bed, peering over the roof with rifles laid flat. Their quarry had been sighted and they were egging the driver onward, slapping the roof in excitement. Two more men were inside the truck.

The white truck skidded in the dirt stopping just shy of The Shoeman. The men in the back laughed and jumped down, just as The Shoeman did from his perch, only the portly shoe salesman clutched his knee as he landed awkwardly. The Rogues quickly surrounded The Shoeman who was fast to clasp his hands together in pleading.

The two Rogues were having none of it. One of them butt-ended The Shoeman in the head, knocking him down. The passenger slid out from the truck and pointed for the men to check the wagon. The passenger, wearing a thick green sweater of all things, searched the pockets of The Shoeman who allowed it, his hands shaking near his face.

"Don't waste your precious bullets on me!" The Shoeman wailed.

"Take what you want! Spare me, please! I am nothing!" I could hear it all, even from where I hid.

"Did I say you could talk?" Sweater Rogue said. "Shut the hell up."

Finally, the driver of the truck sauntered out, the larger among the men, with dark red hair and a firm physique. The Shoeman continued to plead, sobbing, dribbling, even after the other man completed his search. The Red-Headed Rogue listened indifferently while the others in his party looked on, then lifted a gun from a holster and aimed it at The Shoeman.

"Did you see my men come this way?" the Red Headed Rogue asked.

The Shoeman correctly shook his head. I thought for a moment that he might give me away. Instead, he replied, "No, I am but by myself on this lonely road."

"What about the smoke?"

"I don't know the source. I am searching for it myself."

"How far have you traveled?"

"A great distance, sir."

The Red Headed Rogue turned to scour the area as if not believing him. "My men are missing."

"I have seen no one."

"A dark blue Charger. They came this way."

The Shoeman searched his thoughts. "Sorry, I do not recall."

"You're lying, tax evader."

"Me? No sir."

"You've hidden from us long enough, you piece of shit," Sweater Rogue said. "Time to pay up."

"Wait," The Shoeman said and I gulped. "A dark blue car you say? Sorry, I do not know makes or models. I may have seen one drive by about ten miles south. Yes, now I remember. Ten miles south."

The Red Headed Rogue smiled and then fired. The Shoeman's head snapped back. Blood sprayed like a fine mist and The Shoeman toppled on his side. The Red-Headed Rogue studied his work for a moment. "Grab his shit," he barked and the other men began to work.

Sadly, there wasn't much I could do. All I had was the crowbar but that was for close, inside fighting. The fact they wasted a bullet on The

Shoeman told me they had plenty of ammo. So, I hid there, watching them, staying safely out of sight. One of them soothed the terrified donkey who was stomping and snorting after the gunshot. He then calmed it with soft strokes. The man knew horses and mounted the donkey with ease. Another man jumped into the cart. The donkey and cart team then headed back in the direction they had come. However, the Red Headed Rogue and Sweater Rogue got back into the truck and drove in the direction The Shoeman claimed the Charger had been spotted. Driving towards me.

The Charger. It had to be the same car Bower had taken off in.

They passed me but I managed to stay out of sight. I got a good glimpse at them as they drove by, however. The man in the green sweater was a bit paunchy with black stubble. Dark eyes, bent nose. Nothing special, but the redhead driving had a stern look to him, with hard eyes, and a firm chin.

They left The Shoeman there, sprawled in the dirt, dead.

I left him there too. Any sign of care would be a sign that someone else was there and I didn't need the attention.

I biked northward to the 40 Freeway and found it about a half-hour later. With no more car engines and lots of tall shrubs for cover just in case, I had the road to myself and veered west. A planned detour took precedence before tackling that hardy endeavor on the California side.

It was a good time to listen to some tunes too.

Reaching into my backpack, I hauled out the Walkman, placed the earplugs into my ears, and pressed the play button. The volume was cranked up and that scared the bejesus out of me. Ha-ha, Matias. You got me. Once the volume was lowered, I bopped my head and began to smile. The Bee Gees sounded awesome. Yes, the effing Bee Gees.

A few songs were familiar, some not so much. I sang out loud, "I'm a-stayin' alive, stayin' alive, ah, ah, ah, ah, stayin' alive, stayin' alive..." while others I listened to, just because. After one whole turn of the tape, I clicked it off, saving the rest for another time. The batteries were one of the most precious resources anyone can have and full Double-A's can score you some big trade items.

I rode along the 40 Freeway uncontested all day but checked behind me for the white truck which never showed. I passed the town of Peachberry which was overrun five years earlier by Bale's men who slaughtered everyone there and left it to ruin. There was no point to scavenge anything there. Drifters had already done that over these years.

Later, my front tire began to wobble. I stopped to inspect it and heard a soft *shhhhhh* sound that worried me. Air was escaping the tire.

"Damnit," I said to myself. I watched it deflate until it almost flattened out. I couldn't do anything to stop it as I carried no patch kits. After inspecting the tire closely, I saw a small pointy stick stuck inside the rim. Angry, I rolled the bike into some trees and marked the spot by leaning a busted branch against a rock. I would have to hoof it from then on until I found another.

Camp for the night was between a large boulder and two trees just off the freeway. Dusk settled in with a cool wind behind it. I removed my hammock and strung it taught between the two trees which groaned under my weight. Still, it allowed a four-foot gap between my butt and the ground. Sleeping high kept the ground layer critters off me, mainly scorpions and tarantulas that seek out dark places to hide and hunt. Only the giant spider has bitten me, once on the arm, as it climbed over me one early morning. A strong bite that felt like a bee sting, it was thankfully non-venomous but still irritating. Stories of scorpion stabs were generally exaggerated but their sting was venomous. It will cause a painful burn, make you incredibly dizzy, you'd barf your guts out, and you'd start seeing dead people. Nah, the last part I made up, but it was still not fun.

Bundling up after a can of beets, I relaxed with a gentle sway from the wind that eventually lulled me to sleep. Sometime in the night, I heard a pair of engines drive by but I did not see them. Soon, they were gone.

I woke in the morning to cloudy skies, cooler temps, chirping birds, and hunger pains. After my usual routine of push-ups, sit-ups, and stretching, my stomach growled. My gut was getting used to a routine feeding and growing spoiled from Matias. Scoring some teriyaki beef jerky from his bunker, I set out minding to ration the tasty, chewy meat, gnawing and dribbling until my wet fingers scoured an empty bag bottom. So much for rationing, dumb ass.

And so much for a happy tummy. No sooner after I finished the bag, I darted behind a rock and squatted, trying to figure out if it was the canned beets or the delicious jerky. Remembering the toilet paper in my backpack, I wiped with a softness that was just as relieving as the act of depositing itself. When done, I inspected the beef jerky package and realized, stupidly, that there was a best-before-date which was some four years earlier. Why Matias kept it after all these years was beyond me. Maybe he forgot?

Sometime later, and another two pit stops later, my tummy finally forgave me. I picked up my step remembering that a Call Box was ahead.

I had a phone call to make.

The Call Box served as more of a lifeline than a landline. I usually stopped at every one I came across that was working, using it to check in with my family. Not all were in good shape, but some were. Each time, I would cradle the receiver nervously, hoping my family would answer. The Call Box next to a deserted, burned-out big rig further down the 40 Freeway was a favorite of mine, it had a direct line to my family and my kids were always the first to answer. I never bothered to ask how they got into the emergency center, but I never cared. All I wanted to hear were their voices.

Strangely, first responders never answered. Nor did anyone else. Just my family.

One time some years ago, I spoke into a Call Box off the 10 Freeway further south, and an old drifter sleeping next to it woke and mumbled, "Them phones ain't workin' no more, ya dipshit. You're wasting your time."

My response to him was, "Yeah, then who am I talking to on the other end of the line, smart guy?"

"Voices in your head. You're going batshit crazy," he argued. "You're hallucinating." Then, he fell back asleep.

"Hallucinating, my ass," I barked and turned away. "Keep out of it."

He was wrong. I just lifted the receiver and spoke into it. I couldn't explain it.

This new call made me nervous. Not every call was a good one. I flung open the small door and gripped the receiver in my hand. My oldest son came on the other line almost immediately. After some idle chat, he whined. I cradled the receiver against my neck, watching the roads in either direction.

"But I hate homework," Wayne complained. "It's so stupid."

"Dude," I told him. "It never goes away. You have lots of school left. And then you have college."

"Do I have to go?"

"To where, college?"

"Yeah."

"Of course, you do."

Wayne sighed on the other end. "I just want to play hockey. Can I be a professional instead?"

"Hockey players go to college too," I reminded him. "Think about it. What if you don't make it? And, they don't play forever. College is something to fall back on."

"Dad?"

"What?"

"Why weren't you home with us when the world ended?"

"I was coming home, son."

"Is that what we were? Something to fall back on?"

I tensed up. How the hell did he get so mature all of a sudden? My wife. That was it. She was feeding him lines. I gripped the receiver hard.

"Don't listen to your Mom. You guys were always my priority."

I could tell he wasn't convinced. He went quiet on the other end. I imagined him sitting there in his room, one hand on the phone, the other controlling a mouse. He'd be at his desk, not doing homework, but playing a video game and trying to blow me off.

Once I got my other son on the phone, it was more of the same.

Indifference, boredom, yes and no answers, me talking, he not paying attention. "I'll be at your game on Saturday," I told my youngest, trying to end the call. I couldn't wait. I loved watching their games. They were both good at the sport and they enjoyed playing.

The line suddenly went dead.

"Kevin?"

Silence.

"Son, can you hear me?"

Still nothing.

"If you can hear me, tell your Mom I'll call later."

Sadly, I hung the phone up and closed the Call Box door. Of all the Call Boxes I came across, that one worked the best. Some didn't work at all.

CHAPTER FIVE

Coppertown was a newly formed community that took root in a former copper quarry after the gas hit, which was situated almost shouting distance to the Nevada border. Having been a former rock mine, Coppertown had an abundant amount of dynamite that was left behind. The new residents that claimed the quarry as a camp put the dynamite to good use, using it to carve rock for storage and fortify their defenses. I had been coming there over the years to drop in and say hello on my wayward journeys. Rarely did I stay longer than a few days though.

There was only one entrance to the fortress. Manning the gate was the enormous yellow monster, a bulldozer with a massive loader and metal spikes. I had used this terrifying machine once during a raid in the early years and managed to crush two of Bale's men underneath it.

A pair of gun barrels were aimed at me on either side. Riflemen were posted there as sentries and they weren't a patient lot. A young man on one side and a teenage girl on the other. Both were armed and serious.

"Drop your backpack!" the young guy cried out. I complied, my eyes never leaving theirs.

"Let's see your hands!" the girl shouted.

Standing there with my hands high, I rolled my eyes to acquiesce and go through the motions. I was also trying to refrain from smiling.

"Are you alone?" the young man asked, looking beyond me.

Here went my spiel. "I walk my own path. You will never catch me following another's footsteps." That was greeted with silence. That meant I was alone.

"So lame," the girl replied and giggled. She was named Daisy; she was pretty, had brown frilly hair, baby blue eyes, and looked remarkably older than she appeared. The young man rapped the gate with his barrel three times. His name was Ben, after his late father, the latter having died during a cave-in when they were creating more room in the mountain. Ben was thin, geeky, with moppy hair – careless like a typical teenager. Black smoke belched from the exhaust as soon as the bulldozer fired up. The claw jiggled as it rose to a height of five feet. Ducking under with my backpack in my hand, I noticed the dried blood on the spikes and lower jaw of the yellow monster were never cleaned for show. I wondered if I was responsible for some of it.

Hugged by both as I cleared the gate, the two young ones guided me in. "Well, look who's back," Ben said, patting my back. "Drifter Ted."

Daisy said to me, "You can't just stay away, can you?"

Ben interjected before I could answer. "You need a new password by the way. That one is getting old."

Inside, Coppertown reminded me of an Arabic bazaar. It was filled with rows of open wall tents, picnic tables, chairs, and cooking fires they called the "mall." Parked RV's were campground slotted at the left wall while a few cars and trucks sat idle, but orderly, near the entrance. Only a few vehicles ran, though seldom anymore. Last time I was here, they had finally run out of fuel in the barrels. The degradation of gas over five years would have made it useless anyway even if there was any left.

Disgruntled men were attending to the vehicles, tossing tools and parts aside, and I saw more today with their engines ripped apart, needing to be cleaned, than last time. Two cars remained on blocks, having been there on my last visit some months ago.

Outside excursions were common and necessary. Daring midnight water runs to the nearby Colorado River was done from time to time under armed convoys. Otherwise, wells tapped into the groundwater outside the quarry and open barrels rimming the compound enabled the residents to catch some much-needed liquid from the rains. Pens were stocked with chickens, rabbits, goats, a few cows, and horses. There was farming going on as well with soil trucked in from nearby Bullion. Rows of vegetables grew in an orderly garden. Corn, carrots, tomatoes, lettuce, and others I couldn't recall. Fruit trees were rooted next to the gardens. These were all fenced in, of course, and rationing was still part of the law. They took turns guarding the area; that night it was an older lady cradling a candle and a romance novel.

A stage was central in the camp that was built for meetings, discussions, and performances. They met there every night, weather permitting, for games, songs, and general amusement. Other times, serious announcements were made and attendance was always mandatory.

Upon entering, I was immediately surrounded by Marcel and Big Joe with Daisy trailing. They all descended on me like I was a celebrity; Marcel from the bulldozer seat, Big Joe from one of the cars being repaired, strolling over with a carburetor in his greasy hand. Boredom was very contagious within these walls especially if you didn't venture out much. Ben stayed back to keep watch as a hobbling Marcel took his place at my side.

Marcel was a thin, pale-faced older man covered in warts on his face and hands, due to a sickness no one could verify, but wasn't spreading. He once worked the quarry and I pegged him about fifty, give or take ten years. Big Joe was a scrawny black man with a long beard. Another quarry alum in his mid-forties, he had a deep scar carved into his left cheek from breaking up a knife fight. Sometimes, even the good folks at Coppertown can fall victim to stir-crazy. Staying within the secure walls can still make one feel isolated and claustrophobic.

They parked me near the stage in a ratty lawn chair. They asked me where I had been and what I had seen. Soon, the group became larger with familiar faces all welcoming me back. I rehashed my journeys since the last visit. They listened intently and nodded in unison. Same old shit, different month.

As I spoke, I searched the grounds for Sara, the woman I rescued from Crown Valley and brought to this place five years earlier. She was nowhere to be seen and I hoped she was faring better. Each time I stopped by, she opened up a bit more and I could sense the old Sara was reemerging. We had never been intimate or romantic, but we once had a friendship I missed terribly. She was heavily traumatized from what Bale had done to her and took a long time to recover. I knew she felt alone and my leaving never helped. The poor soul was crushed in more ways than one and I knew that. I restrained from pursuing anything further with her. My family was always my number one priority.

The others egged me on to continue with my stories. I spoke about The Shoeman and the Rogues I had just encountered. Their concern grew as if a mighty storm was on its way.

"Filthy Rogues," someone spat.

"The Shoeman paid us a visit last year," Big Joe said and showed his new boots. "Good man." Everyone was in general agreement on that.

I went on to tell them that there are other small communities set up like this one, some starting to get back on track and establishing trading since the greenback was still worthless paper. Trust was hard to come by though and most places didn't just take in anyone. That was still a staple from the early years. Still, there was safety in numbers, and the scrutiny was lessening, especially when it came to protecting yourself again from the Rogues.

Talk about the Rogues perked everyone up like birds in a tree but not in a good way; everyone voiced an opinion, some getting animated and heated. It was an old argument with no resolve.

Flustered by the Rogue talk, the group eventually broke up and went about their business. Only Marcel, Big Joe, and Daisy remained and we sat there in silence for a few minutes. I was tired and hungry, glancing woefully at the fruit trees, hoping I'd score something to eat besides digging into my stash. Canning was used to preserve the fruit during off-season times of harvest. I was always allowed a few jars each time I left and I rationed them well. They were marvelous and my mouth was beginning to water.

"Where's our manners?" Daisy asked and raced off to a nearby tree.

She quarreled with the old woman, who was reluctant at first to budge, then flipped her hand to allow Daisy access to a pear tree. Returning to me, she slipped the gorgeous pear into my hand and I tore into it. She dropped another in my pocket that she was able to steal.

Scurvy was a bitch. You saw it on some drifters; swollen gums, red-blue spots on their skin, and deep, purple bruises all over. They seemed to be in pain as they walked, usually hunched, always out of breath. Lack of Vitamin C would do it every time. Death came slowly by way of infection or bleeding. Like all the diseases that rose out of nowhere, scurvy was not pretty.

"About time you quit wandering, don't ya think?" Marcel asked me, patting me on the back like a chum, trying to divert the conversation. Here we go again, I sighed, chewing slowly, savoring each bite. Another recruitment talk.

"You know me, I won't stop until I find them," I reminded him.

Daisy rolled her eyes. "You should give up, with all due respect. We got a good thing here. There's talk we may move out." The others rolled their eyes at her and I could tell it regarded the last item. I couldn't see them leaving, not just yet. Daisy didn't catch their expressions; they thought her young and naïve. Poor thing must be eighteen now. She barely got to be a teenager, stuck in a rock quarry with mostly middle-aged men. Slim pickings in here with only Ben as the only available suiter about her age. Ben was not into *those things* and was probably asexual, she once confided in me. The "mall" itself there was a contradiction.

"Did you see Harley and his wife?" Big Joe chimed in.

"Harley..." I said, trying to think. The name didn't ring...

"The guy who owns the Harley," he said, somewhat sullen. "Don't you remember? You played cards with him last time."

Now, I remembered. "That's right. New guy, right? Rode the Harley? Duh. No, I haven't. Why?"

Daisy responded, "He and Cherry are long overdue. Should have been here three days ago at the latest." She quickly eyed Marcel and Big Joe, getting nods from both.

I shrugged. "I haven't seen them. I came up from the east. Where did they go?"

"The Digs," Daisy blurted and Marcel coughed. "Northwest of here."

The Digs was the Rogue camp that was making moonshine in vast quantities. The dregs of society flourished there. Although dangerous given the habitants at that camp, most people went there willingly for the booze.

"Why would they go there?" I asked.

"Running low on fuel and..." Daisy said and she caught herself. Fuel was another benefit of the high-level spirit. Luke had told me that the newer cars could run on the white lighting, but it wasn't easy.

"No matter," Big Joe replied. "They'll be back. So, how long do you want to stay?"

Coppertown was alive all around me and the smell of cooking meat got me extra hungry. The population grew to two hundred with some souls coming and going. Few elderly and kids. There was an order here and I liked that.

"Maybe overnight, if that's okay with you all?" I asked.

"Stay as long as you like," Daisy replied. "Family Feud tonight. Want to play?" Family Feud was one of the games they liked to play, kids and adults alike. Many of the RVs carried board games inside them. Poker and charades were also common too. Someone was writing a play last I heard.

Just as I was about to answer, Daisy nudged me. "Sara is doing well. I know you want to know that."

I breathed a sigh of relief. "Good to hear. I want to see her."

Daisy grabbed my hand. "Daddy would like to see you first."

Daddy was Daisy's father, Luke. He was also the leader of Coppertown, a former cop-turned-lawyer-turned-city council member from somewhere in the San Fernando Valley, just north of Los Angeles. He could speak, motivate, and lead wayward people once too frightened to hold a gun or even face one. A good decade older than me, the taller man with a full head of gray hair welcomed me with a hug as I entered his trailer. When I first met him, the grays were only wispy. He and Daisy still lived in the trailer which also served as "city hall." A hair stylist's chair sat in the corner in front of a mirror. Daisy found a new and convenient trade-in cosmetology and was getting better at it. She lopped off my hair last time and it hadn't been cut since.

"Sit, sit," Luke said to me and we sat on old office chairs with the mayor behind a large desk cluttered with paper. I stared at a wallet-sized photo of his late wife taped to the wall who had been left behind at home when the gas hit. She had been pretty, younger, a second wife, but lost to the gas. Luke and Daisy had been returning from Laughlin after seeing a concert by some R&B artist known as Camille de Pente. Daisy had her autograph, signed backstage after the show, and showed it proudly. I barely knew who Camille was.

A photo of Daisy sat centered on his desk, taken recently. He had others but kept the more up-to-date images upfront. It was a Polaroid camera, left behind by an older gentleman who passed away at the camp. It was mostly used for the dead. I know Luke snuck one in on his daughter and placed it inside an old frame after the man passed. Speaking of the deceased, I turned left and saw the "death board" where the other images of the deceased were pinned, starting with the old owner of the camera in the top left. There were five rows of the unlucky ones, eyes eerily open for the show. Most were from the Hellion attack that I helped defend against some four years ago. Eddie, from my earlier days, was up there. A stroke victim two years ago. That was a sad one for me. Vanessa stayed in their RV and became somewhat of a recluse after. I never saw her on my last visit here. There were at least five more added since I was here last. One was a kid, the youngest here at the camp. Carlos was his name and he was number eighty-one.

"What happened to Carlos?" I asked.

"Appendicitis. It was an awful death."

"Damn."

"So, the wayward drifter came back to lovely old Coppertown," Luke chided with a slight smirk. He knew I came across similar communities like this that were just as nice, protective, and filled with hope. The struggle wasn't necessarily about keeping bad guys out but keeping the good ones in. People left the confines of a tranquil place all the time. Sometimes, it was to see if a better-suited society flourished elsewhere. Better medicines, better food, better people. Sometimes, it was strictly out of boredom.

"Decided to stay I hope," Luke said. "Room in Big Joe's trailer. He's a snorer but he keeps to himself."

"You know I can't. Not yet, anyway."

Luke mulled the answer over each time I said it. I know he thought I was wasting my time and I didn't give a rat's ass that he thought that. I couldn't stay here even if I wanted to.

"You know what I'm going to say," he said.

"Then don't."

"Come on, Ted," he sighed. "You belong here. You know you do. You're surrounded by friends. You helped us fight for this quarry. You're family to us. We could use you. Build morale. Keep the place safe."

"I only plan to stay the night. They had me at Family Feud."

He looked me square in the eye like a father to a child. "Each time you leave us, I think it'll be the last time."

"And yet, here I am again," I reiterated.

Luke snorted. "Did Daisy tell you about Harley and Cherry?"

"Yes, they said they went to the Rogue camp."

"We all have our needs," he surmised. "I couldn't stop them if I tried. They took the bridge at Dregger Road. There's less *activity* there."

"Activity," I repeated.

"Trolls," he responded.

"Did you send them?"

Luke shot me a stern look. "They went on their own accord."

Arguing that matter would have been useless. Fact was, if you travel by vehicle, any vehicle, you'd attract attention. Vehicles make noise. Harley and Cherry were on a two-wheeler with very loud pipes. Dumb, dumb, dumb.

"Ginn leads the filthy bastards," Luke continued. "He's like some master warlord now. We think he took the other groups over by force."

"Ginn, huh," I replied. "I didn't know that."

Ginn, the old hotel concierge who framed me for cheating on my wife back before the gas. The man who gave me the scar on my hand. The man was responsible for separating me from my family. The man Matias called the Trickster. Still alive and creating havoc. After all these years.

Luke continued. "Even we are compelled to trade at times there, albeit with lots of security. Usually armed with the gas and dynamite."

The former meant the Rogues still saw the jar of gas we took from Bale as a threat. Bower had spread the word long ago when we released him and none of the Rogues had figured out that the original jar was used by Darcy to wipe out their comrades in Crown Valley. It could be they assumed Luke had the original or maybe they knew of more jars that were still out there. That was scary. Even the Rogues didn't take any chances. The rope that bound the jar was a distinct, braided relic with symbols and letters in Latin. No one second-guessed its origins.

The latter meant a bomb-on-wheels. For extra security, dynamite was loaded into a cart surrounded by rocks and shards of metal. It was then hauled by horses to the camp. Not to trade, but to deter any attack. If there was any threat, the shrapnel alone could wipe out a city block. The group here traded fruit and eggs mostly and was always given a wide berth by the Rogues. Extra space was for the moonshine on its return.

Luke reached down into a drawer and pulled out a half bottle of whiskey and two shot glasses, as per our ritual. Upon leaving here last time in the spring, I told him I ventured west to Central California on the off chance that my wife and my kids ventured north to the Bay Area for no other reason that I was striking out everywhere else. There had simply been no sign of them anywhere, despite all my queries and searching. I was acting on the fact that my wife lied and she had taken my kids much earlier than she admitted and they were further than I originally thought.

A SkyBlue flight attendant, Rebecca Shutt, admitted to me years ago that my mother-in-law flew out to Orange County the day before the worldwide gas attack. My wife never told me Kathryn was coming out to see her and my boys. That meant plans were in motion *not involving me*.

"I suppose you want to know about Sara," Luke said and filled our glasses. "She's doing fine. Great actually. Talks, laughs, is more integrated now than ever." He paused and eyed me. "She is still beautiful."

"Any suitors?"

"None," Luke said with a shake of his head. "She's turned down every one. If you ask me, she's waiting."

"Waiting for what?"

Luke shot me a look. I felt awkward.

"Tell me what you saw there, in Central California," he said, changing the subject, raising his glass and we drank.

I told him the flat, arable land was fertile again, and that migrants were able to recover the fields to a degree and resume farming a few crops. "There were attempts to unite the groups that remained there but that was filled with some hostilities. Spanish is the preferred language with many calling the region La Raza now."

"The Race?" Luke asked. "That's what that means, right?"

"They're taking back California," I responded. "No significant leader among them though. They can't agree on that yet. But they have tons of fruit to fight off scurvy."

"Any troubles?" he asked.

"The usual," I shrugged. "Not just the Hispanics, but others. Most folks are trying to better their lives. Lots of trading going on. I heard a census wagon from Sacramento is making the rounds too. Trying to count who's left."

That brought him a smile. "Did you see our new trees? Grapefruit. We figure another year or two and they'll start producing," Luke stated, changing the subject. "We've succeeded with other crops too, but the camp is quite small. We need to expand our growing efforts."

"How?"

"We need to find open land."

"That means leaving Coppertown," I pointed out.

"We've sent out scouts to see if there is arable land. We've found some near the river. A good spot for all of us."

I figured as much. They were land-locked but growing. They needed to move.

As he poured again, I told him that during the late summer, I cut back around the Sierras and headed north to Utah where I found the polygamists were happily united, armed with an *I told you* so arrogance and a walled city to keep non-believers out.

"They were in the boonies already. They were lucky the gas from Las Vegas didn't reach that far north," I noted.

"Did you get in?" he asked.

I shook my head. "It was like talking to a wall. I was not welcome. My wife and kids were not in attendance either. No way my wife would have consented to sharing a husband or even wanting another one after my alleged track record," I said. I then wondered if she was still admitting she was married anyway.

"Doesn't anyone realize with all those wives, you have that many more mother-in-laws?" I asked him with a serious look.

He laughed and said, "I'll drink to that." And he did, swallowing the glass entirely and gasping loudly. Grabbing what was left of the whiskey, he shook it and said, "Soon enough, this baby will be gone and we'll have to go to the camp myself."

"Getting dry are we?"

"Bone dry." Luke then reclined his chair. "Speaking of boning, I hope to God you're abstaining from sex."

Odd statement. "What do you mean?" I asked.

"STDs are making a whale of a comeback. Syphilis is the big daddy, but we're seeing signs of the clap and crabs. There's no lack for people getting their freak on, but try finding a Doctor when your dick is dripping."

"Inside Coppertown?"

"Afraid so," he sighed. "Lack of condoms will do that. They get red sores all over like bad pimples, some get lesions and scarring. Then, you see the ones that look like zombies from hell, missing noses, lips, hair, and skin. Eventually, they die."

He was exaggerating, I knew that. Having abstained though, I felt lucky. I looked bad enough as it was. I didn't need my kids to see me like the undead on top of it.

Luke shifted in his chair. "If you need a spot check around the genitals, Manson will do it." Manson was a resident Doctor who had stayed for five years on. They kept the young man busy here. That earned him a spot in one of the mobile homes where the weather in the winter wasn't exactly favorable.

"We even have a herbalist here too who swears on these new remedies to fight off infection, but I'm not convinced," Luke admitted. "Where's some amoxicillin when you need it?"

Shaking my head in disbelief, I let him know that I had abstained and rightly planned to continue.

"Don't you ever get lonely?" he asked, sincerely.

"Sometimes," I confessed.

Luke stared at the photo of his daughter and turned it to me. "She thinks the world of you. She's not my little girl anymore. She's a grown woman. She's twenty-one now."

"Twenty-one? I thought she was only eighteen. Wow. Time flies."

"You two could make a good pair," he suggested.

I coughed. "Yeah, right."

"Is it weird that I might be pawning off my daughter?" he asked.

That was awkward and out of the blue. "I'm sure there's a lot of boys nearby."

"I found blood in my stool," he admitted. "Sometimes the pain is unbearable. Daisy doesn't know. Only myself and the herbalist and we're scrambling. Not so much for the leadership of Coppertown, I'm not worried about that. There are plenty of good people here that can take over. Before I go though, I want to see her with a man, a suitable man that can take care of her. That's my biggest concern. And despite your age gap, you're it."

I did the math in my head. Biologically, I was clearly old enough to be her father.

Luke interjected. "I trust you. I know you'll treat her well. Your devotion is admirable and you're certainly one not to fuck around with."

"Luke..."

Angrily, he rose from his chair. "Your family is dead! Why won't you admit it?"

A tear streaked down his cheek, the first time I had ever witnessed that from the normally stalwart man. The awkward pause between us was jolted by a knock on the door. With a look of contempt, Daisy entered the office eyeing the both of us like a mother to her warring kids. It was her turn to act the adult with a righteous glare and Luke calmed, settling back down in his seat. I wondered how much she had heard.

"What's going on?" she asked.

"Nothing sweetheart," Luke gasped and wiped a tear. "What can we do for you?"

"The rototiller needs more fuel," she said with her hands on her hips. "We want to open another row for carrots. Can we get more fuel?"

Luke looked at her incredulously. "Why are you asking? You know we can."

She stated, "I just want to make sure. You and your rations."

"Sure," he said and waved her off.

"Don't be that way," Daisy barked. "Fuel is important, you know that. If we ran out, you'd be all up in my grill. Then we'd have to head off to the Digs to get more."

"Third-world problems," Luke told me with a wink.

"Well, you nominated yourself as the leader," Daisy interjected.

Before she left, she snatched the bottle of whiskey and mumbled that her father shouldn't be getting the guests plastered. We stared at two empty shot glasses wishing for more but neither one of us was willing to chase her down. "Maybe you don't want to be around her after all," he sighed. "She's just like her mother."

"I already have a wife."

"And if not for her, maybe Sara. I get it."

"Don't confuse me any more than I am," I sighed.

Sighing, he leaned back and dismissed the prior conversation. "Anyway, tell me more of what you saw out there in the wild," he said. "After, we'll have dinner."

So, I did.

After dinner, which was a bowl of jackrabbit stew mixed with potatoes and corn, I paid a visit to the outhouse after my stomach rumbled uneasily. Food often got to me that way when I wasn't used to spices and herbs. Since toilet paper had been used up years ago, their method of cleaning was scooping a ladle of water to wash one's backside. Some people preferred to bring in their cleaning devices, like washcloths, but simple water did the trick for most, while the coolness of running water back there always gave me a jolt.

When I was done, I washed my hands in a communal bucket where I cleaned with homemade soap. They had a disgusting way of making it by use of animal fats, bones, and lye which I learned was wood ashes, liquified. All of it was boiled together and then allowed to harden. Because of the overwhelming stench of boiling these ingredients, they often only did it every few months, usually late at night. The saving grace was the numerous desert flowers like acacia, lavender, and chia that were added afterward, that not only masked the smell but livened it to what we used to expect from a soap.

Sara still hadn't made an appearance, not even at dinner with the rest of us. She had to have known I was there as word spreads fast.

I ventured for a walk around the camp by myself, visiting some of the locals and catching up. I was greeted warmly by the denizens as always and I enjoyed hearing about their lives since the last visit. The walk was an excuse to eventually meander to the mobile homes where Sara worked, as a nurse, so I could pop in and say hello.

At one point, amid a deep conversation with an older lady named Ruth about boils and how best to clean them, I was thankfully rescued by a tap on the shoulder. It was Sara. She smiled at me and looked as beautiful as ever. Her blonde hair was cut around her shoulders, her face radiant, her eyes still a sparkling blue. "How are you, stranger?" she asked me and then hugged me.

"So good to see you," I said and hugged her back.

We held each other for a long time. Ruth got the hint and walked away. "Will you walk with me?" Sara asked after we parted. "My shift ended so I have some free time."

We began to walk. "They keep you busy here?" I asked her.

"Yes," she admitted. "But I enjoy it. Manson taught me a lot over the years. He's a great instructor. He's dating Rebecca, the flight attendant. They're hot and heavy. They sneak off into the desert to hide it, pretending to go on hikes. But we all know better."

Dating was very incestuous in Coppertown. With limited available suitors, it was inevitable and always awkward. Fights often broke out. People left too. "Wasn't she recently married to Brad, the SkyBlue Pilot?" I asked.

"The *supposed* marriage only lasted two months It was a simple swearing-in over a bible with Luke winging it and acting as a minister. Brad accused her of having a fling with a man who's no longer here. Brad took it hard when they broke up and he supposedly added peyote to her soup. She went berserk, hallucinating and crying. We forced her to throw up but she bit Manson on the finger in the process." Sara laughed. "His finger was taped up for a week but Rebecca was grateful, if not ashamed, and came by often to apologize. I guess they hooked up after that."

"Wow," I responded. "What happened to Brad?"

"Banished. Haven't seen or heard from him in months."

"That's too bad," I sighed. "I liked Brad. He was a good guy, or so I thought."

We walked past some kids inside the tented school. While it was after school hours, they often took to arts and crafts to cure their boredom.

"How have you been these days?" I asked.

"Much better. Most of the sting had worn off. I recall a lot of what happened but have come to push those memories away. Being raped by that slob Bale put me in another world. I had headaches. I was fearful and anxious. I lost any sexual desire. It put me on guard. I couldn't trust people. We had a psychiatrist in here for a while and I was able to talk to him. He said I suffered from post-traumatic stress disorder. Working in the clinic with Manson made me help others. It helped me to heal."

I didn't recall any psychiatrist before. "What happened to the doctor?"

"He was only here a short time. He left to find his sister up in Oregon just a few months ago." She paused and admitted, "It was too bad too. He was cute."

I didn't know what to say. I just smiled.

"What about you?" Sara asked and stopped. "Did you find anyone else?"

"Why would you ask me that?"

Her face flashed a *duh* look. "Because if you found your family, you wouldn't be in here. You'd be with them."

I paused. "No, I haven't."

"I feel sorry for you. All this time you wander, full of hope. I can see the pain on your face. I hate to see that in you. Before, when we first met and made our way here, you were jovial, kind, and optimistic. Now, that man is mostly gone. All I see is a broken-down guy carrying on as if that's all he can do. Maybe you too suffer from PTSD."

"I hadn't thought of that," I replied. Although I should have.

She gripped my hand. "We are much more alike. I think we need each other."

"If things were different, Sara," I said. "I'd be next to you..."

She kissed me hard on the mouth. At first, I didn't let go. Eventually, however, I came up for air and gently pulled back.

"Sorry," she mumbled. "I shouldn't have."

Before I could respond, Daisy came running up to us, grabbed my hand, and said, "We're going to play Family Feud right now!"

Lying on a cot outside next to Big Joe's trailer, I stared up at the Heavens and marveled once again at its majesty. The million pricks of light never bored me and on a cloudless night, the scene was as marvelous as ever. I squirmed for comfort as the middle rod of the damn contraption bore into my back, a problem I never had with my hammock. I could have slept on an empty bed in the RV, but Joe kept a ton of engine parts on it and I told him to leave it. He had a cot, a flimsy fold-up that was as uncomfortable as it looked and I took it trying to be polite. The springs whined under me and I thought sleep would never come.

Family Feud had been a blast. Sara and I played together on a team with her faring better than I at the answers. We played the game in front of a whiteboard, outlining the boxes on a black erasable pen. The questions themselves came from the board game named after the TV show. I lost, of course, and only got a few answers before perpetual and contagious yawning broke up the festivities and we all herded to bed.

We all went our separate ways. Sara kissed me on the cheek and wished me a good night's sleep before trailing off to the clinic's trailer where she usually slept in one of the beds. As a nurse, she was expected to stay close by at all times.

Most of Coppertown was asleep. Only a few awakened souls kept guard. I could hear random snoring coming from a few trailers. One RV was rocking back and forth and the thought of sex crept into my mind for the first time in a very long time and I felt a stirring down below. I became flustered, then angry, because my thoughts circled to Sara, asleep in the trailer when I should have been thinking of my wife.

Naturally, I assumed my wife Tracy was still alive. The possibility of her shacking up with another guy was a realistic scenario I couldn't fathom.

What if Tracy believed me to be dead? Quite the quandary I was in. I had many thoughts over the years on what we'd see in one another when we finally met up. I had been faithful. Had she?

Thankfully, the trailer stopped the rocking a second later, replaced by a grunt, a giggle, then two sets of snoring. My libido died with it as well and I closed my eyes.

After only a few hours of sleep and waking just before dawn, I rose from the obnoxious bed, grabbed my backpack, and tip-toed to the yellow monster as I didn't want to create a scene. Ben was nodding off inside the cabin of the machine with a men's fitness magazine on his lap when I got to him. Just before I could poke him, Sara tapped me on the shoulder suddenly from behind, a blanket wrapped around her.

Angry, she asked in a loud whisper, "Where do you think you're going?"

"I don't want to wake anyone," I confessed. "I have to go."

"What, like right now?"

Turning it back on her, I asked, "What are you doing here?"

Huffing, she searched for an answer, then said, "I had to go to the bathroom."

Not sure I believed her, I softened my tone. "I can't stay."

She paused. Her mouth started to speak, but no words came out. She reached out, held my hand, but then she snapped out of it and said, "You'll just wake everyone up if you let Ben operate this thing. No one is allowed to leave until seven am." She tugged on me and led me to a corner of the front gate where metal plates were welded together. Pulling back on it, one plate separated and came apart, exposing a hole to the outside. Enough for one to squeeze through.

"Sometimes, we just need to leave the camp, you know?" Sara admitted. "It can get stiffly in here. I used to ride a bike out to the old ninety-three and be back before anyone knew it."

The 93 Highway was a four-lane thoroughfare connecting Kingman and Lake Mead. "That's a hell of a dangerous ride," I pointed out with some concern. It was best to stay away from that road, ambushes and attacks were common.

"It was for exercise and to clear my head. I found the bike by a ditch near Bullion when we went out gathering seeds and plants one day. It was in pretty good shape. I can tell you where I hid it."

She told me where it was parked, behind some rocks on the trail I was heading, and I knew approximately where she meant. When she was done, she had a tear in her eye. "Every time I see you go, I think it's the last time I'll see you."

"I have to know. It's my family."

"This feels different though..."

"Why does everyone say that? Maybe I'll be back sooner than you know," I said and motioned to leave.

"This place isn't as strong as you think," she said. "We need you. I need you."

"Everything will be fine."

She pulled me back. "What if you finally find your family and it turns out, she is with someone else? That's a possibility, you know. Five years is a long time."

"Thanks for your concern."

"I see the way you look at me. You're in pain every time you leave. You should consider alternatives."

"Don't make this harder than it should."

"I guess you have to go then," she demurred. As she held the plate open for me, I thanked her and shoved my backpack through. Just as I threw my legs into the opening, she stopped me, kissed me on the mouth again, and said, "I hope you find what you were looking for. I really do."

Wanting to say more, I just said, "Thanks."

"I can't wait forever, you know."

My heart sank. With a fake smile, I replied, "I hope you don't."

She paused. "You didn't find it yet, did you?"

"Find what?"

"Never mind." With that, Sara turned and trudged off.

CHAPTER SIX

The mountain bike Sara gifted me was in good shape. It had ten gears, faded paint, loose brakes, and semi-pumped tires. I had spent a good hour riding since I left Coppertown and stopped at the Colorado River once again facing a new challenge ahead of me; where to cross to get to the California side. Unlike the northern Arizona crossing I took a few days ago, bridges were more numerous between California and Arizona but they were most certainly guarded. Ferries and boatmen worked the river there too. Luke mentioned that Harley and Cherry crossed at Dregger Road believing it was one of the less violent crossings and small enough for a motorcycle to cut over without much of an issue. In passing, Luke gave me directions as to where it was, only the trek seemed much further north.

Most of the squatters along the river watched me as I rode by on a cracked roadway. Fish bones, carcasses, and garbage lay scattered there too. I rested my crowbar on the handlebars, keeping it visible, just in case. Some of the river dwellers nodded to me. Others gave me a wide berth. Boats crisscrossed the river and I was propositioned at times, mostly for sexual favors in exchange for the trip. They were all from men and I declined with shakes of my head.

A sign for the Dregger Road Crossing finally came to view and soon, I saw the low-level expanse. The sides were made of wood while the rest of the bridge was made of steel. Thick weeds grew at each end around the supports. I slowed my pace and dismounted the bike. I noticed the bridge was empty, except for a man at the opposite end, watching me as he leaned on a car parked diagonally there. Another car was parked opposite, so the front bumpers kissed. Asphalt led the way with a thick yellow lane marker splitting it in two.

I studied the man and searched for signs of a possible ambush. Seeing nothing obvious, I still suspected he was not alone. No way would he conduct business by himself. I began to walk forward with my bike anyway. Still, no one else at the other end showed up next to him, and halfway across the span, I got the feeling others may have been hiding at my end, possibly under the bridge, ready to deny me a U-turn.

From a distance, I could see the man was ugly and dressed shabbily. He held a fishing gaff in his right while his left held a cup. He watched me advance, tilting his head as if I was an illusion. About three-fourths the way over, I twirled my skull crusher like it was a cane, daring him or anyone to *fucking* try it.

My adversary fidgeted nervously as I approached, lowering the gaff as it mattered. His features were indeed repulsive. His hair was brown, oily, and wily. His forehead was thick, and his eyebrows were massively hairy. Dark eyes, a pointed nose, and missing teeth. Lumps grew from his neck. With his haggard clothes, he reminded me, fittingly, of a troll.

Troll Man then wobbled when he stood and I realized he was drunk. In one of the cars behind him, a sloth of a woman rose from her sleep in the driver's seat. With blackened teeth, gums, and sunken eyes, all under a black mop of hair, she looked like she rose from the dead. She then began seductively stroking a shotgun barrel and rolling her tongue. I wasn't sure if that was an invite or a warning. You go, girl.

Sipping from the cup, the troll gawked at me and my crowbar but then manned up suddenly. "Stop right there. Can't cross unless you got something to give up," he said. We were about twenty feet apart.

I kept my eyes on the woman, making sure her barrel didn't come down. "A couple on a motorcycle. Big one. A Harley. They come by?"

"Yeah, yeah, they came by a few days ago," he slurred, through bleeding gums. "Headed north to the Digs." He fidgeted and kept glancing from side to side.

"You ain't lying to me, are you? You didn't try to gobble them up?"

Puzzled, he looked back at the woman, then returned. "Didn't hurt them at all. They traded fair and square. We let them go."

"They come back this way, Troll?"

"No, sir. Wait, what the fuck you say?"

"You seen any Rogues?" I asked him, then brought my backpack around. I was sure there were more trolls under the bridge. The witch in the car wasn't his backup.

"Nope," he replied and averted his eyes. That was a lie.

Reaching into my backpack, I brought out a package. "Beef jerky. Teriyaki flavor. When's the last time you had that?" I asked him.

The beef jerky was gladly accepted but then he got spoiled. Lowering his gaff at me, he hit me with, "What else you got? Because, this ain't enough, sugar."

"That's all you get, Troll," I stated.

"I don't think so," he responded and rapped his gaff on the ground twice.

Just then, the woman hit the horn three times and two more trolls emerged on either side of the bridge. They had come from below, trying to look intimidating, holding weapons at their sides. A blond one on my left had spikey hair, was covered in dirt and rags, had blotchy skin, and was missing teeth too. He carried a machete. The troll to my right was taller, bald, and leveling a golf club at me. It looked like a three-iron. He wore a dinner jacket over a pair of boxers. His legs were covered in purple rashes and his left wrist looked gimpy.

I wasn't in the mood.

Machete Troll to my left was my first concern. He had the deadlier weapon. I dropped my bike and began walking towards him with a confident stride. The image of Polecat entered my mind and my stomach churned. I felt the rage building within like a slow boil. I twirled my crowbar, gritted my teeth, and eyed the poor son of a bitch, knowing he was going to be in a world of pain. Machete troll suddenly swung nevertheless, completely wildly, and missed. A forward kick from my right leg connected with his chest before he could return. He slammed into the bridge and dropped the machete. I then smashed my crowbar down on his left shoulder with a dull whump that snapped his collarbone. He screamed and fell to his knees. His eyes bulged and he gasped in pain, slobbering and muttering in gibberish.

Behind me, I heard my bike wheeling away. Golfer Troll had snaked it and pushed it to the edge of the bridge where he had been standing.

"Give it back!" I yelled.

"Splashy splash," Golfer Troll giggled.

Golfer Troll picked it up and tossed it over the side. It splashed into the cold depths below. "You asshole!" I shouted and made a move towards him but Machete Troll suddenly found his weapon again and stood quickly, backhanding the large knife. I met his return with my crowbar, stepped inside, and smacked his jaw with a right elbow. He crumpled like a rag doll and fell against the railing. I used the toe of my boot to kick the machete over the side. It plopped into the river below. Machete Troll didn't move.

One down, two to go. Golfer Troll was next and I hiked toward him quickly. The main Troll just watched me walk by and I paid him no attention. Golfer Troll began to giggle but urine flooded his boxers as he strangely stood his ground. He cupped his mouth like a child who did a bad thing and raised his club. Not to strike, but to keep me away. I took no pity on the man. I brought my crowbar down on his hand, heard a bone crack, and watched the golf club bounce on the ground. His mouth contorted in pain and he was too shocked to utter a word. It wasn't until I drove my right heel into his left kneecap that he moved, jackknifing to the ground.

I went back to the main Troll. He blabbered some nonsense, leveled his fishing gaff, and charged me but I easily sidestepped him. With a downward swipe as he passed me, I knocked the weapon from his startled grasp. When he turned around, I underhanded my tool, whomping him in the groin with the backside of the claw-end. He dropped instantly, cradling his privates and blubbering loudly. I'd like to think I damaged his chances of ever procreating with the blow. Especially with the witch in the car. I'd hate to see what those two could produce.

Speaking of, the woman in the car looked aghast. Her head suddenly jerked and she glanced behind me. I turned and saw yet another troll at the other end of the bridge holding a long piece of wood like he was in the batter's box. That troll was supposed to keep me from backtracking. I stomped my foot down and that troll scurried off.

Stepping between the bumpers, I flung the jerky package to the woman who snatched it mid-air and subsequently flipped me off, cackling like a witch. Nice.

Enjoy the jerky, bitch.

Dregger Road wound westward around small hills and became less inhabited the further I walked. Although still a dangerous area, there were small hills everywhere with large rocks for cover. Sightlines were great too and the sound of any engine would provide me with plenty of warning. Another road led north to the Rogue Camp but I wasn't headed that way. A long westward trek lay ahead for me along the 15 Freeway, checking in and scoping the once-busy thoroughfare. Harley and Cherry supposedly traveled north to the camp. As far as I was concerned, they were on their own after they crossed the bridge.

My new plan of attack was to try to hit the California coast, up by Santa Barbara, and maybe try Tracy's brother once more. I hadn't seen Johnny since he forced me at gunpoint to leave and wander the desert four years ago.

Maybe he softened up.

Anyway, if he was going to be tight-lipped again, I'd make my way up from there. The ocean breezes would cool me down in the summer. After I left Johnny four years ago, I checked Santa Barbara and neighboring towns but Tracy and my boys weren't listed anywhere. I'd have to try further north this time. To get there, I'd have to move around Barstow, travel the desert above the grapevine north of Los Angeles, then hit the coast as I did before. The central California coast was an area I hadn't really considered. We didn't know anyone there but nothing else provided any answers. I had a really good feeling about it.

With the Bee Gee's tape back in the portable player, Barry Gibb's voice enthralled me a second time. I found myself hitting the rewind button to hear the better songs. Childhood memories of the sound-track. Disco beats the maddening quiet of the daytime desert. Hell, yeah.

I chose the moment to sharpen my crowbar with a rectangular, six-inch rock meant for sharpening as I walked and listened to the tape. Matias gave me the oil stone years ago and it was well-used. At both ends, I flicked the blades with my fingers, feeling the deep ridges there, nearly cutting myself in the process. I kept those babies sharp.

Later in the afternoon, I stopped to rest on a roadside boulder. I tipped my canteen back and guzzled semi-warm water. A brown lizard with a blue tail came up one side of the boulder to greet me, then quickly dashed back down. I was growing tired from the long walk and decided I should set up camp for the night. I wouldn't make the 15 Freeway that night, anyway. Not on foot. I'd scope out a secluded spot in-between hills, the view from which could not be seen from the road. Being so close to the Digs and Rogue activity, I was taking a risk as it was.

A glint of metal down further down the road gave me pause and I did the same with the Walkman – paused it. Crouching low, I scanned the horizon and saw nothing, except the sun setting in the west and circling birds. California Condors and crows were rotating high above a certain spot. That meant death was directly below. Curiosity got the best of me and I got off the road, putting the oil stone back but keeping the crowbar out.

I wandered parallel to the road, hugging bushes and rocks, a good twenty feet off the shoulder. Like a mirror flash, the shine of metal lay between a set of small hills that resembled skiing moguls, with a bush partially obscuring the source. Still weary, I realized the best view would be from the road, of course, and that could be a dead giveaway, but annoying crows began to caw away at my presence in the shrub, so my cover was blown. They took to the air angrily, announcing to all that a threat was coming and that menace was little old me. The condors hopped safely aside but never took flight, finding a perch along some rocks and rocking their heads in disapproval of my presence. The raptors would simply wait for me to leave.

The glint of metal was a motorcycle, standing upright, the handlebars to the side, leaning against the kickstand. Like someone parked it and had to take a leak or maybe stopped to rest. Rounding a bush for a better view, I kicked a motorcycle helmet on accident, the head gear rattling and rolling in the rocks. So much for surprise. When the helmet came to a stop, there was dried blood inside. The motorcycle was a Harley and the forks were bent. It didn't look rideable.

Behind another bush, a man was sprawled on his stomach, his face turned to me. The birds had pecked some skin and had gotten inside him. Ants and flies competed for the same holes.

Harley himself, but no Cherry.

Crouching again, I surveyed the area more closely. No movement, except the damn birds. The crows especially, cawing, hopping from rock to rock, agitating the condors that hissed back at their competition. Looking behind me, the road seemed vacant; ahead, more of the same. A flat rock on a ledge about halfway up the closest hillside drew my attention. A blur, like a flash of blue on top of a rock.

Then, an impact on my chest slammed me backward, causing me to stumble and lose my footing. A split second later, the distant crack of a gun pierced the air, echoing off the hills. Falling to my back, I landed hard on my backpack somewhere amid the sand and shrub, smacking my head on something firm. Dazed, I fought for breath, trying to assess exactly what had just happened, looking right and seeing Harley's dead gaze upon me. At that moment, as I tried to suck in air, I realized then that my instincts failed me miserably and that I had been gunned down.

CHAPTER SEVEN

A whoosh in the air was felt as if the birds had taken flight leaving me alone with a dead Coppertown resident I barely knew. The back of my head ached and throbbed as it lay against something hard, probably a rock. My chest felt hollow and caved in. I trembled with muscle spasms and shook until every part of my body tensed up. Then, I calmed myself by slowing my breathing and trying to gather my wits.

My toes moved first, then my fingers. I clawed at sand and small rocks at my sides, squeezing them, then letting go. I coughed, finally gulping air, slowly moving my hand to my chest, caressing the spot where it hurt most and dreading the worst. There was no wetness, thank God, and I relaxed a bit, lowering my hand to my side again, feeling underneath me for another discomfort, my crowbar pressed into my right leg. The claw end was facing down and again, no wetness there either.

I heard voices coming towards me and I stayed down, trying to recover and get my bearings. The gunshot felt like a giant weight pressing me down and I'd be useless, even if I wanted to stand. Towards the hillside where I had seen the flash of clothing just seconds ago, I saw two men clambering down the slope towards me. The taller of the two held a rifle and had trouble maintaining his balance under the shifting sand, swearing as he stumbled. The other one, smaller, skipped and hopped like a child, whooping and hollering as he skied down. As far as I could tell, that was the entire ambush right there and I needed more time to defend myself, hoping there would be a delay before they fired off shot number two. I kept my eyes open and turned my head towards them but played dead, hoping I wouldn't have to blink.

They slowed their approach, spreading wide. I couldn't tell if the smaller one was armed as he had moved out of view. The tall one with the rifle hung back, staying a safe distance from a counterattack, his barrel aimed directly at me. He was big, gangly, dark-skinned, and his neck had shriveled skin, like a burn victim. He wore black leather, head to toe. The smaller one was bald, wore a blue tracksuit, and suddenly came back into view, hovering over me. He regarded me with an unusual cock of his head and I saw why; his left eye was gray like a cloud.

Later, I would learn they were called Leatherneck and Cyclops. What a pair.

Hacking a gob of spit, Leatherneck sprayed a brush, bent down, and studied me more closely, his gun not wavering. "Is he dead?"

"He ain't moved, but he's on life support," Cyclops said as he knelt next to me, holding a knife at my throat. I could feel the steely edge of his weapon digging in. "That was an awesome shot, by the way."

Leatherneck looked around the hills and harrumphed. "Like putting out cheese for rats. You just gotta have patience." He then sneezed and spat phlegm. "We got to hurry though, get back to camp. Torch is gonna be pissed we're so late."

"Check out his eyes," Cyclops said, flashing his blade in front. "I like it when their eyes are open. I like it when they watch." He giggled then, girlish and high-pitched. "Man, he's a cutey. I want to keep him. Can I?"

Bending away, Leatherneck blew snot and then grunted. "Shut up and search him, you sick bastard. Ain't you had enough with the dead chick anyway?"

Cyclops slapped me in the face, knocking my already sore head to the right. It stung and I waited for another but Cyclops went ADD and got distracted, put his knife aside, and began searching my pockets. "After we're done here, I'm gonna prop his ass up. Have myself a party."

"Backpack," Leatherneck pointed with the rifle. "Get that out. Hurry up too, my allergies are sucking big time now."

"Just you wait," Cyclops said firmly. "You know they always hide their best stuff on their person." The smaller man then found a bulge in my right front pants and probed, bringing out the contraband. "Look. Band-Aids, lip balm, salt packets..." Cyclops inventoried. "Hello, what's this? A wallet. Fucker still carries one around."

"What?"

"Wallet." Cyclops showed him.

"Fuckin' forget it," Leatherneck said and sneezed, wiping the excess on his sleeve. He was watching me less, believing I was mortally wounded and not about to spring up and seek revenge.

Cyclops opened the wallet and must have pulled out my driver's license because he then asked, "Dude's from Mission Viejo, California. Where the hell is that?"

Leatherneck lowered his rifle. "Orange County."

Cyclops blinked his one good eye. "Like Disneyland, Orange County?"

Annoyed, Leatherneck snapped, "Just open Goofy's backpack, will ya?"

"Dude's wife is hot. Check it out." Cyclops must have taken my Christmas family photo out. That pissed me off. Images of Polecat entered my mind then. As Cyclops tugged and prodded me, it reminded me of Polecat yanking on my pants. A low growl swirled in my throat.

"What the fuck was that sound?" Cyclops asked as he tossed my wallet aside.

Sniffling, Leatherneck barely batted an eye. "What the hell you talking about?"

Cyclops felt my socks, then began to remove my boots. "I don't know." Then, he stopped. "Check this out, dude has two different types of shoes."

Leatherneck grunted. "Who gives a shit?"

My strength back was coming back. I could feel my muscles tensing, coiling, ready to spring. Out of sight, my fingers probed my crowbar under me. Cyclops was still exploring my feet, unaware that he was going to die first.

First, I needed the one with the rifle closer. He was too far.

"Fuck the shoes. If you don't open that backpack, I'll knock your ass out," Leatherneck said, jabbing the air toward him with the butt of the rifle. Cyclops took the hint and placed his hands under me, rolling me to my side so Leatherneck could see too. Cyclops then leaned over me and peeled the zipper down on my backpack. The contents spilled out.

"Jackpot!" Cyclops shouted, grabbing some of the items I kept inside. "Batteries! Check it out!"

"Told ya," Leatherneck nodded. "Now, pull his backpack off and give it to me. You can search him all you want. I want what's in the pack." Two more sneeze fits and Leatherneck raged. "I'm sick of this shit! My fuckin' allergies!"

Cyclops tugged on my headphones, yanking them out. "Fine, I get the cassette player. I'm the musician here." Cyclops then reached towards the cassette player hanging off my belt when he suddenly stopped. He knuckled my chest and his palm then went flat against it. Cyclops suddenly went slack.

"What is it?" Leatherneck asked, leaning down as he was wiping his snot. "Talk to me."

My hand gripped the crowbar harder and I planted my right heel into the sand. My eyes moved and I saw Cyclops's lips trembling as if he had stumbled across a bomb. My lungs filled with air and my chest heaved. I was ready to strike.

Alarmed, wiping his snot, Leatherneck suddenly asked, "Where's this dude's other hand?"

"Kevlar!" Cyclops screamed and I quickly dug in with my heel, twisting my body to the left, ignoring the smaller man for the moment. Roaring out loud, I propelled my crowbar skyward, aiming for and smacking Leatherneck's rifle barrel with my heavy tool. The rifle barrel bounced off the taller man's forehead, leaving a deep red line square in the middle.

Leatherneck instantly dropped the rifle, cupped his face in pain, and shrieked, twisting away. I had risen from the dead, sitting upright, glaring then to my foe on my right who fumbled in the dirt for his knife, mumbling incoherently. I switched ends on my weapon and jammed the chisel-end into Cyclops' good eye.

It sounded like *glitch*. Yanking it back out, the tool then made a sucking sound. Like oil on a dipstick, the blood level was at least four inches deep. Cyclops surprisingly never uttered a word, but instead, fell face first on my lap with blood and some other goo from his eye streaming down his face. Rolling him off with disgust, I watched Leatherneck regroup and grab for his gun.

Seeing his dead comrade with the deep hole where his other eye used to be, Leatherneck shouted, "Oh, sweet motherfucker!" and lifted his rifle. Flipping the crowbar around again, I slammed the claw-end down onto his left foot before he could aim. Blood gushed up like a geyser as I yanked it out. The tall man wailed and fired uselessly into the air before dropping the gun once more. Bending down, he grasped his foot as blood seeped between his clasped hands and he rocked there, crying, spit drooling to the sand. I put him out of his misery with a crushing blow to the back of his neck and a follow-up bash, breaking his skull.

For good measure, I also split open Cyclops' skull and wiped the excess blood off on his jumpsuit. Seeing no more life in these bastards, I calmly rose to my feet and wobbled a bit. My legs felt like they were asleep. I rubbed them to get the sensation back.

The stillness around me proved very tranquil again. There were no more attackers and I was left alone once more. Looking up, I saw more birds circling the soon-to-be all-you-can-eat buffet. As soon as I leave, they'd descend and gorge.

"You're welcome," I said quietly to my fine feathered friends.

I then smelled shit. One or both of the men crapped their pants.

A quick pat down on my body revealed no injuries except the gunshot to my chest. Removing my jacket caused me to wince and I hesitated a moment. I felt the indent under my shirt, the impact crater thin on top, and a deep groove below in my vest. The bullet was flattened like a mushroom and fell to the ground. Picking it up, I studied it, realizing it was a decent size caliber. Had the bullet been a bigger caliber, the gunman closer, and the shot a tad more to the right, I might not have been so lucky.

Matias had given the vest to me in the early days and I wore it ever since. Removing that as well, I saw the bruise directly behind the impact and thought, *that's gonna be smarting for a while*. I touched the other two areas on my chest, small bruises and spots from other times, and kissed my finger.

"Third time is the charm," I said to no one. "How lucky can I be?"

I picked up Leatherneck's rifle and checked the barrel. No more ammo. They used their last bullet to cover me and it fired freely somewhere into the desert. I laid the rifle down and stared at my two opponents. Both had red, splotchy skin. Flies began to circle. Other insects would soon invade as well.

Rummaging through their pockets and holding my breath from the shit smell, I didn't find much. Condoms, gum, and a few buttons. I looked up at the hill from where they came and I then noticed it. A pair of lines ran from here to there, twisting, as if a body was dragged. By the looks of it, the person had been fighting back. What did Leatherneck say to Cyclops "Ain't you had enough with the dead chick anyway?"

I groaned. Cherry.

I kicked both dead men, then picked up my wallet and photo, and hiked towards the hill. The sand shifted under my weight and avalanched below me. I knew I would find bad news. Harley was already proof of that.

Along the way, I thought of Harley and Cherry. They were supposed to go to the Digs. That was north. Did they get lost? Did the troll give bad directions?

It was a camp alright, situated on a flat outcrop of rock and sand. A good vantage point where I could see across the desert quite easily including most of the road below. I knew then why these thugs chose this spot to snipe. A red two-seater dune buggy was parked here, hidden from view, enclosed by a metal cage with large tires and tread fit for sand. A pair of headlights mounted at the front, a gas can attached to the rear along with a spare tire. Fast and rugged, it screamed.

From the looks of the trash, they had been there a few nights. A pair of sleeping bags lay near a campfire filled with ash and surrounded by a small ring of rocks. Cigarette butts smoked to the ends lay nearby. Those were hard to come by. Very valuable items for trade.

I found Cherry by the sight of swirling flies. She was hidden behind a brush, naked, all four limbs tied to stakes on the ground. I could tell she had been raped repeatedly, even in death. Her legs were spread apart wide and the sand between them was unsettled with knee indentations. She was in her mid-forties, I guessed, but the new world could age you. Her face was distorted, cemented with anguish and as I closed her eyes for her, I felt ashamed that my fellow man would commit such acts of brutality.

As I sifted among the trash left behind, using my boot to push and nudge the crap aside, I discovered the following: animal bones, children's toys, magazines, a pair of drumsticks, discarded fruit, a couple of empty jars and a mystery jug half-filled. No bullets anywhere. The jug piqued my interest. I picked it up and removed the cap. I sniffed inside, took a swig, and immediately coughed.

Moonshine. I hadn't tasted hooch in a long time and it burned my throat. I sat on a rock and rested, still angry at the men who shot me. They mentioned the name of their leader, a man named Torch, who said that he'd be pissed they were late.

Late for what? Who the hell was Torch anyway? He couldn't be much if he was in charge of these fools.

What little food I could afford from my stash, I ate, and then relaxed on the dune buggy's wheel, watching dusk settle upon the hills. The desert was growing dark and it was obvious I was going to spend the night there. No one would see the condors and birds circling at night. The birds would simply stay grounded and feast. If someone happened along the road, they'd sound the alarm. I figured this spot was as good as any and I could see threats coming from a mile away. I told myself no more than one night though, tomorrow was another day and not to be wasted. I was chancing it staying there already. The dead girl's smell alone would become unbearable anyway.

I made a small fire in the ring they used, using a lot of the trash left behind. I kept it small so it wouldn't be seen from a great distance. It warmed my hands and I thought about meat and what I could cook when the dune buggy drew my attention.

The key was in the ignition, dangling there, too tempting not to try. I reached in and turned it. The buggy coughed, then idled. Black smoke puffed from the rear and the metal cage vibrated. A few other squeaks from under the hood but all in all, good running order. While it had a fake skull as a gearshift, a dried human hand dangled upside down from the rearview mirror. The middle finger was extended. I ripped it off and flung it far.

Last I saw, Harley and Cherry still had theirs attached. The hand belonged to someone else.

I decided I'd use the desert hugger if I had to hightail it out of there. I killed the engine and pocketed the keys, just in case.

The scope on the rifle could come to good use, much better than an empty rifle. Guns got challenged in those days, and bullets were a rarity, so what was the point? Rogues were the only ones armed anymore and even these two were down to two remaining slugs when they dealt with me. After using the crowbar to pry the scope off the rifle, I dropped the weapon into a crevice where it tumbled into darkness. With my newfound toy, I sat down against a rock and peered through the scope at the desert floor below me. The condors were gobbling and squabbling with themselves. The crows fought back and yelled as well, silly because they were all fighting over ample carrion. Seeing nothing else, no other Rogues or humans, I settled back, removed my wallet, and stared at the photo of my family. It was getting dark.

Little boys and cameras don't mix. Just trying to get them to sit still was a challenge. I missed the hell out of them. I wondered what they looked like now. How they aged and grew, how their features were morphing into a glimpse of the men they would become. Where they were, how they were coping.

Did they think I was dead?

I was about to lift the jug to my lips once more when a patch of fur crested the rock in front of me; pointed ears and glossy black eyes rose then and peered over. A long snout, black nose, and white fangs followed, surrounded by whiskers.

A coyote.

"Hello, friend," the Coyote said to me.

CHAPTER EIGHT

Underneath the coyote's head, a human face materialized, belonging to a little person. Boyish, and young, I could make out brown curly hair under the flappy pelt, along with brown eyes, a small nose, and a scruffy, but short beard. He stood about four feet tall and he held his hands out in a calming gesture. I became distracted and kept looking up and down at the two faces, unsure which to follow. The rest of him wore the coyote skin, draped like a bad taxidermist job.

"I come in peace," he said, with a cautious grin. The coyote fur was matted and fluffed in places, well-worn, and in need of a cleaning. A mix of wet dog and BO gusted from him. The chest area was tied together with string in a crisscross pattern while two pieces of long fur dangled out front which appeared to be the former owner's front legs. Underneath, he wore a plain brown t-shirt. Black jeans and sneakers filled out the rest of the attire. Both dirty and full of holes.

I was on him fast, first pulling him down to the ground. I then checked the ridge below him, making sure there was no surprise attack from others. I hadn't seen him before so I didn't know his story. Seeing no one else, I whipped him backward and he fell hard into the trash, scattering cans, bottles, and the rest of the rubbish. Before he could react, I was on him, pushing him down face first, frisking him.

"Hey, not so rough. I don't do that..." he complained, flinching as I searched. Besides finding a few essentials in a small backpack under the coyote fur, his weaponry consisted of a slingshot, a bag of ball bearings, and a small buck knife. Dwarf or not, I trusted no one, so my actions for being rough were tantamount to making sure he was no threat. I spilled the contents of his backpack on the ground, looking for evidence that the man had an alternative motive for surprising me, and found nothing else. Action figures spilled out, as did dice, Star Wars cards, and comic books. I flipped him over and he called out panicky saying, "Easy, hey, don't ruin those, please!" The rest of the contents was much of the same and I regarded him not as a man at all, but as a kid.

Examining the slingshot, I found it to be a high-power weapon, the kind that has a stress band on your forearm with thick, rubber strands. It could do some damage, especially with the heavy metal ammo he was stocking. Rising off him, I confiscated the slingshot and knife, jamming them into my waistband. He rolled over, sat up, and brushed himself off.

"What are you doing here?" I asked him.

"Take it easy, man. I told you I come in peace," he said, scooping up his toys and memorabilia back into his backpack. Once they were carefully placed inside, he got his bearings and breathed hard. "That went well," he said, shaking his head. "What was I thinking? You can't up and surprise a man like that. My bad."

I regarded him with suspicion. I probably treated him too rough, but I'd been duped before. I said nothing and watched the little guy study the campsite, the hills, then me. He was taking it all in, like he had found a new home.

"My name is Jock," he said to me and offered his hand. It was dirty, scarred, with stubby fingers. His fingernails were long and dirty. Keeping my right hand at my side, I ignored the shake.

"Jock? What the hell kind of name is that? You some kind of athlete?" I asked.

"It's Scottish, a derivative of John. And no, I don't play sports."

"Why not John then?"

"Ask my father, maybe he saw me as some kind of derivative."

Jeez, that was deep. I caught myself smiling, as did he. My hand stayed at my side though. "You're a coyote, huh?" I asked him.

Tipping the coyote's head, he said, "In the flesh."

I noticed a full moon rising in the distance. Hard to believe this little guy was traveling alone but the desert floor would soon be illuminated so I'd see then if he was really by his lonesome.

"What do you want?" I asked him. "Why are you here?"

Jock was quick to answer. "Not selling, trading, or anything."

"Then what?"

"I don't know," Jock said. "Company?"

I grunted. "Are you following me, Jock?"

"You walk with a purpose."

That caught me off-guard. "Purpose?"

"Yeah," he said. "Most drifters tend to wander, but you seem determined. You walk fast. Like you have a purpose and I was curious."

"Curious for what?" I asked him.

"To see what your purpose is," he stated. "Like what's your plan, Crowbar man."

"What did you say?"

Jock sat up excited. "People talk of you. I heard about it up and down the river. They say a man walks alone carrying a crowbar and instills justice in the wasteland. He's quick, stubborn, and downright ornery. He'd kill you sooner than blink."

I scoffed at that. No way that was meant for me. Sure, I came across people, but I was hardly the judge, jury, and executioner type. People have a way of talking out of their asses. I shook my head. I just looked out for one person. Me.

"Your legend is growing," he said in all seriousness. "They say you have superhuman strength and can take on ten men."

"Now you're lying. You made that up. That's from your comic books."

He smiled. "I wish."

I felt like he was trying to butter me up for some reason. "Is that where you live? The river?"

"River, mountains, forests, wherever," he admitted, waving his arms like he was covering the land. "I roam, just like you do."

"Legend," I muttered and held my crowbar out. Newly stained blood was still on there. "I'm just a survivalist with a home wrecking tool. What legend eats leaves off trees and craps in the sand? Crowbar Man? More like Cro-Magnon man."

Jock tilted his head. The coyote's nose flopped to the side. "I never pegged you for being modest."

"Yeah, well, a few days ago, I almost cried when I was given some toilet paper."

"Funny man, you are," he said in a voice that sounded like Yoda.

The desert floor was given another check one last time after the moon was able to provide some light. There was no movement on the desert floor below anywhere, except for the carnage I created. Or added to. I could hear the odd squawk and crow's caw down below. "You alone?" I asked.

He nodded sincerely and I could tell he wasn't a threat. This little guy was probably lonely and bored. No way was he a Rogue nor associated with them either. They'd tear him apart, but not before having some fun first – sick and demented at that. Sitting down on a rock, I grabbed the jug and held it close. I took a swig and belched.

"What you did to those two noobs...that was sick!" he said, pointing down below. "They deserved it. I saw the whole thing. I thought you were dead. Good thing about the vest. Dope move."

"Dope move would be to not get shot," I pointed out. My chest hurt again at that moment, like some subliminal thing. "I fell for their trap."

"The motorcycle you mean?"

I shook my head and pointed up. "The birds. They left the dead guy there to attract suckers. Meat is precious out here. The fresher, the better. Circling birds are a dead giveaway. Thank you."

"Good one."

I feigned indifference. Had to admit, I liked the comradery we were sharing. Since Coppertown I had little, except for the Trolls and the cackling witch.

Jock leaned in, just like a kid, ready to hear a story. "How many times is that for you? Being shot?"

"Three."

Jock jumped up. "That many? Holy cow!"

Shrugging, I went on. "I've also been stabbed with a knife a few times, even got nailed with a pitchfork once." I used my finger to outline the various cuts and slices I incurred. Doing so, I realized just how lucky I was. Some legend. If not for the vest, I would have been dead by now.

Leaning in, he then surmised, "The vest saved you each time."

"I don't leave home without it," I admitted and then took another swig. "I can't believe you want to follow me," I said, realizing I was tapping the vest itself as I spoke. "I am a nobody. Going nowhere."

Jock stood up and wandered the filth. "It's not like there's a mall or theater to go to anymore. Dude, you find something interesting, even remotely fascinating, you stick with it."

Dude got that right. I once watched a rattlesnake devour a rabbit, completely mesmerized that the smaller snake could open its jaws as wide as it did and swallow the damn thing whole. Another time, I saw two scorpions battle to the death, one finally stinging the other to death after an hour-long dance that reminded me of a knife fight. The little bugger then ate his foe. Little iotas of a world turned bland and bleak.

"How long were you following me?" I asked, thinking back to when I should have first noticed him.

Jock thought about it for a moment. "The river. I was hiding in the weeds, trying to figure out how to cross the bridge when you showed up and nailed the ugly sucker in the balls. He was still down when I ran by, by the way. He left me alone."

"There were two others on the bridge," I said. Jock searched his mind, then said he hadn't seen them. They probably slunk back down under the bridge, never to rise again. And I went easy on those guys.

"What about the witch in the car?"

Jock giggled. "Barfing over the side. Didn't even see me. Dude, she was gnarly."

"Nice." I nodded at his costume, amazed he stayed wrapped in its entirety. "That get-up work for you, dressing up like that?"

"Look at me," he said and tugged at the fur. "Low to the ground, I can pass for a coyote easily. I've been spotted more than once and left alone. The fur also keeps me warm at night."

"No one took a shot at you?" I found that hard to believe. Coyote meant meat and animals were hunted every chance you got. No one was that selective anymore.

"Yeah," he replied. "That was a while ago when guns were everywhere. Now, I'm left alone. I'm a small target and can hide well enough. You didn't know I was following you, right? See, I got that aced."

Jock then motioned for the jug.

"You old enough?" I asked. I wasn't sure I wanted to part with it.

"I'm twenty-four," he said, crossing his arms. "What, are you going to card me now, Dad?"

"You're twenty-four?" With all the kids' relics he was carrying, I figured a decade less. I handed the jug to him. His face contorted as he took a swig, most of it spilling over his chin.

"Amateur," I told him.

Wiping his mouth, he then said, "I don't know how you can stand the stuff." He stuck his tongue out and waved off more. "Yuck, it burns." He spat out what remained the rest.

"You take what you can get out there. Like you said, there is no mall," I said. With that, he nodded and laid back, hands behind his head. Or, rather, the coyote's head.

His easiness got to me. "Who said you can stay?" I asked him.

"You know you want the company. I do too. Besides, you don't seem like the mean sort or a bro who gets on other bros."

I rolled my eyes and took another drink. "What happened to the coyote?" I asked, pointing to his cover.

Jock reached over and grabbed his slingshot, hesitating until I nodded. "Found him caught in a bear trap. He was in the middle of chewing his leg off. I put him out of his misery." He then stuck his finger through a hole in the coyote's head behind the left ear and wiggled it. "I can hit a moving rabbit at forty yards."

Coyote. Rabbit. My stomach growled thinking of meat. Jock heard it too. The little man then stood up and walked over to the ledge. He reached down and pulled up a dead rabbit.

"How about some dinner?" he asked me. "Just killed it on the way here."

CHAPTER NINE

"Keep calm and eat rabbit," Jock said with a grin as I casually watched the desert floor below. He confessed that the little desert dwellers were his meal of choice and the Mojave was full of the little buggers. Add a couple of old McDonald's salt packets, a can of asparagus spears, and we had a home-cooked meal. We roasted the meat over a small fire, holding the meat over the flame with a pair of musical drumsticks one of the Rogues left behind. The can of asparagus spears was placed over the fire as well, held between two rocks, boiling the green veggies to a warm, soggy stew that when sprinkled with salt, was delicious as hell. We mostly ate in silence, savoring the meal, gnawing down to every bit of meat on the bone.

Jock lifted his and said, "Drumstick on a drumstick," and giggled as if Carrot Top was looking for a protégé. The little man was a marrow sucker too; he'd bite hard on the bones with his back teeth, crunching off the ends, and then he'd suck the innards that completely grossed me out. He reminded me of a child, his twenty-four years on this planet highly in question. I was surprised he survived this long in the wasteland.

The fire was a risk, the yellow light from the flame could be seen for miles. The scent of the hoppy dish would also spread and attract animals and humans so we'd have to remove all evidence and quickly cover it up. Not long after the meal was done, I doused the pit with thrown sand. The evening would get chilly but nothing a couple of layers couldn't handle. Without the crackle of the fire, the only sound that followed were crickets and the occasional sigh from both of us as we sat back and rested.

Something nagged at my side. I leaned over and Jock plugged his nose. "What?" I asked him as I pulled out the Queen from Matias' chessboard from my pocket. I forgot I tucked it there. I wondered what he would have thought of me as I dispatched those two assholes down below. Worse, watched me wander into a trap set by those amateurs. Just like he did in chess, he'd set me up for a flank attack at those times I thought I had an easy shot at his Queen.

"You can't be one step ahead," I said. "You got to be five steps ahead."

"Oh," Jock said, eyeing the Queen. "I thought you were going to let one rip."

That's what my sons would have said too and I laughed.

"Can I see it?" he asked, and I flung it to him. Catching it midair, Jock studied it like it was an ancient relic and I thought he'd try to add it to his collectibles.

"Why do you have this? Do you play chess?" Jock asked me.

I told him about Matias. As he listened, he twirled the piece between his little fingers. "Why did he train you?" he asked and then leaned forward like a child ready to hear a story. Cross-legged, arms folded, hands under his chin.

"He was bored. He believes in underdogs."

"You were an underdog? How?"

"I was just a Corporate bigwig with no survival skills. Now, thanks to him, I'm a man on a mission and nothing is going to stop me."

Jock nodded. "I knew it. Man on a mission. You do have a purpose. So what is it? What's your mission?"

"Find my family."

Jock thought about that and asked, "Where are they?"

"I don't know," I replied. "I got word they were alive after the gas and I'll find them soon enough."

"Where did you live?" he asked.

"Orange County."

He thought about my answer, but instead of making up his mind, he grew concerned. He asked, "Where were they when it happened?"

"Not home. I was trying to get back to them when I crashed my car in the desert. That is why I was not there with them."

He perked up. "So, they weren't home. That's a good thing. Because Orange County, LA County, the whole area…"

"I know," I interrupted.

I took out my wallet and showed him the photo. "Cute kids," he said. "She's a knockout too." His uneasy glance told me he had no one and I wondered if there ever was one. He didn't seem to be missing anyone. "You married up," Jock added with a grin.

"Thanks," I replied, nodding. I shoved the photo back into my wallet and tucked it away. My wife did look good in that photo. I wondered if I told her that.

Jock asked, "Why did she leave with the kids?"

"Argument. Personal." I shot him a look to change the subject. And he did.

"What about Vegas?" Jock continued. "Did you try to go in other directions?"

I shook my head. "No point. Vegas was gone. Phoenix too."

Jock agreed with me. "I got close to San Diego once and had to leave. That's where I am from. I threw up for days. I don't go close to cities anymore. Not worth it. Plus all the diseases out there now. You see people? Shit, everyone has some sort of sickness. And no one to cure it."

I took another slug of moonshine. It felt better going down now. I was getting used to the bite. *That* was my cure.

"Are you going to drink it all?" he asked, pointing to the jug.

"Hopefully," I said with a shit-eating grin. If he was going to be one of those sermonizers, he was going to be lonely again real fast. I deserved my drink. It numbed my brain, enough to let me forget and relax. I once found a bottle of Jack Daniel's hidden in a closet of an abandoned trailer and I savored every drop until it was gone. I was sure someone stashed it there. That was a good two days.

Antsy like my kids, Jock got up and walked to the dune buggy. "Can I ask that you maybe stop drinking?" He then studied the vehicle, tapping the headlights, and pulling on the metal cage.

"You can ask, but I'll say no," I replied, not moving.

"Hear me out first. Then decide," Jock said and kicked a tire, then walked around the vehicle kicking the others. Like a car buyer inspecting his new ride, he studied the sand cruiser, tugged the steering wheel, opened the gas cap, sniffed inside, and nodded. Hands in his pockets, he came back to me like he was going to propose something.

"There's a good place out west," he said. "We should check it out."

"Out west where?"

"Once a month, there's a plane in the sky," Jock proudly stated. "A small one, a white Cessna. It comes from the west, lands, stays for a day or two, then returns to the skies and heads back. I saw it fly over the mountains towards Barstow and it stayed in a westerly direction." He waved his hand in the air like a child mimicking the plane's supposed flight trajectory with sound effects.

"A plane," I said, incredulously. "Like fly through the air kind of plane?"

Jock shot me a dumb look. "What other planes do you know of?"

"None," I groaned and flung the stick away. "Nothing survived out west past Barstow. Besides, even if there was a plane, the Rogues would have it by now. They wouldn't even land if they knew Rogues were here. Landing a plane would be suicide. End of conversation."

Jack shook his head. "Dude, they fly at night and circle the skies to confuse everyone on the ground. Then they switch off their engines and glide. A small Cessna can glide for miles. It's so sick. They land in a place that's hidden and well-protected. I hiked under their flight plan, starting near Barstow and walking east in the Mojave. Watching, waiting, kind of forever. Finally, I figured out their operation and discovered where they land. I've seen them do it and they fly in and out, like, every four weeks. That's why I was hanging around the river. I had time to kill between landings."

"When did this happen last, Sport?" I said with a pang of pessimism.

"Like four weeks ago. They are due to arrive tonight. First full moon."

I looked skyward into the night, stars filling my view, the moon's light growing in intensity. The thought of an aircraft sailing up high over the desert would send its denizens into a frenzy. Rogues would certainly want to find it. How it can fly in, land, and then take off without anyone knowing seemed like a miracle. The desert held many secrets, but there aren't many places to hide a plane and runway. I turned to him and asked, "Where?"

Jock walked to the dune buggy and rapped the door confidently. "Normally I avoid cars but we are pressed for time. You got the keys to this thing?" he asked.

CHAPTER TEN

The dune buggy jostled and jolted like an aging theme park ride. Our arms and legs took a constant battering against the metal cage we were encased in, smashing side to side with every bump as we wound through a rough and uneven road, most of it uphill. The loose steering wheel and grinding gearbox added to our misery. My frustration was redlining, almost forcing me to stop and heave the stupid thing over a ledge.

Hills appeared and disappeared on each side of us. We were able to use the moonlight to guide us so I kept the headlights off. We passed a shell of a campervan that was burned out many years ago. I saw a mountain goat another time, although it hopped away before I could point it out to Jock. The engine did us no favors either, sputtering and belching at will, with me thinking it would quit at any moment.

Jock was leaning forward and gripping the dashboard with both hands. We didn't seem to be getting anywhere but Jock insisted on continuing. He would shout, "Keep going!" or "Watch this curve!" every so often. Occasionally, he'd point to rock piles he made to point the way, like breadcrumbs on a trail. I never saw them and concentrated on the road, fighting the demon buggy and cussing under my breath.

We began climbing again and the buggy slowed. At one point, Jock hit my arm. "Want to see Mos Eisely?" he asked above the noise of the grumbling engine.

I didn't understand what he said so I slowed down. "Mos what?" It didn't seem like English.

He rolled his eyes. "Mos Eisley from Star Wars. Remember the scene where Luke Skywalker, Obi-Wan Kenobi, R2-D2, and C-3PO approach Mos Eisley and stop to watch the city from a cliff's edge? That viewpoint is Dante's View and it's close by. They filmed that there. After we're done with the plane, we can check it out."

That brought back some good childhood memories. "I used to love Star Wars," I admitted, recalling that my boys liked the newer versions of the movies better.

"Mos Eisely Spaceport," Jock said, mimicking Obi-Wan Kenobi. "You'll never find a more wretched hive of scum and villainy. We must be cautious."

We passed a couple of boulders in the middle of the road, maneuvering around some with only inches to spare. Driving was arduous on my stomach too. I was growing nauseous, not used to the motion of the vehicle. I was on a full stomach which was also a rarity too.

"It feels like we're flying through an asteroid belt, doesn't it?" I asked him, trying to deflect my uncomfortableness. That brought a smile to his face. I could tell he was feeling nauseous too but he tried not to let it show.

Jock suddenly stiffened seconds later as if he forgot something. Then, he stood up in the seat and craned his head in all sorts of directions, searching the night sky. "Stop the car!" he cried out.

"It's a dune buggy," I protested, being a smart-ass.

"Stop the damn thing!"

So, I did and slammed on the brakes. Jock bounced off the metal bar in front and landed back in his seat. Dust swirled us like a fog. Some got in my eyes and I blinked, waving it off. He coughed too, whining about my stopping skills.

"I didn't mean like that," he said, righting himself.

"Well, shit. Be more precise next time..."

"Shh!" he said and stood back up again.

I heard it too. The unmistakable sound of another engine. Up in the air. Damn, he was right! That sounded like a plane, but a sudden flashback caused me to flinch. My thoughts returned to Bale and his war machines killing innocent lives years ago. This time, however, no grenades were being dropped from the skies.

Hoisting myself up with the roll bar, I stood in my seat too and scanned the skies. "Can you see it?" I asked him. The sky was white from the moon's glow and I couldn't spot anything. Looking down below, I could see the desert valley below us. If nothing else, the scene was breathtaking and we were higher than I thought.

He shook his head. "No, you won't either. They don't fly with lights on. They removed them, I think."

Then a thought occurred to me. You need fuel to fly and the Rogues were the only ones that had any semblance of it. Moonshine, however, was not a good choice and no one dared to try. "Are Rogues flying it?" I asked him.

"Hell, no! Their hooch isn't that good! You need pure gas to do that!"

That was almost too good to be true. Someone else besides a Rogue was commanding the skies, but how could someone be this manic to fly out there and potentially lose a vital piece of machinery to bloodthirsty pirates? "What about the Rogues? They'll hear it," I sighed, shaking my head at the obvious.

"Far away they think it lands," he stated, doing Yoda again.

I looked at him. *Really?* He shrugged and spoke in his normal voice, "Sound travels far in the desert."

Spotting a plane enveloped in a light sky should be easy, a white one at that, but the moon's glare caused some confusion. There seemed to be some lingering clouds overhead too, making the job much tougher. The sound did take some time to reach us so the trajectory of where you thought it was versus where it *actually* was could be confusing. Jock had a point; in a vast desert arena, where sound can bounce and travel great distances, the plane above had the advantage, echoing and rumbling in all directions. The engine's exhaust sounded strong. Jock was right. They were probably using gas for fuel. Whoever was flying it was well stocked but batshit crazy to be cruising out there.

And then, without warning, the engine high in the sky quit. All went quiet. "Did they run out of gas?" I asked and searched the sky, slightly worried for them.

"They're gliding," he said, matter of fact. "We're close. I told you."

Jock turned to face ahead and sat down, content that not only was he right, he knew where it was headed. Without being able to pinpoint its location, I saw nothing, heard everything, and wanted to doubt whether it existed at all. There was no crash, just silence. He said it could glide for miles and I wondered how far exactly.

"We won't hear the plane gliding, amigo," Jock said. "It will be too quiet."

No one in their right mind would fly over in this hellhole and return to brag about it. Would they? And why would they? Some thrill ride? What was their purpose?

"So, you know where it lands then?" I asked my smug passenger.

Jock folded his arms and nodded.

"Arrivals is dead ahead," he said.

CHAPTER ELEVEN

The ghost hovered over the desert floor, her long white robe flowing behind her. Like an angel, she was graceful, seemingly sweeping across the sand. Suddenly, she came to a halt. She shifted and fidgeted, her gaze searching the night skies. Clearly, she was expecting something or someone as she glanced around repeatedly. Her eyes did not find us so we were able to sit where we were, undetected. Jock was calm next to me, unfazed, calmly watching the spirit. The hair on the back of my neck rose. One could see how apparitions such as this would lead to tall tales of spirits haunting the wasteland.

The ghost was a mere woman in a white coat. She had long, gray, wavy hair that floated over her collar. I couldn't see her face clearly, but then suddenly, orange lights bathed her grace as she waved a pair of flashlights in windshield wiper arcs, the same tubular flashlights they used to use in airport tarmacs.

Earlier, Jock and I had arrived at our viewpoint just in time, the shoulder of the road had provided a ledge to look down and study what was happening below. The road itself continued, snaking onward and upward carving a path along the hillside. The demon buggy was parked behind us and we hiked to this spot so as not to give away our position. Crouched low and hidden from view, we watched side by side, my knees digging into hard rock and gravel. My scope was centered on her.

Behind her was a row of buildings, two of them, one larger than the other.

"It's an old airfield," Jock said. "She's trying to catch the plane's attention. See the buildings behind her? The big one is the hangar."

The area below was flat, about the size of two football fields laid end to end that could easily accommodate a runway. We heard the crackle of a walkie-talkie but couldn't make out any voices. I felt a small breeze flowing our way and I thought I caught the scent of aloe.

Illuminated by the moon's glow, the buildings behind her looked to be in rough shape. The walls appeared blackened by fire, full of holes, with the roof caved in on the smaller of the two. The hangar stood firm and intact, but a gaping hole remained where the door should have been. Inside that structure, it was pitch black. I could also make out the outline of a perimeter of some kind, a fence that contained the entire airfield.

I don't recall ever seeing this place. Were these people successful in hiding from the Rogues or even other drifters? How was that possible?

"Can you see the runway?" he asked me.

"I do," I said and nodded. A long, flattened stretch in the middle. The woman in white stood in the middle of it. I then heard a single word over her walkie-talkie.

"Copy." It was a man's voice.

I frowned at the setup. It was too easy. A fence wasn't enough to deter a curious Rogue or drifter and they would have been through there years ago. Maybe the crumbling structures presented themselves as a place where there was nothing to see or take. In other words, why bother? Still, something was amiss. There had to be some sort of deterrent.

"That's the signal. They spotted her," he said smiling. "Showtime."

And then I saw it, coming in low about two hundred feet in the air, approaching from the south, a small white plane with the wings above the cockpit. It dropped quickly, hung low, and then soared over the fence at the far southern end. It hit the ground hard, skipped twice, and then cruised down the runway, past the woman in white. Wind and sand blew at her, forcing her to turn away. The front end dipped as the brakes were applied and it turned towards the big building where it coasted inside and stopped. The Pilot, a man, quickly leaped out and grabbed a chain by the entrance. He yanked hard twice, pulling down a large metallic door where he and the plane soon became sealed inside, hidden from view. Just like that.

"A plane," I said. "An actual fucking plane. And I barely heard it land."

"I told you, planes can glide for miles," Jock said. "I read somewhere that the glide ratio is nine feet horizontal for every foot vertical. Depending on how high he was to start, he could've glided for miles until he landed here. They don't need an engine to land. Planes used to practice landing with engines off all the time."

That astounded me. "No shit? They can glide like that?"

Jock was smug. "Aerodynamics, amigo."

I was still blown away. They landed here in complete silence. No wonder Rogues couldn't find the airstrip. How do you chase something that was whisper quiet?

"The day I found this place? I was nearly run over, bro." Jock remarked. "It was hot and I only traveled at night. I was walking at the south end, there's a road over there. Barely visible. I heard a strange whistling sound. I couldn't pinpoint what or where it was coming from. Then to my left, I saw the flashlights, and then suddenly, to my right, the plane flew just feet above my head just like they did right there! It scared the shit out of me. I ducked and fell to the sand. I swear the wheels sailed just feet over my head! What you saw tonight? That's exactly how I saw it that night! The plane sat there for three days! They follow the same drill each time! It is so sick!"

"Who are these people?" I asked.

"I don't know. I never saw anyone until the third night," he said and pointed. "You know what though? It's hard to see from a distance, isn't it? You see a couple of old buildings, right? And then just a heap of whatever. No big deal. Really not worth checking out, probably picked clean already. There are abandoned houses and shacks everywhere in the Mojave so this spot doesn't matter."

I glanced at the compound. There was no activity in the buildings. It didn't make sense. Where the hell did they go?

"Then, on the third night, I saw them. The Pilot came out first, then the woman. They opened the hangar door and the plane took off. Only she stayed behind. And just like that," he snapped his fingers, "she vanished again. Like a ghost. The plane didn't return until the next full moon. I've been watching the whole thing from up here, each month. No one has seen me. No one was alerted I was here." Scrunching his face, he then added, "At least I don't think they know I'm here."

A million questions came to mind, but one was obvious. "Did you check it out? We should go see."

I was about to stand when he grabbed my arm and pulled me back down.

"Wait," he said. "There's more."

"I want to know who they are," I said and stood back up again. Just then, I heard an engine. Coming from the south, a throaty rumble. I shook my head. "Rogues. Damnit. They heard."

"No," Jock pointed south. "Friends bringing gifts."

A large truck pulled up to the south end of the compound and stopped. An older model flatbed with wood sidings, it had what looked like jugs in the open rear cargo hold. I scanned the cab of the truck with the scope but I couldn't make out who was inside. The truck idled for a moment and then the driver stepped out, stretched, and walked up to what looked like a gate. He was short, stocky, and dressed in black clothes. The driver fiddled with the gate, then swung it open. Climbing back into the truck, he put the truck in gear, moved it forward about twenty yards, then stopped again just inside the compound.

Jock mentioned, "He always shows up just after the plane lands. I think he waits for it out there somewhere."

The driver got out and walked to the rear of the truck. He leaned in and picked up something long that had what looked like limbs. It took me a second; it was a dead body. Hiking it over his shoulder, he carried a man's corpse inside the fence a few yards, then dumped it on the ground. He went back, grabbed another body, a woman, then flung it about ten yards away, not caring how it landed. All inside by the gate.

"Doesn't give the place much curb appeal," I said.

"He didn't kill them," Jock said. "At least I don't think he did."

Dead bodies littered the front gate. "So, what's the angle? No trespassing? Violators will be shot?" I said, believing their deterrent was a sign, but a bad one at that. "Not very convincing if it is," I added. Rogues would ignore that statement in a second. They had more firepower.

"No," Jock remarked. "Much more than that."

"I hope so," I said.

A quick scan of the buildings showed no movement. I shot my scope across the field once more, saw the fence clearer then, and figured it was electrified somehow. That had to be it. That, or trained dogs, but there was no barking. Swinging my line of sight back to the driver, I saw that he was locking the gate. Like someone proud of their handiwork, he then stood over the dead he sprinkled on the desert floor with his hands on his hips. I huffed in frustration. The lock and a couple of dead bodies couldn't keep the bad guys out. No way.

"This part always makes me want to hurl," Jock sighed and looked away. "There are a lot of deceased down there. They like to put fresh bodies on display."

"I'd prefer grass, maybe a few flowers," I said. "Then again, maybe he expects them to push up some daisies."

Jock looked at me weirdly. "Was that a joke? Know what? Never mind..."

Seconds later, the driver grabbed an axe and began hacking off the limbs of the dead he planted, scattering them every which way like he was laying seed. "Oh, man. What the hell is he doing?" I cried, slapping my forehead. I could hardly believe it. What the hell did Jock bring me to? Jock shushed me as I may have said it too loud but I pointed out his whacks were much louder, some striking rock that sounded like *chink*! After having gone lumberjack on the dead, the driver tired himself out and strolled back to the truck bumper where he wiped his forehead with a rag. "All in a day's work, eh?" I surmised for the guy.

"That takes a lot of effort," Jock pointed out. "They prefer their limbs severed."

Not to miss out on the opportunity, I asked Jock, "Quick, what do you call a man with no arms and no legs who sits in a hole?"

Jock shook his head. "Jeez, you want to go there?"

"Doug."

Unamused, Jock faced me and then said, "There's a reason why he does it, you know. There are many dead bodies over there. Some have been there for months."

"Yeah, well, he's good at his job," I remarked. "He's killing it out there."

"Stop."

Tossing the mike aside, I returned my gaze to the hangar and back to the truck again. No woman in white, no Pilot. No nobody. This axe-wielding psycho wasn't a concern to them. I assumed he was welcomed and expected.

Jock nudged me. "He's moving again," he said.

I returned my scope to the driver who now held a rake in his hand and began smoothing the sand where his tires made tracks entering through the gate. Satisfied at his chore, he then took one last glance around him, chucked the rake back into the bed, climbed back in the truck, and drove it forward. He followed a straight line up to the buildings where the hangar door was open again and he tucked the truck next to the Cessna inside the larger building. The Pilot was there, as was the woman in white, waiting inside, and they both yanked down on the chain and the door came back down once more.

They then disappeared again.

"General Patton used airfields out in the Mojave for practice in dubbya-dubbya two," Jock told me. "Good conditions for the African assault on Rommel. I bet he used this one too."

I looked at him. "Patton was here? Serious?"

Jock nodded with sincerity. "Maybe. The desert has a few old army bases they used for training. I read there are also ammunition depots with some bombs still stockpiled. Some ticking too, stuck in the ground from war games."

"Like watch your step?"

Jock lifted an eyebrow. "Kaboom."

"This is nuts," I said and stood up. "We should go see what this is all about." Below us, the hillside was sloped with shrubs and loose rock, but I could make out a small path from the moonlight. Forgoing the bumpy tin can we come in, it would be all foot power from here on in. Sand gave way as I trudged downward, not waiting for my little friend to join. I was beyond curious about this place.

"You can't just walk in there," Jock shouted and hurried alongside. "They could be armed. Don't be such a noob."

More loose rocks tumbled as we hiked down. Some of it flowed over my boots. "You never went in?" I asked him.

"No. Are you kidding me?" he replied, huffing, struggling in the shifting sand. "They could be mean."

"Only one way to find out then."

The perimeter was a fence, chain-link, about eight feet high with corkscrewing barbed wire. Standard *stay the hell away* kind of fence. As we neared, the cover was really limited, so we would be completely visible if the ghost appeared again. I kept an eye out on the structures just across the way and saw no movement there, no ghosts, airmen, or horror movie axe-murderers. Behind me, Jock fell, rolling in the sand, and tried to rise gracefully.

"You done having fun?" I asked him. "Want to go back up and roll down again?"

"This is crazy," Jock said, smiling as if he completed a dare. "I mean, I got down to the fence once but I ran back up. I'm so nervous."

"Good," I nodded. "I'm nervous too."

"There's just one thing though," he said, catching his breath. "It's a biggie."

Jock had been holding back on me and I was beginning to lose my patience. I hated the fact I didn't know. "Well, I doubt it's electrified," I said. "Still, we need to find out. Go ahead and touch it."

Jock shot me a look. "It's not, but remember what I said about bombs in the desert?" he asked and pointed at a square sign on the fence.

DANGER MINES. I looked up and down the fence line. The signs were posted every fifty feet.

"What, they going to have us believe they have actual mines in there?" I asked.

Jock didn't answer and only smiled.

"I don't believe it," I said, yet I searched the ground inside the fence, hoping to see some mounds that might be dead giveaways to the mine locations. Like little metal rods or cylinders poking through the sand. If it was that easy, we could leapfrog those suckers. If they existed, that was. I highly doubted that they did.

"That's why I never entered," he stated and pulled on the fence, shaking it. We could hear the chain links vibrating down the fence line, rattling in a wave. Jock wasn't zapped either, so the fence wasn't carrying any juice.

I stared at the buildings. Still no movement or sign of life. We could hop the fence although the barbed wire looked mighty pokey. Seizing the moment, I asked Jock, "What do you call a woman with no arms and no legs, stuck in a fence?"

Jock gave up at that point. "What?"

"Barb."

"The driver got in safely at the gate," Jock pointed out, changing the subject. "Maybe we should go over there."

"He did, didn't he? Let's buzz the front gate then," I said.

CHAPTER TWELVE

The lock looked old and rusted yet it remained firm as I yanked and pulled in every direction. At first glance, it would appear strange to be still in place, guarding an empty field, but maybe that's all it was meant to show. A long-forgotten protector to a long-forgotten field. Nothing more.

Inside the compound, the driver did a good job of covering his tracks. I could barely see the strokes from his rake and only because I saw him do it and knew where to look. We were the ones that knew people were inside and they got in safely.

The DANGER MINES signs were posted all over the gate and when the wind shifted, I smelled death. The dead bodies lay sprawled right where the driver left them, their limbs littered, blood and clothes carpeting the sand. Two men it was; I was wrong about one being a woman. He was slim, somewhat feminine with long hair, but still male. I didn't recognize them either, they were probably drifters left for dead roadside by the Rogues. One looked as if he had been run over, his legs were crushed and bent at odd angles, despite the hack job provided by the driver.

I had second thoughts about meeting those folks.

"They're just props, right?' Jock said, frowning. "Scare people away?"

"Let's ask this guy," I remarked. There was another body, a younger male, who was long dead, weeks for sure, with body parts strewn to my far right. He had both arms, but his legs lay next to him. Not neatly, just there, as if dropped. "He's just laying around," I pointed out.

Jock smiled. "Matt," he said.

"What?"

"Guy with no arms, no legs, lays at your front door?" Jock grinned. "Ah, forget it," he waved.

"I dig your style," I said. I snapped the lock in two with my crowbar. We squeezed through the gate, then quickly stopped, minding the mines. No obvious dirt mounds or metal rods were sticking out or up, all that lay before us was a flat driveway surrounded by shrubs on either side leading up to the buildings. "As long as we follow the path the truck took, we should be fine, right?" I asked.

"I think so."

"You go first," I told him.

"Why me?"

"You're lower to the ground than I am."

"So, you go with a height joke?"

"Well, your eyes are closer to the ground than mine," I remarked. "That's all."

Jock stepped aside. "How about age before beauty?"

We bickered like that for a bit longer, then decided to move together. Straight in, follow the truck tire tracks that were visible the further you strolled inside. "I still don't know what to look for," I whined. "What does a mine look like?"

"Let's assume that if there were actual mines, they wouldn't be placed between the tire tracks, so let's start there," Jock said with some confidence. "Heel to toe, like you're performing a sobriety check at a DUI checkpoint. I'm sure you've seen your share. Make sense?"

After a few careful steps, Jock began to zigzag tread to tread and bent down like a scent dog. With the coyote fur hanging off him, he fit the part. "Get the scent. That's a good boy," I told him.

Soon, he straightened as if the signs were bogus. I followed behind him knowing I was pretty much safe wherever he had already stepped. "The more I think about it, the bodies were planted there to act as if the airfield is loaded," he said. Suddenly stopping, he then pointed to a mound of dirt and said, "Don't step there." Yards further, he pointed to another mound. "That step's a doozy," he giggled.

The closer we got, the less the rationale for flying in was apparent. Besides the hangar, the other building looked condemned. There was nothing of value to be seen. So why would they fly in here? Collecting water? That could be it, but would it take them three days to load it?

We arrived at the first structure and while I was confident there were no bombs under our feet, the place did look like a bomb was dropped *on top* of it. The walls were cracked and damaged while large holes exposed rebar. Planks of wood jutted from blocks of cement, while moldy insulation hung from a fallen roof. It could've been some former control tower or office; I could make out a desk and chair near a broken window.

Behind the building, however, was a greenhouse of sorts, still intact, save for some plastic sheeting where the glass used to be. Under it, plants were growing and it appeared to be…maintained.

That was interesting. And not visible from the entrance.

Next to that was the hangar. Inside, I could picture the plane and the water truck sitting there, maybe with the keys in the ignition. Little good that would do, I couldn't fly and I had no use for a loud water truck.

A shut door caught my attention on the side of the tower/office building. It was the remaining portion of the structure not collapsed, painted the same color as the walls, and hard to see from our earlier viewpoint.

Jock sensed what I was about to do and stopped me. "You're not going in there, are you?" he asked above a whisper.

"I'll pretend we're Mormon," I shrugged, reaching for the door handle. "That'll blow their mind."

Jock wasn't in the mood to joke and he got all serious. "You sure this is a good idea? What if they shoot to kill? Take no prisoners?"

My gut instinct said to run and I, of course, was going to ignore it.

"No, as a matter of fact, it's a pretty fucking stupid idea. But I want to find out who they are. The plane has me curious."

"I'll stay out here, keep a lookout," Jock said and ducked behind a nearby wall filled with cracks and holes. Only his coyote ears poking up were visible.

"Whatever," I mumbled and walked to the door. I took a deep breath and paused.

Jock whispered to me, "Take out your crowbar at least."

I wanted to show I meant no harm, however, so I shook my head and kept it in the quiver. These people had an airplane, an actual working airplane. To me, that sounded civilized in today's world, despite the axe-wielding truck driver planting the dead out front. Bale's attempts to conquer long ago were the last I saw of any plane. Soon after, gasoline turned gummy and clogged most engines without the refined resources required to liven it up again.

"What the hell," I said with resignation and twisted the handle. Surprisingly, the door opened, creaking a bit, and swung wide. After a five-second count, no gun barrel poked out, no meet and greet, and I thought I was free and clear. I kept the bear in check. No need to start a rumble when there was no visible threat.

A small room was before me. A set of stairs descended into the ground ahead. A dim light shined up from a floor below. That's why we couldn't see where they went. Those people we saw earlier? They went gopher.

I left the door open in case I needed to flee. I walked soft to the stairs, peering down below, seeing more of what lay underground; a large room with plants atop tables, with neatly stacked boxes next to the staircase. Then, suddenly, I heard the click of a gun and a voice from behind.

"Don't give me a reason to shoot," the voice said. "Turn around slowly."

Turning and abiding, I saw it was the Pilot behind the door. I noticed he was clean cut and shaven, with brown hair parted in the middle, brown eyes to match, healthy looking and fit, maybe mid-forties, armed with a .9mm. "Backpack off," he instructed. "Drop it on the floor."

Obliging, the backpack dropped with a thud, obviously full, but the Pilot barely registered as if what I had in my possession meant nothing. A strange calmness flooded me. They had more than what I could offer. They were better than me. I didn't even try for my crowbar because I was curious to see more. Even with the gun pointed at me, I deduced he wouldn't shoot unless I provoked him. I wasn't so sure about the man with the axe to grind, however.

Speaking of which, the Driver of the water truck, aka the body butcher, came up the stairs from below, eyeing me the entire way up. Upon closer look, he was older than I thought when I spied him through the scope. He was graying, had some facial scars on top of plump cheeks, and carried a week's worth of salt and pepper stubble. His expression suggested indifference, even after he sized me up. He was comfortable that the Pilot could handle me on his own as he didn't appear armed. No axe, especially. Thank God.

Both men looked healthy. Both men showed no obvious sicknesses. That was a rarity in the desert.

"Arms on top of your head," the Pilot told me and I complied.

The Pilot frisked me, found a couple of obvious knives and sharp objects, and tossed them to the floor. He was a professional at it and by watching him hold the gun on me, I guessed he was either a cop or army in a past life. The Driver shuffled the contraband away with his shoes.

"Bulletproof vest, huh?" the Pilot asked me, rapping it with his knuckles.

"It was taken from a cop," I said.

The men looked at each other. "You kill him?" the Driver prodded.

"No."

"I'll see if he has friends," the Driver suggested and brushed past me, removing a gun from his waist. When he reached the door I just entered, he opened it more and took a few quick peeks. Seeing no one, he exited, calmly shutting the door, and from the shadow under the door, I could tell he hung a right. Jock, thankfully, was hiding to the left so hopefully, he'd stay hidden, at least for now.

Hauling my backpack and crowbar over his shoulder, the Pilot waved the gun. "Turn around," he said and pointed. "Move down the stairs, slowly."

"Sure thing," I shrugged.

"Keep your arms above your head," the Pilot advised and nudged me forward. "Go down the stairs. Don't make any sudden moves. Don't move fast or you'll be shot."

"What is this place?" I asked him.

"Shut up," he responded and shoved me hard.

CHAPTER THIRTEEN

We descended into a large room that resembled a laboratory. It was filled with tables, microscopes, lights, bottles, beakers, and test tubes. Textbooks were opened to various pages while nearby, plants thrived under lights. Along the walls, boxes were stored, filled with various seeds and packets.

"Keep going," the Pilot said, nudging me. "Eyes front."

"No problem," I replied. Planters lay on tables, packed with an assortment of desert flowers and small shrubs. The room was rectangular, about twenty feet wide and fifty feet long. A door led to a hallway on my right where I could see more rooms. In one, a cot with blankets and a pillow captured my attention. In another, a Men's sign on a door, and that intrigued me. A real bathroom? In working order? That I got to see. Assessing what Jock had told me, this appeared to be a former military bunker.

A table with coffee mugs and plates covered in crumbs lay ahead. Orchestral music played softly from an old tape deck. Playing cards were stuck midway in a game of interrupted solitaire.

The Pilot guided me to the middle of the room and said, "Stop right there. Don't move." Walking around to my left, he kept his gun trained on me. I was positive it was loaded. By the looks of the lab, these people could probably make their own ammunition.

The woman in white was in the middle of the room, bent over some plants, gently spraying them with water. She looked to be in her fifties, her gray hair about shoulder length but tied in a ponytail. When she finally stood, I noticed she was as tall as I was, healthy and fit. She looked slightly irritated and studied me as if I was a new specimen. She had hazel eyes, a slim nose, and small lips. She clicked off the music with a push of her finger and I wished it stayed on. Music was hard to come by and the Bee Gees needed a break.

"Congratulations," she said breaking the ice. "You're the first to make it all the way inside. You're incredibly brave or incredibly stupid. Now that you broke our defenses, I don't know what to do with you."

Ignoring her, I took in the room itself, trying to ascertain what all of it meant. Not the size necessarily or the activity, just the organization and planning. Everything there worked and everything was clean. Even she, along with the Pilot, was apparently disease free. Besides me, that was rare. However, I became modest at that point and looked down at my clothes. I was probably a mess.

"Do you have a name, Rogue?" she asked me.

I stared at her, taken aback. She assumed I was a bad guy.

The Pilot motioned to her. "Here, I found this on him." He flung my wallet at her.

She caught it and looked surprised. "A wallet? Really? Now we're getting somewhere." She inspected it as if it was a relic.

"I am not a Rogue," I told her. It came out weak. "I travel alone."

She didn't answer me but instead opened the wallet. "May I?"

I shrugged. "You're going to anyway. I have nothing to hide." Except for my modesty which was sucking pretty badly. There was a tear on my jacket and dried blood on my sleeve. I looked like a wreck. No wonder she thought me a Rogue. I fit the part.

"I need to go shopping. I have a gold Amex card in there," I said as I tugged at my shirt. Was that my blood? I caught the Pilot glaring at me as if I was a nut job.

She pulled out my driver's license, then looked at me. Her gaze fell upon me with an accusatory glare, like a judge to a prisoner about to be sentenced. She then studied the rest of the license and tapped it against her hand. "You're far away from home."

"Ted," I told her.

"Excuse me?"

"Ted," I noted, nodding at my license. "Call me Ted. I am not a Rogue."

Glancing back at the license, she then spotted it. "I see. Well, Ted, we were almost neighbors once. I was from Newport Beach."

"What's your name?" I asked.

She paused. "You can call me Doctor."

"Doctor? Like, cure people, Doctor?"

"Something like that," she surmised, then regarded me closer. "You don't seem to be sick. Are you? Any virus or condition we should be aware of?"

"Nope, clean bill of health," I mentioned, proudly. "I get a physical once a year, take my vitamins, eat my veggies. What the hell is all this?"

The Pilot sneered at my comments and then glared at the Doctor. "We know he's been whoring. They all have. We should be wearing a mask," he said and nudged me with his gun. "There's no telling what this man is infected with."

"I abstain," was all I admitted and left it at that. "I'm married."

"That's hard to believe," she said to me, dismissively, then followed with, "that you've led a clean life out there."

I took offense to that and firmly asked again, "What is this place?"

She smiled, "It's a laboratory. And nursery. And supply depot."

"He doesn't need to know," the Pilot reminded her.

"Laboratory," I repeated, like an idiot. "In these times? Where are you from?"

The Pilot stepped forward as if to block her answer. "Don't tell him, I don't trust him." I could tell my presence unnerved them, to the point they didn't know what to do with me. I hoped the next step didn't involve the axe man joining the party. Suddenly, she motioned for the Pilot and he walked back to her, the gun still pointing. They spoke in hushed tones.

"You've got a safe place, haven't you?" I asked, stopping their discussion. "I know it. It's somewhere in the west." The Pilot grew incensed but she quickly calmed him. Then, unequivocally, she placed an upturned hand on him and spilled the beans to me. "I won't lie to you. Yes, we do. But even we have our limitations. Some plants only grow in the desert. Some have medicinal qualities and we've got a growing op outside hidden in all the rubble, not visible from the fences. Water supply from the Colorado River, salt from the salt flats, these are much-needed resources. No place is perfect. You have to make do with what you can get. We are not sustainable on our own at times. We've needed to branch out."

The Pilot shook his head. "Stop, please. You've said too much."

The Doctor eyed me some more. Studied me even, as if we met in a past life. I tried to place her somewhere, but nothing rang a bell. Newport Beach was only a few minutes from Mission Viejo but I was positive we had never met. Even if she knew me before, my current looks and attire wouldn't resonate with my wife.

Slyly, she confessed, "I have to admit, I am intrigued by you. You don't seem as rough as the others."

"Looks like a scumbag to me," the Pilot remarked.

"Don tells me he sees all kinds out there. Ferocious, disgusting types. It's not difficult for him to find bodies. The Rogues leave quite a trail."

"Don?" I asked.

She nodded to the ceiling. "The driver of the water truck. He stays with me for weeks on end, then leaves for the Colorado River days before the plane arrives. Mostly drives at night with the help of moonlight or night vision goggles."

"He keeps a beautiful body garden out front," I stated but no one laughed.

"You don't appear to be sick, no sign of infection or wayward symptoms, reasonably healthy, maybe sane even," she pointed out. "That is indeed rare." She opened the wallet again and found the family photo. She pulled it out. "Your sons?"

I nodded and bowed my head. She could tell she was intruding and she apologized. "I'm sorry," she said, and it sounded sincere.

Suddenly, she cupped her mouth, shock showing on her face. Back and forth her eyes went from me, to the photo, back to me, the photo again. Her eyes widened as if staring at horrible news and she mumbled, quite clearly, "Oh my God."

"What?" I asked. Even the Pilot noticed her reaction and he slid closer to her.

"Who is in this picture with you?" she asked me quite loudly, her voice changing.

Was she kidding? "What is this?" I asked.

Angrily, she tapped the photo to make her point. "The woman. Who is she? Who are these kids?" Her tone was accusatory as if I had stolen it.

"My sons and my wife." Panic set in and my heart raced. She knew something from the photo and I wasn't prepared for it. My knees shook. I felt like falling. I hoped it wasn't a mistake and definitely not bad news.

Showing the Pilot the photo, she demanded that he look at the woman. "Holy shit," he mumbled. He then studied me and squinted. "Is this a joke? Is it true?"

"Tracy?" she asked me. "Tracy is your wife?"

My jaw dropped; tears began to well in my eyes. "How do you know her name?" I stuttered. "Why...are you asking me this?" It was hard to catch my breath.

"Answer me!" she bellowed.

It all came out in a blur. "Yes, my wife is Tracy! Of course, she is! Who carries around a photo of someone else's family? What the fuck do you think? I found a photo on the ground and kept it, believing I was the man in the fucking photo?"

"I know her," she then said. "We know her." She emphasized *we* using her finger to go back and forth between them.

Rage built inside me. My fists clenched, my muscles tensed up, and I was ready to bring out the bear. This was the first time I'd heard any news of my family in years. Almost five long years of silence, wondering, hoping, searching, finding nothing. Fighting the urge to give up. Fighting to stay alive.

And those two knew something about them.

"I know Tracy and her two boys!" she said to me, her hand over her heart.

"What? When? How?" I stammered. My throat went dry and for some reason, I kept the bear in check. Confusion set in. Memories flooded my mind, visions of my kids, of my wife. My jaw was working but no words came out. I could feel my eyes fluttering. The Doctor and the Pilot were looking at each other and all I could do was blubber.

She quickly studied the driver's license again. "Oh my God," she said. "I should have realized this. Your last name. Ratelle. It matches!"

I was truly dumbfounded and confused. I stepped forward and tried to reach her, but the Pilot grabbed my arm and held me back. "What are you saying? You know her? Know her now? Who are you?" I twisted my right wrist under my sleeve, shifted the fabric under it, and felt the screwdriver I kept there hidden slide down into my palm.

"What does your wife do?" she asked, then corrected herself. "I mean, what did she use to do?"

"Let me go!" I shouted at the Pilot. Amazingly, after a nod from the Doctor, he did. I searched her face. She was crumbling, caught in a dilemma, unsure herself of what to do next. I wasn't sure I was going to trust what she had to say. This was unexpected and uncomfortable all around.

"Nurse," I told her. "She was a nurse after college. Before my kids were born. She quit after becoming a stay-at-home Mom."

As if expecting that answer, she followed with, "What sports did your boys play?"

"Tell me where they are," I said, gritting my teeth.

The Pilot stepped in. "Tell her what sport they played!"

"Ice hockey!" I shouted at both of them.

"Ice hockey," the Doctor nodded and then looked up. Her voice lowered. "She told me that. Her boys used to play ice hockey."

I felt like I had been robbed. I pivoted and grabbed the Pilot's gun hand and twisted backward, his finger still on the trigger. It caught him by surprise and he yelped, his finger bending back, and I slid the weapon from him, dropping it to the ground. I then drove my fist into his gut and that knocked him to his knees. I leaped at the Doctor with my screwdriver out, but she was too stunned to move and I caught her with the Phillips end under her chin. My other arm locked her right arm and I held her in place.

"Tell me where they are!" I shouted. "Are they still alive?"

Shaking, she managed a nod. "Please don't hurt me," she whispered.

The Pilot was on me, trying to pull me back. I kicked backward, at his knee, and he shrieked in pain. I knew he'd go for the gun next and I spun the Doctor around to shield me, holding her tight. "Then where are they? Tell me!" I yelled in her ear.

Gasping, she admitted, "She told me she was a widow! She said she lost her husband, that he was dead in the desert somewhere!"

"She knew I was alive!" I screamed in her ear. "I spoke to her!"

The Doctor shook her head. "She thought you possibly lived shortly after the attacks but that you wouldn't last long in the wasteland!"

I took offense to that. "Why would she say that?" I asked, gripping her tighter.

As if searching for the correct words, she mumbled, "Because..."

"Because what?" I demanded.

Her nails dug into my arm but I brushed the pain off. "She said you were just a Corporate weasel and doomed to die out there with the rest of the filth!"

Gritting my teeth, I snarled, "I don't believe you."

"There's something else you should know!"

"What?" I asked.

"She had taken another lover!"

A simple phrase can knock you back worse than a bullet. Caught off-guard, I froze, staring straight ahead at a light fixture, loosening my grip. I dropped my screwdriver and the Doctor freed herself by lifting my arm and sliding out. Lips trembling, head shaking, I doubled over then, ready to vomit. Nothing but bile rose from within yet my stomach rocked and heaved, churning and rolling. My hands came up and covered my face, the shame I felt was worse than death. My worst fears were confirmed. By telling others of our story and who I was, Tracy was rejecting me entirely. My wife harbored deep hatred and I could only imagine what my kids thought. I failed them in my past life and that had carried over to the present. I wanted to hide. I wanted to die.

In my wife's mind, I was already buried.

The Doctor and Pilot weren't lying. They knew her. Lifting my head, I didn't expect sympathy from the two and I wanted to apologize, but words failed me and all I could do was moan. The Pilot has his gun out again, aiming at me, furious, himself shaking. The Doctor righted herself and rubbed her sore neck.

My face must have shown total anguish as I muttered weakly, "My family..."

"You didn't have to kick me!" he shouted, limping towards me. "You son of a bitch! I should shoot you right now!"

"That's enough!" the Doctor yelled and stopped him mid-charge with an arm out. He reluctantly stopped and obeyed, swore under his breath, then grabbed at his knee again. The Doctor collected herself, her hand flat against her forehead as if a migraine was building. I did not make a good first impression but they had no right to keep information from me.

In a soft voice, I pleaded. "I'm sorry. I didn't want to hurt either of you. This is my family we're talking about. Please tell me where they are. I've been searching for so long. Five years now."

"We can't," she stated angrily. "It's too dangerous for the rest of us."

"What are we going to do now?" the Pilot asked her. "You've said so much. He might figure it out."

We were interrupted by a small explosion from outside that rocked the walls. The roof shook. Both of them were caught off-guard as the Doctor and the Pilot looked up like the ceiling might cave in. It was clearly unexpected. I was clueless, unsure what to make of it. The Pilot condescendingly asked me, "Friends of yours?"

"Was that an explosion?" I asked. "What blew up?"

"Answer my question!" the Pilot demanded. "Are they friends of yours?"

"I don't have any friends. Well, except for Jock, but he's small..."

Another explosion shook the foundation. "We need to move," she informed the Pilot. The Doctor ran to some books and papers on a table, gathering them into her arms. "Quick, grab the plants by the door!" she shouted to the Pilot who was already on it. They left me there alone, unsure what the hell was going on. The Doctor peeked back at me and requested, "Little help?"

Gathering my backpack and crowbar, I followed them as they headed toward the stairs. Reaching her, I asked, "What's going on?"

She piled the papers into an empty box, then stopped to survey the rest of what lay around. A lost cause was reflected on her face. The Pilot had already ascended the stairs, taking what he could, and disappeared from view. "We're being attacked, obviously," she replied to me as the impact finally hit her. "Can't you tell? Do you think those things just go off by themselves?"

"What things?" I asked, incredulously.

She stared at me in disbelief. "Mines, you imbecile. Didn't you see the signs?"

"The mines are fucking real?" I asked, completely astounded.

"How else could we stay here protected?" she said, grabbing a box of cacti. "Here, take this, please." She handed me a box filled with the same. "Help us take it to the plane," she begged.

"Where are you going?" I yelled. "You don't know what's out there!"

"Were you followed?" she stopped and probed me. "Did you invite others here?"

"No, I wasn't followed," I countered, unsure if I really was. "What about the truck driver? Maybe he took a bad step," I suggested.

She sighed and made her way to a panel on the wall, opening it with one hand, and cradling the cacti box in the other. Grasping a lever inside, she glanced around and glared at me. "He was one of the men who planted the mines. He knows where they all are. He isn't stupid enough to walk out in the field. He's ex-military, for God's sake."

I thought of Jock but he was too smart to wander off the main area. It had to be someone else. Someone dumb enough to ignore the posted signs and make a beeline for the buildings. Gunshots suddenly rang out. I shuddered and thought the worst. What if I *was* followed and didn't know it? Did I bring them here? Was it the dune buggy tracks? Were they shooting at Jock?

The Doctor squealed at the gunshots. Then, she shook her head and yanked the lever down. Turning to me with a look of sadness, she said softly, "You need to come with me. You can't stay here."

"Coming," was all I could say but I followed her, wondering what pulling the lever would mean. The power inside was still on.

"This place took two years to complete," the Doctor conceded, reaching the top step and taking one last look at the lab below. "It took us so long to build. So much research, so much insight, so much good. And now..."

"Now what?" I asked, cresting the top of the stairs next to her.

"Rogues," she said, opening the door. "The bastards finally found us."

CHAPTER FOURTEEN

Single file, the barbaric brethren known as the Rogues had been making their way across the minefield. It was just the Pilot, the Doctor, the Driver, and myself facing down a slow train of killers light-stepping the uneven ground. We had the plane and the means to escape the airfield, but time was not on our side, despite the mines planted under the horde's feet. Eventually, they'd luck out and follow the safe footsteps created by the less fortunate before them. No doubt they'd block our attempt to flee.

Two of the sons of bitches had already blown up, causing the loud booms we heard underground. From my vantage point outside the door and with the help of the moon's glow, the remaining eight or so Rogues were frozen, like deer in headlights, too afraid to move after the last blast. Their comrades lay sprawled ahead of them, various parts and limbs scattered about, smoke wafting from a few severed, burnt limbs. Behind the train of degenerates, I could make out a hole in the fence where Jock and I first stood when we studied the airfield earlier. Headlights shone from a small car parked there, providing extra vision for those attempting to cross. Up high to the left, I could see headlights from more vehicles next to where we left the dune buggy and I groaned, realizing they must have followed Jock and I somehow.

The Pilot was pulling the Cessna out from the hangar, having already opened the grand door. The Doctor was tending to Don, the water truck driver, who looked to be gut shot, propped up on his elbows, with blood pooling under his shirt. The Doctor had laid her boxes down next to him and began checking his vitals. Although the good guys required my immediate services, I was more concerned with the bad guys and their trans-minefield attempt. Specifically, the engine of the train, by default, who was maybe fifty yards from the runway and only feet from his dead counterpart. I knew he would trudge on and it was like a car wreck waiting to happen. I didn't mind rubber-necking that one.

Goaded by his moronic brethren behind him, the Rogue out front, in tears and visibly shaken, finally began walking again, his face splattered with dirt and blood from the last blast. He bypassed his fallen comrade who was leading the charge up until that fatal step just moments ago. The first victim lay off to the side yards back, passed up by the others.

Stepping over the small crater created by the most recent pop, the blabbering fool still had a lot of ground to cover. I was afraid he could be lucky and miss the rest of the planted bombs. Then, we would have to face him head-on. However, just as he side-stepped a shrub mound, we all jolted at the sound of a small thunderclap as the ground erupted and the Rogue went flying. When the dust settled, he was on his back, his legs gone, his comrades laughing and nudging the next victim forward.

Animals, I thought. Such a disregard for life.

"Help me, Ted!" the Doctor shouted at me as she helped Don to his feet. I rushed over and lent him a shoulder for him to grasp. Together, we three made our way to the Cessna where the doors were propped open, the Pilot inside starting the engines. As Don was helped inside the plane in the front, the Doctor smoothed his hair in a caring fashion. When she kissed his cheek, I knew then they were lovers. I gave them space and checked out the interior of the plane. It was a four-seater; two in front, two in the rear, and not much storage behind. There were five of us, including Jock. I supposed he could jump into the storage hold, I thought. There had better be room for us.

The Pilot turned to me in the cockpit which was full of gauges and lights, some of which looked modern and completely foreign as of late. Eye-popping displays of lights and instruments were mesmerizing and I felt awe-inspired like a kid. "Drop the boxes in the rear cargo hold," he directed me, breaking my glare, and then he climbed out of the plane. "Follow me to the water truck!"

Sliding the box to the back of the cargo hold, I noted the boxes were quite bulky. And now some water jugs? There was only so much room. I began wondering where Jock would fit into all this.

Where the hell was the little dude anyway?

I sprinted to the water truck where the Pilot already had a jug ready. "Grab this one," he said and handed me a jug. "Put it on the seats at the back." Heavy and awkward, the water sloshed on the inside as I carried it back to the Cessna.

"You sure we're all going to fit?" I asked worried, turning to him as he was right behind me with one himself. He didn't respond but simply nodded ahead. We made it to the plane with some difficulty and plopped the jugs into each seat. Another explosion rocked the ground and I heard more maniacal laughter.

"What happened to you?" I asked Don, who was watching me with disdain.

The Doctor answered for him, arriving with her boxes. "He said a Rogue entered from the front gate and ran up firing."

"Front gate?" I asked and turned around. There, more Rogues had assembled, their vehicles splashing lights across the entire field but staying well behind the perimeter. Only the Rogues deep in the mine-field had the balls to try entry so far.

Still not trusting me, the Doctor let the driver know I was there to help and not a Rogue myself. Don swallowed and pointed, holding a cloth over his wound with his other hand. "They sent that guy over there in first. I didn't see him until he was almost upon me." He winced when he said it. His face showed a tremendous amount of pain.

Thinking of Jock, I asked him, "What guy?"

A Skinny Rogue was lying on his back in the dirt about ten yards off from the runway. "He came up from nowhere, firing his gun at me, and then his luck ran out," Don replied. "He stepped on one of the mines I planted over there."

I approached the Skinny Rogue as he laid on his back, noticing he had blond flowing hair with a seventies mustache and only one leg. His other was a bloody stump, severed above the knee. I stared at him, astounded that I missed seeing him just moments ago, he had only been a few yards away when I first exited the door. His eyes were open and he was watching me. He didn't speak. More blood seeped from his side and I realized shrapnel from the mine must have done more damage than just his leg.

The Rogues began whooping it up and hollering louder. It was unnerving, like monkeys screeching at a zoo. Cars revved their engines, gunshots rang out. The front gate suddenly swung open and a car drove inside. A few men scampered inside too and I assumed the worst, believing if they stayed the course of the driveway somehow, they would make it here in one piece like Jock and I had done. It would be a free-for-all and no one to stop them. I ran back to the plane to warn them.

"Did you set the charges?" the Pilot asked the Doctor.

She nodded yes and said, "Just a few minutes ago."

"Quick, get inside the plane! We don't have much time!" The Pilot shouted to her.

A mine detonated and I heard a mixture of shattered glass and screams behind us. About a quarter of the way past the gate, the initial car coasted to a stop, the hood popped up, smoke billowing. The other cars lined up behind braked immediately and got stuck in a traffic jam. They started cussing loudly, and then another thump sent a Rogue cartwheeling. Those still intact hightailed it for the fence, leaping to safety, laughing as they did. The cars stayed put. It was like I was reliving the dynamite blasts back at Coppertown all over again.

Maybe the mines would hold them off, after all.

Jock finally appeared, emerging from behind the concrete wall, frightened and jumpy. The Doctor saw him but didn't flinch, despite Jock being a little person in a coyote costume. Still, introductions were necessary.

"This is my friend, Jock, who I neglected to tell you about," I informed her above the sound of the Cessna. "It's just me and him though. He's a good guy too." The fact Jock and I had wandered into the compound, uninvited, wasn't going to bode well. I just hoped they'd be sympathetic regardless. Jock was the one who discovered their secretive airfield after all.

The Doctor shook her head, ignoring the meet and greet. "Our base has been compromised. We won't be returning," she shouted to me.

That was fine by me. "You can take us though, right?" I asked her.

"Too much weight, pal," the Pilot pointed out over the roar of the engine. The Doctor looked at him to see if it was possible. He stared at her and then said, "We need the extra fuel to land in the sky. Remember?"

Nodding, she acquiesced. "He's right. We can't take either one of you," she said, flatly to me. "We need as much fuel as possible to make it home."

The Doctor climbed into the open, rear seat. Before she could shut it, however, I grabbed hold, preventing her from closing it. "Take the water out! You can't leave us!" I yelled.

"We need the water!" she shouted back and tried to pull the door shut. A bullet pinged off the plane. Glancing right, the Rogues in the minefield were making a go of it, one of which held a gun high.

"But my family!" I reminded her. The engine was revving louder and the plane was starting to move forward. "I have to go with you!"

"I will talk it over with the group!" she said and the plane began taxiing. I jogged next to them, trying to keep up. Somehow, she managed to shut the door on me.

I banged on the window, shouting, "You said you won't come back! You have to let me inside!" My voice strained above the engine. The plane rolled faster and I was clawing at the door. She rolled down her window and placed her hand on top of mine, gripping it with sincerity. I didn't want her to let go.

"Where is this place? Where's my family?" I asked desperately, running then. I then noticed we were heading south, towards the front gate, which caused the ruckus back there to erupt even more. "I'll go there myself!"

She shook her head. "I can't tell you that! If you were to be caught, you'd give it away! Our very survival is our secret! You have to understand!"

"What about my boys?" I cried. "Are they healthy?"

"Yes, they are. And they are beautiful," she smiled at me. Another shot rang out and just missed us. The plane began to move faster. They were going to take off. More shots rang out from the Rogues and a bullet penetrated the wing.

"Be a dear and clear the runway!" she shouted and waved me clear. "Use the shrubs! There are no mines underneath them so hop to each one!"

"I need to be with my family!" I shouted back, not caring. "I'll stand in the middle of the runway!"

"Don't be a fool!" the Doctor shouted above the roar of the engines.

"I don't care," I cried. "I'll do it!"

She offered me a look of sympathy. "I promise I will tell them about you! Please watch yourself!"

I ran as hard as I could. "I'm coming for them! I don't care what it takes!"

"Stay away from the buildings!" she warned me, waving goodbye. "Leave this place at once! It's booby-trapped!"

The plane began to pull away from me. "You have no right to keep me from my family! My kids deserve to see me again!" I yelled.

The Doctor and Pilot eyed each other.

"Do you have a car?" she asked/yelled to me.

"No!"

She leaned out the window and shouted, "Make your way to the Salton Sea! Find the place of judgment! If you are truly worthy, head north and you'll find redemption!"

"What?" That stopped me in my tracks.

"You heard me! I can't tell you more! Figure it out! We'll be there in a few days! Goodbye for now!"

Out of breath, I doubled over, hands on my knees. I hadn't run that far and that fast in a while. "What the hell does that mean?!?" I shouted after them, knowing they wouldn't hear it.

The plane traveled south even more towards the front gate which got the Rogues delirious. More gunshots, more yelling, more engines revving. The plane then slowed, turned around, goosed its engine, and began to race back toward me. Soon, it thundered past me, the wind buffeting my face, the Pilot giving me a thumbs-up. I saw the faces of the only people who knew where my family was fly by me, literally, and all I could do was watch.

Dirt and dust kicked up as it roared down the runway, lifting into the air at the northern end. It banked left after a couple of dips, then flew into a steep climb eventually soaring over some hills. It continued to climb, then headed westward, a small white blot in the white evening sky. I then lost sight of the plane and my hopes diminished.

Salton Sea, she said. Fuck it. I was going to go there. She said they would be there in a few days. I knew what I had to do.

First though, we needed to leave somehow. She said to stay away from the buildings. They were booby-trapped. Jock and I would have to find our way out of this mess. As I neared the buildings, I froze on the spot and removed my crowbar.

The Rogues from the minefield had made it across in one piece. They had given up on the plane and began scouring the buildings, howling and screeching in anticipation of the possible loot. None of them had approached me as I stood there armed with my weapon. I heard one of them shout out that they found the water truck and that got the others riled up. I was simply ignored.

Jock hurried over to me. Together, we began looking for an out. Crossing the minefield would be tricky. "She said step on the plants," I informed him. "No mines underneath them."

"I don't know if I can jump that far," Jock groaned.

The only way in seemed to be the only safe way out and that was a straight shot toward the front gate to where the rest of the animals were. Somehow, we would have to make our way by them but the Rogues there figured out the same game plan Jock and I mastered earlier. They entered the compound much more brazen this time, staying in the middle of the roadway leading up, probably following the same water truck tread we did. No explosions occurred as the first vehicles made it toward me, engulfing us more in their light.

Jock was clearly worried. Rogues in front and back did not bode well for the little man. He'd be torn apart if we gave ourselves up, the sick fetishes of these beasts would make the remainder of his life miserable, to say the least. "Hide," I told him. "Hop from bush to bush the best you can and hide in one of them. Just stay away from the buildings. I'll take the heat."

"Promise?" he asked.

"Promise what?"

He shifted on the balls of his feet. "You'll come back?"

Our eyes met. He looked as if he was going to speak, then stopped himself.

A window shattered at one of the buildings. One of the Rogues shouted out that he found stairs. They discovered the lab and all that was below would be stolen and trashed. Years of hard work were wiped out by short-sided marauders.

I placed my hand on his shoulder. "I promise, man. I'll come back for you. I owe you, Dude. This means a lot to me. Go."

With that, he nodded, bent down, and leaped atop a set of bushes. From there, he hopped to the next set, his feet seemingly staying above the ground.

"Keep it up," I told him. "Stay on top of the shrubs."

The coyote fur ruffled in the wind and soon he was gone, hidden among the shadows of the next few shrubs. Even the moon's radiance didn't betray him. The action was all around the buildings, so I doubt they'd hunt for him, especially in the field.

"Don't go far," I said to him and made my way towards the gate, acting indifferently, as if I intruded on this mess and would best be going. A car passed me along the same driveway, then another. Rogues ignored me, more interested in what their comrades had discovered back at the structures.

A white pickup truck, the same Toyota that I saw with the Shoeman encounter, was parked behind the gate. The headlights blinded me, causing me to look to the side as I approached. The same red-headed Rogue that killed the traveling shoe salesman stepped out, the light from inside the cab giving him away. I recognized him instantly. He barked at a couple of Rogues to secure the perimeter and they spread out with their weapons drawn. As soon as I reached the gate, guns cocked and leveled at me. At least a handful of them by my count. None were fired, but I didn't think they would.

"That's far enough," the Red-Head Rogue instructed me with his hand up as I reached the gate. "Put down your weapon."

Outnumbered and outgunned, my options were limited. I did have one advantage in my favor; answers they will seek about the plane. I relinquished my crowbar after a few seconds of contemplation, juggling it to show the confidence and severity of the tool I carried. It ended up on the ground at my feet along with my backpack.

Redhead Rogue walked up to me and sized me up. He had green eyes behind a smattering of freckles atop high cheekbones. Below those was a sturdy chin with some stubble. Not uttering a word at first, he just looked me up and down and then gave me a hard stare. I didn't look away and met his glare.

Finally, he asked, nodding at the sky, "Friends of yours?"

I shrugged. "I don't know them personally. Just a tad socially. Happy hours, that type of thing."

Unamused, he then asked, "Where's the plane headed?"

"No idea," I sighed. "I got bumped. Red eyes these days. You know."

The veins in Red-Head Rogue's temples flared. "Keys," he ordered of me.

I played dumb. "Keys?"

"The Dune Buggy, asshole."

I fished out the key from my pocket and dangled it in front of him, the ring wrapped around my index finger, my empty palm facing out. No sense in keeping it. "Sorry, the valet gave me the wrong set," I said.

Seeing my palm, Red-Head Rogue did a double take. His demeanor changed, and he harrumphed, grabbing the keys from me.

"You get to live. For now," he said and kneed me in the crotch. I doubled over, the pain rocking my whole lower body. I crumpled to the dirt, moaning, trying not to throw up and give him any satisfaction. He hit me square like I had never been hit before. Under some wrathful gasps, I swore and made a mental note to kill him. The bear would have to be kept in check at the time, however. I would have to wait it out.

"Put him in the back of the truck," he demanded. Rough hands pulled me up. I lurched forward as the numbness between my legs felt like cement. My toes curled as I was dragged by my arms, me twisting, holding my legs together. I could actually walk fine enough, but I made it hard for them, acting like dead weight.

When we reached the truck, blood had pooled in the back of the bed. Two bodies were laid down near the gate. It was the same two men I disposed of a few hours earlier. The tall one with the shriveled neck and the other with the gray eye.

The Rogues had a hard time lifting me in and over, but once my limp body cleared the rear gate of the truck and the bodies, I quickly and nimbly found a seat against the passenger's side fender.

"Faggot," one of them called me.

"Meet your old friends, Leatherneck and Cyclops," the Redhead said to me as he leaned over the truck's side.

I glanced over and simply smiled, despite the dull throb from below.

"I'm sure you're responsible for their demise since you took their dune buggy," he noted, somewhat impressed. "We'll be leaving shortly. Make yourself comfortable." He then eyed my privates. "Too bad we don't have ice for you."

CHAPTER FIFTEEN

Minutes passed and my nuts felt whole again. I glared back at the Redhead but he seemed to be taking an interest in the airfield. The other Rogues around me were jumpy, anxious to join the fray beyond the gate. The Rogue wearing a sweater, whom I also saw terrorizing The Shoeman, walked up behind the Redhead and said, "Torch, you might want to hear this. Cholo's got some news for you."

A Hispanic Rogue with a shaved head walked up, carrying another Rogue on his back. It was the blond Rogue I saw earlier next to the runway. Cholo twirled to have the piggybacked Rogue meet Torch, and blood splashed to the side.

Torch jumped away. "What the fuck, Cholo?" Torch asked, avoiding the splatter. "Better not get any of that shit on me," he warned, checking himself out.

"Surfer here knows where the plane is going," Cholo said and stayed put.

Surfer's lifetime was ending quickly. Blood was nearly flowing down Cholo's legs. Torch leaned in and asked Surfer, "So, what's up?"

Surfer's blond hair was matted with dirt and sweat. His mouth trembled and he whispered, "I know...where they are going. I...heard...

it all." His mouth opened and closed like a fish. "Was beside...the runway. Before...they took off."

Torch bent toward him as if listening to a child. "Tell me then."

"Water," Surfer said, his eyes fading, heavy eyelids about to shut forever.

"No. Tell me first and I'll take you back to camp," Torch demanded. "Get you all fixed up. Get you a new leg. Prosthetics. We got a new supply just last week."

Gasping and nodding, Surfer struggled to get the words out. "They said...go to...go...to..."

"Go to what?"

Torch leaned in close to the poor man's bloody mouth. Surfer's eyes rolled and he finally whispered. "Salton...Sea..."

Surfer wheezed and died right there, on Cholo's back. Cholo grossed out and tossed Surfer to the ground. Other Rogues laughed and playfully kicked sand on their former comrade in an attempt at a half-assed burial.

Torch grinned at me. "Salton Sea, eh? Interesting." I tried to hide my disappointment, but I was somewhat relieved that he only knew part of the riddle and not the rest. I merely shrugged it off but I could tell Torch believed he had the upper hand.

"You," Torch spoke out to a Rogue with bad teeth who was standing alone, scratching himself, grinning at the horseplay around the buildings. Torch looked lost for a moment. "What the hell is your name again?"

"My real name or the one y'all gave me?" the man asked.

Torch eyed him and the man gulped. "It's Crabs. Call me Crabs," the man said.

"Who's got basic army training at the camp, Crabs?"

Crabs thought a moment and scratched. "Latrine."

"Go fetch Latrine and bring him over here. See if we have a metal detector at camp too. I want you guys back here looking for mines. Map it out."

"Fuck that," Crabs said and laughed.

Torch pulled his gun out and placed it at Crab's forehead. "Get him or I make you run laps out there."

"Alright, okay, whoa, easy," Crabs said, pleading with open hands. Crabs then bolted, scurrying off to another vehicle.

Smart plan. An army could hold out there as long as they knew where to step. Might be worth it if they could somehow locate the mines.

A large explosion jolted us from behind. The ground shifted under our feet and the truck heaved. Pieces of concrete and debris showered us from high above. I covered my head with my arms. All around, men were shouting and coughing. Dust and smoke swirled, mixing like a dark gray vapor, engulfing us to the point where I could not see feet away. When the smoke finally cleared, Torch helped himself up on the truck, dazed, making sure I hadn't bailed.

I peered over the truck's roof. A Rogue ran screaming into the airfield, his back aflame. He was trying to pat it out when a mine exploded underfoot, causing him to cartwheel into another mine where he bounced up but fell to the earth like a puppet. More men screamed and ran in every direction, most with shattered eardrums I guessed, losing their balance, running into one another. Forgetting the mines, they ran blindly, some making it further than others into the field, but all meeting their ends as the foot bombs went off, each sounding a *foomp!* at different intervals.

I hoped Jock was okay. He was about midway down the driveway and my ears were ringing from where I was.

"Let's go," Torch grumbled.

The sweater-wearing Rogue asked Torch, "What the hell happened out there?" "Went up in smoke, Froggie," Torch answered. "That's that."

"What about the others?" Froggie nodded at the men scrambling in the dirt, some now on their knees, wailing, too afraid to move an inch.

Torch asked, "You want to go fetch them?"

Froggie glanced back once more, then shook his head. "Assholes, all of them," Froggie said and turned. "Thinning of the herd."

"Let's roll," Torch agreed and tossed Froggie his keys.

"You want me to drive your truck?" Froggie asked, surprised.

Torch nodded, pulled a gun, and said, "I'm going ride with my new friend."

CHAPTER SIXTEEN

Pretend inferiority and encourage his arrogance. I read that passage in a Sun Tzu motivational poster once, inside the office of my former boss. A competitive strategy when undermining your foe, he'd tell me. "Let your enemy think they are above you; they will then underestimate you and lower their fucking guard. That's when you strike when they least expect it," he'd say.

Matias agreed with him when I told him of that.

That was Randall alright, always looking for the edge. It had been years since I saw him when he and Maggie made a pitch to be welcomed to Coppertown as new residents. Maggie was a woman who drugged me in a Las Vegas hotel room and somehow filmed us naked, the images sent to my wife. Randall and Maggie ended up teaming together after the gas but were sent on their way when I kicked them out of Coppertown. I knew Ginn was behind the scheme and had sent the wayward couple in to be spies.

Torch, the Redheaded Rogue, sat opposite and stared at me. His gun rested in his right hand. With his left, he lit a lantern and propped it against his leg. The bed lit up. I returned his gaze but when the truck lurched forward and turned around, I eyed the rest of the bed. A thin, one-armed man in a dinner jacket sat facing us at the truck's gate. Underneath him were the bodies of Leatherneck and Cyclops.

"So, what's your name?" Torch asked me. I didn't respond.

"Well, as you already know, I go by Torch. That's FuckStick," Torch told me, nodding to the rear. "Not worth much at all, but he's got a finger left at least."

"Thanks a lot, Torch," FuckStick replied. FuckStick's eyes were dark and beady, his cheeks bony, his neck and chin full of squirrelly black hair. His neck was full of boils, some looking ready to pop. He only had one arm yet cradled a sawed-off shotgun in his lap. I scoffed at the man, then smiled at Torch as if to suggest, *you command fools*.

I laughed inside at the notion many Rogues died with the earlier underground explosion, hearing their cries and whimpering. The incessant ground pops chasing those running blindly for the hills. I recalled the lever the Doctor pushed down. It must have been a slow fuse of some sort that decimated the Rogue battalion by a number that made even me envious.

A pothole jarred everyone in the back of the truck and Torch slammed the rear window. "Easy, Froggie!" he shouted. Froggie waved sorry.

Torch nodded to the man driving. "We call him Froggie because he always wears that fucking sweater and it reminds us of the frog in the Sugar Smack commercials."

I couldn't have cared less and didn't react.

FuckStick spoke up. "I could go for some Rice Krispies, right Torch?"

Torch didn't respond to him but said to me, "FuckStick here was a minor celebrity back in the day if you can believe it."

"Minor? Torch, dude, I was the shit!" FuckStick cried. "Fuckin' cameras, autographs, chicks, blow..."

"Give me a break," Torch spoke out, cutting him off. "You were on a reality show about riders finding love on the fuckin' subway."

"Did two seasons of Subway Seduction. Found love twice," FuckStick announced. "I was a star, man. Got recognized everywhere."

Torch rolled his eyes. "Don't get too excited. I doubt our friend here is fainting over your presence."

I wasn't even the slightest impressed.

Torch kicked his partner. "Tell our guest how you lost your arm, FuckStick."

FuckStick demurred, lowering his head. "Come on, Torch. It's not right."

Torch continued anyway. "FuckStick lost it to a rattlesnake bite. See, he thought he was reaching under a rock for a gopher snake, but this wise New Yorker didn't check for the rattle at the end of the snake's tail. And boom, he gets bit."

"Those snakes got the same coloring," FuckStick stated. "You know that."

"So, the guys decide to save this wretched man's life. As he's crying like a baby, the other men grab a hatchet, and hold his arm down." Torch turned to the poor man. "How many whacks did it take, FuckStick?"

"Five," he said, softly.

"Just below the elbow. Turns out, only about a third of rattlesnake bites contain venom. It was a defensive strike. So, poor old FuckStick carried his withered arm around for a good two days and it had no poison in it. What happened to that stupid arm?"

"You threw it into the pig pen," FuckStick acknowledged.

I finally spoke up. "Why the hell are you telling me this?"

Torch grinned and said, "Because Scarred-One, you're one of us and it's nice to know your peers."

About a half hour later with no more useless chitchat, we began passing people on either side of the road, some ducking away, and I could guess we were coming close to the Rogue camp. I figured we had been heading in a northeast direction and was trying to map out my return to the airfield. Wherever we were going, I wasn't going to stay long.

My backpack was at Torch's side tucked under his arm, my crowbar poking out. He was resting his other hand on the claw end of the tool, flicking the edges with the underside of his fingers. Do that too many times, you'd get a nasty nick and an infection.

I kept those babies sharp.

Leaning back, I took in the ride to think of my boys. I would see them soon. All I had to do was make my way to the Salton Sea. My mind drifted to their hockey games, which were a thrill for me to watch. They were good at it, fast skaters, good stick handlers, and not afraid to mix it up in the boards. It was too bad I never got to see them grow with the sport and see how far they could go. I doubted hockey was played very much, or any other sport for that matter, anywhere in the world now. We were back in the old west. Technology and peace were waiting to be revived.

We slowed to a four-way stop, yet only three stop signs stood. A scarecrow was hanging on one of the stop signs wearing tattered clothes. A gloved hand was pointing east and that's the route we took. I couldn't quite make out the face but it looked dark, shriveled, and human. There was no straw there.

"That's Woody. He likes you," FuckStick said to me.

We left Woody behind. Woody obviously knew the way.

"Maybe you take Woody's place," he giggled. "Right Torch?"

The recruiting academy for Rogues got stretched a bit thin. You took what you could get out there. Torch was irritated with him and tried to change the subject by speaking to me again. "You busted up those two pretty bad. Leatherneck and Cyclops." He pointed to the bodies under FuckStick. "You must be one badass hombre."

I feigned indifference but snickered inside when I learned their names. FuckStick glared at me suddenly. "You did this shit?"

"How come I've never seen you before?" Torch asked me. "All kinds of people come to the Digs. Maybe you came from a secret society. Some clandestine group hiding in the hills?"

I didn't respond.

"Or a faction in a rock quarry," he continued.

I glared at him momentarily and our eyes met. I looked away unconcerned, trying to steady my poker face, craning my neck, faking as if I had a crick. I regretted doing that and instantly wonder if he saw my tell.

"That's what I thought," he nodded. "Yeah, I know all about you Coppertown guys. The jar of gas. I wonder if it's real."

Disappointed with myself, I shifted my attention to FuckStick at the rear who was smoothing the hair of Cyclops, the dead Rogue closest. "I didn't know it was you who had done this. This dude was a friend of mine. Now you took his life."

I shrugged and smiled. I wanted Torch to grow nervous and fucking with the prospector wannabe would certainly accomplish that.

"You fucked him up," FuckStick whined to me. "Maybe we get back to camp, I fuck you up."

Torch yanked my crowbar out and twirled it like a baton. "I doubt that, FuckStick. This man here didn't need a gun to take down two of our brothers. Think about it. All he needed...was this."

FuckStick rolled his tongue like he was thinking. I figured the hamster inside his head was asleep at the wheel because he rattled his head.

"You want to mess with him now?" Torch asked his comrade. FuckStick did a double-take, drew in his legs closer, and went quiet.

Lights crossed Torch's face momentarily. He straightened and looked ahead. "Almost there," he said to me. "Party time."

"Yeah, you gonna get some," FuckStick giggled at me, and then the one-armed man put his gun down to scratch himself. An opportunity presented itself, the gun lying next to him, but I held back.

Torch shouted, "Pick up your fucking weapon!"

"Alright, sorry. Ain't like it's..." and then he caught himself. "Sorry."

Torch knew I knew, and now he held his gun even higher as if to stress that his weapon was fully armed. With him glaring at FuckStick, I wondered if the one-armed doofus would survive the night.

We crested a hill and I saw a glow ahead. The road descended and the truck picked up speed, but Froggie braked to slow us down. Bright lights were shining in a valley below, casting shadows on the far hills. Far off, I could hear laughter, yelling, and singing, like we were approaching an amusement park. I tilted back to look past the truck's cab and saw more drifters, a cluster of them, single-file along the side of the road. They were pushing carts and wheelbarrows filled with junk, some carrying large items on their back or shoulders. Shovels, tires, paint cans, bikes, clothes, and blankets. Chickens hopping in small pens, skinned ducks tied to a string, and even a thin horse was forced downhill by the rag-tag groups heading towards the lights like insects at night. They all had something to carry and they were slowly making their way forward.

As we rounded a curve, the camp came to view, the lights very bright, forcing me to squint. There were tents, RVs, campers, cars, trucks, motorcycles, and ATVs, all parked like one giant tailgate party underneath huge lights. There were even porta-potties stacked side by side. It wasn't all permanent; it all looked like it could pack up and move within a few hours. The Digs was a mobile camp.

Trade for moonshine was where it was at. What they couldn't steal or plunder out in the desert, they openly traded for. The Rogues needed to remain strong. That meant anything of value was considered whether it was food, drink, goods, or weapons. Sometimes, man. I noticed very few women and children among the drifters. Ironically, for now, they were somewhat safe. Rogues weren't about to make their customers unhappy so they left those parading in to be untouched. Out in the desert, however, you were fair game. Here though, trading was to be made and even the Rogues knew better than to steal. That would make for bad business.

A large distillery produced huge amounts of moonshine in massive vats. The customers, at least a hundred today, looked thirsty and eager. I saw the following carried in: books, animals, water, sports equipment, knives, tools, a prosthetic limb, medications, and car parts. As long as it was worth something to the Rogues, they would estimate the worth with a glance and hand out a slip of paper that would entitle the bearer to *this many* jars for whatever was accepted. There was no bartering either. You got whatever the Rogues deemed a good exchange and that was that. Complain, and you often got dealt with on the spot and your goods confiscated anyway. That was the risk you took and by the looks of it, many were ready and willing to take that chance.

I visited a camp like this years ago, south of here, but it was much smaller. Once I traded a set of golf balls and a bent nine iron for one jar. I was surprised they took the box of Titleists and a club with a lousy grip. Some Rogue still felt the need to practice his chipping, I supposed. Torch wasn't among that group of Rogues back then though. I would have recognized him. He was hard to miss.

I had another purpose that day besides the moonshine, however. See who the residents were. I found neither my wife nor sons there and moved on soon after.

We were somewhere along the Colorado River, just south of Las Vegas and the Hoover Dam, that much I could tell. The truck was forced to honk as the crowd of drifters thickened, nudging some aside. Shouts of protest didn't work; the truck found its path and it was up to you whether you want to be a speedbump or not. The truck divided the horde, carving a path as the drifters fell away and formed a line. They stared at me with contempt as we passed and I wondered if they saw me as a Rogue. We passed the trading area where Rogues assessed the goods while others carted off with the stash. Armed Rogues watched over the proceedings, some holding back large, barking dogs on short leashes. Rottweilers and Dobermans tugging and salivating, eager to be released. They were stocky and well-fed, probably better than most of the drifters moseying in. I was certain human flesh filled their doggie bowls.

Beyond the trading area was what looked like a party; drunken men stumbling and laughing around campfires. A guitar was playing somewhere. A woman sang a country song. Someone had bongos. A fight broke out between two others and order was not restored; they were allowed to scuffle. The atmosphere was jovial and lively, despite the fact the revelry was inside the serpent's nest.

We passed the distillery, huge pipes that ran in and out of a large tanker truck. Buckets of water were retrieved from the nearby river by an assembly line of drifters and Rogues, then emptied into large vats. From there, hoses ran into three other large containers with fires under some of the vats. Vapor came off glass vials atop each one. I didn't understand the entire setup, but I was guessing the resulting hooch was created inside the large tanker. Another tanker next to it dispersed the hooch from a tap, as a Rogue stood before a long line of drifters holding jars. Those tankers could hold thousands of gallons. More than what these people can drink in a lifetime.

A couple of Rogues dispensed moonshine into the jars, one acting like a bartender, the other collecting slips. Not content to wait, some of the drifters pushed and shoved, not wanting to queue, but thrusting their precious paper to the guy manning the taps. The bartender's partner lashed at them with a whip, keeping them orderly. Finally, when calmness prevailed and many were flogged for their conduct, jars were handed out, filled with the elixir they had waited so long to drink.

I licked my lips. I wanted some. I needed some.

We passed pens that held goats, chickens, rabbits, and cows. More dogs were caged in another, barking and pacing as we drove past. A stable for horses was further on, with one that looked like a donkey. The last set of pens were filled with pigs where they wallowed in their filth. A Rogue was busy there, shoveling manure into a bucket. As he neared the pen next to him, I heard a large crash, and the wood next to him splintered. Freaking out, he jumped back and leaped the fence as others looked on and laughed. All I could see in that pen were the backs of two large, humped, brown creatures. I didn't know what they were.

Farther on, a junk pile of worthless trash. Beds, car axles, boxes, microwaves, all piling up. Then, I saw it: The Shoeman's cart. The shoes were long gone, of course. Thinking back to the prior pen, that donkey I saw was his too.

A parking lot filled with cars and trucks appeared as well. I saw welders working on a couple of bumpers. A garage was set up in the farthest corner where cars had their hoods up. Men in overalls tended to those and behind them was a mountain of parts.

Our truck came to a stop near an area where tents and shacks were sprung up. I assumed this was their little ramshackle shanty town and the end of the line. As the engine switched off, Torch jumped out of the truck, unlatched the gate, and leveled the gun at me. FuckStick scrambled down first. Other Rogues circled, curious as to what the cat dragged in.

"Out," he said to me, motioning with the gun.

Just as I slid down, FuckStick neared me, getting in my face. "You and me. We gonna dance. Make you toss my salad." Then he scampered off.

Torch led me past a row of tents filled with whores and drug dealers. Doormen Rogues stood outside them, glancing at papers thrust into their meaty hands. Through an open flap, I saw a woman on her back, a drifter heaving on top of her. The tent next to that had men passing around a joint. Another woman, this one stunning, was topless outside her tent, sitting in a chair, safely away from the parading men, but close enough to be ogled. She had long wavy dark hair with tanned skin. She casually watched the men, apathetic to their desires. Her doorman was the largest of the protectors and he angrily shook his head at every slip. Some customers, he simply shoved away.

I admit I couldn't take my eyes off her. What the hell did you have to give up to get her? She also reminded me of Maggie causing me to do a double-take.

"So, you're not a fag after all," Torch said to me and pushed me again.

"You're disappointed?" I asked him.

Torch laughed it off. "This way," he motioned to me, almost like a cop would to a felon. "Let's go see your new accommodations."

CHAPTER SEVENTEEN

I was led by Torch and a couple of other thugs into a square, ten-by-ten pen of some kind. It was built from wood, some of it cracked, and the ground was covered in black mud. Half the pen was covered by a roof at the rear where a few hay bales were stacked. They cuffed and shackled my hands behind me to heavy chains on a thick wood post next to the hay with enough play that would allow me to sit and stand. A trough was nearby, half-filled with dark, dirty water. Thankfully, the pen was empty.

In the pen directly opposite, however, two massive creatures sniffed and snorted on the other side, partially visible through the slats in the fence. I could see brown hides, but that was about it. I recalled seeing them when I first entered the camp. I thought they were bears at first. Torch excused the other men and then it was just the two of us, alone.

"It's not the Ritz, is it?" he asked me.

I shrugged, eyeing the wall across from me. Torch followed my gaze.

"They're boars," Torch explained. "Razorbacks. Two of them. Brothers. Mean fuckers." He kicked the fence that separated us from them and that sent the boars into a frenzy of squeals and charges, smashing into the wood that reverberated throughout the pen. Their breath gusted between the slats. I wondered how much pounding the wall could take.

"What's your name?" Torch asked again. There was no point in staying mum.

"Ted," I replied.

"Well, Ted. Enjoy the rest of your night," he said.

Torch left me, shutting the door on his way out. I sat as quietly as could be, waiting for the pigs to calm down. The Razorbacks eventually did settle and both plopped to the ground next to the wall. Soon, they fell asleep, snoring and wheezing just feet away. They stunk of rotting meat and some other foulness I couldn't guess.

I stood up to get my bearings. I could see the tents nearby over the fence. The camp was still alive with drunkards and partying. No one paid me any attention and I figured I'd be left alone for a while. I decided to try to sleep and lowered myself back down. I'd have to do so sitting up with my hands behind me and my head tilted back.

A few hours later, I woke with a sore neck to a bright sun, roosters calling, and the camp coming alive with grumbles of headaches and hangovers. A piglet was hauled from another pen down the line by its rear legs, squealing and twitching in the hands of a sniffling Rogue with a black eye. Only minutes later, after the squealing stopped, did I smell meat cooking that made my mouth water.

Midday, a small Hispanic woman with short gray hair entered the pen with a plate of pork and a cup of brownish water. She was old and frail, her skin weathered from the sun. Her clothes were dark blue scrubs. Nurse maybe?

"I don't suppose you have a key, do you?" I asked.

She wouldn't look me in the eye, didn't say a word, and seemed irritated. She wouldn't feed me by hand and merely lifted the plate under my mouth so I had to pluck the meat with my tongue and teeth. The pork was delicious but I only got about half the plate before she whisked it away and lifted the cup.

"You got to be kidding me," I said.

She shrugged, dumped the water aside, and tossed the rest of the pork into the pen next to me. One of the brother Razorbacks gorged on what I didn't.

She then squatted in front of me, grabbed my face, and studied my eyes with a small flashlight. She parted my lips to see my gums and teeth, felt around my neck behind my jaws, and checked my ears. "Tongue," she muttered.

I stuck it out for her and she glanced inside with the light. I guessed she was satisfied with my condition because she soon got up and left without another word.

Through the slats in the wood, I watched the camp scurry with activity as Rogues went about their business. Some were already drunk again. A few onlookers noticed me from time to time but I was largely ignored.

Just before sunset, a tow truck rumbled past my pen and stopped at the one occupied by the two beasts beside mine. A crowd began to form. Curious, I eased myself up to see over the fence and saw more people surrounding both the truck and the pen. Behind me, from a pen further down the line, a naked man was dragged by two Rogues and led to the boom of the tow truck where the tow truck driver waited. The man was twisting and fighting the entire time. I recognized him this time immediately.

Bower.

A rope was slung over his neck and shoulders and he began to cry. The tow truck driver fastened Bower to the boom, tying the poor man's hands behind him. "I didn't mean to leave! I just got lost!" Bower wailed.

Torch split the crowd and strolled up to Bower. The crowd hushed and Torch spoke out loud. "This man was wanted for desertion! He was AWOL! He left his brethren to die! He ran like a chicken! What do we do to those who leave our brothers behind?"

The crowd shouted, "The pen! The pen!"

So, Bower must have been caught in the Dodge Charger after he fled Matias' cabin. Torch took after him when I last saw him murder The Shoeman.

"You know you must pay the price," Torch reminded Bower, but it was for the benefit of the crowd as well. "The penalty for you, Bower, is death!"

The crowd whooped it up again. More shouts of, "The pen! The pen!"

Torch signaled the tow truck driver. The boom was lifted and Bower's body jerked skyward. "No!" Bower cried. "Please, not in there! I'll do anything!" A crowd gathered around Bower as his body reached the top of the fence. I didn't know tow trucks could lift anything that high and wondered if the boom was modified.

Shouts of "Chicken!" "No retreat!" and "Leave no man behind!" filled the air.

Suddenly, Bower's demeanor changed as he was swung over the fence. "Then fuck you all! Bring it, you stone-cold fuckers! I'm free! Free, finally, from this fucking nightmare! I'll be welcomed in hell! Be there in just a few minutes!" Bower began to laugh and the crowd suddenly hushed.

The boom was then lowered into the empty pig pit. The frenzy of squeals and snorts that rattled the cages from within caused the crowd to gasp. Only Bower's head was visible from the top of the fence and he attempted to twirl to see what was happening behind him. The pen gates opened and the beasts within pounced on his lower body.

Bower was flung violently and he began to scream. I had never heard a human make such a sound of torment as his body was thrashed. I could imagine the brother swine were tugging and ripping with such ferocity that they'd finish devouring him within minutes. The crowd went bonkers but the event was short-lived. A sharp snap was heard, Bower went limp and quiet, and the crowd groaned. Ripped apart with such great force, Bower probably died from a broken neck.

After a few grisly minutes, Torch said to the tow operator, "That's enough for now. We need to put the rest of him on display." The boom was lifted, much to the dismay of the beasts as they squealed in protest, banging into the fence, trying to leap up to snatch one more morsel. Those closest to the fence nervously laughed and quickly jumped aside when a plank cracked. The lower half of Bower was swung back over and it resembled dangling spaghetti, with skin and shredded muscle drooping. The boom was lowered and the fence prevented me from seeing what remained of Bower.

The crowd dispersed after that. Torch looked back at me and smiled.

The sun was setting when I had a visitor. Through the wooden slats, I could see someone standing outside the wooden door. For a moment, I smelled perfume, and that intrigued me. When the door was opened, the sun's rays blasted me in the face, causing me to squint. The figure entered the pen and shut the door behind them. They made their way to me, bent over due to the low ceiling but I could tell that it was a woman. Although her face was hidden in the shadows, I could tell she had a nice figure. Long dark hair covered a t-shirt and she wore no bra. Below her waist, only a pair of shorts. No shoes. Strange, since this was a pig pen. She got to her knees and crawled to me, like a cat. I heard a giggle. When the sun's rays finally caught her face through the fence, she was suddenly revealed to me.

Maggie. The prostitute from Las Vegas who helped frame me against my wife.

"Hi, baby," she cooed. She held a small jar and I could see she was buzzed. "I heard you were back here."

"What do you want?" I spat.

She was still stunning, despite the wear and tear of the new world. Her eyes were still a deep blue, her face delicately fresh, her lips full, her teeth white, and her smile completely captivating. She didn't answer at first and just glared at me.

"Leave me alone, please," I said as she lay down next to me.

"That's not what old lovers say to one another," she pouted. "Aren't you happy to see me?"

"What are you doing here?" I asked her again, ignoring her question.

"Surviving the best I can," she said. "I work here for a living now. It's not so bad. Look at me. I think I've done alright." She took a sip and tipped it to my mouth. I was dying of thirst but sketchy as to what she carried with her.

"What is it?" I asked, clenching my lips.

"Hooch," she said. "Come on. I know you want some."

I allowed her to tip the jar into my mouth. I swallowed a mouthful and immediately coughed some of it back up.

"God, I missed you," she said and kissed my neck.

"How? We barely knew each other," I said, wriggling away.

"Now's our chance to get to know one another more. The men around here are disgusting animals."

I decided to switch tactics. "Maggie, can you get me out of here?" I asked her. "Do you have a key to the handcuffs? We can go somewhere else. This *place* is disgusting." The Razorbacks must have sensed something was up because I heard them snort at the wall that separated us. The pigs were a welcomed distraction but when Maggie's hand began to massage my chest and stomach, I knew what she had in mind, pigs or no pigs.

"Please, don't," I said. "Just get me out of here, okay?"

"It's been so long. For both of us, hasn't it?" she said. "I've always saved myself for you."

"You shouldn't have."

Her hand drew closer to my groin. "Don't you want me? Don't you want to be inside me?" she asked.

"Not here. Let's go get a tent," I demanded. It was only a ploy. I didn't want to be seduced there, in a stinking, filthy pig pen. I was hoping she could free me instead. "Do you have a bed we can go to?" I suggested. Anything to get me out. I would have a better chance of escaping then.

Suddenly, two burly men rushed inside, quickly grabbed each of my legs, and sat on them. The one on the left had a green Mohawk and a pudgy face while the other had a bucktoothed grin, pointed jaw, and wily mustache. More men arrived behind me and grabbed the chain that bound my handcuffs through the fence. She ignored the men, brushed my pants with her palm, and slowly rubbed my crotch.

I realized then, this was all planned.

"Maggie! Stop this! Get me out of these chains!" I barked.

Maggie removed her t-shirt and slid out from her shorts. The men began to whoop and holler. She slowly gyrated as she undressed and that got the others into a frenzy.

"Maggie, stop. This isn't going to happen," I said with a firm voice.

"Hush, baby. Time for us to finally party," she replied.

She unbuttoned my pants and began to shimmy them down. I tried to resist but couldn't. There was too much weight holding me down.

Before I knew it, my privates were exposed. The voices were getting louder, surrounding us. Rogue heads popped over the roof. Maggie smiled and climbed on top of me. "No! Don't! I don't want this!" I yelled and tried to buck her off.

"Oh, look! It wants me!" she shouted. Ashamedly, I was growing somewhat aroused. It had been years since I had seen a naked woman, never mind having had sex.

"Don't you fuckin' do it!" I shouted at Maggie and she ignored me.

The bear woke within. Roaring, I gritted my teeth and tensed up, pulling back against the chains which only made them synch harder, pinching my wrists like a snare. I ignored the pain and bucked wildly as she tried to mount me but my writhing prevented it from happening.

Outside the pen, the Rogues were slapping the cage, howling with laughter. The two Razorbacks were going bonkers as well, head butting, splintering wood, cracking the planks in places while dust swirled like a tornado. Their squeals were drowned by the hollering of excited men, some with their cocks through the slats, the men stroking themselves, making the most of the peepshow.

The pen door opened suddenly, the sun blinding me momentarily again. Torch entered, grasped Maggie by her hair, and dragged her out. The other Rogues mumbled and left like kids caught doing something they shouldn't. Torch reemerged and glared at me. He had a gun in a holster.

"Brother, that was unjust," he said to me.

The chain behind me was released and I was able to pull my hands back toward the post. The strain on my shoulders was unbearable.

"I suppose you want to be dressed," he said.

"You want to hike my pants up for me?" I asked.

Torch uncuffed me, surprisingly, and quickly. He stood there with his hand on his gun and watched as I yanked my pants back on. The man was careful and rigid.

"Can I ask for a wake-up call?" I asked when I was done.

"You won't need it, funny guy. Hands behind your back," he said.

He cuffed me again and left.

Just as nightfall enveloped the camp, two armed men quietly entered the pen with Torch standing at the door with his gun out. They were the same men that held my legs down. They unlocked the cuffs and each grabbed my arms.

"You guys are going to die for what you did," I said to the men, yanking my arms away from them. Both men stared at Torch who merely shrugged.

Torch, though, motioned me out. "Time to meet your maker," he said.

I was escorted away from the pens by Torch. The other two men followed. No sooner had we traveled ten feet before FuckStick suddenly made an entrance, rounding the corner of the pens, shuffling his feet towards us with a jar in his hand.

"I got to get me what's mine," FuckStick said, slurring. He teetered on his legs. "That means I get a piece of this shit," he said, referring to me. "Get revenge for my pals. C'mon, Torch, you cocksucker, let me have a go."

FuckStick was in a world of pain within two seconds as Torch grabbed FuckStick's good arm, and slammed the jar into the man's head, shattering glass and spilling hooch all over the poor sap's face. With shards of glass impaled and blood seeping out, FuckStick wailed as the hooch stung his eyes. Torch silenced the one-armed man with a chop to his throat. Torch then decided to shorten FuckStick's miserable life by lifting the slight man like a feather and dropping him into the Razorback's pen.

The Razorbacks were on the former reality star within seconds. FuckStick screamed and lashed about. The fence between him and us took a pounding. As a crowd of onlookers surrounded the pen, drawn in by the shrieks of a comrade and the squeals of the ravenous beasts, Torch ushered me away like the event was a major inconvenience.

"Just when I wanted an autograph from the guy," I said. "I suppose I could be your new BFF right now."

"Don't try me," he warned.

I was escorted towards a large tent. It was massive and elegant, like a large Arab pavilion. Tiki torches were lit outside. Behind the tent was a parking lot, full of cars and trucks. I wondered how many actually ran.

Rogues eyed us as we passed. Some pretended to stroke themselves in jest. They had to be the peepers outside the pen with Maggie and me.

A flap was opened at the tent entrance. A thin, squirrely-looking Rogue with a shaved head, arched nose, and a face full of zits was manning the doorway there with a rifle at attention. Before we got to it, Torch stopped me with a hand on my chest. "You going to mess with us, Ted?"

I didn't answer. I caught a glimpse of my backpack with my crowbar still in the quiver on a table inside.

Frowning at me, Torch continued. "Answer me!"

"I'll be a good boy," I replied.

"Good," he replied. "Ted. Sounds like an old man's name, by the way. What's it short for? Theodore?"

"Yup," I said.

Just before Torch entered, he sneered at the Guard Rogue who was slouched. "Spaz, straighten up, you lousy hack," Torch demanded.

Spaz shuffled and stiffened the best he could. "Yes, sir," he mumbled. His voice was whiney. He seemed jumpy.

"Is the boss ready?" Torch asked.

Spaz danced on the balls of his feet. "I, uh, don't know, sir. He's quiet. Hasn't said much."

"Stay here. Watch this asshole. Shoot him if he moves," Torch commanded then entered the tent. I had no doubt I could have swiped the barrel from Spaz in a split second, but I needed my backpack, so I smiled and began humming *Stayin' Alive.*

The other two Rogues who held my legs down earlier in the pen watched me as well. One flashed a gun tucked in his belt.

I turned my back on them, a sign of disrespect. That earned a cuss word from one of them. The jittery Spaz, however, needed some placating, so I didn't do much else but casually scan the grounds, hoping to ease his mind. A pair of Rogues reeking of fish pushed by and ducked behind the main tent. One man was jiggling a set of keys. I watched them climb into an Acura that was parked next to Torch's white pickup truck. The men in the Acura started their car. It coughed, then shot off in reverse. Sand sprayed as they floored it forward and they vanished down a small road and into the night.

So, those vehicles did actually run. Directly behind the tent too.

Interesting.

Torch exited the tent and grabbed me by my arm.

"Let's go see the man," he said.

CHAPTER EIGHTEEN

The tent was domed at the top and rectangular. Inside, it was plush; leather couches, soft chairs, a dining room table, and Persian rugs, it all reminded me of an Arabian abode as if it was plucked from the Saharan Desert and moved there. A large bed swamped with soft sheets and pillows looked inviting at the furthest end. Jugs, decanters, and carafes were filled to their rims with precious liquids. A coffee table with bowls of ripe fruit made me envious. Whoever owned this pad, the guy did alright for himself and I was starry-eyed.

Candles provided a gentle light. Torch brought me to the dining room table, handcrafted in nice oak, where I was ordered to stand before it and wait. Another bowl of fruit and a wine carafe, filled, sat cruelly center stage. The fruit looked delicious, shiny, and ripe. My mouth watered and my hands instinctively twitched. I was hungry. Beyond scraps of pig meat, I had eaten nothing else. Wine glasses were lined up expecting to be filled. Beside me, Torch played bailiff as if waiting for the judge, still holding me close by the arm. I couldn't care less who he was parading me in front of. What held my attention at that point was my backpack and crowbar nearby. The tent was too much.

"He's all yours," Torch said out loud to a Rogue standing near a window flap, gazing out at the throngs of people roaming his camp. The man was holding a glass elegantly, his body cocked at an angle, almost feminine. There was something familiar there and when Torch summoned him by name, it wasn't until the head honcho Rogue turned to face me that it hit me.

Ginn.

"Welcome home, Mr. Ratelle," Ginn said.

Ginn had long, flowing blond hair with a gray goatee. Last time we saw one another, his hair was shorter, he was clean-shaven, and he always wore a suit. Now, he was sporting a white dress shirt, blue jeans, and cowboy boots. Holstered at his sides were two wild west revolvers with ivory handles. A large belt buckle with a grinning skull centered his attire, completing the get-up which was much more playful than the suited gentlemen I was used to. Ginn looked at me and smiled and I realized he reminded me of Buffalo Bill. I was too stunned to say anything.

"Look who's here. My favorite customer," he said, breaking the ice, approaching me. I was still too dumbfounded to speak. On the one hand, it was good to see someone from the past that I knew. Then again, it had to be this guy?

And then I remembered his partnership with the other warlord, Bale.

"Put her there, old friend." His hand was out for a shake. The last time we did that, my skin opened up, and all hell broke loose. Torch coughed behind me and I acquiesced. The handshake was firm, long, and blood-free this time. "You look great," he remarked. "All things considered."

I could have said the same about him. Rare was it to see someone else fit and strong. Torch himself resembled a gym rat. These guys were doing something right.

"Torch told me he found you at the airfield last night," Ginn said, nodding to the man on my right. "Very interesting place they have there."

"Yeah, well, the real estate market in that area is exploding," I answered.

Ginn didn't laugh but remarked, "And the plane. The mysterious plane that never lands. It mystified me for so long. Now we know where it was landing this whole time."

Torch weighed in. "Airfield is still mostly intact. It's a good spot for us."

"Ingenious," Ginn noted. "Little booby traps in the sand. Careful where you step. That screams organized. A water truck too. Efficient friends you have."

Torch zipped open my backpack "He's got a lot of little goodies in here, plus something I think you ought to see." The crowbar was removed from the quiver and made a loud clunk when he tossed it on the table. Ginn looked it over casually.

"Gun?" Ginn asked Torch.

Torch shook his head. "No, he's clean. Does most of his dirty work with that thing. The crowbar."

Ginn considered that and worked his way around the table. "My, oh my. Mr. Ratelle, I never knew you to be a tough guy."

"There's a lot you don't know about me, Ginn," I replied.

Ginn shot me a look. "But Rambo in the desert? Come on. That wasn't like you. The worst you could have done in the past was maybe stiff our hotel valet."

"Try me," I said.

"Watch your mouth," Torch warned me.

"You and me," I said to Torch. "We aren't done."

Ginn laughed. Torch made a move to get to me. I faced him, waiting for my shot. "Stop!" Ginn yelled and Torch did just that. "This is all wrong," Ginn continued. "We're getting off on the wrong foot. This was supposed to be a reunion." Ginn then walked to my backpack and opened it slightly, peering inside. With a wave of his hand, he casually sighed at Torch, and said, "Leave us, Torch. We're old friends."

Torch cleared his throat. "Sir, you don't understand. He dispatched two of our armed men *without* a gun. I don't trust him."

Rounding the table, Ginn met Torch with a tsk-tsk and placed both hands on his shoulders. "I do trust him," Ginn said softly. "We have a history."

Torch quickly differed. "I beg you to reconsider."

"Leave us!" Ginn suddenly erupted, his eyes turning red. I swore half the camp heard it and it gave me a jolt.

Torch was taken aback. He turned to me and scowled. "He has a vest," Torch said, easing off, making his way past me. "Police issue. Keep that in mind, sir."

How the hell did he know it was a police issue?

I kneed Torch in his crotch as he passed me and he immediately collapsed to his knees, groaning in pain. Hands shot to his privates and I watched the grown man cradle his own balls. He coughed and spat, spewing bad words.

"You get to live. For now," I said to him, repeating what he told me when he kneed me earlier.

"Enough you two. Ted, please sit," Ginn said, patting a nearby chair. He then helped Torch to his feet, whispering something to the red-headed man. Hunched over, Torch swore under his breath and stared me down as he left. I smiled at him. I got the fucker *good*.

Turning to me as he watched Torch leave, Ginn tapped his revolvers by the handles as if he was ready to draw on me. "Colt 45 Peacemakers," he said proudly. "Old west favorites." I was certain he stated the fact as a warning. "Before, they were priceless. Now, they are a necessity."

Unimpressed, I mentioned, "Stanley tools, home remodeling section," nodding to my crowbar. "Before they were cheap. Now, they are a necessity."

Smiling, he pulled a chair out. "Sit," he said to me.

"I'd rather stand," I countered, not trusting him, despite our prior dealings.

I could tell he was not used to being denied. With a slow nod, he strolled to the opposite side of the table where he reached for the fruit bowl. "Ted," Ginn said, picking up an apple. "It's a wonder our paths never crossed since the event."

That was a lie. I knew he saw me at the Bullion airport some years ago. I often thought he was outside Coppertown when Randall and Maggie tried to enter as well.

"I don't stay in one place too long," I answered, playing along. "The west is one big place."

"How have you been? Hungry? Would you like an apple?" He tossed one to me, and I snatched it midair. It was firm, round, and incredibly beautiful. I bit into it and the juices drowned me instantly. The flavor and sweetness were overwhelming. I chewed childishly, using both my hands to gnaw and stuff it all in. My eyes watered as I gulped down huge chunks. Ginn laughed at me and pointed. "You have some...on your chin...never mind."

Belching in-between bites, I shrugged and scanned his new digs. The furniture was impeccable, like a showcase room that IKEA would kill for and this man had it here in the damn desert. All that was missing were the pretty maidens and their waving fans.

"How about a refreshment?" he asked.

A wine refrigerator was opened up, the contents there for an impressive selection. "I have Coke, Diet Coke, beer, water, Perrier, and some French Bordeaux," he said, pointing them out. With the wine, he picked one bottle up from the rest. "Two thousand-five, one of the best years for Bordeaux. Aged well enough by now, the tannins are now smooth. Would you like to try?"

Wiping my mouth with my sleeve, I candidly declined. "No, thanks," I said. I was trying to enforce my uncomfortableness and eagerness to leave.

"Here, you might find this interesting," Ginn said and moved to a large cabinet nearby and opened the door. Inside, were hundreds of prescription and vitamin bottles. "This is all from you. Antibiotics, painkillers, sleep aids, downers, uppers, you name it, it's stocked here."

I shot him a quizzical look.

"In exchange for me turning your life around," he said. "Don't you remember?"

I did recall supplying him with those and regretted it. "Why?" I asked.

"Well, a healthy army is a strong army. Infections and diseases are all out there and they run rampant these days. It helps to be prepared. We are the healthiest denizens out there. It's their grooming habits that need to be addressed."

"Those two morons I killed didn't look healthy," I noted.

"Ah, Leatherneck and Cyclops. Lowest rung," he replied. "Hardly worth it." Ginn calmly closed the cabinet door. "I left Las Vegas that fateful day just in the nick of time. I recall you did as well."

"Yep," I stated. "I was going home."

"You didn't make it, I see."

The image of my car crashing was decimating and it could have been worse. I was lucky to be alive. "No, my car crashed. Even then, I was still hours out."

"Safe, you mean."

"What about you? You were able to leave Vegas?" I asked him. "I thought you would die there."

"You underestimated me. Again."

"That was your city. You got things, you understood what made it run. You were Vegas, man."

Grinning, he declared, "It doesn't matter anymore, does it?"

"Guess not."

Lifting the carafe, he tipped what looked like white wine into a glass. "I spent most of the time in Nevada and Northern California. I traveled with a large group, crisscrossing the deserts and mountains," he said and paused. "I seem to recall that a brother of mine met his fate some time ago. That he is permanently sealed in the mountainside."

"Bale had it coming. He had no right to attack us."

Ginn ignored that comment. "I took control of the Digs and overran the thugs that operated here. Still, the Mojave struck a chord with me. Long had I desired its control."

"You wanted to control the desert? It's harsh, a wasteland."

"Empires don't discriminate and it's a vast piece of property. Especially the Colorado River. That in itself is worth killing over."

"Dream big," I offered.

That earned another smile. "You still know nothing of me, do you?" he asked me. "That I'd be here, now, in control. Commanding an army."

Maybe I did underestimate him. "I didn't know you all that well outside of the hotel. Is that what you mean?"

Sipping his wine, he smacked his lips like a connoisseur, studying the glass. "My guess is, you probably assumed I had no life back then."

Truth is, I *didn't* think much of him back then either. "Good for you," I remarked and hoped that ended that. Ginn was simply a go-to guy for stuff that was illegal and immoral. "I hope you make the best of it," I stated.

"It's even better to plan for the future," he said, dodging my last comment. "And I did that. Long ago."

"So, what are your plans?"

"Expansion," Ginn confessed and poured another glass, handing it to me. "The wasteland needs unity. There isn't any form of government anymore. Just warlords here and there. We've been termed Rogues, as in rogues against society I'm told, but we're all just petty thugs."

I took a sip and it burned like moonshine. "Murderers more like," I coughed, expecting grape juice, not hooch.

Ginn considered that impression as if he'd heard it a million times. "Still, manpower achieves success. I've led other factions, groups, what have you," Ginn stated. "Some held strong, others not so much. Some were deceitful to me and I can't have that," he toyed with the rim of his glass. "It's not a democracy out there anymore. There is no electoral vote. The one who controls the army is the one who leads. And I currently lead the largest army in the desert."

Ginn confidently stroked his beard. The power to influence oozed out of his pores once again. Even with the gas, I had no doubt he came prepared.

"Do you know what has made my operation so successful?" Ginn asked, lifting his glass high. "Moonshine. Best elixir around. The one we are sipping is mixed with apple. The horde out there, for those yokels, that's mostly barrel cactus."

Another sip scorched my throat like the first one. I coughed again. Come to think of it, I could taste some apple, with notes of depravity and debauchery, of course, given the dour mixings of the moonshine trade.

"Amazing power this liquid holds," Ginn continued, marveling at his home-grown product that scores traded for, some of it deeply personal. "Why, even in this shithole wasteland, people still want to get fucked up."

"Why not?" I acquiesced, downing the hatch. "It allows them to forget."

"Come take a look," he suggested and guided me to the open window flap. "They walk in from all over the desert," he claimed, using his hand to sweep as if he collected them like a broom "You get all sorts; drifters, loners, farmers, hunters, trappers, and just regular people. They come from the mountains, the desert, lakes, and rivers. They trade their wares for hooch or whoring. Guns and ammo get you both, by the way," he giggled.

So, that's what the chick outside the tent bearing it all was worth. Remind me to check my backpack.

As if reading my mind, he asked me, "Did you recognize the vixen out there? With the large bodyguard?"

I saw who he was pointing to but her face didn't ring a bell. Men were still trying for her services but the bodyguard was keeping them at bay.

"Camille de Pente," he stated. "She was a famous R&B singer. She won several trophies at the MTV awards. Also has a couple of Grammys in her repertoire I understand."

It took me a few seconds and it registered. "She did a concert the night before in Laughlin," I said. That was the concert Daisy and her father attended.

"Ah," he nodded. "So, you were a fan."

"Hardly."

"Yes, Miss de Penta did, in fact, play a concert that night before. Anyway, I was told Camille was on her way to her next concert in Salt Lake City when like the rest of us, she was stranded midway. She had been living in a small town just inside Utah when my group attacked and took it over. Deplorable conditions there, mind you, despite having avoided the gas in the first place. The town had simply turned to shit but she was kept close to the warlord there, a prize of sorts, and generally left untouched. To the victor goes the spoils, however, and now that lovely creature has been under my employ for years. Miss de Pente still possesses a soothing, harmonious voice. She was a bit melo-dramatic at first, a pretentious bitch more like, wouldn't lift a finger, didn't like the sight of blood, but she was quickly corrected of that."

"You got her whoring," I pointed out.

"They have to earn their keep. Everyone does," Ginn conceded. "She's also hooked on meth. If only the tabloids could get wind of her now. Damaged goods. So tragic for someone once so famous."

I made a mental note not to tell Camille's number one fan, Daisy, her whereabouts.

"Do you know what she first said to me?" Ginn asked me.

"No idea."

"Don't you know who I am?" he recited in a girl's, squeamish voice. With that, Ginn burst out laughing.

"And what of Maggie?" I asked him. "Why is she here?"

"Survival, of course."

"How did she end up here with you?"

"She has always belonged to me."

A cuckoo clock suddenly went off, held high by a pole. A little blue bird flapped its beak nine irritating times. We stopped and stared at the distraction. When done, it retreated between a set of doors under an A-frame house and closed shop. There were some things I clearly didn't miss.

Ginn eyed the piece angrily. "A post-apocalyptic world is just one giant thrift store," Ginn inferred, at the nuisance.

I put my glass down on the table wondering how much longer I needed to be there. I don't believe Ginn would hurt me or jail me. Warlord leader or not, we had a past and I planned to remind him of it. Ginn was coming off as some sort of leader and I wasn't impressed.

"Don't tell me you've had enough," he said, quick with the carafe. "You were always one for overindulgence."

I shook my head and waved him off. The booze was kicking in and I needed to feel in control. I was relaxed but I had the feeling Torch and I weren't done yet. "Just need a break," I said and belched.

"Allow me to continue. But first, I need to make sure that silly bird will no longer trouble us." Hauling a baseball bat out from an umbrella rack, he swung high and hard at the cuckoo clock, smashing it off the post, the clumsy timepiece skipping across the floor in two pieces. As the cuckoo bird popped out from the larger piece, dangling on a spring, he swung down hard, bashing it mercilessly until the bat itself snapped in two.

Having heard the commotion, a wide-eyed Torch stood at the door holding his gun out. "Everything okay, boss?"

Breathing hard, Ginn ignored him and said, "Irreplaceable."

"I think you did it justice," I said.

"No, the bat. Jackie Robinson signed it," he quipped and spun what was left in his hands, showing me a signature. All I saw was a scribble with loops and faded ink. He tossed it aside as if it held no more meaning.

"Sir? You cool?" Torch inquired, eyeballing me. I glared at his crotch and he caught me. I sensed the fury coming from him. He was coiled, ready to pounce.

Ginn waved him off. "We're fine," he confessed. "Oh, have his tent ready. The one next to yours. Evict the present owner." I didn't react to that yet but I wasn't about to spend another night as his guest. Torch smiled at that for some strange reason and disappeared through the front flap again.

"Now, where were we?" Ginn asked, walking up next to me and taking a large gulp from his glass. I don't remember seeing him drink or indulge in anything in the past. He was always straight, prim, proper, and obviously on duty, which meant sober.

Outside, a Maserati rumbled by with gunmen hanging out the window, visible through a smaller set of flaps. "See, moonshine is a marvel. Both you and your automobile can drink from it." Just then, the car belched and a puff of smoke rose from the rear exhaust. "Mind you, it isn't an exact science. Cars run very poorly on the stuff so constant repairs are a necessity. Newer models work best. Still, there's no lack of car parts. The desert is full of them."

"So, this is what you do?" I asked, pretending to look out over the camp, but really trying to see the weak spots. "Make moonshine and trade it, huh?"

Shrugging, Ginn answered, "I give the people what they want."

Maybe it was the hooch kicking in, but this guy was not fooling me and I decided to bring him down a little. "Not much of a step up from being a concierge."

"In the eighteen century, the concierge was once a high official of the kingdom, appointed by the King to maintain order as well as oversee the police and prisoner records," Ginn responded as if having memorized this to feel content.

"Yeah," I agreed. "But you made dinner reservations at Spago."

Ginn seemed to ignore that. Sighing, he leaned forward. "I have scores of men ready to die for me. I rule them. In exchange, I allow them to live a little better. And longer." Slapping his hands together, he then continued as if a decision was made, "Brawn I have, brains I need. I want you here beside me. There isn't exactly a huge talent pool out in the middle of the desert. A Corporate man will do well. After all, you still owe me. I have yet to collect."

I shook my head, ignoring the last comment. "Some of them will die for what they tried to do to me," I informed him.

"Yes, I heard," Ginn giggled. "But it was just mischievous boys, wasn't it?"

My eyes bore into him and I could tell he knew I would follow through. As if understanding, he bequeathed, "I'll make you high on the food chain, just under Torch. You can have your vengeance too. Torch will provide the individuals responsible. See? That's a throw-in."

Ignoring that, I said, "One day, someone will slit your throat and you'll be gone. Your time will come. I'm surprised they haven't already. No offense."

Ginn grinned at the notion. "They will not dare. They are bound. All of them, they owe me."

Rolling my eyes, I said, "Warlords don't last."

"I am much bigger than a warlord."

I had serious doubts. Mutiny was marked on everyone's agenda. Days were numbered. The ginger in the number two slot had a bad itch, for instance. "What about Torch. You trust him?"

"He would eat dog shit if I commanded it."

I had a hard time believing that. Torch didn't look the type to take orders from anyone. Ginn had to have something on the guy.

"Torch has the same scar you do," Ginn stated. "We made a deal obviously, back before the gas. He was a medical devices sales rep, the western region his territory. He had a troubled marriage due to his numerous affairs, mostly in Las Vegas and in my hotel. His wife, who spent most of her time alone in their Phoenix area home, caught on but refused to divorce. Instead, she quit her waitressing job, rooted herself on his couch, and spent vast amounts of his hard-earned money. They were childless."

Sales rep? Torch? Hard to believe.

Ginn continued. "From one of the affairs, however, a child does result. He loved her. Doted on her. The girlfriend, who lived in Henderson, just south of Las Vegas, wouldn't marry him either and he was only allowed the occasional visit. Money was becoming tight too, his wife the cause of much of it, so he came to me with a favor concerning his wife."

I could see where this was going. "Rub her out?"

"Yes. There was a life insurance policy to the tune of eight hundred thousand. One day, while she attempted to jog, she died from the result of a hit-and-run on a lonely side road. Torch was in Las Vegas at the time with me as his alibi. Crocodile tears flowed, but then a part of his misery was corrected."

"Eight hundred thou? I'm sure he didn't complain."

"For that service I provided, he offered his loyalty. It was unfortunate on his part that he didn't know the gas would occur a year later and that I'd require his services so soon. He barely had time to enjoy his wealth."

The last sentence sounded sarcastic. I then recalled the three men, the Weathermen he coached. "You knew the gas would occur, didn't you?" I asked.

"Super Gas. Yes. What, did you think you were the only one I helped?"

I sensed this conversation was going nowhere and quite frankly, I was tired of talking. "If I were you, I'd watch my back on the redhead," I noted.

"There is no need. For one, I command him. I command all. Second, before he was peddling pills, Torch was a former police officer. Worked 77th and Rampart Divisions in Los Angeles until he was fired for misconduct. Mostly abuse on thugs, gangbangers, and drug users."

There it was. Torch was a former cop. "Sounds like a hero," I said.

"Most of the men in my camp had rap sheets. A life of crime. No surprises there. And what they wouldn't give to have a shot at a former police officer," he said, smiling. "Of course, that's a secret between me and him. That keeps him alive."

So, that was it. Ginn held the police issue over Torch's head.

"Police, lawyers, dispatchers, anyone dealing in law, they are fair game out here. Even if you were so much a front desk receptionist at a police station," Ginn said, and arced his finger across his own neck. "You don't want my men to know that. It's like a shark feeding frenzy and sometimes, it cannot be stopped."

The tent only had the one exit but the walls weren't bolted down. I was either going to walk out the front door shaking hands goodbye or take him down and resorting to Plan B. Problem was, I hadn't thought of what Plan B was yet.

"Yeah, well, if you don't mind, I think it's time to go. It's been interesting. Nice to see you, hope it works out," I told him and walked around the table.

"What's the rush?" he asked. "We were just beginning to reconnect."

Stopping, I turned to face him, sounding all serious. "I found out my family is still alive and I'm going to find them."

Suddenly, loud rock music blared outside the tent. Ginn perked up, leaning in. "What did you say?"

"What? About my family being alive?"

"You received word?" he scoffed.

"I got word they are alive," I replied, wondering why he cared. "They escaped somehow. Best news I got in five years."

"Come on," he snickered. "Your wife and kids. Still alive. To this day."

Serious, I glared at the man. "Something I'm going to check up on. Why?"

"Humor me then," he said. "Where are they?"

"I am not sure."

"You're not sure."

"Why do you care?"

"I don't. I just find it hard to believe you do."

"What does that mean?"

Rolling his precious liquid in his glass like a well-aged Bordeaux, he answered, "Well, a man like yourself that preferred to be away from them so much, I would have thought their demise would have provided some relief."

I let that one slide. The rock music was intensifying outside, causing a distraction. "Anyway," I sighed, eager to leave. "I don't know where they are exactly, but I know where to go to find out."

"The plane," Ginn presumed. "Those people there told you that, didn't they? Torch told me they took off without you. Have you thought that these people, on this plane, told you your family was still alive so they could escape, am I right? I wonder if they felt threatened."

"No," I added, "They knew things about them, about them now. There's no way they were faking it."

Rolling his eyes, he followed with, "They admitted this to you?"

I nodded. "Yes."

"But they didn't tell you where they were?"

"What is this, twenty questions?"

"Doesn't that strike you as odd?"

Yeah, it did, motherfucker. And the more I thought about it, the more it hurt.

Ginn approached me and stood just inches away. "Do you recall what I said to you when you departed my hotel years ago on that fateful day?"

With a deadpan glare, I responded, "Thanks for staying with us?"

"Volo quad alienum est."

I want something precious of yours.

Ginn simply smiled. "But it's not what you think."

"What then?"

His eyes settled on my backpack and he reached for it, unzipping. "Let's see what we have here," he said. Fishing around with one hand, he pulled out a compass, matches, then some cans of food. Content there was nothing more to it, he then fixated on my crowbar and lifted his eye brows.

Ginn picked up my crowbar and smacked it against his palm. "Does blood still drip from the end, I wonder?"

I didn't get what he meant and barely heard him right as the volume stayed cranked outside. "When necessary," I told him, my voice getting louder as well.

"I'm told you are quite deadly with this thing. The crowbar. You must have received training somehow."

"Look, I don't want to be a part of any of this. Good luck with conquering the desert. I want to be going. I prefer to be alone." I held my hand out for the backpack.

"We have a contract. You owe me," he replied and put the crowbar back in the quiver. "I cannot let you leave until I get what I want and it's been five years overdue."

"You're delusional."

Ginn grinned. "And you're easily tempted. "Narcotics, alcohol, insider trading..."

My fists balled up at my sides. "That was a long time ago, asshole."

With a sarcastic laugh, he retorted, "You abandoned your family when you made that choice."

My left hand shot out and I gripped Ginn's neck firm. His feet flew into the air as I threw him down on the table, bending him backwards, pinning him there. Clutching my arm and chest with both hands, his face went beet red, trying to push me off but I had the weight and the leverage to keep him there. Some fruit spilled from the bowl while the carafe toppled, leaking moonshine that flowed down the table, the glass thankfully staying atop and not crashing to the ground. That would have alerted Torch and the others in an instant. Dumb move this was, maybe, but his remark set me the fuck off.

He bellowed with a joker's smile, "Maggie was a fine, fine woman!"

Probing with my right hand, I quickly snatched my crowbar from the quiver and I flashed the claw end facing down, the two prongs like fangs on a snake, ready to strike. "I keep these babies sharp," I told him menacingly. "I'll dig into brain. If you have any."

Ginn eyeballed the tool and suddenly he loosened his own grip. "All I need to do is make a sound and my men will come in running. Try leaving through the front without me. You know who's there. You will not escape," he grunted with some confidence in his voice, although I smelled desperation as sweat began to roll down his forehead.

He was right though. I couldn't make a sound. I placed the crowbar down and probed the backpack. Ginn didn't catch my movements.

"Your life. I gave it back to you," he stated.

"I already had a life," I remarked.

"It was I who made the texts to your wife," he suddenly said.

I thought back to that fateful day. The texts to my wife, the photos. That son of a bitch! I knew it.

I jumped back away and hit him with a taser Matias left for me, the air sparking, filling with electricity. Two prongs jammed into his chest fired from the handheld weapon, long, scraggy wires attached, jolting him instantly. He collapsed like a rag doll, his head rolling to the side. His leg jolted a few times like a dog stuck in a dream and he passed out, limp on the table. I tossed the taser and grabbed my backpack.

"I owe you nothing," I spat and walked to the rear of the tent where the bed lay. Checking the front, there was no sign of Torch entering. The sounds of the music and the camp had drowned out the taser sparks and struggle. Shoving the bed hard, I moved it aside and lifted up on the heavy canvas material of the tent wall behind it. The supports that held the canvas were low and tight to the ground. As I pulled the canvas up from the bottom, there was maybe a foot of clearance to crawl under midway. Cupping my hands, I dug into the sand and scooped handfuls out until I created an extra six inches of depth, the length of my chest and head. It was time to go rabbit.

One last look at Ginn, and I saw drool forming under his chin. His finger twitched and it looked like he was waking.

Flipping to my back, I bench pressed the flap as hard as I could and rocked my shoulders back and forth, using my legs as leverage until I cleared and swung my legs through. Once I made it outside, I stood quickly, finding myself in the parking lot.

CHAPTER NINETEEN

An old Chevy El Camino was parked directly behind the tent and I actually stopped to admire the half-car, half-truck creation. Even in the dark, I could tell it was a late seventies model, cherry red, stock as the day it rolled off the production line. *Royal Knight* was stenciled on the side in Olde English and the hood flashed the iconic hood double-dragon decal.

Oh, baby.

A pristine Mercedes was parked nearby as well and I figured that to be Ginn's. Beyond that, a mixture of other newer cars and trucks; Fords, Toyotas, Mazdas, all modified on the inside with roll cages. On the outside, larger than normal tires on lifted suspensions, while comically bad weld jobs of exaggerated wings, armored plates, and sharp edges like knives or spears were mounted out front. Spray painted graffiti was common with intimidating slogans of allegiances to death and mayhem. Only the El Camino stood out as a classic and older than a two decades. Torch's Toyota Truck was parked next to it, hardly modified itself. Besides those three before me, the rest in the parking lot look like entrants to a demolition derby contest. They were all hemmed in like a bad valet parking job and the lot was overflowing.

The open desert was just beyond the lot. A small dirt road led out a makeshift gate. That much I could see but what was beyond, I had no idea as we had entered the camp from another entrance. The spotlights shone inside the camp, not out, so all I saw was darkness beyond. The moon would be full again tonight, but it was low on the horizon and only casting a dim light. Behind me, a bottle crashed and the music got amplified. While it was a hell of a party, I needed to hightail it before Ginn fully woke.

A snore stopped me cold. Looking down, I spied the outline of a filthy Rogue passed out, propped on the front bumper of the El Camino, his legs splayed out front, one of which was missing a shoe. An empty jar of hooch was next to him and his lap looked soaked. He probably pissed himself. Since he wore overalls and his clothes were full of grease, I guessed he was a mechanic of some sort.

I didn't have a lot of options. If I made a run for it in the desert on two legs, I was sure Ginn would use his dogs to hunt me down. I needed speed to leave.

The El Camino was not hemmed in by other cars and I could see keys dangling in the ignition. The Toyota truck wasn't blocked either, and I opted for it instead, as I knew it ran. I quietly tried the door but it was locked. The Mercedes was blocked by another car. My only option was the El Camino. I hoped it ran.

I returned to the Snoring Rogue who shifted in his sleep and moved his own arm. His hand landed on my boot with a thump and that caused him to wake. Looking up, he squinted and whined, "Hey, you ain't supposed to be back here."

Bending down, I grabbed his thick hair and slammed it against the bumper.

"Ow," he wailed, cowering. "What the fuck you doin', man?"

A toe punt the next time sent him to la-la-land as his head bounced off the bumper with a loud thud. He flopped forward, off the bumper, out like a light. I ran around the driver's side and jumped in. I took a last look around and turned the key. The El Camino whirred a few moments, then the engine came to life. The noise from the raucous camp seemed to be drowning out the idle rumble from the V8 but even I knew that wouldn't last long. There was three hundred and fifty cc's under the hood and I'd have to remember to keep my revs down (I knew the engine block size because a buddy of mine had a similar model in high school). I kept the headlights off since the camp spotlights casted enough glow for me to maneuver.

The El Camino backed up easily. I shifted to Drive and turned the wheel. Lucky for me, the tent appeared quiet and undisturbed through my windshield as I spun the car around. I left the parking lot without protest, hung a right, slowly chugged along a dirt road, and watched the frenzy of the camp disappear out the passenger window.

Once I cleared the camp outskirts, I had to dodge drifters who gave me a wide berth. Only then, when the drifter's numbers became few, did I open it up. Soon, there were none and I had an open road to myself.

The muscle car flexed its might, but the iconic machine was hard to keep straight. The steering wheel had a lot of play, the brakes were frightening, it felt heavy, and it lagged the punch I thought it deserved. After the lug chugged to fifty mph, I realized my BMW sports car would have dusted this old timer easily. Still, it was comfortable with bucket seats that kept me snug and it was cool to drive a piece of nostalgia. The engine produced an odd cough and sputter at times that would have freaked out the average driver just years ago.

Moonshine became the new fuel but it did a number on engines and had to be potent to burn properly. You had to keep your speed to less than forty to keep everything somewhat happy and in good running order. Engines weren't designed to run on moonshine, obviously, but the combustible nature of the white lightning was all that was needed to ignite and keep the crankshaft rolling. Luke, back at Coppertown, told me once that spark plugs had to be cleaned every month or the gunk that built up would delay the firing order and cause a few cylinders to stop working. Another reason why I abandoned having a car long ago. Too much work.

Still, I used the El Camino to my advantage. I didn't have the head-lights on and I was finding it hard to see the road. Sometimes, the moon's glow can only do so much. Later, I managed to connect to a real road with pavement under sand. The car lurched forward and the ride smoothed out. When I came across a stop sign, I hung a wild right. I was trying to recall where we had come from when I was escorted into the camp.

Since most newer model engines will run on moonshine, but poorly, I knew I was on borrowed time with the El Camino. While it chugged and seemed to thrive for the moment, most older cars were susceptible to wear and tear from the new energy type. Luke junked anything from last century and beyond; they were simply too hard to maintain and parts were harder to find. Newer model cars were willing to chug more of the hooch.

After a few miles and having trouble guiding, I decided to risk it and flicked the headlights on. By doing so, I flooded the desert with two funneled beams. Cacti danced before me, cast in white, swaying like ghosts in the wind.

I found the interior light and illuminated the cabin to see what she held within. The interior was mostly stock and clean. Whoever owned this, kept it up well. The dashboard was polished, the carpet free of dirt, and the cigarette holder empty, never having been used. The speedometer read in the high thirties so it was garaged in its lifetime. Only the leather seats showed some wear, but that was expected.

Rounding a bend in the road, nothing looked familiar and I become concerned that I might be lost. I had been sitting sideways in the back of the Toyota truck on the way in so I wasn't privy to landmarks. I passed a call box but resisted the urge to stop and use it.

"Next time," I muttered. "I promise, Tracy. We will talk."

My thoughts then ran to my wife. The Doctor at the airfield said she had taken another lover. Who the hell was it? A guy from her past? Someone new to her now? Images of random men floated in my mind. The waiter at the café where she used to have bagels and coffee in the mornings. An ex-coworker, a doctor, who drunkenly called her cell-phone after she left the hospital – but that was years earlier. What about Facebook? Did she reconnect with an old boyfriend? My jaw

174

clenched as I drove, thinking back to the possibilities of neighbors, friends, and old coworkers. I honestly drew a blank. Convinced it was some new guy, I slumped at the notion. She thought I was dead. She had moved on.

Or was she carrying on an affair that I didn't know about? Maybe Tracy was hiding out with him? Paula said she wasn't with her in San Diego. Did she meet some guy there?

I gripped the steering wheel hard and I increased my speed. The speedometer reached sixty and the engine grumbled with an odd knock that I tried to ignore. My wife assumed that I was dead. I would have considered the same, had it not been for Matias and his training. By now, however, she surely knew I was very much alive. The Doctor had to have told her as soon as they landed. She seemed the type to divulge that. My wife would also realize that I was coming for them.

The boy-toy better be gone when I get there.

I snapped out of it when I hit a pothole and the car shuddered. Gripping the wheel harder, I promised myself to not let my mind wander and concentrate on the road. I then noticed a CB Radio under the dash.

"What the hell, let's see what happens," I said to myself. Reaching over, I turned it on and got loads of static. Nothing else. "What did I expect? A convoy of truckers looking out for *smokey*?" I turned it off.

The rearview mirror reflected only dark. Thankfully, no headlights in pursuit. They had to have discovered that both myself and this fine car were gone by now. I just don't know what Ginn and his men would do. I then saw the four-way stop ahead and the scarecrow. He was on my left this time and he was smiling at me.

"Shh," I said to him with my finger to my lips. "Don't tell anyone where I'm going, Woody."

Woody just grinned back and I thought of the poor soul up there, wondering if he was a Rogue, or some simple drifter caught along the road, robbed and beaten to death, then strung up for eternity. He served a purpose up there, I had to admit, the roads in the desert all looked the same and he showed us where evil and temptation lay. Many signposts have been knocked down so unless you had a map in hand, or in your head, a dead man pointing the way was a surefire hint of where you were, and probably shouldn't go. I know Woody would keep the secret of my venture as I cranked the wheel and I liked to think his grin was for me, one-upping the desert dogs and making a run for it. Better yet, I realized an important facet of my trip thus far.

I knew where I was.

CHAPTER TWENTY

My wife used to say that you'll never find a more heartfelt hug or kiss than at an airport. A white-knuckle flier herself, she shared the fear of crashing with many other passengers and often held my hand when we flew. However, as I stood at the entrance to the airfield, I knew the Cessna had landed safely, somewhere in the abyss, and I was determined to find out where.

I wanted to stand there and savor the place, clinging to the encouraging words from the voices of good people. There was a connection there to a past life, one where I belonged. I heard the joyful news *right there*! as I glared at the runway. Then, reality sank in, there was death all around me, the bad men with their wafting stench and missing limbs, not from any crash, but from pure and simple greed. It was a fitting demise for the fate of the ruthless who shared the same space as I.

I had found the airfield quite suddenly, pumping the brakes having almost passed by it. While the moon did a remarkable job in providing guiding light to get me to the airfield, the explosion that decimated the structures made the complex harder to find and only when I saw the rotting body of a dead Rogue lying nearby that I did stop and see the front gate.

The airfield was littered with bodies. My guess was, the remaining Rogues left the area, too frightened to scour the leveled playing field, possibly realizing there was nothing left to scavenge anyway. The smell of ammonia lingered and I figured that was from the explosives. Many other mines were waiting to pop and I knew better than to stay out front. I exited the muscle car and strolled down the safe driveway.

From the corner of my eye, there was movement in a nearby shrub. "About time you came back," Jock said, popping up like a Jack in the Box, brushing himself off. Tired and haggard, I guessed he rode out the day, freaking out over where to step and sit.

"I couldn't find departures or arrivals," I said with a smirk. "So, I had to circle."

"Can we go now?" he asked and started down the driveway. I followed, watching for sand humps, reminding myself to stay the course. Naturally, I was behind the little guy who seemed quite cocky in his exit and I guessed a full day of sunlight gave him more confidence to stake out where the underground body-splitters may be hiding.

"I'm surprised you stayed inside here," I said.

"I thought it safer than to be out there," he said pointing back at the ridge where we first staked it out. "The Rogues left after you were taken. More died trying to sneak back in. I guess the mines did their job. This place has an effective force field, you know?"

Another sci-fi reference. I smiled and asked, "What did you do all day?"

"Tip-toed over the safer tracks. The ones that didn't blow. Scrounged for pieces of food. Hopped from plant to plant. You don't know how scary that is. Dude, some of what your friends had buried below came up from the explosion. I had a granola bar, a bag of chocolate chip cookies, and a can of RC cola. I'm stuffed."

I could hardly believe it. "Cookies? You didn't share?"

"Dude, I didn't know if you were coming back!"

"Should have saved me one at least," I mumbled. I couldn't remember the last time I had a cookie. Probably the early years when foraging vacant homes produced something. Jock had eaten chocolate chips too. God, I missed chocolate.

We reached the front gate and Jock paused once he saw the El Camino. I had to admit, it looked impressive in the moonlight, with a nice sheen coming off the hood. I couldn't wait to climb back inside. Speaking of which, we needed to get a move on.

"So, what now?" he asked, stopping before the car.

I patted the hood. "We ride."

"In that thing?" he asked. "Is it supposed to be a car or a truck?"

"Good question. Anyway, it's ours. Road trip," I said, then waved him on. "Come on, it'll be fun."

"That will make noise."

"Yeah, but we'll get there quicker," I said, opening the driver's side door and climbing inside. I slammed the door shut and propped my arm up.

Jock hesitated as if getting in would be sacrilegious. "Hey, you want to play tourist guide for the rest of the Rogues, your call," I shouted to him. My fingers drummed the roof, impatiently. I fired up the engine, revving it just a touch to egg him on.

"They're coming after you? They're coming back here?" He rounded the hood and opened the passenger door, jumping inside. "What did you do?" he asked, finally shutting the heavy door.

"A little shock therapy," I said and goosed the throttle twice, not elaborating on what I meant. The engine rumbled, waiting to be put into Drive. *Oh yeah, I dig this ride.*

Panicked, Jock sprung in his seat, peering through all windows. "Please don't do that again! Someone will hear it! Sound travels in the desert!"

I rested my arm on the steering wheel and pivoted to stare at him, waiting for him to come to grips. Finally settling in, he sat with both hands folded on his lap.

"What?" he asked me as I stared back at him.

"Ass, gas, or grass. No one rides for free."

"What?"

"I would have accepted a cookie."

"Forget about the cookies," he snapped.

"You had a bag, you said. That meant more than one," I pointed out, then dropped the car into Reverse. "Do me a favor. Check your window for traffic. See if it's clear."

"Funny," he said but still looked anyway.

Having backed into the main road, I shifted into Drive and we headed west on a two-lane road decimated by erosion and neglect. Cracks in the road gave way to weeds, some a few feet high, while sand and small rocks filled the course too.

Calmed then by the steady reassuring grumble of the V8, I kept the speedometer to less than fifty and the mental map of the surrounding area came to me. The Mojave Desert still had squirrelly roads, some paved, and some not, and as long as I headed in the right direction, each mile would count towards reaching our goal. The windy road became confusing at times and the compass in my head spun unnervingly. Are we headed west still or did it seem like it was north now? Tempted to press harder, I had to remind myself to remain cautious. Throwing a rod or blowing the heads would not be a smart move but we needed to create a gap between us and the hunting party that was sure to come. Bored, Jock poked around the interior and popped open the glove compartment, pulling out a repair manual.

"Guess how old this car is," he asked as he opened the front page.

Watching the hillsides for fires and activity, I answered, "I would say seventy-seven or seventy-eight."

Squinting first, he then brought the manual towards the window, allowing for moonlight to capture it. "Seventy-eight Royal Knight. Older than me. Who owns it?"

I shrugged. "Mine now."

Flipping through a few pages, he grew bored, folded it, and placed it back. Glancing back through the rear window, I could sense he was becoming impatient like a child. "What happened to you, anyway? Those Rogues took you away."

"Oh, you know. A couple of drinks, a couple of laughs," I responded.

"I waited all day and then was going to leave in the morning," he said. "I thought you were dead."

"And yet, here I am."

"Does this run on gas?" Jock asked me after a few minutes passed.

"No, moonshine," I told him.

"Really?"

"Flammable liquid is all you need," I stated. "But it has to be highly concentrated. Or so I was told."

Jock looked confused. "How flammable is flammable?"

"Engines have been known to explode. Mostly older cars. Gaskets wear away, the hooch seeps through the block, and kaboom, motor kaput."

Jock laughed at that as if I wasn't serious. I told him, "Once, I found a Buick Regal and it blew up on me. That's why I have no more hair on my forearms."

I caught him looking.

"We'll be fine," I said.

"Think this is a good idea?" Jock continued with some concern. "This will make noise. I can hear cars all the time when they are far away."

"Whatever. We need wheels and we need to go."

He moped and slunk into his seat. "It will draw attention is all."

"But everyone will think this is a Rogue vehicle, won't they?" I pointed out.

Jock jumped at that. "And that's a good thing?"

I had to admit, I wasn't so sure. We might be well received with the impression that the person who owned this car was widely known to the wasteland - so we could be left alone. On the flip side, this car could be viewed with hate and loathing and we could be attacked because of it.

"Where are we headed?" he asked.

"Salton Sea."

Jock must have figured as much as he didn't reply or object. He had heard the riddle too from the Doctor just before takeoff. He was welcome to join me in the quest or be dropped off partway. It was up to him. I owed him for this and there was room enough for two. I just didn't know if there was a reservation for him on the plane ride as well. That might be a difficult situation.

"You don't have to come if you don't want to," I said.

He shrugged. "I got nothing else going on."

About a half hour into the drive, I noticed the temperature was slowly edging up. The fuel gauge wasn't looking good either. I pulled out an old compass from my pocket and stared at the dial, hiking it out the window to capture some light. The compass said we were headed northwest. "Damn," I said and almost dropped it.

Jock glanced at me. "We somehow got off track," I admitted. "Next road, we are going to turn left and head southwest." I handed the compass to Jock. "Here, you hold this and explore like Magellan."

It had been a quiet ride to that point, but Jock seemed a bit uneasy being in a car. He'd been staring out the window, like a child going to school, and I knew he had a butt load of questions stored up. I eased on the gas and Jock noticed it.

"What's wrong?" he asked.

"Just want to take it easy," I said and pointed at the dash. "She's running hot."

Jock glanced over but I could tell he wasn't sure where to look. "Right there," I said, pointing. "Temperature gauge. It was about halfway before."

"It's getting close to red," he noticed.

"If it gets hotter, we'll pull over."

"What's this thing?" he asked and pointed to the unit under the dash.

"CB radio."

"A what?"

I went into my best hillbilly accent. "Breaker one nine, this is rubber duck, we got smokey on our tail."

He looked at me weirdly. "An actual radio?"

"Used to be," I answered, realizing the man was young, too young to remember them. I was too but saw them on reruns. "Big back in the seventies," I added.

"Should I turn it on?"

"Knock yourself out," I shrugged.

With a press of a button, the power came on. All we heard was static, just as I had before. He twisted the dial and we heard different pitches of static. No voices, no music, and no traffic reports. Just dead air. After a few more twists, Jock gave up and switched it off.

"Salton Sea, huh?" he asked.

"What about it?"

"Your family," Jock said. "The woman in white knows them?"

"She calls herself Doctor," I told him. "Yes, she does."

"No fooling? You believe her?"

"She saw the photo of my family and called my wife by her name," I pointed out. "It makes sense that she knows her, my wife was once a nurse. She being a Doctor, they probably work together wherever they are. They also asked what sport my boys played. I told her about ice hockey and she remembered that. My wife must have told her that in passing. That's Tracy for you, she loves to talk about our boys. She can go on and on."

Hesitating, he then said, "But this Doctor didn't tell you where they are."

That was a stickler in the scenario. If they trusted my wife and kids, why wouldn't they trust their husband and father?

"No, they didn't," I admitted.

"Do you know why?"

For a moment, I hesitated but then responded. "Well, for one, the plane couldn't take all of us. It was too heavy with all of them and the water and boxes and other shit in there. And second, they told me to head to the Salton Sea. That's where they'll pick me up. They are doing this to protect me and themselves." I eased back in my seat. That made total sense. I was convinced of it.

"How would your family react if they saw you?" Jock posed to me.

"They would be happy." I smiled at the notion of seeing them again. "I know my boys would run into my arms and I would give them the biggest hug of their lives. And my wife would be crying tears of joy. She would be relieved too; we had been apart for so many years. There's a lot of catching up to do." The last part was a lie but I didn't want him to know that. Truth was, I had no idea how she'd react.

"You seem more upbeat since we first met," Jock said.

"I've got good reason to be," I admitted. "It's the first good news I've heard in over four years."

The stupid temperature needle was hovering near red. I frowned and wondered how much longer we could go before she'd heat up. I didn't want to risk blowing a hose or the radiator.

"So, what about you?" I turned to him. "Family?"

He sighed. "I'm an only child. Grew up in San Diego. Both my folks were normal size. Dad left us when I was ten. He and I weren't close. I have no idea what happened to him. One day he went to work and never returned. Mom thought he had a girlfriend in another state. Mom died a few years ago when I was in college. Brain aneurism. She died while making dinner for herself. A neighbor found her on the kitchen floor two days later. Mom had just sat down to eat spaghetti when she fell off her chair. I was supposed to join her for dinner but I had to study for an exam."

"That's rough," I said.

"Mom made the best spaghetti too," he said as if I wouldn't believe it.

I tried to change the subject. "So, where were you when all this went down?"

"Mount Palomar Observatory," he said. "Northeast of San Diego. I was taking astronomy as an elective and we were invited to visit the observatory. Almost the entire class went. You got extra credit if you went but I would have gone anyway. A bus took us from school. We were going to see out of their gigantic telescope. I was thrilled. Being a huge sci-fi fan, it was dope."

We came across a row of trees that showed up on both sides of the road. I slowed the car down again to about twenty-five miles per hour. The temperature was in the red then. I was going to pull over soon. The car was going to overheat and conk out anyway.

"We drove up the mountain and watched a show on the heavens and the stars. Had to stay inside because of the rain. And then afterward...," he said and trailed off.

"What?"

Jock eyed me seriously. "We walked into hell."

The car started to jackrabbit. "We need to pull over," I said and drifted onto the shoulder. We hit a bump and the car rattled. "Find some water, let the engine cool down."

Frantic, Jock leaned out his window. "Dude, we need to, like, hide it."

I saw a break between some trees and steered for it. The El Camino bucked again, steam rising from under the hood. The car stalled and I shifted to neutral and which allowed us to drift behind a large bush, coming to a stop there when water suddenly splashed from under the hood. Jock jumped out quickly as if the car would blow sky-high. I merely opened my door and grudgingly stepped out.

Besides the trickle of water dripping on the ground and some sizzling from the heat atop the manifold, all was quiet. Lifting the hood, steam hit me square in the face and I backed up, waving at the heated cloud. It would soon die down.

Jock hovered behind a tree. "How do you know it won't blow?" he asked.

"It just overheated," I said, still waving at it. "Don't you know anything about cars? Auto-shop at school?"

"No," Jock admitted. "But it was driving on moonshine and you said they catch fire. Like your Buick story and the fact that you have no more hair on your arms."

That made me laugh. "You're adorable," I said. Smiling then, I walked to the road and looked around, taking in the straight road hugged by trees and bushes as if it led down a long driveway. The car was visible from my vantage point but you would have to be stopped and looking for it. Anyone driving by would miss it. In the darkness, that was. In the daytime, the red car would stand out, even in that thicket. We had until morning to decide on how best to fix it or else we would risk it being spotted. "We need water more than anything," I pointed out. "Maybe get some rest too."

"Aren't we in a rush?" Jock asked me, staring back down the road we came.

"I suppose, but the people in the plane have to know I'd be getting there by foot since they probably figured I didn't have a car. No way I could get to the Salton Sea in a day or two by walking. So, we should have some time," I mentioned, but then some doubt crossed my mind. "I think."

Walking back to the El Camino, I noticed there was a tarp over the bed. I hadn't looked under it before so I unhitched one end and lifted the flap. Jugs of liquid were there. Lots of them. All of them were full. "Holy crap!" I shouted.

Jock ran over, stood on the tire, and peeked in. "What is it?"

I lifted one out and unscrewed the cap. I sniffed it, then took a small sip. The hooch burned as it always does. I leaned my head back and smacked my lips.

Jock eyed my reaction. "Moonshine?"

"Good stuff," I croaked. I had more of my share today. A couple sips of this and I'd be out like a light. "Sleep should come easy tonight."

"I think we solved our fuel problem," Jock offered and climbed inside the cab. "There must be ten jugs in here. Enough to take us all the way, you think?"

"This here is gold," I reminded him and took another swig.

Jock frowned at me. "Dude, just don't drink it all," he whined.

"No promises, Dude," I said and grinned.

A soft tune suddenly carried in the wind. Jock heard it too. I walked back out to the road and look westward. There was a soft glow of light in the air, hovering about twenty feet in the air like a streetlight.

"Do you hear a piano?" Jock asked me, incredulously.

CHAPTER TWENTY-ONE

Softly, deftly, the music of the night brought us to the Jupiter Playhouse. The name was etched on the white stucco walls, curved around the image of the planet Jupiter painted on the side, complete with a small red blot that served as the storm that circled the humongous orb. The two-story structure was a large adobe building with a tile-sloping roof that shone brightly in the moonlight and was visible from a good distance. The soft glow we had spotted from afar was provided by a candle in a second-story window. A soothing female voice from inside drew me closer as I remembered a time my wife and I once attended Phantom of the Opera.

It sat at the corner of a three-way intersection, T-boned to the street Jock and I walked down. The front door opened away from the road, into an empty parking lot filled with weeds. The lit candle served as a signal, to tell others there would be a performance tonight. I was sure of it, like an *On Air* button. Why else would it be there? Behind the theater, smaller buildings surrounded it like a motel but the Playhouse held all the glory and took center stage.

Jock and I had walked along the road following the sound of the piano that got stronger and stronger as we neared the structure. We watched for a while behind an old tractor, peering over a large flattened tire that smelled of soggy rubber as drifters calmly walked in and out of the joint. I doubted any Rogues were in the Playhouse, the music here was too mature and serene.

"What do you think?" Jock asked me.

A drifter stumbled inside, uncontested. "I say we go see a matinee," I answered. Brushing myself off as if I could become more presentable, I then hiked my backpack over my shoulder. I strutted towards the entrance like I owned the joint.

"No, the back of the place over there," Jock said and pointed to the rear. "They may have a pump for water. You know, for the car."

"Back where?" I asked, without looking back

"Right over there. Behind the cars and farm equipment." Jock said, then whined. "You're not even looking!"

"We should ask first," I stopped and pointed out the obvious. "That would be the polite thing to do."

Jock hesitated. "We don't know who they are inside there."

"Come on, my treat," I said, and jay-walked towards the main entrance as the piano started up again inside and the crowd cheered. While crossing, I did notice the rear lot contained a lot of cars and parts, much like a small auto yard.

Racing up to me, Jock tugged my arm. "Did you see that guy back there?" he asked, nervously. "I think he was following us."

A bearded teenager stood at the intersection behind us in dark clothes, his hands on his hips. Tall and thin, he had dark curly hair, squinty eyes, and a long nose. The beard he grew resembled the one Abraham Lincoln once had, long and thin. While he didn't appear to be armed, he made no intention of hiding, even as we approached the front entrance. He just gawked, making it known he was watching us.

I made it to the front door, unchallenged by him or anyone else. A woman's soft voice began to sing again. I opened the unmanned door that had a speakeasy grille, half expecting a doorman to open it and slam it shut on me, saying my kind wasn't welcome, but no eyes appeared there and the door opened with a gentle push. Jock didn't follow quite yet; he was content to spy on Abe Lincoln from a distance. I chuckled at the irony; Abe Lincoln at a theater. That would not end well for the ex-president.

Inside, I was awestruck by the spectacle of the playhouse. Murals of space stuff decorated the walls, the paintings bright, cheerful, and characteristic. Rows of wooden seats with pink cushions were divided down the middle by an aisle but the sides also provided a pathway to move up or down. The seats faced an old wood stage, four feet off the ground, with a small staircase off to the left. Red curtains hung loosely at the sides. It looked like it was designed in the thirties, an era when the stage was still strong compared to the silver screen. The wood was ornate, hand-crafted, and meticulous. Somehow, this place dodged the destruction and looting that almost every other structure had suffered in the desert and that truly amazed me.

Planets and stars adorned the walls. Comet trails guided you toward the front. Cartoonish spaceships and UFOs floated in-between. Torches hung on the walls while candles helped light up the theater. At center stage, a pregnant woman in her thirties sang, sitting on a stool. I didn't recognize the song; it sounded operatic as if from an Italian play and she moved her arms like a maestro. Her voice bellowed, then mellowed, rose, and fell. It was captivating, mesmerizing, and relaxing all at once. She had straight blonde hair, was dressed Bohemian, her clothes looking loose and soft. I pegged her for a vegan, even by today's standards.

There was a crowd of drifters watching, nearly all of them smiling at the show. Mostly older men but a few older women were in the audience. None paid attention to me, they were fixed on the performance. I didn't blame them. It was not often you could get entertainment out here. Civilized entertainment, anyway. The fine folks at Coppertown tried their best, but no one came close to the talent before me. I could have sworn she was a ringer, someone who pretended to be humble, yet knew deep down she could have been a professional once.

Off to the right, another teenager, this one thin with an eye patch over his right eye, played the piano. He was energetic and passionate, his fingers dancing effortlessly on the keys. Eye Patch's dark hair was cut short and he was beardless, so someone he knew was good with a knife or shaver.

A third youngster was bigger than Eye Patch and Abe Lincoln. Six-two, pushing two hundred easy, the blond kid with a chubby face was a sizable dude and probably carbo-loading somehow. He hovered near the staircase and kept watch over the performance like he was security. A high school wrestling logo was on his shirt, ripped and torn in places, the name long since faded. Arms folded across his chest, he acted like he'd dare anyone to bum-rush the stage. I doubted anyone was willing to try. The Wrestler's eyes met mine as I strolled down the aisle and they didn't waver until I plopped into an empty aisle seat three up from the stage. I placed my backpack at my feet and sat back. My crowbar rested on my right knee.

Jock joined me suddenly, sitting in the chair directly behind me. He leaned forward, a bit excitedly. "I lost the kid out there," he said to me, gripping my shoulder. "He was there one second, gone the next. I don't know where he went."

"Don't worry about it," I told him without looking back. "Enjoy the show."

He did a double-take. "You're smiling," he said to me. "You like this?"

The song ended and the singer caught her breath. The crowd cheered enthusiastically. She fanned herself with her hands, thanking the crowd, and smiling at the fanfare. She took a leisurely bow which seemed to cause some strain as she held her back and then retreated to the stool. Wrestler grabbed a bucket and I thought he'd place it in front of her as she might be sick, but instead, he began to walk along the front row on the right side, shaking for handouts. Drifters reached for their pockets depositing whatever they could into them. Their offerings were anything from dead animals to assorted veggies. The singer looked steadier now and watched the proceedings.

"Does anyone have an apple? Orange?" the singer asked the crowd. "My boys need vitamin C." An orange was mysteriously dropped in the bucket.

"Thank you. My name is Song for you newcomers, by the way," she told us, somewhat looking my way. "That's it for tonight. I perform each evening. Watch for the candlelight and don't forget to tip." She ended her quip with a gentle smile.

Drifters slowly rose and wandered out of the Playhouse. All were in good spirits, many were hesitant to leave. They slowly shuffled and looked back hoping for more but none came. Song was wiping her sweat and looked truly beat. She was done for the night.

"Phew, that was a long set," she said to Eye Patch who spun on his seat, facing her. Wrestler walked in between rows and drifters continued to drop whatever they could afford to leave behind. I remain seated waiting my turn, as did Jock. Wrestler stopped suddenly, looking behind me and I pictured him staring at Jock, possibly surprised at the sight of the little guy. I picked out a can of baked beans from my back-pack and held it out. The bucket was at his side but he didn't present it to me so I reached over to drop it in. He smacked it out of my hand, the can rolling under some seats.

Behind me, I heard a small shriek and turned around. Abe Lincoln, the teenager from outside, had a knife at Jock's throat. Eye Patch whipped out a bow and arrow from behind the curtain and aimed at me, steadying his arm. Song produced a screwdriver from under her dress and lifted off the stool. The rest of the drifters had filed out, so we were all alone. What was this? A ruse?

I slowly sat back assessing the confusing situation. How the hell did this go from something so good to getting eighty-sixed from the joint? "What, you don't like hickory and maple sugar?" I asked them with a smile, then grew serious. "I was saving those baked beans, you know."

"You won't be raping or killing here, Rogue," Song said to me.

Ah, there it was, and I was offended. "I am not a Rogue," I told them. They weren't convinced and kept their weapons ready. Eye Patch was uneasy with his bow and was starting to shake. It took a lot of strength to have one cocked and ready. Last thing I needed was for him to tire and release. Song held her tool out firmly and she looked to Abe Lincoln for an explanation.

Abe Lincoln held Jock tight. "I saw them walk in from down the road like they owned the place," he said, gritting his teeth. "I saw their headlights come up and watched them ditch their car. They hid it back there about a hundred yards. They thought we wouldn't know shit."

I nodded and shrugged. "You got me. Our car overheated. All we need is water and we'll be on our way," I said, somewhat dejected. "I liked the show though."

"What kind of car is it?" Song asked Abe Lincoln.

"Red El Camino," he stressed.

Eye Patch's one eye opened wide. Song started to fret, her lips trembling, her eyes darting around the room. "Are you sure?" she asked him. The car had her concerned.

Abe Lincoln nodded, "Oh, yeah. Red fucking El Camino."

"Watch your language," Song snapped at him and shot me a look. She then returned to Abe Lincoln and asked weakly, "Are there others?"

Abe Lincoln shook his head. "No. Just the two of them."

"There will be more," Eye Patch offered. "There always is."

I leaned forward and Wrestler stepped closer. "I am not a Rogue. Look at my Buddy," I pointed out. "Would he last long as a Rogue?"

She considered that but then responded by asking, "So, if you're not a Rogue, what are you doing in *that* car." Big-time emphasis on *that*.

"It's a courtesy vehicle," I said bluntly. "They treated me like shit, so as a courtesy, I took it."

She searched my face. "I don't understand."

"Okay, I stole it. Better?"

They didn't seem convinced. They knew the car. Some Rogue who drove that must have had a reputation.

"We don't offer whoring here," she said to me.

I shook my head in disbelief. "Come on, I'm not looking for whores. I'm only looking for water. Jeez, do you guys shake down all your audience members like this? I'm going to post a bad Yelp review about this joint."

Abe Lincoln grunted, "He's lying."

"Trip Advisor then," I said.

Nobody moved. This conversation was going nowhere, no one was laughing, and I was getting annoyed. Unfortunately, I couldn't get to Jock so he'd have to play this out. I made a move to stand. "Look, I really liked your show, but all we are looking for is water and we'll be on our way."

In a flash, Wrestler pinned me back down, and admittedly, that caught me by surprise. He had incredible strength but he was standing over me, holding me down with both hands on my shoulders in my seat. He probably thought his dominance and show of strength was enough to scare most, but this left him incredibly vulnerable to a strike anywhere on his body. I went for the easy shot and kneed him in the balls, quickly shoving him off after. It must have been a glancing blow because he was back on me in seconds, grabbing my arms and lifting me out of my seat.

"Take him down! Go for the can opener!" Eye Patch shouted.

Wrestler threw his right arm under my left and pinned his hand behind my chest, drawing himself in close. By doing so, he locked my left against his body and I couldn't move it. Having been seated, my movements were already limited and I was taken aback by his speed and strategic move. The kid knew his stuff. His left forearm then jammed my throat, pushing it back hard, the pressure intense so intense, I found it hard to breathe. However, he neglected my right hand, which was free, and I drove a low punch below his ribs. It stunned him and he mumbled, "oh," and I felt the tension loosen on my neck. Believing I was going to punch again, his left arm came off my throat to ward off another low blow. However, I changed tactics, tilted my head back, leaned forward, and slammed the bridge of his nose with my forehead.

Big boy released me and dropped to his knees whimpering. Blood was pouring through his fingers as he cupped a possible broken nose. No one moved. They were all fixated on their fallen member as if it had been the first time the big lug had been defeated. What they didn't know, was that there was more to come.

Seizing the moment in the stunned silence, I hauled the crowbar out from the quiver, grabbed Wrestler by the hair, and spun him around. I then whisked the claw end of my crowbar under his chin, cupping it, and pulling back. Song and the other boys freaked. Hauling Wrestler up to his feet by his hair, I then used his body as a shield. Red air bubbles formed under his nose, some of it dribbling down his chin to my crowbar snug at his throat. Eye Patch aimed his bow again but was unsure what to do.

"Don't you hurt him!" Song shouted and jabbed the air uselessly with her screwdriver. Eye Patch wavered, his eyes darting to Song, then me. Glancing back, Abe Lincoln hadn't released his grip on Jock who looked like he'd faint any second.

"Everyone drops their weapons or big boy here loses his pipes," I said aloud, tugging on my crowbar for extra emphasis. Wrestler was barely holding on, visibly shaking. The claw part of the crowbar was digging into his skin and it would not be pleasant if I yanked harder. I didn't want to hurt the poor kid, but enough was enough.

"How do we know you won't hurt us?" Song asked, and then I felt warm piss running down my left shin. It was not from me. Song noticed it too.

"It hurts...please do what he says," Wrestler mumbled, finally speaking up.

"Release my Buddy!" I shouted at them. "Right now!"

She hesitated, then pocketed her tool. "Let him go," Song told Abe Lincoln.

He shook his head. "I won't do it. They'll kill us."

"Damnit, you release him this second!" She yelled and suddenly bent over, clutching her stomach. Eye Patch dropped his bow and rushed to her.

"Song, no!" he shouted, cradling her. She looked to be in pain and I became spellbound, wondering if she was going to deliver right there and now.

From the corner of my eye, I looked back at Abe Lincoln. "Drop the knife. Go help her out. She needs you."

He closed his eyes and complied, his knife dropping to the floor. The two boys gently lowered Song into a seat in the first row. I loosened my left arm on big boy, lifted my crowbar up and out, and shoved him towards the stage where he tripped and fell to his knees. Instead of rising, he sat down and resumed cupping his bloodied nose.

"You're lucky the bear didn't come out," I told him. Wrestler opened his eyes between his fingers and nodded.

Suddenly, miraculously, Song got up from her seat. "I'm okay, I'm alright."

"But you may have hurt the baby," Eye Patch protested. She waved him off and told him, "I'm fine, it was just a little tummy ache." She then stood quite firmly and faced me. Eye Patch contemplated going for his bow again but Song motioned for him to stop. Abe Lincoln was stuck in no man's land.

I twirled my trusty crowbar. Jock appeared next to me.

"You okay?" I asked Jock.

He brushed himself off and adjusted the coyote headpiece. "Just a bit freaked out," he admitted. One of the coyote ears had flattened during the scuffle and he tried to straighten it.

Song looked us over and softened. Her stance was more resigned, her composure without the luster she had before. "What do you want from us?"

"Water," I reminded her.

Hesitating, as if there was more, she then relented. "We have a well around back."

I walked up to her with my crowbar out. She stood her ground, her gaze on mine. The boys were too timid to move now, their bravado squashed and shamed, and their fate surrendered to me. One of them whimpered and I suspected it was Eye Patch. I was pissed that this meeting had gone to this extreme. As I closed in, I smelled perfume and it tickled my nose. It was lovely, stopping me like a wall. That eased me and the tension I felt moments ago began to fade and I soon relaxed.

"What else do you want?" she gulped, conveying her tell that she was frightened.

I glanced at the stage, placed my crowbar back in the quiver, and sat back down in a seat on the front row.

"How about an encore?" I asked, settling in. Feet crossed.

—————

Song sang once more. It was another classical melody that I'd never heard of nor knew any of the words. She was moved by her performance. I could watch her all day. My partner had other things on his mind and squirmed in the seat next to me.

After she was done, Jock asked me, "Can we go now?"

I sank deeper into my seat and pulled my arms behind my head.

The seats were amazingly comfortable, softer than sand, and less rocky. The El Camino could wait.

Eye Patch and Abe Lincoln watched us with contempt a few seats over. Wrestler was out front somewhere taking over watch at the front door, his nose bandaged.

While I didn't know their story at all, I assumed they were all related, she the mother to her sons, only the husband and or father missing, maybe dead. I didn't know if I would press the issue, nor know how long I'd stay. I still had a plane to catch and the fuming El Camino needed to calm down.

"Thank you," she said. "Unfortunately, that's about all I can do these days." She patted her tummy. "I am easily tired."

"I thought it was great," I told her. My elbow hit Jock.

"Yeah, yeah, groovy," he said softly.

Song stared into the bucket of offerings. "Let's see what we can make for dinner."

CHAPTER TWENTY-TWO

Soup was served outside where the junked cars and farm equipment were parked out back. My butt was stiff, parked on the hood of an old Subaru, the wheels gone so only rims remained. The front end dipped so low into the dirt that the bumper met the ground. Jock stayed close to me on a hood as well, still with the coyote skin, obedient like a loyal dog. I didn't think he'd ever take the smelly thing off. The boys were lined up on a set of drawers that had been hauled out from one of the motel rooms where it turned out, they all slept at night.

I caught Abe Lincoln and Wrestler staring at Jock, making him feel uncomfortable. So much so that Jock threw up his hands and asked aloud, "What?"

Song glared at the boys. Abe Lincoln spoke up and confessed, "It's just, you know, we've never seen anyone like you before."

"Boys, I've talked to you many times about manners," she scowled.

"Well," Wrestler stuttered, "He's right. We don't see midgets at all."

"Little people," Song offered with a smile.

"Jock," Jock replied.

Eye Patch strolled in from the road with his bow and was handed his bowl. "Nothing to report. No cars, no drifters. They all went nighty-night." I heard that from a cop once, most crimes died down after two am. Bad guys get tired and have to sleep too.

The subject of Rogues then arose and we all talked of our experiences. They sometimes stopped in for the shows but rarely caused a fuss; the Playhouse was a good collection and as long as the tax was paid, they went on their way.

"Tax?" I asked.

"Whatever we can offer," Song said, spooning some soup into a bowl and handing it to me, then serving Jock next. Abe Lincoln frowned in protest, but she reminded him that Jock and I were guests and that was the polite thing to do.

"Once they are satisfied, they leave," Song continued, casting a sad look. I thought of Song's predicament and wondered again if she was part of the tax. I then wondered how she would give birth and if the child had a fighting chance. That brought me to think of my boys, and how they'd handle these conditions. I doubted they'd handle it very well.

"I've been moving around a lot and I avoid the Rogues," I said as I bit into some meat. "I mostly travel alone. I haven't seen them in some time, spent most of the summer up north."

Song pointed out, "But you're in that car."

"Yeah, it's a cool ride too," I said with a shit-eating grin.

Abe Lincoln huffed and crossed his arms. "Don't you know whose car that is? Haven't you figured it out?"

"Mine now," I said, shrugging. Truth was, I could've cared less.

"Ginn's car," Abe Lincoln answered.

I almost choked on my bite. "Serious? That's Ginn's car?" Wiping some of the soup off my chin, I couldn't help but laugh. The boys eyed me like I was crazy. Even Jock looked stunned and began gawking at me. Ginn owned a muscle car? I pegged him for the Mercedes I saw if anything.

Song grew concerned. "Do you know him?" The campfire suddenly grew tense and I calmed them with open hands, putting my bowl aside – which was delicious.

"It was in a past life," I said, trying to reassure them. "He was a hotel concierge and I was a frequent guest at his hotel. My work had corporate rates so I stayed there and I saw him often. We weren't friends. That was in a past life. This is all just coincidence."

Alarmed, Jock suddenly asked Song, "Who's Ginn? Is he a crazy person?"

The boys laughed. Song told them to settle down. Jock couldn't make much of it, Wrestler made horns with his fingers on his head and Abe Lincoln "crossed" himself. Song looked at Jock and slighted at her boys. "Mind them, Jock. They're trying to be funny but in reality, they are being rude."

Eye Patch stated, "Rumors of Ginn have spread everywhere. He is a demon."

Wrestler added, "They say he drinks blood."

Rolling my eyes couldn't have been more evident. Now I had heard it all. Abe Lincoln cocked an eyebrow at me and cast a disbelieving look. "How can you not know the man? You've got his wheels," he pointed out.

Song wiped her mouth with a small cloth. "Actually, how did you get his car?"

Sighing, I conjured the meeting in my mind, resisting to speak of the plane and the Salton Sea at this point, however. Some things don't need to be said. "I was taken hostage and I decided I did not want to be a hostage anymore so I found a car I liked and took it."

"Simple as that?" Wrestler asked in disbelief.

"Well, I had to knock some heads, but you get the idea."

Song looked at me with deadpan eyes. "Ginn is not to be taken lightly. He is evil. He won't stop until he finds you."

"If you say so." I grinned at that notion and saw sullen looks all around. "Oh, come on. Ginn? The same guy who scored me coke and got me good seats at a heavyweight bout? The guy whose hair was never out of place and gave steakhouse recommendations to tourists? That guy? Give me a break."

Song spooned her food. "Anyway, the Rogues are getting bigger and stronger. This Ginn has the desert in total fear."

Wrestler perked up. "Rogues are dirty, filthy assholes who kill and rape. They're like the pirates of the desert." I said the same thing.

Abe Lincoln threw his food aside. "They'll spread this way. You watch."

"Don't waste your food," Song told him and grabbed his bowl.

"Not that hungry anymore," Abe Lincoln pouted. The boys stayed silent after that. They were all in deep thought.

"Eat up," she said to everyone. "Enjoy what you can."

"Tired of rat stew," Abe Lincoln said and walked off.

"Same as yesterday," Wrestler admitted.

"Well," Song sighed. "The menu doesn't change all that often. But beggars can't be what?"

"Choosers," Eye Patch said.

"Beggars can't be choosers," Wrestler jumped in and high-fived Eye Patch.

Amen to that. I cleaned my bowl and slurped the soup. Song collected it from me when I was done. Jock devoured his too and she took his bowl as well. As expected, he looked at her longingly, wondering about seconds, but she commented that the soup was devoured entirely. There was no more to be had.

"So, stranger, what do we call you?" she asked me with her hands under her chin. She then pointed, "We know he's Jock. What's your name?"

"Ted," I told her.

"Ted," she repeated. She got up and sat next to me. She then took her hand and gently stroked my hair. "That's not a good look for you, Ted."

CHAPTER TWENTY-THREE

Hair and beard trimmings had fallen at my feet as if I was at a salon, some of it a mass of curly brownness that looked more animal than human. Idle chit-chat made Song and I strangers no more. I had no choice but to be cooperative, she was the one holding the blade at my throat after all and used smooth strokes to clear away the fuzzy concealment I tried so hard to grow. Well, not really. Laziness had a lot to do with it. That, and a shortage of clean razor blades.

It was an old straight razor, long with a wooden handle. I have never used one before. We were sitting near the well, me squatting on a tire, she on a small stool, her legs astride, and I imagined she had done this, numerous times on the boys and possibly others who stopped by. Smooth, even strokes. A propped flashlight provided her with some light and she barely needed it. They had found boxes of packaged, small bath soaps in the motel, and one of the bars was mixed with water to be used for lather.

Daisy was going to do the honors as well the next night back at Coppertown, but I skipped out before I could take her chair. With all the hair and beard gone, it felt good on my skin.

"So, you think your family is still alive?" she asked me. She sounded sincere, unlike most other folks. We had been talking about what we had done in the past, me doing most of the jib-jab, not divulging too much of the crap I had been through for the last five years, but centering on most on the dull parts. The conversation, of course, steered towards me getting caught and taken hostage by the Rogues, the escape, and then me backing up a bit to explain the airfield and what transpired there. She was still very curious as to what we witnessed and somewhat impressed that I was able to escape but not fond of the result; hillbilly trackers who were probably scouring the desert for me. And there I was, at their Playhouse.

I finished with, "I know they're still alive. The Doctor and the Pilot confirmed it."

She smiled at me. "The plane," she noted. "That would get me excited too."

"Have you heard it? Flying above you?"

She stopped and looked skyward. "No. I stopped seeing planes years ago."

Jock had no interest in being groomed. He lay beside us, resting up against a log, his hands folded across his chest. Underneath the coyote skin, I could see the outline of his slingshot, close at hand, and I could tell he was weary being there.

As Song dipped the shaver into the bucket, I took it upon myself to feel my face. My skin was smooth and I ran my fingers over both cheeks. I was anxious to see what I looked like but she wouldn't let me see until she was done. A small mirror in my backpack rested temptingly nearby.

Eye Patch was somewhere in the Playhouse keeping watch from the window on the second story. Behind Song, Wrestler and Abe Lincoln were tinkering with an engine under an Audi hatchback. Wrestler tried to hold a hand-crank flashlight steady. Abe Lincoln was under the hood and he swore loudly. Song turned to them.

"Language," she said.

"Sorry," Abe Lincoln replied.

"Doesn't bother me," I said with a shrug.

She shook her head. "There's no use for it. I'm trying to teach them better manners. They don't need to learn bad habits now."

The Audi looked to be in good shape. A newer model. Well, new as new could be. "They get that car to start?" I asked her.

She sighed. "They've been trying for weeks. It's the best one out here. We almost got it running today. We found an old battery in a shed not too far from here and the engine cranked over. They're troubleshooting everything."

"You sure you want that?" I asked. "A car? That will draw attention."

"We need something in case we need to flee and there isn't a lot to choose from." She nodded to the right. "That minivan would be ideal but she won't even turn over. We think the cylinders are seized up. It's clean inside though. You're welcome to sleep in there tonight."

"Is one of them your son?" I asked, nodding toward the boys.

She stopped and dipped the shaver, rinsing it. "No, they were students of mine. I was a teacher."

"Where's the father then?"

"Of my baby?" She stopped altogether and stared at the boys. "I don't know."

It hit me. "One of them?"

She didn't answer at first. She struggled to reason with me and finally said, "Don't judge me." She then grabbed the shaver and moved my neck gently to the side. "Tilt your head, please."

"Sure."

"They hunt for me, they protect me. I wouldn't survive on my own. In return, well, we all make sacrifices, don't we?" she stated.

I didn't answer.

"I am a woman too. I just turned thirty," she continued, hardly abashed. "I'm entitled. I have feelings. They are all eighteen and nineteen now."

She brought a rag up to my face and wiped me down. Admiring her work, she sat back and told me their history.

"We were on a field trip coming back from Death Valley. I was their science teacher. It was pouring rain and traffic was backed up. Our bus stopped at a gas station to get snacks for the road when the clerk behind the counter suddenly stared in horror at a TV hanging on a wall. The news was talking about a gas or virus that was spreading fast. A news station from LA. We all came in to watch. A newscaster gasped and died on camera. The camera itself wavered and we all heard screams before the TV went static. A kid had a cell phone and called her parents in Riverside. All we heard was screaming on her phone. Next thing I know, the bus driver freaked, got into the bus, and drove off. He had some students with him. We heard him yell a woman's name like he was going to rescue her. We never saw him, those students, or the bus again."

"I was caught in the same storm," I mentioned. "No far from here, actually."

"The rest of us stayed at the gas station, waiting for rescue. None came. Some students decided to walk back home. That left ten students who stayed behind, all of us camped out at a gas station. We left soon after, people started coming by stealing fuel. They were harsh and not nice at all. A few held on but then seven of them trekked west to search for help. That left three students with me."

"What happened to the seven?"

She thought for a moment, wadded up the rag, and then smiled. "You know what? They found a good place to live. I'm sure of it."

"How long have you been here?"

"Quite a while," she replied. "We wandered a bit, stayed with some groups, then wandered again until we found the Jupiter Playhouse. But we four have always been together. I feel responsible for them."

Nodding towards the Playhouse, I said, "The show must go on."

"No, we need to leave," she admitted. "The audience members around here spare what they can but they're getting smaller in number and giving out less. You probably didn't notice it, but there's a small makeshift town behind this place. Like a homeless encampment. Anyway, we'll head east to the Colorado River. We plan to start a communal society, like a kibbutz. We'll grow vegetables, raise farm animals, and maybe open a school. Won't that be grand?"

She hoisted a mirror up for me. I pivoted the flashlight towards my face and barely recognized what was staring back. "There, much better now, don't you think?" she asked. I was amazed.

"Yeah. Wow," I replied.

"You could go on a job interview now." She was right. The long, scraggy hair was gone, as was the bushy beard. Jock would freak out when he woke up.

I yawned. Song caught me and glanced at her watch. "Time for beddy-bye."

I reached into my backpack and doled out all my canned goods. "For you," I told her. "This is all the food I have. I won't need it where I'm going."

Smiling at the motherlode, she thanked me.

As I went to place my backpack away, she stopped me and touched my right hand. Flipping my hand palm side up, she saw the scar. I pulled it back instinctively, not wanting her to dwell on it.

"That's an interesting scar," Song said.

"Just a cut."

"How did you get it?"

"Long story..."

"Let me see it again," she asked and gently pulled it towards her. I let her take my hand. Her touch was wonderful. Light, caring. It felt good. My hand was spun and overturned a few times as if she was looking for more but then she lifted my hand high, palm facing up as if presenting a find.

"The right hand is strong, powerful. It can ward off evil," she told me, tracing the scar back and forth. "Use it decisively. When the time comes." Song leaned over and kissed me on the cheek. "Be thankful for the good things. Remember the times your family made you smile. That's gold." She then stood up. "Go find them, Tiger."

"Listen," I said to her with all seriousness. "If your plan does not work out, there's a small community called Coppertown. They have a good thing going there, well protected. They are always looking for good people. They would welcome you. Just use my name. On the other side of the Colorado River near a town called Bullion."

She dismissed me with a passive wave. "We'll be fine."

Just as I was about to retort, she suddenly stiffened and touched her belly. "Ooh. That was a kick right there. He's going to be a soccer player for sure." I smiled at that and wondered if anyone of us would ever see that. A simple soccer game.

Eye Patch suddenly came sprinting in from the Playhouse.

"Trouble!" he cried. His face was full of worry. Song went wide-eyed, looking to him and myself.

"What is it?" she finally asked. Then, we all heard the distant sound of an engine. Then two.

"Rogues! Everyone inside! Hurry!" he cried.

Wrestler and Abe Lincoln dropped their tools and shut the good. Eye Patch helped hoist Song from her seat and they all hustled inside through the rear door. Jock and I followed, unsure that was the best tactic.

Once inside, they all scattered. Wrestler ran to the front to make sure it was shut and slid a heavy bolt across the door. Abe Lincoln ran to a side window. Eye Patch and Song gathered near the piano.

"Coming from the east! Two of them I think!" Abe Lincoln said, peering his window. Headlights loomed inside the theater through his glass that faced the street.

Song grabbed Eye Patch. "Are the candles out upstairs?" she asked aloud.

Eye Patch nodded and shouted, "Of course! That's where I first saw them from!"

"Stations everyone!" she yelled. Eye Patch picked up his bow and ran for the rear of the building. Wrestler remained at the front door, peering through the speakeasy door. Abe Lincoln left the side window and rushed to the piano, shouldering it, and moving it sideways. A carpet underneath was kicked aside revealing a trap door.

"Last resort going below," Song said to me, glumly. "A tight squeeze. Never needed it before but we all managed to fit in during a practice run." The hole looked to be a four foot drop down that ran under the stage. I couldn't see how far it would go but the snugness suggested Jock and I were odd men out.

Not that I'd hide like that anyway. "Do Rogues usually stop here?" I asked her, contemplating my next move. There were other buildings outside, but that would mean we'd have to stray outside and risk being seen. The only fight would be inside, at ground level, and we would have to draw them in.

And I probably brought the fight to these poor people.

Song sat on the edge of the trapdoor, her legs lowered inside, ready to drop in. "It's been awhile since we've seen any Rogues," she stated.

"Except for you," Abe Lincoln said, looking at me, holding his knife out again. "They're your pals, aren't they?"

"No, but they are probably here because of me," I admitted. "I'll deal with them alone if I have to."

"Enough," Song told Abe Lincoln. "Everyone remain quiet."

The engines grew louder. Mufflers must have been in short supply as one of them had a nasty belch. One of them popped from backfire and it sounded like a gunshot. That made everyone jolt.

Wrestler peered through the peephole out the front door, shifting left to right, hopping on his feet. "I don't see them. They must be back at the intersection," he whined.

"Shh," Song said to him. "Quiet."

Jock tiptoed to the side window that faced the lights, propping up a chair under it. He climbed up and ducked to the side. I made my way over too, keeping my head down and taking position at the other side of the window from Jock. Both of us kept most of our faces away from the window.

The headlights were on high beams and that extra glare caused us to wince and blink repeatedly. However, cupping some of the brightness, I made out two distinct shapes. One was a car, the other a truck.

A white Toyota truck. Torch. *Greeeeaaaaat.*

They had stopped at the three way stop sign as if abiding by the rules of the road. A Chevy Camaro idled next to the truck. I heard voices but it was hard to understand what was said above the rumble of the mufflers.

A bright flashlight surfaced, shining from the passenger window of Torch's truck, splashing its glare at the Playhouse, then behind it. The truck moved forward and then turned right where the flashlight centered on the rear where the motel, abandoned cars and farm equipment were. The Camaro jumped forward and then hung a left where it then entered the front parking lot. One vehicle around back, one around the front. We were surrounded. That was not good. I couldn't cover two entrances; these boys would have to man up quickly.

"They're looking for someone," Wrestler said hushed. "They have a flashlight and they're aiming it all over."

"Unlock the door," I told him as I ran over to him.

"What? Are you crazy?" he asked me. I gently nudged him aside and peered through the peephole myself and saw the Camaro sweeping the grounds.

"We don't want them to torch the place," I said, backing up. "If they can't get in, they will burn it down."

"Are you sure?" he asked.

I thought back to what happened at Matias' cabin. "Quite sure."

Wrestler trembled and asked me, "So, we just let them in?" His bravado was long gone. Before me stood a child, one who knew his boundaries and that didn't extend further than managing an aging drifter audience. Rogues were out of his league.

"Use the crawlspace. I'll handle the rest," I said, reassuringly, and motioned for him to go.

"What if there's more than two of them?" he asked and slid the bolt back.

"Wouldn't be the first time," I replied.

As I watched Wrestler slump his shoulders and walk back to the stage, I told Jock to arm himself with his slingshot. "Don't forget to yell when they come in," I added, and ran for the back.

"Wait, where you headed?" Jock asked me, pulling his chair.

The rear had me concerned. Torch was one bad dude and I couldn't let Eye Patch confront him. After I ran to the back, I relieved Eye Patch immediately and took position at a rear door, which was boarded up with a deadbolt, the top portion once having served as a window. Not all of the theater had escaped vandalism after all and I peered through the slats where glass used to be.

The white truck slowly cruised the rear lot, meandering the assortment of cars and farm equipment. I couldn't see who was driving but I could hazard a guess; my friend with fiery red hair and throbbing balls, courtesy of *moi*. The flashlight beam darted between the cars, then flooded the motel walls with looping wide circles like a prison yard guard looking for an escapee.

The truck found no purchase back there, so it turned around and cruised back, settling its search light on the Playhouse. The beams crisscrossed the backside of the theater until they almost found me, but I ducked in time.

Suddenly, the truck gunned it back to the road and turned a wild right and out of sight. I ran back to the stage area. Song, Abe Lincoln, and Eye Patch dangled their legs inside the trapdoor. Only a wearied Wrestler stood outside, trying to pull the piano closer to the hole. Having grown a pair, I guessed he would cover his friends and take the heat along with me. I felt a sense of pride in the poor kid.

"Grab a weapon," I told him and he nodded, picking up the bow and arrow.

I made my way back to the front where I saw the truck pull up alongside the Camaro. The two vehicles idled side by side again in the parking lot.

"I think there's two of them in the Camaro," Jock said to me, standing on a chair under the speakeasy door. He leapt down for me to look.

"Makes sense," I nodded. "Rogues usually don't travel alone."

That would make four, minimum. Conversation went back and forth outside, seemingly forever. I couldn't hear the lingo but I imagined it involved a lot of grunts.

The doors to the Camaro opened and two men exited. The driver was a large man, clean cut, and dressed very casual for a Rogue. Nice shirt, slacks, nice shoes. In contrast, the passenger was paunchy, dressed like a slob, and holding a sawed-off shotgun. The doors to the truck opened as well, and just as I assumed, Torch exited. He walked around the back of his vehicle with a walkie-talkie in his hand though. His passenger was Spaz, the Rogue who had been guarding Ginn's tent. He was holding a baseball bat and a large flashlight. He was fidgety like before and almost dropped his bat.

Casual Dressed Rogue popped his trunk, pulled out a jug, and handed it to Torch, who ignored him. Shrugging, the nicely dressed Rogue then handed it to the Slob Rogue, then another to Spaz. All three eyed the Playhouse and I knew they were going to flame us out. Torch continued to talk into his walkie-talkie.

"Don't go under the stage," I said in a loud whisper.

"What's going on?" Song asked, worried.

"Not sure yet," I lied and thought of alternatives. Not a lot of options. "They may come in." Coming in was one thing. I could give myself up, hoping they wouldn't need to enter. Flaming the place was another. That would wipe us all out.

Song stifled a small cry. The boys tried to console her.

Outside, when Torch wrapped up his call, the four Rogues began walking towards the entrance.

CHAPTER TWENTY-FOUR

Through the speakeasy door, I could see the men assemble but I noticed the three other Rogues seemed to distance themselves from Torch. Torch surveyed the Playhouse and at one point, his eyes focused on the front door where I was. It was dark inside, so he couldn't see me, but I was still on edge.

The Slob Rogue whisked out a lighter and flicked it on and off. "Knock that shit off," Torch said. "You're like a child, Utah."

"Just trying to scare them is all," Utah remarked.

"We don't even know if he's here," Casual Rogue pointed out. "We didn't see the El Camino."

"This seems all for naught," Utah said. "Maybe we should go."

"Shut the fuck up, Utah. Leave no stone unturned," Torch reminded them. "That's what the boss wants."

Torch's walkie-talkie chirped again and Torch took it aside like a personal call. It was mostly whispering and the other Rogues began talking to themselves. The one called Utah was shaking his head, nodding at Torch who wasn't watching. Utah looked irritated.

Song asked me, "What's happening outside?" She was still half in the hole.

I turned my head. "I'm not sure. There is some uncertainty."

Torch ended his call with a "Roger," and made his way back to the group. Pointing to Spaz, he said, "You, go to the rear and start the fire there. We'll cover the front. See who comes out."

Spaz nodded, juggled his jug, and walked towards the side of the Playhouse. That got the others excited. "Fucking A. About time," Casual Rogue said and brought out his knife. "Easy pickings when they leave, right?"

"Put the knife away, Smiley. You don't harm the man."

Smiley, the Casual Rogue, pleaded with his hands. "Where's the fun in that?"

Torch took a menacing step towards him. "You heard me. Mr. Ratelle is not to be harmed. If he's in there, he'll be driven out."

"Someone watch the front door," I pointed and rushed towards the rear. "Tell me what's happening."

Wrestler ran up and took the position. "What are you going to do?"

"Snuff out a flame," I replied, then heard a gasp. Bad choice of words, I realized, but I didn't have enough time to correct myself.

<hr />

Spaz didn't anticipate any company. I beat him to the corner of the building having moved the deadbolt at the rear door and taking a quick right. Like a kid with a new toy, he juggled the jug with care-lessness, spilling some, swearing when he did. He was also trying to hold the baseball bat and was paying more attention to those two weapons more than the one I held. As he approached, I could see the yellowness of his teeth as he grinned at what he thought would be a tremendous bonfire. When he rounded the corner, I swung my crowbar into his left thigh and he dropped both the bat and jug. The claw-end sunk in deep and he muffled a cry, more surprised than anything. From behind, I grabbed his neck with both my hands and snapped his neck. Spaz went limp like a rag doll. The moonshine sloshed on the ground. There was almost a gallon of it, enough to splash the entire rear walls. Thinking I had to get back inside fast, I bent over Spaz and placed my foot atop his leg and tried to wedge the crowbar free.

Just as I hauled my crowbar out from the dead man's leg, I heard a gun cock behind me and I believed it to be loaded.

"You did me a favor, Theodore," Torch said. "Thinning of the herd."

I was led at gunpoint to the other Rogues, Utah and Smiley, who held jugs in hands. Their faces dropped in disappointment. They wanted some fun with little old me and now their boss was in sole possession of their quarry. I just hoped they wouldn't still burn the Playhouse anyway.

"Where's Spaz," Utah asked, looking over our shoulders.

Torch stopped me just before we got to the vehicles with his hand gripping my collar, his gun at my back. "My friend here disposed of him." Torch nodded behind us to where Spaz's final resting ground was.

"Dead? For real?" Smiley said, not smiling anymore. Instead, the big man began to cry. Utah hugged him. "I just got to know him," Smiley babbled. "I loved him."

"Get in your Camaro, you fucking baby," Torch instructed. "Let's roll."

"Can't we light up the place at least?" Smiley whined through his tears. "We came all this way."

"No. We've got orders to meet the boss pronto," Torch said. "Now that we have his man. We meet up as planned. I'm not going to waste time so you can light up the joint and jerk-off to it."

"That's not satisfactory, sir," Utah said. "We need revenge."

"I want a go with him then," Smiley said staring at me.

My collar tightened. Torch was growing irate and he was squeezing his fist. "You guys are new, right? Just joined us, what, three weeks ago or so?"

Utah puffed himself up. "Boss said he likes us mechanics."

"You know what the boss likes too? Orders. You don't want to fuck with his orders. You've seen what happens in the pig pen, am I right?"

"No way Ginn does that to us," Utah barked.

"Then how about I call Ginn, have them bring the truck over and drop the Razorbacks out here in the parking lot. You want to do that, shit for brains?"

Ginn had the Razorbacks with him? Silently, I breathed out a tad.

Utah and Smiley were not amused but ended up agreeing. "Then you know what awaits if you don't cooperate," Torch said and left it at that. That was scary, that they transport those mean suckers around.

Consoling his friend by patting his shoulders, Utah said, "Smiley, I got the wheel. You just relax, big guy."

"No," Smiley said, waving him off. "I drive my car. No one else."

"I'm not that particular," Torch told them, then shoved me towards the driver's seat of the truck. "Ted, you drive."

CHAPTER TWENTY-FIVE

The Toyota drove much more smoothly than the El Camino. The steering was easy, the power decent. The seats were firm and there was less of a knocking sound under the hood. Inside, it was as clean as the muscle car. Torch kept this well maintained, although I wondered if he had his minions do the actual detailing. My rival rode shotgun, leaning towards me, his left arm up on his seat, his right holding his gun. "Keep the speed to fifty," he said. "No rush."

I checked the rearview mirror and saw the Playhouse vanish behind me over a hill. It was left untouched and I knew those inside, including Jock, were confused and worried. At least they were left alone. Torch hadn't reported this on his walkie-talkie yet and I thought that strange. "Where are we headed?" I asked.

"Just keep going south," was Torch's reply. "I'll tell you when to turn."

The Camaro was three car lengths behind us. I imagined Smiley wanting to do some very nasty things to me but through the conversation I heard, I was not to be harmed. That gave me some solace. I had some pull with these thugs for the time being. What Ginn had in mind for me, though, I had no clue.

From the corner of my eyes, I could tell Torch was studying me. He then began his questioning. "Who trained you?" he asked.

I played dumb. "What are you talking about?"

"You snapped Spaz's neck like a chicken. You took out Leatherneck and his fuck buddy Cyclops. Even the boss himself. That's quite a skillset you have. There's more to the Corporate bullshit Ginn claimed you did. I'd say MMA fighter in your spare time but you don't seem the type."

"Just called survival," I said and shrugged.

"Okay," he sighed. "But my bet is, you met someone and they trained you. Maybe in Coppertown. Maybe somewhere else. Five years is a long time to train."

We slowed around a curve. I kept my foot down, tempted to drive off the side. If it wasn't for Smiley and Utah behind me, I would have chanced it.

"So, what was your deal?" Torch asked me, then held up his palm. The scar was prominent on his hand, it appeared deeper and longer than mine. "Mine was a big-time insurance scam."

"You rubbed your wife out and scored some cash," I said. "For pills. I heard." I wondered if he knew I did the same.

Torch considered that. "Well, well. Seems you and the boss are tight."

"Boss? Don't you mean watch commander?" I had a friend who worked in a police station and remembered some of the department lingo.

Torch ignored that and quickly changed the subject. "I know all about the woman and the boys in the Playhouse," Torch said and that caught me off-guard. "I had no plans to burn it. There's no sense in doing so. They're good providers. I figured we'd flush you out if you saw us with the moonshine and the lighters. And you did."

"That place was empty," I said. "I don't know who you are talking about."

"Yeah, and you got your hair cut and shaved by yourself."

I forgot about my new look. One thing wasn't obvious though. The El Camino. It was hidden. "How'd you know we were in there?" I asked.

"Call it intuition."

"How about being a former cop?"

It was his turn to be surprised. I could feel his eyes burrow into me. "That's a good guess," was his reply. "But you're wrong. I was a Marine."

"The other Rogues," I said, then looked at him. "They don't know you were a cop, do they?"

"Go ahead and tell them," he remarked, trying to call my bluff. "They've heard my Afghanistan stories around the campfire."

In the rearview mirror, the Camaro was closing in on our bumper. "They'd kill you on the spot if they suspected you were a badge, am I right?"

"Why don't we shut up for a while," Torch suggested.

Smiley's Camaro suddenly roared past us on the left, the valves rattling, and I swerved. Torch grabbed the wheel with his free hand and pushed us back in the lane. The Camaro must have hit, sixty, then seventy. It crested a small hill and the red taillights vanished. Torch was not amused. He twisted both his body and his gun hand to face the front. "What the hell is Smiley doing? That faggot is going to blow his engine! He's fucking supposed to stay with us!"

Gripping the steering wheel, I seized the moment and stomped on the brakes. The Toyota's tires wailed as we came to an abrupt halt, my chest smacking the steering wheel. Torch face planted into the windshield and dropped his gun. For a moment, we both coughed as smoke from the tires outside engulfed us. Torch sat forward, feeling his face, and blood began to trickle down his mouth. I twisted in my seat and drove my left fist into the side of his cheek. Due to the distance between us, however, it only grazed him. My second punch, with my right, found his kidney and he roared in pain. Torch, however, sprung up fast and with little room for me to duck or weave, he hit me flush on the chin with his right that stunned me. My jaw ached and my neck felt sprained. I was woozy, but clear enough to see that Torch had recovered his gun once more. "Fucking try that again!" he yelled and jammed the barrel into my cheek. "Do it!" Just when I thought he'd pull the trigger, headlights filled our cabin and the Camaro was returning. However, it didn't pull along my side and swerved to pull up to

Torch's passenger seat. Torch didn't bother to face them as they stopped just inches from his door.

"I ask you a question, Torch?" Utah said from his open window.

"What?" Torch shouted but still had his gun digging into my cheek. "What the hell do you want, Utah?" Seconds passed and Torch was gritting his teeth. He wanted to pull the trigger badly.

Utah, however, needled him again. "Torch! Bro! Look here!"

Relenting, Torch eased off me and pivoted to Utah. "What the fuck is so important? What? Tell me, you useless piece of shit!"

Utah gave him a leer. "Word around the campfire is that you were a cop."

Too angry to process, Torch screamed at him. "Is that your fucking question?!?"

"No, but here it is. Are you ready?" Utah didn't blink. "Do you cry like a bitch when you bleed, pig?"

A sawed-off shotgun flashed outside Utah's window, similar to the one FuckStick had earlier. Utah was careless with it, not really aiming, using it more for show. In the driver's seat, Smiley was kissing a large knife.

In a flash, Torch whipped his gun around and fired. The bullet sheared off Utah's lower jaw and pinged off Smiley's knife. Utah dropped the gun to the road and cupped where his lower mouth used to be while blood gushed between his fingers. Smiley stared at two missing fingers, too shocked to move. The Camaro began to roll, however, as he must have released the brake and the car veered to the shoulder and bumped into a large rock where it stopped. Torch twisted to me, pointing the gun again. "Don't you fucking move!" he said, then removed the keys. A second later, Torch leapt out of his truck and ran after the Camaro.

Smiley made it out of his car with the knife in his left hand, but he had nowhere to go. Through the rearview mirror, I saw Torch confidently stalk his prey. A bullet singed Smiley's arm and he dropped the knife. Shaking, Smiley fell to his knees, trying to grasp his new wound with his mangled hand. He also tried to cast the blame elsewhere. "Sir, please, it was Utah's idea! I swear! He was going to say you killed Ted!"

Rounding the hood of the Camaro, Torch planted the gun at Smiley's forehead. "Who told you I was a cop?" Torch asked.

"We didn't mean anything by it," he said.

"How did you know?"

"Spaz said so. He heard the boss tell that to Ted earlier. In his tent."

That seemed to register. Torch paused a moment, as if to reflect.

"Who else knows?" Torch asked, as if softening.

"No one, sweetheart," Smiley said. "I didn't mean to do this. It was Utah's idea to take you down. I can forget about the fingers, if you'll forget about the whole thing."

"You got me confused with someone else," Torch noted and fired. Smiley's head kicked back and disappeared from view, but Torch soon became confused as well.

I had Utah's sawed-off shotgun planted at his neck after having left the truck, finding the weapon, and sneaking up behind the former cop.

"You can't kill me," Torch said, dropping his gun. "They'll hunt you down."

"Kick it towards me," I instructed him. Torch did as I said and I slowly picked up his gun. Over his shoulder, Utah was making gargling sounds inside the Camaro. "Hands high," I insisted.

Torch raised them. "I'm supposed to check in every thirty minutes. If I don't, Ginn will come up here. I reported my destination at the Playhouse just before we caught you. I believe I only have five minutes to make another call. You won't escape. Neither will the people back at the Playhouse. They will get the blame."

I contemplated wasting the man right there, but that would mean going back to the Playhouse, rounding up Jock, Song, and the boys, and taking off. That would also mean in a different direction I needed to go and that would slow me way down.

Sensing my plight, Torch lowered his arms, "Point the gun away. We need to talk. You and I."

"What for?"

"I might be a dead man already. Smiley was lying. Someone else knows."

"That you were a cop? He said no one else knows. I heard it."

Torch nodded. "His eyes told me different."

"Because you were a cop."

There was no point in hiding it now. "That asshole Spaz must have heard you and the boss talking. I was only gone a few minutes too, to clear your new tent beside me as I was instructed. Ginn can't protect me from these animals all of the time. Sometimes," Torch said and trailed off.

"Sometimes what?"

"Sometimes, I think he wants us all to attack each other." Torch walked to the Camaro. After he flung the door wide, he hauled out Utah, throwing him to the road. Utah moaned and barely moved. I saw his tongue snake around his mouth, probing his upper teeth. His breathing sounded like a whistle.

Torch seemed to think we were comfortable now and walked past me to his truck. "Where's the El Camino?" he asked me.

"That old piece of shit? It broke down. I had to ditch it."

Torch seemed to believe it and opened the gate to his truck. He brought out thick rope and attached one end to his bumper. "Seems about right. That old piece of shit was a pain in the ass to maintain. But if you know the boss, he's very *traditional*. Now you have a Camaro. Can I have my gun back, please?"

I emptied all his bullets into my palm and threw him his gun. He caught it mid-air and shoved it back in his holster. "How are you going to explain this?" I asked, waving at the roadside carnage.

"They got bored, tried to leave. Go AWOL and Ginn doesn't like that. These assholes were new members."

I lowered the shotgun. What he said could probably pass.

Again, Torch strolled past me lugging the rope. "Look, we all know you're heading to the Salton Sea. But the sea is a big fucking sea and we don't know exactly where. I can delay them for you, tell them I didn't see you. That will give me time to assess who knows my secret before it leaks out. We can make another arrangement, down the road. Once you're captured."

"Arrangement?"

"The plane. I go with you," Torch said, and began wrapping the rope around Utah. "I have no desire to serve Ginn anymore. This life is a brutal one and I want out."

"No way."

"You don't know what Ginn is capable of. You don't give him enough credit. And right now, he's in-between us and the finish line with a bloodthirsty armada."

"I overheard I wasn't to be harmed."

"If he's around," Torch noted. "But when he's not..."

"How many of you are there?"

"Was twenty. Now, seventeen because of these three idiots. That's still plenty," Torch replied and finished up with a knot. "Whatever arrangement you had with Ginn, it must be epic. He's got a hard-on for you. I've never seen him act like this before."

"What are you doing to your man there?" I asked and pointed the barrel at Utah squirming on the ground.

"Leaving you a trail. Show which way I'm headed." Torch replied.

"You could just tell me."

"There's no fun in that. Besides, they could be moving again and I might find out where down the road. I don't have an extra walkie-talkie for you either," he said and then nodded at his victim. "Look at Utah. The prick is kind of quiet now, isn't he?"

Torch was clearly enjoying this. "He doesn't have half his jaw," I pointed out.

"I'll enjoy the silence then. We good?"

I didn't answer. I was still mulling over my next move. Watching his plight against his own team made me think he was in direr straights compared to me, so I didn't stop him.

"The only deal I am making with you is now. And that's letting you go, so they don't come up here," I informed him.

"You'll need me again and then we'll make another deal. See you soon." He climbed in his truck. I took one last look at Utah and felt no remorse. His eyes found me and they closed.

The truck started, the rope went taught as the truck rolled forward, and Utah began to slide.

The Camaro was a beast. The car leapt forward with the slightest nudge of the gas pedal. It was a big, thirsty engine and hovering around a quarter tank full. The seats were race car snug, the ride firm, but the visibility sucked out the rear. I found Utah's lower jaw on the floor, made a face, and nudged it under the seat. Blood had splattered the gearshift and a tooth was deep inside a cup holder. I didn't believe Torch was using Utah's parts as a trail for me to follow by tying him up like he did. My bet was, he was doing it for revenge. Maybe set an example for the others.

Torch was in a bad mess. All because of Ginn's loose lips. I smiled at that.

I neared the Playhouse and saw the lights still out and no movement. I parked in the rear and stepped out. I was tired and looking for sleep. From the rear door of the Playhouse, Jock stepped out and met me halfway.

"They still don't trust us that much," he said. "They went into hiding again."

I planted the Camaro keys in his hand. "Tell them I got them a new set of wheels. Forget the Audi."

"How did you get this car?"

"We have a new ally," I said. "By default. I'll tell you later."

"Will the Rogues be coming back?"

"No," I said, and was confident with that. I handed him the sawed-off shotgun as well and added, "I'm going to bed. It's been a long day."

CHAPTER TWENTY-SIX

I woke up on the stage in the morning with the backpack as my pillow, my jacket as my blanket, and my back stiff and sore. It was bright inside and I realized then that daytime was already a few hours old. I rolled to my knees and yawned. My arm was also a bit sore. I sat back on my heels and arched my back, groaning like an old man.

I fell into my morning ritual of stretches and exercises. Just as I was wrapping up my push-ups, Jock interrupted me as he entered the room from backstage. "Finally, you're awake," he said, smiling. I could tell he wanted to tell me something but was holding back.

"Hope you brought doughnuts," I said as I got to my feet.

"Don't worry, bro. It's good news."

"Tell, tell," I urged as I grabbed my backpack and jacket.

"The El Camino is full of water and we have extra. Come on."

I forgot all about the damn car. We had left it hidden back down the road. "Yeah? Where are the others?" I asked him as he strolled to the rear of the Playhouse. It was unusually quiet. Last night, I laid down on the stage alone. I preferred to sleep that way, just in the slight chance Torch and his brethren returned. The others said they'd sleep in the motel rooms.

"They left," Jock stated. "Amscrayed, vamoosed, beat feet, fled, bolted."

"What?" I stormed out the rear doors, squinting at the bright sun, hoping it was a gag but the rear lot was void of people. It looked as it did yesterday but something was missing besides Song and her troop.

The Camaro was gone. "They took off in the Camaro?" The Audi they had been working on was still there, parked with the hood up.

"And they took the sawed-off shotgun you brought last night," Jock informed me.

"Why didn't you wake me?" I asked him.

"I just woke up myself," he shrugged. "Took me awhile to fall asleep, then I was out like a light."

"When did they leave?" I asked, blinking my eyes.

"Dude, I don't know, I was sleeping like you," Jock said. "Only I was in the backroom. Did you know you snore? Like really loud?"

Dejected, I suddenly felt alone again. "They could have woken us." Maybe I felt rejected instead of dejected?

Jock tapped my arm. "Oh, they left these." He pointed to a couple of water jugs. "These are backup, just in case. They took some moonshine for themselves. Probably used some for the Camaro."

Song and her boys were gone, headed towards the Colorado River in a mode of transportation that made a lot of noise. If the Rogues were out there still searching for me, they could easily spot their car. I found it even further unsettling that they left this place in a hurry, in the night, a sanctuary they called home. Why didn't she say goodbye?

Jock nudged me, pointing to my right. "Check it out, bro."

The El Camino. Lifted in the rear with new, larger rims. Yellow flames painted on the side. A fake human skull on the hood. "The kids must have worked on it all night. It's pimped out. I dig it," Jock admitted with a devilish grin. Something told me he knew what they had done. Perhaps he watched. Perhaps even helped.

I frowned. Seriously? "It just lost its resale value," I sighed.

"I think it's bad ass," Jock quipped holding the keys in his hand. "Ginn's going to be pissed. Whoever he is."

Moments later, we took a last glance at the Playhouse and hit the road. The El Camino's new rims allowed the tires to better grip the road. The fake human skull was a distraction and I thought of ripping it off, but Jock seemed to like it.

"I'm still nervous in this thing," Jock said, however.

"I told Torch the El Camino was junked. He thinks we have the Camaro. Besides, you liked the way it was pimped out."

"Wait. You said Torch. The guy in the truck. You guys made a deal?"

"No. And I don't totally trust him either. He's a former cop and that doesn't gel well with his butt buddies so he wants to leave. He was trying to make a deal with me, but I declined."

Jock turned to me. "What's his plan then?"

"Buy some time, try to figure out who else on the team knows he's a former cop and take them out. Meanwhile, he's sure we'll need his assistance later on and we will make a deal then." I shook my head. "Whatever."

"What deal does he want?"

"The plane," I said. "And I figure he wants it whether I like it or not."

"What if he demands it?"

"I don't plan to see him anymore."

"Oh. Good."

The engine still rumbled with the odd cough and sputter that Jock was trying hard to get used to. We left the Playhouse taking the same road that Torch used last night. He'd be long gone but it was in the general direction we needed to be heading and there wasn't a lot for roads to choose from anyway. It's either take the road back from whence we came, or head north. Salton Sea was south. No brainer.

I just hoped there was no roadblock. Or ambush.

The El Camino was kept under forty mph just in case we'd happen across the Rogues unexpectedly. Around corners, I took my foot off the gas and slowed until the road was clear further ahead. Jock sat sideways some of the time, looking behind us, keeping watch every which way. My eyes focused on the temperature gauge. It seemed stuck halfway, which was good. There wasn't much cover and if we had to ditch or hide the car, that would be tough to do.

Outside, the temperature was rising. However, a quick search revealed that the car didn't have AC and that struck me as odd. Ginn was a devil about details and I couldn't imagine the finely tuned prick driving with a sweat. The ancient fan in the dashboard just blew hotter air into our face and I eventually moved the lever over to shut it off. Jock told me he thought it was October, just as I had assumed, but the daytime temps in the Mojave could still be a scorcher.

"Look for shiny objects," I reminded him. "And birds overhead."

"Birds? Oh, right."

The drive was peaceful except for the guttural belch from the eight cylinders working under the hood. Jock stuck his head out the window like a dog, the wind sifting through his hair, his coyote head flapping like its nodding vigorously.

"What do you know about the gas?" Jock asked as he retreated his head back inside. "Who did it, you think?" he asked.

"Doomsday cult from Siberia."

Jock turned to me. "How do you know that?"

"I spoke to one of them, just before he died."

"You mean, before he let out the gas?"

"No," I said. "This was after, months after. The guy's name was Vlad and he admitted that all to us. My friend and I cornered him in a motel in Crown Valley and the terrorist spilled the beans."

"What happened to the guy?"

"My friend slammed his knife into Vlad's temple."

Jock sat back and took it in. "Wow, Russians."

"It was a cult of people. Followers. Not just Russians. I'm sure blame will be tossed around everywhere. Maybe one day we'll find out in a history book."

Jock changed the subject. "Why were you out here in the desert and not at home?"

"Why would you ask that?"

"Earlier you said you were out here when the gas hit."

Feeling a bit defensive, I replied, "Yeah. So?" I wasn't sure how much he heard between Song and I last night but I didn't want to be put on the stand at this moment.

"So why weren't you home?" he asked and I imagined him, lawyer-like, waiting for me to spill the secret and admit my crime. I wasn't going to give him anything, so I offered a short retort.

"Was working in Las Vegas," I said. "Was driving home to my wife and kids."

"I had a girlfriend once," he blurted out. "Her name was Misty. She was normal, stood five foot two. Does that surprise you?"

Shrugging, I said no, and he went on. "She and I met in a psych class in college. We sat next to each other. I thought she was beautiful. She had the greenest eyes I'd ever seen. Long dark hair. A body that wouldn't quit. I finally got the nerve to ask her out, to a movie, a chick-flick of all things, and she said yes. We went on four dates after that and I finally boinked her."

"Boink? Is that what the kids say today?" I laughed.

"We were both drunk on white wine. I can't stand the stuff. I was a virgin and she was fine with that. We went out for three months and then broke up."

"Were you the dumper or dumpee?"

"I dumped her. Told her that we weren't right for each other. Truth was, I felt she would leave me and I was falling too hard for her. I protected myself from a break up that maybe would have never happened."

I nodded. "You felt insecure about her."

Jock looked down. "I wasn't good enough for her."

"Because of your height?"

"I'm sure she's dead now."

Frowning, I said, "Jeez, why'd you go there?"

"Because I'd be dead too. I wouldn't have gone to the Mount Palomar Observatory that day. I really went because we broke up days before. I would have stayed with her otherwise. The bus trip was an excuse to get away. I was so bummed."

"So, you blame your being alive on a premature break up?"

Being overly dramatic, he looked out the window like an actor from an old movie. "Part of me died when I broke up with her." He even toyed with the window handle for added effect.

I was buying none of it. "Don't give me that, you sap. You were too damn young to feel that way," I responded.

Jock pointed out the obvious. "You don't know how I felt."

"Sure I did," I said. "Many times."

Turning to me with a shocked look, he asked, "How can you say that?"

Rolling my eyes, I said, "Dude, if I do the math, even five years ago would make you, what, eighteen? Nobody falls in love at that age. Virgin or not."

"Sure they do," Jock countered, straightening for effect.

"It's called lust. Sooner or later, you'd get over her and move on. Lust after another, do it all over again. You have to weed out the bad ones to finally get the good one. That takes time. Women come and go. At eighteen?" I shook my head for effect. "You don't know shit. You were too new at the game of love."

Maybe he contemplated that, maybe not. After a few moments, he looked at me and stated, "You're wrong. She was my soul mate."

"The best way to get over a girl is to get under another," I said, matter of fact.

"I don't believe that."

"Okay, then don't. Continue to dwell over what never was. See where that gets you. Good luck."

I let that sink in. Then, Jock spoke up.

"Tell me about Ginn," he said.

Him again. "He's nobody."

"He has to be somebody. How else could he lead the Rogues and why is everyone scared of him? Is he as dangerous as they say?"

"Hardly," I remarked. "You know, I can't put my finger on it. He was very charismatic; I'll give him that. Knew what to get, how to get it. Could read your mind. Always a step ahead. But slimy, like a used car salesman."

Predatory birds swirled in the sky ahead. As we drew closer, I could tell they were after roadkill. They fled as the El Camino neared, bolting to the tops of rocks on the nearby hills. There was a clump of something in the road and I assumed it to be some dead animal. I steered left around whatever it was the birds were attacking and then Jock looked out and saw it.

"Is that...a body part?" he asked. "Gross!"

A human leg still encased in a pair of pants, sheared off at the thigh. The foot was bare, heavily scraped and scratched. Skin had been ripped off.

"That there is a piece of Utah," I pointed out as we continued on.

"Utah? Someone was named that? Like the state?"

I nodded. "Torch was teaching him the fine art of bumper-skiing. Popular with the kids in the snowy areas, I hear."

"There's no snow though."

I faked being surprised. "There isn't? Well, that's not good."

Jock paused and then asked, "Who are we up against?" he asked.

"I'm not sure."

Further on, another leg, and it was moving. We then spotted a badger behind it, dragging it off the road. As we approached, the leg and badger quickly disappeared into the shrubs. More parts were on the road ahead. Entrails like tossed spaghetti, organs covered in sand. A bone here and there. An arm finally. Then another, with bits tore off.

I hit Jock on the shoulder. "Can't wait to see the head."

"Dude, this is getting grosser by the mile."

"Is grosser a real word?"

"It is these days."

We drove further on, steering over the odd red scrape and chunk of skin from good old Utah. Besides those few tufts of bloody moguls, only the occasional vehicle shared the road, all of which were discarded long ago. Car parts and glass were commonly strewn about.

"Didn't sleep well," Jock said. "You snore, you know that?"

"Yeah, you mentioned that already."

"So tired," he quipped and settled back. The coyote head flipped back as well, but got scrunched so the snout and face of the deceased desert dweller faced me. Odd that such an animal normally afraid of human contact would end up hitching a ride with such in death.

"Go head and nap. I got this," I said.

"Gracias," Jock replied.

"I was talking to the coyote."

Moments later, when I shifted to avoid a leg cramp, I looked over and saw Jock already asleep. And just ahead, down the road, I saw a Call box.

I had a call to make.

A grasshopper landed on my leg. I shook at it, and the green creature finally let loose and fluttered to the ground nearby. I wasn't in the mood for the leg crawler. My wife wasn't listening to me and I leaned against the Call Box pole for support. This was going to take a while.

"I can't be traveling and taking the boys to hockey practice at the same damn time, Tracy," I steamed. "Why don't you understand that?"

She groaned on the other end. "All I asked you to do was drop them off on your way out. I would have picked them up."

The air was getting hot. I started to sweat. There was no breeze to help either. I glanced back at the El Camino and the doors were still closed. Jock was in there, still dozing and I was thankful he wasn't hearing this back and forth conversation.

"Have you thought about our future?" Tracy asked.

"Many times," I replied and turned around.

"Do you think we'll make it?"

I slowly banged the receiver against my head. A lizard came out from under a rock. It saw me, extended a flap under its neck, jerked its head up and down, then darted back under it. Yeah, fuck you too.

Softly, she then said, "Maybe we should see someone. Like a therapist."

"I'm not paying for some quack. You'll choose some lady therapist who will side with you. You know, *Team Chick*. Then you two will gang up on me and say this is all my fault."

She sighed. "Then you choose. A man. I don't care."

"You really think our marriage needs to go to that extreme?"

"Our marriage is an extreme!" she yelled.

We both fell silent. Then, out of the blue, she said the following, "You know, each time you leave for Vegas, you're hurried, like you're eager to go. And not once have you offered to take me with you, even overnight, where we can spend some time together, alone, just the two of us. Not once."

That was true. I never did.

"I wonder why..." she ended and then she hung up.

"Bitch," I said to a dead line. I slammed the receiver on the cradle over and over, breaking the plastic. Then, as I turned to walk back to the car, I almost bumped into Jock, the little man standing just inches away, watching me with both a concerned and confused look.

"She suspected something," I said and pushed past him.

CHAPTER TWENTY-SEVEN

Jock didn't pry; he just sat quietly but shot me weird glances with his arms folded across his chest. I know he heard much more than I wanted, however. To dispel some of the peace in the car, I tipped a jug of moonshine that I retrieved from the back and belched loudly. The clear liquid burned a hole in my throat. That jug had a different bite and it reminded me of barrel cactus that had a kind of a sour, lemony flavor. All my muscles tensed and I jammed my right leg down. The El Camino shot forward and Jock planted his hands out on the dashboard. Easing up, I lodged the jug safely between my legs and continued onward like nothing happened.

"Tell me if you see a DUI checkpoint," I said, nodding forward, breaking the silence again. I tapped the jug too, for effect.

He shook his head. "Is that supposed to be funny?"

Jock the buzzkill. The ride got quiet again with the little guy focused, his eyes up front. I could tell he wanted to talk about the phone call, because he started to fidget, but I was not in the mood. My feud with my wife was personal.

Finally, we came across Utah's head, or what was left of it, in the middle of the road and I slowed the car down. The mouth was gaping, some upper teeth visible behind ripped and fleshy skin. I could see an ear and some hair in a mass of a bloody, ball-sized pulp. I didn't even stop and just drove over it, the object thumping the underside of the car. Jock lifted up as if it might come through the floorboards.

"You aimed for that on purpose," Jock whined.

"Maybe."

I took another swig and Jock grunted, "Four."

Great, the little man was counting my sips now. Just for that, I took another swig. "Five," I said and belched again. That time, I couldn't hide some disgust from my face and I shivered with my tongue out.

"You alright?' Jock finally asked.

Nearly gagging, I slapped my steering wheel, "Whoo-hoo! This shit has some bite!" A bit came back up and I swallowed, watering my eyes. I made a mental note to save the rest for later.

Ignoring my discomfort, Jock asked, "What happened back there?"

I answered, "I don't know, I can't wrap my head around it."

"I meant the phone call."

That was none of his business and I deflected the conversation by addressing the problematic cooling system. "Car is running hot again," I said. "I need it to cool down a bit. See that?" I said, pointing at the temperature gauge. "Needle is getting too close to red again."

Jock continued his inquisition. "So, you stopped back there? By the Call Box."

"Good spot as any. You didn't seem to mind."

"I was asleep."

His eyes bored into me but he had no stake in the game. I would trust the opinion of someone who had been married and in a similar predicament, much more than a single guy who never once said, *I do.*

"Want to talk about it?" he asked.

I played dumb. "Talk about what?"

He placed his hand to his ear, holding his thumb and pinky out, like it was a phone. "That was an interesting phone call, eh?"

"Same argument over and over," I said, and then tried to put a spin on him. "Do yourself a favor and don't get married."

Jock laughed and nodded. "I'll keep that in mind."

"Women don't know what they want and they make you pay for it."

"Uh huh."

"Actually," I corrected myself. "They want everything but not the sacrifice it takes to get them."

I settled back, resting my left arm on the steering wheel allowing that to sink in. "She wants me to be successful, make a lot of money, but doesn't want the long hours. Where the fuck does that job exist?"

"I have no idea," Jock admitted. "I wanted one of those too."

Turning to face him, I got serious. "You know where? I'll tell you where. Nowhere. That's where."

Jock crossed his arms. "So, you and your wife were having problems?"

"It's called being married. Spoiler alert; it's not all fun and games."

"For her too, right?"

I glanced over at him, incredulous. "What did you say?"

"You were married to her. You took her life and promised to make it better. Don't tell me you got married for yourself."

"That's deep," I said.

"Just stating facts, bro."

"You're an asshole," I said. I then wished he'd shut the hell up. I was tempted to pull over for dramatics but I needed to defend myself and put this to bed.

Not missing a beat, Jock continued. "So, you were in Vegas on business?"

"That's right," I nodded. "We had offices out there. I was required to visit every quarter. Being an Executive, something I am sure you were not, that is generally something mentioned as part of the job description. Sometimes I went more than that."

"Just business," he said with a quizzical look.

"What are you getting at, Jock?"

"Just that you were headed home and you told me they weren't home."

"Right."

"Why were you headed home then?"

A small sign ahead said Caliber Road. "Oh shit!" I said aloud and slowed the car.

"What is it?" Jock muttered, hands out to the dashboard as the El Camino braked hard and into a partial skid. There were no air bags back in the seventies and the seatbelt was not on so Jock nearly crumpled into the dash. I was able to push back on the steering wheel. "I wish you wouldn't do that!" he yelled.

I pointed to the sign outside. "I know where we are."

Still grumbling, Jock looked out the window. "Caliber Road?"

I cranked the wheel left and concentrated on the road. While the area didn't look familiar to me, I knew I'd come across what I was looking for soon.

"Where are we going," Jock asked.

"Detour. I need to check something."

Jock then muttered, "I hope it's not another Call Box."

My old sportscar car was right where I abandoned it some five years ago. Sand covered half of it as the desert tried to reclaim anything and everything in its path. The paint had faded, the tires and rims gone, the engine picked for parts, rust and corrosion covering the rest. The leather had been chewed and rabbit pellets were all over the place. Staring at my old ride was a downer. I loved the damn thing. The crash was still vivid in my memory, the whole scene a connection to my past, the last day the world was real. I picked off a piece of glass from a headlight with ease and flung it aside.

Jock was on the other side of the car, peering in. "Nice car," he said.

"Was."

I came around the other side and frowned. My old sign on the door used to say ALIVE FIND ME. Instead, someone found the can of spray paint, crossed out ALIVE and wrote DEAD.

DEAD FIND ME it now said.

"That's kind of morbid," Jock said behind me.

"Someone else scratched out 'alive' and wrote 'dead' in there. That was meant for my family in case they came out here." I kicked the car out of frustration. "Damn, I wish I could be driving this again. I loved this sucker."

Jock looked around the area. "So, this is where you were the exact moment the event happened?"

I told him what happened right up to the moment after I crashed. He seemed to accept it. A glint of metal then caught his eye. He peeked inside the old, mangled mess and pulled out a can of spray paint. The marble inside rattled when he shook it. Jock nudged me out of the way, bent down, and went to work.

"What are you doing?" I asked him, hands on my hips. "No gang signs, right?"

Jock rattled the can again and after a few waves of his hand, he stood up and admired his handiwork. "Better," he added.

FIND was blocked out and AT was added to ME.

DEAD MEAT

"Suits your situation better," Jock said, proudly.

"Asshole."

CHAPTER TWENTY-EIGHT

As we continued down the very same road I first encountered five years ago, I noticed little change to the landscape. Maybe a few cacti grew, possibly more flowers, but that was it. Sand still blanketed the desert floor, tumbleweeds still rolled. It takes time for nature to make a difference out there. Man's contribution to the landscape was one that only provided trash and death, and that was usually in the form of abandoned vehicles and human remains.

The heat climbed outside and the wind poured in through our open windows. I grew annoyed at my discomfort and began to fiddle with knobs and levers.

"It's bullshit, you know," Jock said to me out of the blue.

"What's that?" I assumed he was going to talk about the weather.

"All those movies about Vegas road trips," he said. "You always see them driving from LA but they never take the freeway. LA to Vegas is a four-hour drive along the 15 Freeway and that's the fastest route. That's four hours *minimum*."

I could do it in three hours, twenty-seven minutes from the OC, I was going to say. Having a four hundred horsepower sports car and a baggie of blow waiting for me was a good motivator too. I also had the machismo ability to bypass outlet malls without easing off the gas. I refrained from admitting those things, however.

"So, why do they get off the Fifteen Freeway and take these single lane roads?" Jock whined. "Who wants to make that boring four-hour trip *longer?*"

I hadn't thought of that. Good point. Movies always showed the yahoos in convertible cruising in the middle of nowhere, drinking beers, amping themselves up with Sin City on their mind. The rest of the world must think there's no highway between LA and Vegas. There was, and it was usually clogged, but far faster than any dippy side road.

"Guess the desert highway is too boring to shoot. A small road adds emotions," Jock added. "Like only the carefree travel here."

Caliber Road looked like it would continue to head west but at some point, we would have to move a bit south. If I kept heading west, I'd hit Barstow which was not only too far in the wrong direction, but a small city filled with death and disease. Surprisingly, the Minivan with the crazy lady I camped at during the second night of the gas was gone, and I missed seeing Jimbo's body, if it was even still there. Further, we passed the part of the road where I was ditched by the older couple, Charles and Susan, and their son, Freddy, the latter being stabbed and dead beside me in their car. Later that fateful day, I stumbled across the gas station where the gun battle and ensuing cigarette induced inferno took place. When Jock and I drove by that spot and hung a right, all that was left there was a vacant lot littered with mounds of mortar and twisted metal amid weeds and tall grass. I wondered if the skeletal bodies of Susan and Charles were still there, left up the road and up a small hill. I didn't tell Jock what happened. I'd be bombarded with questions.

A paved road at small juncture came up on the left. I stopped the car.

"What's wrong? Should we take it?" Jock asked, sitting up.

I didn't move and kept eyeballing the lonely road. "I don't know. It's the first obvious street from where we were coming," I replied.

"Torch. You don't trust him."

"Hell, no."

Jock sank back into his seat. "Then let's keep going."

A few minutes later, we happened across a bullet riddled sign that said KELSO 1. That meant, of course, that a town bearing that name was a mile ahead. Kelso sounded familiar, I strolled by it once a few years ago, lost in a wander without a compass or a plan. I did that a lot back then, just wandered aimlessly, zigzagged and strolled, sometimes avoiding people, sometimes not. There were people in Kelso but they weren't kind to stragglers like me back then. A portly Sheriff, armed with both a gun and an attitude, encouraged me, at gunpoint, to go around the small town that last time and keep on riding. Bikes were my preferred method of transportation then and I could cover a lot of ground so I didn't mind. Now, I had a stolen car and everyone would know it. I wondered if the same Sheriff was there and if I'd get hauled off to jail. Was it a crime to steal from a criminal?

"The town with no TV," Jock said out of the blue.

Taking the bait, I asked, "What do you mean?"

"Back in the seventies, TV reception was lousy. Kelso was too far to reach a signal. So, the townspeople had no TV."

"No Saturday morning cartoons?"

"No Simpsons either."

"How do you know that?" I asked him. "That there was no TV."

"Read it in a book once," he sighed. "I used to love to do that. Read books."

We crested a small hill and railroad tracks appeared next to us on the left. Two sets running parallel with scattered, dead brush mostly covering. In a few areas, sand reclaimed the land the tracks once covered like small hills. Only a couple of empty railroad cars, three of them in a row, hooked together, would suggest that a major line once crossed through here. No engine, no caboose either. As we drove, the tracks followed us and I wondered where the rest of the train was.

"Conjunction junction, what's your function?" I sang in my best Schoolhouse Rock voice. Deep throated, like a jazz singer.

Jock followed with, "Hooking up words and phrases and clauses."

"Conjunction junction, how's that function?"

"I've got three favorite cars that get most of my job done."

We smiled at each other. We would give anything to hear that again.

Dark smoke in the horizon stopped our happy little jingle as we topped another hill. I slowed the car down to a crawl, trying to see around brush and small hills. A building on fire, half of it collapsed on itself, came up on our right. There was a mix of white and black smoke beyond that. Other buildings and structures were on fire, I assumed. Nothing else can burn that much out here. Cacti have too much liquid in them to stay lit. Behind a large, faded billboard, a double wide trailer smoldered. Another still burned, the remnants of aged two-by-fours resembling charred sticks. A house or store, I couldn't tell which, was long reduced to blackened timbers.

Kelso didn't look so hot.

Especially with dead bodies littering the ground ahead.

***

Despite the lingering smoke from the fires, I was able to count eight dead men, all spread out and laying behind parked cars and trucks that formed a roadblock. Some of the vehicles had been pushed aside to clear and already pilfered for parts. I had to steer wide to get around the dead, narrowly missing a hand or foot as the El Camino idled by at slow ten mph. I steadied my boot ready to stomp the gas if more trouble surfaced.

Jock peered out his window. "Who did this?"

"Probably another warlord," I suggested. "Someone who was a crack shot too." I assumed this was Ginn's work. The roadblock faced east. I didn't want to bring his name up again. I had to make sure too.

"Like a war zone," Jock noted. "I imagine Vietnam was a lot like this, with the smoke and death."

"Rogues. Got to be," I finally said under my breath.

"Do you think there's anyone here alive?" Jock asked.

We heard yelling and laughter. Distant, but there. That answered his question.

We hadn't quite hit the main part of town as far as I could tell as a bend in the road appeared before us. Tall trees and thick shrub blocked our view, so I opted to be safe and drove into a vacant lot between a set of small hills, parking the El Camino in some dirt. It would be foolhardy to drive any further without knowing what else lay ahead.

"What are you doing?" Jock asked me as I shifted into Park.

"Need to check out the party. See if it's worth attending."

"Maybe we should find a different road."

"We don't have a lot of options."

"We can at least try."

I leaned over and said, "First, we got dead Rogue pieces back on the road from whence we came. And now, we come here, there's road-kill everywhere. Now, the body count is rising each mile we go, so don't you think we should play CSI and figure this shit out before we head out?"

"Okay, you're right," Jock replied. "But CSI does forensics, not recon."

I smacked his arm for reassurance. "You don't want to be stuck here, do you? In the town with no TV? What fun would that be?"

"Ugh," Jock said, absorbing the blow. "And by the way, you said *whence*."

As I parked the car, I noticed the temperature gauge had climbed again. Good thing we stopped, but I was confused as to why it ran so hot.

When we exited the car, the laughter grew louder. Whooping and hollering erupted somewhere close by. Jock hesitated, staying near the door. I opted for a small climb up the hill and took out the scope. The more I climbed, the darker the smoke got. I could feel the heat from a fire as ashes tumbled by me.

As I crested the hill, I had to duck as Rogues were parked about thirty yards away. It was a good idea to park where I did because we would have been spotted instantly had I driven more around the bend. The Rogues surrounded a man tied to the ground with four spikes, just like I found Cherry yesterday. I whipped out my scope and zeroed in on Rogues kicking and spitting on the man who wrestled and fought against the restraints. It was useless for him. The stakes didn't budge. Even from a distance, I could tell the man was bruised and bloodied.

Bodies of what I assumed were other residents laid about there as well. Rogues were rifling through their pockets and stealing their clothes.

One Rogue stood above the man, between his spread legs, and opened his fly. Other Rogues wedged something between the poor guy's teeth and held his head in place. The standing Rogue urinated on the man, aiming for his mouth.

"Gross," Jock said to me, having plopped down next to me. "Why would they do that?" Even without specs, Jock could tell what they were doing.

Other men waited behind that Rogue, lining up for their turn. I turned my head away, feeling powerless to do anything. Nobody deserved that.

More commotion was further down, along the main road. Pivoting, I spotted the man I knew all too well in the middle of the town.

Ginn. The former hotel concierge was laughing with his buddies. The reason was, a man was hanging up in the air on a railroad crossing. Rogues were throwing rocks at the guy.

Next to Ginn was Torch, seemingly a part of the celebration.

"Oh my God," Jock said and pointed back towards the center of the town. "What's in the back of that truck over there? Bears?"

A flatbed truck carried a pair of rectangular cages and two men were lowering the bed to the ground. Inside the cages, two large beasts charged and slammed into the metal sides. As I zeroed in, I recognized what they were.

Razorbacks. The same ones I saw back at Ginn's camp. A shudder ran down my spine. "Hogs. Big ones," I stated.

"What do they eat?" Jock gulped.

"Anything they want," I said and lowered the scope. I didn't have to use it to see what was going on. The pair of Handler Rogues readied to open the cage doors. I figured they'd be set free to attack the man staked on the ground but a thin, dark haired man was suddenly hauled out of a car, his hands bound behind him. He wasn't disheveled like the Rogues, so I assumed it was another local Kelso man. As one handler steadied himself at the front of the cages, the other handler ripped the Kelso man's shirt off. That handler then wrapped the man's shirt around a pole and stuffed it into the cages, near each boar's snout. He'd jab at them with it until the boars raged.

"What's that guy doing with the shirt?" Jock asked.

The handler at the front of the cages whistled to everyone and they all paid attention. Rogues began to seek higher ground. Even Ginn hopped on the hood of a car.

"Letting the boars acquire the poor guy's scent," I said.

The Kelso man was set free, cut loose from behind. The handler who jabbed with the man's shirt kicked the Kelso man in the butt and motioned for him to go. The Kelso man hesitated, maybe cluing into what was going to happen. It wasn't until another Rogue fired at the Kelso man's feet, that he finally began to run and he headed directly toward us. Jock and I flinched, thinking we'd be exposed until the cage doors were opened simultaneously and the Razorbacks shot out.

The pigs squealed as they gave chase. They were larger than I suspected, a couple of hundred pounds easy, with large, white tusks and long brown snouts. Tufts of brown hair were raised up like a lion on their thick necks. Muscles in their front shoulders flexed and pumped. Two Rogues wisely jumped high to tree branches as they raced by. The Kelso man heard the hogs and turned around to see what was happening. His face bore sheer terror and he nearly fell. His arms and legs began to pump harder.

"No, go away," Jock said quietly. "Don't run this way."

There was a strange harness on both pigs. I couldn't tell what purpose they had, but they looked like metallic collars.

The first Razorback caught up to Kelso man and slashed the man's legs with his large white tusks, causing him to fall just as he reached halfway to us. The momentum carried the beast past the fallen man, but that was where the second Razorback rushed in and grabbed a hold of the man's pants and shook him vigorously, tossing him like a rag doll. The man cried out unintelligibly as the Rogues laughed. The first Razorback returned and clamped down on the man's arm, tearing a bloody chunk free. The second brother buried his snout lower, somewhere into the man's stomach and grunted, driving in deep. The man screamed an unholy scream and I finally looked away.

I scanned with the scope and found Ginn and Torch once more.

They laughed at the pig buffet but then Torch whisked out a map. They laid it down on the hood of Torch's truck and began to study it, ignoring the pig-feeding frenzy behind him. Torch pointed to the map and then flung his arm, aiming his finger to the south away from us. He drew an arc behind himself and ended with his hands on his hips. Ginn thought a moment, surveyed Kelso, then nodded and followed that with a clap on Torch's shoulder. I guessed Torch had convinced his boss that we were much further south.

So far, he was upholding his end of a deal I wasn't going to honor.

Torch then whistled to his troops. Everyone began to scramble to their vehicles. The pig handlers looked as if they were caught off-guard. From the flatbed truck, they grasped two long poles and hiked towards the Razorbacks that were still feeding. Two other Rogues reluctantly joined in.

"They use poles to haul those suckers back into the trucks?" I asked aloud.

"I can't look anymore," Jock said and turned around.

I was curious to see how they'd get the beasts back into the truck when Jock hit me in the arm. Hard.

"What?" I asked, annoyed.

Suddenly, behind us, I heard guns cocking. We whirled around quickly as two men approached us, rifles drawn at the bottom of the hill. They were Rogues.

"Arms in the air, fuckers, and get your asses down here," one of them said. That man was on the left and he had a small frame, dark hair, scarred cheeks, and a bushy mustache. Jock and I complied and slowly made our way down. The other man came at us quickly, he being older, and taller, with long gray hair below his shoulders, a flattened nose, and predatory eyes. When the second one smiled at me, through yellow and brown stained teeth, I knew the wrinkles in his face as I had seen them many times years before.

"You are so fucking predictable, Teddy," the second man said.

He was Randall. My old boss.

Randall didn't bother with a handshake this time. Instead, he greeted me with a butt-end strike from his rifle to my midsection. The blow caught me by surprise and I fell to my knees. Maybe it was the shock of seeing him after all this time. That, or knowing he had a part in the carnage that claimed Kelso.

Randall shook his head. "I knew you'd chicken out. Lay low somewhere, stay out of harm's way. Observe from a chicken shit outpost."

"Having fun out here, Randall?" I quipped, holding my side.

"I figured you hadn't traveled that far. This town is the dead center of the Mojave with three roads intersecting. Since we knew you hadn't come through yet, I knew you of all people would eventually. I didn't buy that shit you went south."

Wincing, I got back to my feet. "How did you know I didn't come through yet?"

"We tortured the residents. They had squat to say. Now," he said and nodded around with a mock surprise, "they aren't speaking at all."

The other Rogue was jumpy, eyeing Jock on the side. "Look at the little feller, Randy! Goddamn, he's just like a toy!"

Randall ignored his comrade and continued with me. "I've been waiting for this moment a long time, you piece of shit. You fucked me over back in the day. My own subordinate, ratting me out. Then, of all damn things, you deny me entry into that rock quarry. Even with the hottie Maggie at my side. I figure you must have gone faggot because nobody would turn down that tail. But denying me? Now I got hard feelings."

"What are we going to do with them?" the other Rogue asked.

"We don't need this other guy," Randall said of Jock.

"Shall we feed him to the pigs?" the other Rogue asked.

"Sounds good to me, PornStar," Randall agreed.

PornStar still looked confused. "So, we just hold Ginn's friend here then? Call the boss man back?"

"Yeah, but I figure we'll play awhile first," Randall said and dropped his rifle. "See, I want to get me what's owed to me. If I hand him over, I don't get my revenge. I still think of Teddy here as a chickenshit and I want to prove it. He's always been a fucking pussy."

I casually dropped my backpack and didn't say a word. Instead, I drummed up the image of Polecat and felt my insides churn.

"Shoot him if he runs," Randall said to PornStar. "You're going to see the pussy bleed. Scar or no scar."

"You got it," PornStar replied, hopping on his feet.

Randall walked up to me confidentially and said, "Sorry, Teddy, but you were always useless." He swung a wild left that I easily saw and ducked. Then, he tried a looping right that caught air. Randall fell into a typical boxer's stance and tried to jab at me. I blocked his left, then slid away from his right. Nothing had hit me.

From the corner of my eye, I watched PornStar. He had his rifle lowered and bounced on the balls of his feet. "Get him, Randy! Come on! Smoke his ass!" he yelled.

Jock watched me nervously. I was his only hope.

Enough was enough. When Randall stepped in, I blocked his overhand right, cupped both of my hands and slammed them on his ears as hard as I could. It took a second to register, but I had probably shattered both his eardrums and his equilibrium became shot. His mouth worked like a fish and he had trouble standing suddenly. Then the pain hit him and he wailed, bending down, holding his ears.

"What's wrong, Randy?" PornStar asked aloud. "You okay, Dude?"

I walked up to my former boss, stood next to him, raised my arm, and smashed the back of his neck with my elbow, just below his skull. He crumpled to the ground, twitching in the dirt. I had severely damaged the nerves behind his head. Maybe even permanently. My concern turned to Pornstar who still had his rifle out.

Until a ball bearing shattered the other Rogue's wrist. PornStar screamed and dropped the rifle. Since PornStar was fixated on the fight, he forgot about Jock who was quick with his slingshot. Jock then readied another ball bearing, drawing the rubber back.

I watched Jock steady his aim, but the little guy didn't have it in him. I sighed and strolled up to PornStar who was flapping his hand like it was on fire. I balled my right fist and broke his windpipe with one punch. He gasped heavily, clutching his neck, and fell to his knees. Only PornStar made any noise, gargling and spitting as he writhed on the ground. Randall stayed still.

"What do we do now?" Jock asked. He looked stunned, unsure, and resigned all at once. He was eyeing both men. PornStar finally stopped moving.

"Let's blow this town," I said and headed for the El Camino, leaving PornStar and my former boss to the elements. Neither one would be moving anywhere for a while.

Or at all.

CHAPTER TWENTY-NINE

We waited for the rest of the Rogues to finally leave and that took about twenty minutes. We discovered Randall and PornStar shared a motorcycle that was hidden behind some trees nearby but I'd forgotten how to ride one effectively and Jock sneered at it. During the wait, we sat in the El Camino. At one point, Jock asked, "Was he really your boss? That guy over there?"

"Yeah, but he was a terrible one at that," I replied as I pulled the car forward.

"How many of these guys do you know?"

"Too many," I said with a frown. Jeez, that was true, wasn't it?

Once we returned to the road, we drove slowly. A large, Spanish-style building loomed, untouched by fire and smoke. It was a two-story that looked like a school but a sign said KELSO RAILROAD DEPOT painted on the side with the train tracks leading to it. And further on, VISITOR CENTER in bold letters was above a small office door.

We passed the staked man. His eyes were bugging. The man's white shirt was stained yellow. His wrists were red, cut deep by the ropes that bound him. Clearly, he was dead.

"How did he die you think?" Jock asked.

"Probably drowned," I groaned.

The temperature gauge was nearing red, of course. Good timing.

"Do you think everyone is dead?" Jock asked.

Convinced the depot was unoccupied given the massacre that unfolded, I said yes, and we drifted further on. The wind picked up coming in from the west and blew sand across the ground. Ashes from a fire drifted past us and got sucked into a small dirt devil whipping by. We watched it spin until it fizzled out. Trees swayed in the wind, a fire crackled somewhere, and insects buzzed in shrubs close by. I took in Kelso and what remained. Sadly, it was little.

I didn't have a lot of choices in roads to take to the Salton Sea and the El Camino needed exactly that - roads. It was not built for travel over sand, the tires would sink fast and the suspension was too low for dips and hills. We'd be stuck in ten minutes, wheels spinning, fists pounding the hood and *I told you so's* back and forth.

"Oh God," Jock suddenly said and pointed out the windshield.

The body hanging on a railroad crossing sign ahead appeared to be moving.

The bloated body wore a Sheriff's uniform, tied high up with his feet off the ground. A badge was impaled into his forehead, the corner dug into his flesh like a ninja throwing star. Just when I thought the man was alive as I saw movement, I quickly realized that the man wasn't moving at all.

A crow was attacking the hanging man's face from behind.

The bird jumped up on the sign above his head, then flew off, its black massive wings carrying it to a nearby telephone pole. In its beak, I saw something that resembled a golf ball.

Just then, the El Camino quit on us, spewing steam and water from under the hood. "Great, just great," I muttered.

"What happened?" Jock asked.

"She got angry," was all I said and I stepped out with my backpack. Jock opened his door as well.

"It's going to blow up again, isn't it?" he asked, worried.

I surveyed the area and didn't see any movement except for

lingering fires and smoke. The car continued to fizz and spew water. Jock suddenly poked his head under the front bumper.

"Is that liquid supposed to do that?" he asked, pointing under the car.

When I bent down, a stream of water was spraying the ground, pooling there, creating a small river. All the water we had been provided by Song and her boys was leaving. That told me a broken hose. Sure enough, when I lifted the hood, steam pushed me back and I saw the rip in a hose near the radiator after I waved the cloud clear. I felt helpless unless I could score something to fix it with.

In the meantime, Hanging Sheriff got me curious.

I made my way to the body casually, turning, scanning for movement elsewhere. A short distance away, a handcar sat idle on the tracks. One of those contraptions you can pump with levers.

"See anything?" I asked Jock as he smartly walked backward.

"No," he answered.

"Hear anything?" I asked.

"Still no."

Hanging man offered us little. Where he once had dark hair was matted red with blood. He was big, clean shaven, but his mug was reduced to nothing more than a mass of pulpy flesh. Dried blood was caked on one cheek like bad makeup. On the other, a small trickle of blood flowed down and under his jaw. Welts and bruises pockmarked his body. His right eye was reduced to a squint, his left eye gone, and the socket oozed out a clear, jelly-like liquid. I thought back to the crow with the round object in his beak that took off when we came up and deduced that the black bird took the poor man's eyeball.

Hanging man kind of looked like the Sheriff who convinced me, at gun point, to beat feet the last time I came here but I wasn't so sure. His arms were tied behind his back to the large X's on the sign so his entire body was prostrated forward. He reminded me of the feminine statues you saw on the bow of old ships, except those were majestic and beautiful, not gory and revolting.

Around our feet, rocks covered in blood were everywhere. Jock picked one up and scrutinized it like it was a specimen, making a face.

"Gross!" Jock yelled and dropped it. "There's skin and blood on these rocks!"

I picked up a rock and hurled it at the crow. The rock sailed past and the crow simply ducked, not leaving, and that annoyed the crap out of me.

"Check for a pulse," I told Jock, picking up another rock. I found a good one that had some red on it. Winding up pitcher style, I beamed this one hard and it smacked the fencepost just an inch below the eye thief. It freaked out squawking and took flight, the large wings pumping for a further perch.

Jock still considered the poor guy a disease. "I don't want to touch him," Jock told me. "You do it."

"Fine," I said and then walked around the dead Sheriff. Just as I reached for his hand, I saw it.

A scar on his palm.

Then, suddenly, behind me, I heard "Going, going..."

Turning, I caught a brief flash of metal coming at me and I ducked reactively, bending down and away. What looked like a baseball bat grazed the side of my head causing me to stagger off balance. I managed to right myself, but then I was met with a hard thump to my chest and I stumbled, landing in the dirt on my back. I managed to throw my arms up to ward off the coming blow but none came however. The image of a kid looming over me, holding a baseball bat, was something I found entirely improbable.

"Gone!" It was, in fact, a kid's voice. Rail thin, he was twelve, thirteen maybe, holding a baseball bat cocked, ready to swing again. The kid had dark hair, wore a bandana, aviator sunglasses, and a Def Leppard Pyromania t-shirt. He reminded me of Chachi from Happy Days.

Jock wisely stayed out of range. I could tell he was shocked to see a kid as well.

Content that he has us at a disadvantage, Chachi poked around the cab of the El Camino. The little prick even hoisted out my backpack and threw it over his shoulder. He then lifted the tarp and grabbed a jug. "What is this?" he asked, pointing the end of the bat at me.

As I rolled to my knees, a new pain in my chest gripped me

momentarily. The kid connected right where I took a bullet the other day and even though I still had my Kevlar suit on and that still smarted.

Chachi opened a jug and sniffed. "Shit, skull cracker? That all you got?"

"That hurt, Chachi," I informed him as I got my bearings. Where the hell did he come from? In about ten seconds, the little shit was going to regret his time at bat.

"This ain't t-ball, dipshit," he replied, opened the cap, and took a long slug like a pro. "Barrel cactus?" he coughed. "That's all you assholes make. You guys need to make better rotgut." He dropped the jug back inside the cab.

"It's a good vintage," I mumbled.

"Mine now," Chachi reacted and peeked inside the car. "What else you got?"

"Mismatched boots apparently."

Finding no amusement in my comedic delivery, Chachi turned to me and leveled the bat. "Tell me what else you got and I'll finish you right now. Won't leave you out here for the coyotes."

Jock had his weapon cocked and ready to fly. Chachi swiveled and shook his bat at him then, having turned his attention away from me.

Big mistake.

"What?" Chachi said and opened his arms. "You gonna fire that peckerwood sling my way now, little man?"

I swept my leg and Chachi crashed to the ground. I then cocked my fist back and hammered the kid at his temple, knocking him out.

———————

Chachi was unconscious next to the El Camino, his head laying on its side in the sand. I was tempted to mush the little snot's face into the ground for the line drive he did on me. His hands and feet were bound by some twine I found, tied tight so he couldn't go anywhere. Chachi had been lights out for about fifteen minutes. I didn't tie him up to protect myself; I did it so he wouldn't run away. I didn't feel like running. Jock and I watched him stir finally and the sight of us probably jarred a bad memory.

I also had his sunglasses on. Jock gave me the thumbs up in the looks department. If Chachi's answers didn't suffice, guess who was going to get some killer new shades?

"Give 'em back!" Chachi protested, blinking, squirming in the dirt. His arms and legs strained against the twine as he was kicking up a fuss and flopping like a fish. He fought to sit up, but it was awkward as his hands were behind him. After a mighty struggle, he got his own butt under him with his legs spread out. He rested against the car door, breathing hard.

"You struck out, Chachi," I said, staying on the subject of baseball. "Back to the minors for you, T-baller."

"You're a Rogue scumbag!" Chachi spat, trying to keep up with the tough guy persona. The kid did have some bruises and scratches on him, not done by me.

I pulled at my clothes. That was the second time someone called me a Rogue. True, there were some holes, a couple rips, but I'd like to think I didn't resemble those thugs. Jock smirked at me, *kids these days*. Maybe I did need new threads.

"I am not a Rogue and I am insulted," I told Chachi. "Besides, what good Rogue would I be if I beat up my fellow Rogues?"

Still unsure, Chachi asked, "Then what you doin' in this fancy ride?" Chachi shouldered the El Camino door for dramatics, but I could tell it hurt him.

Lowering my new shades to show I was serious, I leaned down, towering over him. "Stealing it."

Unimpressed, he looked away. "Yeah, right."

Why didn't anyone believe me? Chachi stared at Jock who rolled ball bearings in his palm like they were Chinese *ben wa* balls. I could tell the sight of Jock confused the wannabe teenager-thug and after a few moments, Chachi glanced back at me again. "Swear you ain't no Rogue?" he finally asked. "I mean, you ain't one of them?"

Hey, the little prick was starting to think. I held up my last finger. "Pinky swear."

Finally, Chachi caught on and looked me up and down. "You're Ted then, right?" Chachi asked me. "The dude he's looking for?"

"Tell me what went down," I demanded.

"Said a man named Ted stole his El Camino and was heading this way," he said, then spied Jock. "Can you untie me, please, dickwad?"

I kicked his leg. "Why would you, alone, attack a Rogue?"

"Shit, after what he and his asswipe friends did to my town and Gruff?" Chachi said and puffed himself up. "I can take on two of you, but not, like, fifteen. I ain't scared of them Rogues no more."

I stared up at the man tied to the sign. "That sad sack of bird feed Gruff?"

Chachi lowered his head. "Yeah. I can't get him down myself and that fuckin' crow won't leave."

"The bird has his eye on something, that's for sure," I said. Jock rolled his eyes at me.

"You wanna untie me?" he asked and wrestled on the ground.

I placed a heavy boot on his ankle and pressed down. "How do you know all this? Why are you alive?"

Chachi winced and squirmed under my weight, trying to slide his foot away. "I hid under the handcar over there, was able to sneak around. It was dark when they first attacked and they hung out all night and into the morning," he said, gritting his teeth. "I heard it all. Alright?"

"You're an angry little man," I said, lifting my boot and nodding to Jock. Jock removed a small buck knife from his back pocket, pulled the blade out, and flashed it to Chachi with a dead-eye stare. Chachi's eyes widened and he shifted uncomfortably. "Don't," Chachi whined, like a child. "Please."

Chachi wasn't so tough anymore. Even Jock saw through him. "Promise to be a good boy, Chachi?" I asked him. It wasn't so much a question, but an order.

"Why you keep callin' me Chachi?" he asked.

I hauled Chachi to his feet and found him to be surprisingly light, then threw him against the car and told him to relax. Jock nicked the rope between Chachi's wrists and quickly the kid twisted back around.

"Dumb, dumb, dumb," Chachi said rubbing his wrists, rolling his neck, trying to grow a pair. "You a wanted man and you're drivin' the shithead's own wheels. You might as well eat a bullet and save everyone some time." Sliding past me, he then marched over to Gruff and sat down in front of him, cross-legged, and pouted.

I needed to interrupt Chachi's moment. Walking up, I sensed a bond there between the two but I really didn't want to pry. Kids grew up fast and the few that I came across were not treated well and really didn't know any different. Such was life in the desert. You did what you did to get by and survive. Chachi scratched at the sand, kind of zoning out. "There another ride here?" I asked him.

Without glancing up, Chachi said, "Nah, Gruff's cruiser was the only one working now. We ran out of moonshine so it didn't move that much." Chachi pointed to a looted cop car. "We had to push the other cars to form a roadblock," he continued.

I wondered if the hoses were still in good shape in Gruff's pilfered car.

Chachi closed his eyes. "Took Gruff an hour to die. They kept throwin' rocks. There was nothin' I could do." His eyes welled up. He wiped it and his lips quivered. Gruff was close to him and the loss was personal.

So, it was an old-fashioned stoning that did him in. How ancient.

"Why'd they stake that guy to the ground?" I asked, changing the subject.

Chachi turned to look behind him. "Ernie? I don't know. Sick people? They asked him over and over if you came through and he kept saying no. Each time he said no, they hit him harder. They staked his ass to the ground, tied him up and he died."

I left Chachi alone for the time being. Jock and I needed a new game plan. We were merely following Ginn and maniacal warlord stood between us and the Salton Sea.

And there weren't many roads in the Mojave Desert.

Chachi found some duct tape for me and I used it on the busted hose. Water was pumped from a well into a bucket and I filled the radiator after a couple of trips. When done, I slammed the hood, startling Jock who had a stick in his hand. Lines in the sand lay before him.

The lines showed where the airfield was and where we drove to, a westerly direction that he made out to be much straighter than it really was. "The Playhouse is up here, in the corner," he said pointing with a stick to the left. Then he backed up and drew a circle a few feet away and said, "This is where the Salton Sea is, way down here."

The Salton Sea was in a southwest direction. Then, Jock used the stick and came back up to the Playhouse. "So, we started here this morning, heading south. I figure we came back a bit this way to see your dumb old car for no reason," he noted using the stick to move slightly right, "Then, we hooked on another road that came this way to Kelso, which is west and right about here."

"Okay, smart ass, we're here," I said pointing in the middle. "Salton Sea is down here. We need to drive south."

"Where was the Rogue camp?" he asked me. I walked over and made a small circle with my boot north east of the airfield. "Right about there."

Jock thought a moment then drew a straight line from the Rogue camp to Kelso. "They came this way and beat us here. While we went west first and then came south, they came south west diagonally."

"We got to watch a pretty good show at the opera house though," I stated.

Jock took a deep breath and used his stick again. "So, if we head south, we may run into him. Chachi said they took that road over there that heads down to the 40 Freeway. My guess, form a roadblock."

Behind us, Chachi came back from the Depot rubbing his eyes. "There's no one left. I checked all the hiding spots. The Rogues killed them all."

Chachi couldn't hide the pain. Poor kid was alone. Here we were, planning our road trip to glory and his town was massacred. This was his world and we were drawing maps showing the best way to leave it. His friend Gruff was still tied to the crossing sign too. Chachi needed our help and the pang of guilt stung me. I was worried for the kid.

Sometime later, the three of us lowered Gruff, clumsily, to the handcar. Gruff's body was heavy, despite all the blood loss, and I bore most of it hoisting the former Sheriff by his shoulders. It was awkward to look down on the big man, his head was covered in purple, bloody bumps, his skin torn in places from sharper rocks that pierced his skin. He lost his bowels too but we all ignored that.

Chachi knew where there was soft ground where they buried others in the past. It was when I untied Gruff's hands that I saw the scar up close. It ran from his palm to his fingers like mine. I instantly hid mine but my reaction was one of surprise. Chachi seemed not to notice, but Jock did and he glared at me.

"What do you know about Ginn?" I asked Chachi who was untying Gruff's legs as they dangled off the car. I turned Gruff's hands back over and folded them on the dead man's chest, palms down.

Chachi was quick with his reply. "He's as wicked as they come."

"How was their relationship recently? Gruff and Ginn?" I asked, watching Chachi slide the man's legs on to the handcar, one leg at a time. Jock took care of the middle grasping the man's belt for leverage.

"We didn't see Ginn hardly," Chachi replied. "Gruff would go see him, do some trade for bush whiskey. Do some whorin' too, I heard," he laughed. "They had an understandin', you know? Like you stay there, I stay here."

"So, Gruff was allowed to stay on as Sheriff?" Jock asked.

Chachi took a seat next to his friend. "Yeah. Some warlord chiefs were allowed to stay in charge where they were from, you know?" he said and blinked. "Gruff was a Sheriff here and kept order even after. There's other small towns that do that too, Gruff told me. So long as you traded and obeyed the son of a bitch Ginn and paid your taxes, he was cool with it. But Gruff didn't call himself warlord. He was always Sheriff."

Glancing around, the former railroad depot looked like a war zone. "What do you have going for you here? Now?"

Chachi shrugged. "Nothin'. I don't know."

"Parents? Family?" Jock asked.

"Mom and my real Dad were divorced. Mom shacked up with Gruff. Gruff nailed her on a speeding ticket when she blew through town trying to find a shortcut from the Fifteen. She came back to contest it saying she was only doing fifty in forty-five. I guess he was feeling guilty and got her off with a warning, then took her to lunch for all the fuss. Soon, they started dating and we moved out here to this place for a year. One day, when I was in school, Mom went to Lake Elsinore, where we were originally from, to get my deadbeat Dad to sign the divorce papers and that was the day when the world ended. I never saw her again. Gruff looked after me since. He was cool with me, long as I stayed quiet and didn't cause shit."

"Sorry to hear," I added. Must have been rough waiting to see if your mother would show up. Worse yet, she was trying to make a better life for Chachi and herself, although one would wonder why Kelso made sense, if at all.

"One more thing," Chachi said. "Ginn said he was after you because you broke some deal."

Jock shot me a look. "What deal?"

"I have no idea," I replied and let it drop.

Later, we were back at the handcar, ready to say our goodbyes. Flies buzzed Gruff's corpse and Chachi shooed them away.

"You going to be okay?" I asked Chachi.

Chachi sighed. "I'll deal. Gruff will want a proper burial." He stood up and manned the lever.

"Need help?" I asked, sincerely.

Chachi brushed me off, "Nah, it's best if you go. If Ginn and his men came back and found your sorry asses here, I ain't sure I'd be any help for you."

I grabbed a couple of jugs of moonshine from the bed of the muscle car and brought them over. I put them on the handcar next to Gruff. "Don't drink it all," I said to him. "Use it to trade."

"Whatever, Dad."

I nodded to Jock and motioned that we hit the El Camino and get going. Truth was, I wasn't happy about following Ginn and his merry men but it seemed like the only route was to go the same way they did. We'd just have to deviate somehow.

"Listen up, man," Chachi said as he climbed on the handcar. "There's a small road about ten miles out, about a quarter of the way to the 40 Freeway. Take a left at Homer Road. None of them will go that way. Road is all windy and twisty, goes up into the hills and you'll backtrack. Ginn wanted to hit the Forty fast because he thinks you're way ahead and you wouldn't get off the faster tracks and make your trip longer."

Jock hit me in the arm. "See? Just as I said about Vegas road trips in the movies. Why get off and make it *longer*?"

"Hell," Chachi said, "He may even be at the Salton Sea by now waiting for your ass there."

All the directional talk was getting confusing. "But where does Homer Road take us?" I asked.

"Way back on the Forty I think but at least it ain't where he will be. If you want to get to the Salton Sea, you got to cross the Forty anyhow." Chachi grabbed the handle on the handcar. "Also, stop by Drambooey's for a laugh. You can't miss it."

Feeling bad, I then told Chachi about Coppertown. He didn't react either way.

Chachi began to pump the handcar. It creaked and groaned as he leaned hard on the lever. Finally, the handcar began to move. "You got balls driving the man's car," he said to me, grunting.

"Makes me look dope," I called out.

With a wry smile, Chachi said, "Dude, you got minivan written all over you."

Jock snickered and strutted back to the El Camino. Just then, Chachi stopped for a moment. I thought he was going to take us up on the digging.

Turning back, Chachi shouted, "Salton Sea, huh? Watch out for the Mud People!" Then, with shake of his head, he began pumping the handcar again and it creaked down the track. "You boys are in for some laughs!"

"Mud People?" I asked Jock and got nothing. I shouted after Chachi. "Mud people? What the hell is that?" Chachi ignored me and continued pumping.

With the last word in, I yelled, "That's an awesome shirt by the way, Chachi!" He flipped me the bird. Soon, he was about a hundred yards out, the handcar moving along. At that rate, he could end up at the Arizona border soon, maybe take my advice about Coppertown. That made me feel better.

"How we doing on fuel?" Jock asked as he rounded the car.

"Good idea." I came up on it and unscrewed the gas cap. As I poured the precious liquid into the aging car, we take one last look around Kelso.

"Town without a TV, eh?" I asked him.

Jock nodded in Chachi's direction. "Why didn't you call him Opie next? Yet another timely TV reference."

I emptied the jug but saved the last swig for me. "Do me a favor. Point to the sky and say, "The plane. The plane.""

That earned a smile from my buddy. "That almost works, doesn't it?"

"I came from a town that had TV," and coughed. I tossed the empty jug back into the cab and looked back at the tracks.

Chachi, Gruff, and the handcar were nowhere in sight.

I didn't even pause to think about the condition of Randall and PornStar.

CHAPTER THIRTY

Homer Road wound up a small mountain with terrain full of colorful brush and large boulders. Certain plant life preferred higher climates and I saw some I hadn't seen in a while; a mix of reds and purples, some atop cacti. The views were great too.

After leaving Kelso, we talked little since we took a left on to this new road. The 40 Freeway was still further south, so we opted to take Chachi's advice and backtrack a bit so as not to run into the backsides of the Rogues.

"Do the Razorbacks concern you?" Jock asked me, his voice a slight octave lower, like a child.

"Not as much as the Rogues do." I then glanced at him reassuringly. "But if we don't run into them, we're good."

Sighing, Jock quipped, "Be a horrible way to die, bro. Being eaten alive."

The image of the Razorbacks tearing into the poor Kelso man stuck with me. Probably forever. Why would Ginn bring them? I wasn't to be harmed, he said. It didn't make sense.

Jock turned to me and said, "They are probably cross-bred with other wild pigs like those from Europe. They could weigh, like, a couple hundred pounds and their tusks are razor sharp." He ended with, "Oh, and they freak out at the sight of blood and not in a good way."

"How do you know all this?" I asked.

"Comic book," Jock answered. "A vampire from Romania kept them as pets. I forget his name, but he preferred pigs over dogs as his hell hounds. Said the pigs were trainable, ornery, built like a train, and always hungry. It kept me awake for days." He shuddered and then I noted that the pigs, or boars, were probably his height. Like someone my size facing a bull. Not a meeting I would like either way.

Jock then thankfully changed the subject by remarking about his knowledge on cacti. "Shrub and cacti everywhere here. That means there's water to be found."

I agreed. "You'd probably have to dig but as long as you knew where, it wouldn't take long. Canyons that face north will collect dew at the bottom and dried riverbeds will have water just below the surface." I looked at him and asked, "Tell me you haven't drunk from a cactus."

"Drinking from a cut cactus is for fools," Jock said with a wave. "You know those old westerns had cowboys lopping off the tops and sucking out the water?"

"No, but go on," I said.

"The juice inside is dangerous and can cause you to be sick. I found out the hard way once," he said and added, "Projectile from both ends of your body."

I agreed. "I hacked a cactus once, tried a bit, and immediately spat it out. The Rogues somehow tamed the liquid when they made moonshine though. How they did that was beyond me."

Jock fiddled with the CB radio again but this time, he was more determined. He moved the tuner only ever so lightly for even the faintest change in static. Someone could be broadcasting out there, even the Rogues.

"Should we have invited Chachi to come with us?" asked Jock.

"He wouldn't have come anyway."

Jock turned to me, still twisting the dial. "But is he going to be okay? If I was his age, I'd be scared to be alone. Hell, I'm scared now."

"He's more resilient than you think," I suggested.

"He's an angry little boy. His parents caused him a lot of hurt. Divorce can do that to a kid," Jock informed me. Jock would know. I wouldn't. My parents stayed together.

"If he has any sense," I said, "He'll go to Coppertown like I told him."

"Tell me about this Coppertown place," Jock insisted and sat back, giving up on the CB.

As I reminisced, Jock checked the speedometer and the side mirrors as he listened. Every now and then, he'd nod and smile, ask a question, make a comment. Coppertown was a good place to set root and he'd be welcomed there. I, on the other hand, had other places to go first. When I wrapped it up, he sank back in his seat.

"You're crazy for leaving it," he said to me with a look of resentment.

"You can get too comfortable there. I don't do comfortable." I then got the sense he had something to hide. Again, I wondered how he survived on his own for so long. "Did you come from a good place?" I asked.

"Promise not to judge me?"

"I promise nothing," I answered.

"I did," he admitted. "I spent the first few months tagging along with these other people from my school. We went all over the place but settled in a community outside Temecula. It's just north of the Palomar Observatory. I lived there for about four years."

"Temecula. Wine country. Nice."

"We grew lots of fruits. I can't touch another grape," he then said and smiled. "Actually, I could, just had so much of it. We made wine too. We were a large group at first, all living in tents and homes in the area. It was fun, we rarely got attacked. Then, I got banished."

That caught me by surprise. "Banished why?"

Jock leapt up in his seat. "This guy stole some fruit to feed his family! I was on watch and saw him do it! He pleaded with me! I let him go! The man took more than I thought and I got blamed! He was kicked out of the community and so was I!"

"That's rough," was all I could muster.

"Zero tolerance, bro. The law was the law."

I had heard that often enough. Even Coppertown was succinct in their laws. Once you broke them, you were out. "So, you spent the last year on the road?"

"I've been wandering around, went north around Palm Springs, then up to the outskirts of Barstow. I was planning on going up through Nevada when I saw the plane."

"Why Central California?"

"I had a cousin up in Fresno. Only living relative," Jock admitted. "I don't know if he made it, or if he would welcome me in. We weren't close. I never found out. The plane was more exciting anyway."

We didn't talk for a minute. I kept the speed around thirty miles per hour since we left and had not seen another Rogue or vehicle at all. The drive had been so far surprisingly uneventful, winding and slow like Chachi had said. Thankfully, no more body parts were strewn across our path either. We were heading in a south-east direction and I doubted any Rogues would have come this way.

Guilt began to weigh on my mind. Was Jock's life in danger because of me? I was certainly heading towards an inevitable conflict and Jock didn't mind riding beside a man with a target on his back. Would he survive better if we split up? Would the plane even take him too? I wondered what Jock's motivation was in all this; it couldn't be because of boredom, could it? Or was he planning to join me at my side where he'd be provided with safety and friendship? I traveled alone and preferred it. At some point, we were going to disband, and it was either because of a sold-out plane, or a futile effort that led us nowhere. I made the decisions on where I wanted to go and I didn't want any outside influence suggesting to me to give up and find solace in a rock quarry. The only company I wanted was my family.

"Doesn't it bother you that Ginn is looking for you and he knows where we're going?" he asked me, returning to the tuner.

"Can't help it if the man is a whack job," I shrugged. I did that a lot, shrugging. Remembering Ginn the way he was made his impact a nuisance. I should have taken it more seriously though, the fact Ginn's got well-armed friends and a couple of hellacious hogs does not bode well for this team of unimpressive underdogs.

"What's this deal he says you broke?" Jock asked.

Lying, I said. "I told you I have no idea."

Jock thought that was a lie too. He knew Ginn and I had formed some sort of partnership. You don't chase a man through barren desert to say hello. You chase him because he owed you. Something big.

Jock looked up from the CB. "It must have been some deal."

"There was no deal. End of subject."

Suddenly, the CB chirped, the static ending. A male's voice filled our car, loud and clear as if coming from the rear seat – if there was one.

"This is the emergency broadcast system," the voice announced. "This is not a test. I'll repeat this one last time." It was definitely Ginn. He caught me by surprise and I felt the desert suddenly stifling. He was broadcasting somewhere and I was sure I was going to be the topic of discussion.

With his mouth open, Jock cranked up the volume. "This message is brought to you by Ginn, supreme ruler of the desert," Ginn said and then his voice grew stronger. "My fellow Wastelanders. There is a fellow among us that is wanted for desertion. As you all know, I do not take kindly to those who disobey me. This man must be apprehended at once."

I stopped in the middle of the road. Ahead, the road was clear. Behind us, the same. Jock, he panicked, twisting in his seat, searching high and low thinking we are being followed. "What the heck? Can he see us? Do you see anyone?" he asked.

This tactic wasn't something I expected. I wasn't sure there was even any radio traffic out there besides walkie-talkies. "Relax, he's nowhere close," I said reassuring, but not very convincing.

Ginn continued, "This man goes by the name of Ted. He is dashingly handsome, armed with a crowbar, driving my beloved red El Camino, and is heading towards the Salton Sea."

"Shit!" I yelled. Torch assumed I'd take the Camaro because I told him the El Camino crapped out. Problem was, obviously, that we were in the damn muscle car anyway. Torch really wanted us to avoid capture and was still feeding Ginn lies. Torch *really* wanted a seat on the plane. Too bad he was going to get bumped.

Ginn added, "Bring him to me, unharmed, and you shall be

rewarded with all the moonshine you can carry. But harm him, and you'll witness my fury. I can be reached via CB radio. You all have the channel. Relay this information on your HAM radios and other devices. Spread the word. Report to me at once. This concludes the emergency broadcast system." The CB then went back to static and Jock calmly turned it off.

The damn car was cursed. We stayed there silent for a few moments. Only the rumble of the V8 idling permeated the air. The desert suddenly felt small. The El Camino had to go.

Grinning as if to satiate the issue, I said to Jock, "At least he said alive." However, the little man, predictably, was not amused in the slightest. He sat stone faced, staring straight ahead now. If he wanted to bail, I wouldn't blame him.

"Swell for you, but what about me?" he asked, his face deadpanned.

"I'll put in a good word."

He suddenly pounded the dash with his fist. "We need to ditch this car! I told you it was bad news! Why would driving a Rogue vehicle make any sense whatsoever?"

Seeing no chance for rebuttal, I shifted the car into Drive and spoke up in a positive tone. "Don't worry about it. We'll figure something out. We just need to get some distance going and then we'll move on foot."

"Was there a woman involved in all this?" Jock asked.

"What makes you think that?"

"There usually is."

Giant boulders appeared on each side of us and I half expected a Rogue or two to jump out brandishing a firearm. Homer Road led us even more uphill and we were quickly hugging a rocky terrain that split a couple hills in two. I caught Jock peeking behind us, catching the same view I saw in my rearview mirror. We would crest the hills soon but the road had more twists and turns than I wanted. The temperature gauge was toying with me, urging for us to pull over and rest. It was dangerously close to red again and I wondered if Ginn and his crew had ever heard of engine coolant.

Although making better time than walking, driving in the El Camino was becoming a liability. We needed it to take us as far as possible though. Maybe we'd find another ride along the way and switch out the cars. I didn't want to walk; it would take too long and there were still hills to climb. I had thoughts about the plane landing and looking for me and then taking off due to me being a no-show. The Salton Sea, I thought, was still over one hundred miles away. Walking would put us way behind schedule.

Suddenly, the El Camino jumped and sputtered. The steering wheel rattled in my hands and I fought to control it. There was a loud cough and the car rumbled and shook.

Terrified, Jock asked, "What was that?"

A puff of smoke poofed out from under the hood. We lost power as I rounded a corner and the steering locked up on me. I gripped it hard to keep the wheel from turning and it coasted towards the cliff side and a couple of large rocks.

"Stop!" Jock shouted.

The poor El Camino scraped the side wall of rock and slammed into a large boulder parked on the shoulder. We both pitched forward; me banging into the steering wheel, he crumpling into the dash. With dust wafting the windshield, I half-expected the radiator to blow but it didn't. I sat back, coughed, and checked myself. Nothing more than maybe a bruise on my right side. Jock, on the other hand, rose slowly, eyeing me as if it was my fault. Ignoring his glare, I faked a cringe at the dent I caused. The scrape didn't sound too good either. We were halfway across the road, the back end taking up the lane opposite we were traveling.

"I guess that's one way of stopping," Jock said, sarcastically.

The car wouldn't start. It just turned over and over. After a few attempts, I gave up and tapped the wheel with my palms.

"Is there enough fuel?" Jock asked, peering at the fuel gauge. It was hovering above Empty but not quite all the way down.

"The car is running a bit low. I'll put some more fuel in." I then wondered if we had enough moonshine in the back to cover us.

"Yeah, you do that," Jock replied and sat back. His attitude was a little pissy and I didn't blame him.

The air was cooler and the sun was leaning midway in the afternoon sky. I'd say it was three o'clock plus or minus two hours. I really had no idea anymore.

Once done, I tossed the dead soldier into the pile with the others counting only a few jugs left. I checked the damage to the front and found the bumper dented. Along the side, a big scrape about two feet long was running from the left fender to my driver's side door. It was sliced inwards, long and about an inch thick like a cigar, the paint peeled back, exposing the metal underneath.

"Ginn is going to be so pissed," I said out loud but Jock didn't hear me.

Luckily, the El Camino fired up right away. I backed the old car out and we continued down Homer Road, downhill then, the setting sun casting shadows as we ducked behind the hills. We could see the valley floor ahead of us but windy Homer Road was making it difficult for us to gain any ground.

The El Camino's engine ran rough, like the timing was off and that was making my blood boil. It didn't feel like it would last long and I began searching for places to ditch it again. And that was when our fate took a strange turn.

We both saw it. A sign painted on a rock.

THIRSTY? DRAMBOOEY'S STRAIGHT AHEAD.

"What do you think?" he asked, and we both knew the answer.

CHAPTER THIRTY-ONE

The once-white Winnebago was hardly recreational. Resting in a gravel-filled lot by the side of the road, it was as if it had been parked there for decades with its flattened tires melting into the landscape. Sandy mounds climbed the sides like a snowbank. The only saving grace seemed to come from within though, as colorful images and slogans on the camper's walls said it all: GET WELL, TERRIFIC TONICS, and FEEL BETTER were scrawled with medicinal devices crudely drawn. Slowing the El Camino, I studied the hillsides around us, watching again for movement from a possible ambush or attack. I saw none and returned my gaze to the trailer.

Plastic chairs were stacked neatly against the trailer. Except there was neither people nor vehicles to be seen. Only us.

DRAMBOOEY'S MAGICAL ELIXIRS another sign read.

Reminding me of a circus, I half expected clowns to appear. The letters were ablaze in a rainbow of color, red, blue, green, and purple. It was both ugly and captivating. There was ample parking out front and gravel grooves reflected tire treads from past visitors. I stopped the El Camino which only seemed to motivate the damn car to shut down as it conveniently stalled anyway. Wisps of smoke rose from under the hood suddenly, steam whooshed, and I feared a tow truck call was in order.

"We're stopping, huh?' Jock asked. "Duct tape didn't hold?"

I flicked the dashboard, the thermometer screaming red again. "I don't think we have a choice."

Through the cloud of steam rising from the hood, we saw a slight, limber man dash around the camper, dressed in a black jacket, red striped shirt, black pants, top hat, and cape. Strutting like a penguin, he twirled a cane and the quirky man stopped short of the El Camino, ogling us through the windshield.

"Welcome folks!" he sang to us waving the cane. "The name's Drambooey, not the drink, but the purveyor of drink, and I am the proud owner of Drambooey's Fine Elixirs!" he proudly announced, standing aside, waving his cane at the camper. "Yes sir, I possess the ultimate refreshers known to mankind and the largest, cleanest source this side of the Mississippi!" He then wiggled a finger at us, cocking his hips. "Say, you two look a little parched and in dire need of nature's true liquid refreshment!"

Drambooey stood poised, waiting for an answer, tucking his cane under his armpit. We were quiet, taking this in, wondering if we were being had, our attention diverted by this loon. My eyes drifted to the mirrors, searching behind us for anything out of the ordinary.

"Is this guy for real?" Jock finally asked me.

I reminded Jock, "Chachi did say to stop by here for a laugh."

"We exit on the count of three," Jock reminded me.

I cheated, opening my door on two. Jock grumbled and exited but not before the superstitious shit reached his quota.

"My, oh my. What a fine specimen you are!" Drambooey appraised me as I closed the door. I kept one eye on him, the other on the trailer. I held my backpack in my left hand, my right ready for the crowbar if needed. Beyond the Cheshire Cat grin, I noticed the man's hair was short, his skin smooth, his jawline clean shaven. Hell, he looked clean all over. Maybe his elixirs were the answer to desert glum. Or maybe he was hiding something.

Drambooey didn't hide his surprise when he spied Jock and slapped his knee. "Look at that! Wee man, you're most welcome here! There'll be no harsh words coming my way! Heck, I could give you a job today! Would you like to be my sidekick? Just joshing there!"

That stopped Jock. He was not amused and had second thoughts.

I concluded that the showman was like a desert flower; prim, colorful, and seemingly out of place. Curiosity got the better of me and I asked, "What you got?" I then wondered how the man came to be out here, by himself, and remain so soft and slender. He was ripe for attack by a Rogue. Unless this was under their control, this joker was easy pickings and my gaydar was going off.

"Whoo! The man is a questioner, right here I reckon!" Drambooey said to the skies, then sized me up with a squint, leaning forward. Then, wiggling his finger like he's got me, he stated, "That depends, oh sir, what it is you have in your fine possession?" My backpack was near empty but I was hauling a different precious liquid in the back of the El Camino.

With my own reveal, I hauled up a jug from the bed showing my hand. "Moonshine," I said, propping it on the roof, the semi-clear booze sloshing inside. I knew it would sell, even as an open container. Some of it was gone, courtesy of *moi*.

Drambooey licked his lips. "Would that be barrel cactus?"

Confidently, I stated, "Best to drink now. Not hold." I *heard* Jock rolling his eyes at my vintage wine reference.

"Well, step right up and sit a spell," Drambooey said and motioned us to follow with his cane. "Yes, my good man, we'll embark on a trade! Some folks say an eye for an eye, but in these parts, we say a glass for a glass! And dear fellow, a little nip of the catdaddy goes a long, long way!"

Drambooey excitedly shuffled to the camper and that bought Jock and I some trivial glances. We weren't going anywhere for a while so we might as well make the best of it. Jock commented, "If he starts speaking in tongues and juggling snakes, I'm out of here."

The quirky dude was frantic like a mad scientist and just as giddy. "Say, good men, that's a fancy ride, that one is! Is it supposed to be a car or a truck?" he asked.

Before I could answer, Drambooey slapped the trailer's wall and suddenly a plank of wood dropped and landed flat like a shelf. Inside the wall were jugs and containers of all types of liquids in what used to be a storage compartment. Now, it was a makeshift bar and he busily wiped it down with a rag, trying his best to make it all hospitable. Time was of the essence and he didn't want to lose our interest.

"You alone?" I asked him.

Nodding, Drambooey stated, "Yes, yes, please make yourself comfortable." A couple of plastic chairs were immediately dropped into place, facing the trailer as if a show was to be performed. Jock was checking low, under the trailer, searching for feet on the other side. We had a pretty good routine going here and I gathered that no one else was hiding in the hills.

Drambooey was a classic nutjob out to make a trade and nothing else, dancing on one foot to the next, brushing dirt off the furniture. You'd have to be, out there alone, but I was a betting man and this dude had to have some protection somewhere or something was up his sleeve. My guess was, business had been slow. Even Jock seemed at ease and for the first time and he actually walked in front of me.

"What are those?" Jock asked him, pointing to the containers in the wall.

"Well, shorty, it's my secret formula. It's from God's great creation and will cure all types of ailments. A spring not far from here, and only known to me, is chock full of vitamins!" Drambooey excitedly grabbed two glasses, spat inside both, wiped them and then reached for a container. "But don't you dare ask, as I will not pray tell!"

Jock turned to me and whispered, "Snake Oil Salesman" and I nodded *duh*.

The secret formula was poured into two glasses and handed to us. The liquid looked like water, probably from a well or a spring like the man admitted. We studied it like a fine wine, swirling and sniffing it, but neither one of us drank. Bits of leaves and dirt floated but nothing to get a tangent over. Beggars couldn't be choosers, right?

"Oh, very well," he said and gulped down a mouthful to prove it was safe. Seconds later, Jock eagerly did the same, some of it spilling over his chin. I tipped my glass to my mouth and swallowed a little. It tasted bland, convinced it was spring water and nothing else.

Wiggling his cane, Drambooey asked us, "Got a problem with your liver?"

I glanced at Jock. "My liver?"

Drambooey leaned forward. "Cleaned! Constipation got you down?"

"No..."

"Cleared!" Drambooey shrieked. The medicine man then cocked an eye and winked. "Erectile dysfunction? Charged!"

Slapping his hands together as if to get this moving along, he then tapped two chairs eager to get our company. "Fear not! The gas took away your past but it shall not claim your future!"

This guy could be a source of information so I'd need to pry on prior customers that had ventured this way, namely Ginn and his fun boys. Jock sat straight away, not moving the chair at all, but I cocked mine at an angle, splitting my view from the road to Drambooey's happy trailer. I wanted no surprises coming to us from either direction.

"Yes, sir," Drambooey smiled and took a seat as well, sliding in delicately, posturing as if the chairs were antiques. "I don't get many customers but when I do, I make them feel at home!"

Jock suddenly rose from his chair and Drambooey jolted as if his chair caught fire. "What is it, sonny? You can trust me," Drambooey asked, unnerved.

"Men's room," Jock said and puts his glass down.

Weary, I examined my glass more carefully.

Jock said to me, "It's not the liquid, Ted. I had been holding it in for a while. I was waiting for the next pit stop anyway."

"Well, little man, the desert is your oyster," Drambooey said and swept his arm out. "Just make sure you dig a hole. Remember, I have to live here." He winked at me, like one parent to another. Jock rolled his eyes and made his way around the camper.

Sitting there, I got the sense the man truly believed in his elixirs. A true salesman proud of his product despite the desert world we lived in. As the wind shifted, my nose tickled again with scents of lavender. The whiff of perfume wasn't lost on me. Whenever I caught a scent, it stopped me, taking me back to a time when smells were pleasant and attractive, just as it did with Song. His skin noticeably smooth, I surmised Drambooey had been doing well for himself, trading in simple water for the finer things such as cosmetics and other health related remedies. I wondered if he had ever taken in a performance by Song and her boys. Some of the scent I got from him was very similar.

Eyeballing my jug, he licked his lips. "Now, as for the trade..." he said, casually leaning forward with his hands to grab it. I blocked the jug with my leg and he backed off. "I thought we had a deal," he said, straight-faced and concerned. His voice crackled, losing the giddiness. It was whiny and not jolly. Where did the Snake Oil Salesman go?

Drambooey was an act. Grinning, I slid the jug to him with my leg and he sunk back into character. "Now," he said to me, nodding to the glass, "Is that not the best refresher there is?"

Pointing to the moonshine jug I shoved to him, I asked, "Won't you try it?"

"Oh, well, I never touch the stuff. Alcohol that is. I'll use it for trade, of course. And to light my fires. I spend many a day boiling my precious resources assuring they are right for human consumption! I discovered a spring not far from here, a secret spring with amazing remedies..."

"Enough with the water. Have you seen any Rogues?' I interrupted.

"Excuse me?"

"You heard me."

Tilting his head skyward as if the vast blue might jar his memory, his eyes fluttered and I saw that he wore dark makeup and long lashes. "I do believe I was paid a visit, quite possibly three moons ago, by a pair out for collection. For their warlord. Just a bit. To wet his beak."

"Taxes," I corrected him.

"Correct, but none since then."

"Has anyone else been through here last night or today?"

"No, you are my first customers in nearly a week," he sighed, losing the snarky dialogue. "This spot is not easy to find. Why, just the other day..."

Drambooey stopped talking. I heard a rumble and thought earthquake. I hadn't felt one in years but I felt no vibration at all. Drambooey's eyes lit up and he straightened suddenly, gawking back over the road like he saw a ghost. His mouth widened and I saw his teeth, white and even.

Alarmed, I turned and saw a black Jeep coming towards us, blue smoke belching out the rear. It was an older model with a lot of wear. The Jeep pulled up and parked directly behind the El Camino, blocking me from reversing out of the lot. Only one man was inside with no other vehicles following. The driver killed the engine and watched us, not making a move to exit yet, possibly studying us as we were of him.

Drambooey steadied himself. "My lucky day," he muttered to me. "Stay cool, okay?" Nerves got the best of him and he twitched his gentle fingers. Whoever this was clearly made him worried.

The Jeep door opened with a bang and the driver finally stepped out. Stocky and bald, he had a flattened face and nose that mimicked a bulldog. His attire was suggestive; shirtless under a leather vest while jeans and boots claimed his pudgy lower half. The slobby man wore some tattoos and piercings, like a middle-aged punk rocker trying to fit in at an eighties concert. Handcuffs dangled from his leather belt. Since this was the circus, one could assume these two were partners but Drambooey was beside himself, more jittery than before. I knew right away that the man in the Jeep was a Rogue.

The Rogue straddled the El Camino, whistling in admiration, even cupping his hands at the window to cut off the glare so he can peek inside. Running his hand along the fender soon after, the man pulled at his groin and spat, simultaneously burying his keys in his front pocket. A toothless grin flashed us as he walked up.

"Welcome my good man!" Drambooey said aloud, arms spread out to the Tattooed Freak. His voice cracked; his enthusiasm downgraded a few notches. Drambooey was about to have a coronary.

My backpack drew closer so I could reach the crowbar. The slob knew the car, pretending not to. He wanted me to be relaxed. Being a Rogue, he'd be armed and he was too far for me and my crowbar.

"Say friend," Drambooey said and slid Jock's chair over to meet the new customer. "What's your health worth? Won't you sit a spell and enjoy goodness that'll put you in the pink?"

"In the pink?" the Rogue asked, dumbfounded, stopping in his tracks.

"Just a silly phrase," Drambooey shrugged it off and dismissed his own axiom with a flick of his wrist. "I have some divine liquid refreshment, a pick-me-up guaranteed to give you a much-needed boost. That is all."

"A pick me up, huh?" the Rogue asked and hiked forward. "What's in it?"

Drambooey relaxed a bit and then patted the empty chair. "Sit, sit." He was quick with the rag again and wiped it down, slapping it against his thigh when he was done.

The Rogue was glaring at me as he rounded the chair and took a seat. Tats for death mostly covered his skin that included graves, skulls, a scythe, and a nuclear mushroom, as far as I could tell. Most were crude and random images of death and destruction inked by amateurs. He hadn't taken his eyes off me and he was taking me all in, up and down.

He reminded me of Polecat. Only a fatter, sloppier version but just as foul. Leering back, I downplayed his gay advances, showing no interest, but switched to assessing whether he was armed or not. While his see-through vest revealed most of his pudgy body as being weapon-free, I couldn't see what was at his back.

Clasping his hands together, Drambooey started in with his spiel. "I, of course, would inquire of a trade," he quietly mentioned but the response from the disheveled customer was a merely a wicked eye and a grunt as if bothered by nosy waiter. The Rogue seemed to be focused on me more than our fortuitous salesman.

Visibly nervous, Drambooey reached for a glass. "Nature's rectitude," Drambooey explained softly, still carrying on with the show, and poured from the same container Jock and I were served just minutes ago.

"That sweet car yours?" the Rogue asked me.

I didn't answer. My hand was now covering the claw end of the crowbar. So far, he hadn't seen it.

"That's one fine ride," he pointed out. "I'd say that sucker is probably a seventy-eight. Am I right?"

"Sure."

"Sure, huh?" he said and laughed. "What man don't know the year of his ride? What did you do, steal it?"

I winked at him. "As a matter of fact, I did."

The Rogue's smile went stale. His brow creased and he leaned forward. Drambooey sensed something was bound to happen and placed the glass in front of the man like a peace offering. Without taking his eyes off me, the Rogue took the glass, chugged it, and then gargled and allowed it to spill right back out all over himself.

"That shit is good," the Rogue stated as the liquid spilled over his chin, some dripping to his boots. Tilting his head, he muttered to me, "I could chug all night."

"What brings you to these parts?" Drambooey asked him, taking the empty glass from him.

"As opposed to what parts, Sissy Man?" he grumbled.

"Well, usually you Rogue types aren't around out here," Drambooey replied. "Not unless you've come to, you know, collect."

Returning to me, he said, "Maybe I come looking for a thrill."

Casually, I glanced away as if indifferent, taking in one last glance, searching for the rest of his gang. It was no accident he was there and he might not know that I know about the broadcast. Either way, he was there for me. "Man hasn't traded," I said to Drambooey and the empty glass he held. "Man's full of shit."

Drambooey's lips quivered. "Well, I'm certain a man of his convictions, would certainly honor..."

"What's it to you, Sweetheart?" the Rogue interrupted, looking at me again.

Nervous, Drambooey stepped up. "Now, fellas, we don't want trouble, do we? No trouble at all. I would not deny a man a drink and I am certain that repayment could come in another form."

"You got that right," the Rogue answered and his hand gripped the armrest and when I saw three letters on the back of his right wrist.

JKL

Drambooey saw it too. "That's an interesting tattoo. What does the JKL stand for?" he asked, trying to quell the oncoming fight.

"Jackal," the Rogue answered. "That's who I am."

"Sounds like an asshole name," I said.

"Ain't you a pistol," Jackal said and blew me a kiss.

The bear instantly rose from within. Planting my leg, I pivoted, and hoisted my crowbar up with my left, quickly shifting it to my right. Jackal was faster, however, somehow erupting from his chair like a spring with a gun produced from the small of his back. His chair toppled behind him and he slid back a step. I didn't anticipate that and now the man gained some distance between us, the gun proving the advantage when space was an issue. His trigger was suddenly pulled and the gun fired into the air as a warning shot, the deafening boom echoing off the walls of the hillsides. Drambooey shrieked, covering his ears. I froze on the spot knowing I couldn't cover the ten feet or so in time and was now staring down the barrel of an actual loaded gun, the light smoke curling off the end like a cigarette.

"Drop it, Ted," Jackal said to me, motioning downward with the gun. I did, reluctantly, and the crowbar landed at my feet.

"Such a blessing I was told to come back all this way. And to think I didn't want to at first. Thought it a waste of time. No way would Ted be this far back. What did he do, get lost?" Jackal laughed. "Whole gang is down yonder, waiting for you there, having their fun and little old me gets the rabbit."

Jackal unhooked his handcuffs and tossed them to Drambooey. "You, skinny feller, cuff him to the rear suspension." Drambooey didn't have to be told twice, shuffling quickly to the trailer, whimpering the entire time.

And then the Jackal howled.

I sat against the wall of the trailer, my right arm cuffed to a rocker arm under it. Drambooey hovered over me, whispering 'sorry' to me and it was sincere, even though the cuffs were convincingly taught and painful. He wanted no part of this and his hands shook badly. Jackal had his gun leveled at us a safe distance away. When he was done, Drambooey stepped back to show that I was immobile. Jackal grunted his okay, then scratched his groin with the gun.

I snuck a few glances at the desert behind us. So far, Jock had avoided the skirmish and Drambooey hadn't let on the little guy's presence either. Jock was safe and I know he'd hidden well. Word around the Rogue campfire suggested I was traveling alone. That was a good thing.

I took comfort knowing that I wouldn't be harmed. Ginn wouldn't permit it, per the broadcast. Torch said so too. I just needed to know if this halfwit was capable of following orders. I grew angry at getting caught again. Gritting my teeth, I found myself not remaining calm, but straining against the cuffs, feeling for them to loosen. The cuffs resisted as they should and my wrists hurt from trying. I felt myself beginning to lose it.

Bottles were suddenly tossed as Jackal harshly inspected Drambooey's inventory, making a loud, clumsy racket. Some bottles he shoved aside, others he visually inspected with a stare and a sniff. Finding my moonshine jug on the ground, he winked at me and lifted it high for cheers, taking a long, impressive slug. Hardly content, Drambooey himself rose to assist but Jackal shoved him back. A thunderous belch erupted and Jackal rubbed his stomach like he was growing bored. My backpack suddenly caught his interest and he hiked it high, unzipping it, and dumping the contents. What he found further jaded him until he removed my crowbar. He snickered as he yanked it from the quiver, turning it over for inspection.

Twirling it, he asked, "Serious? You fuck people up with this thing?"

"Uncuff me and find out," I offered.

"Gun is better," Jackal scoffed and pretended to hit Drambooey with it, which only caused the slight man to whimper and duck uselessly. Jackal laughed, then returned his attention to me, bending down, smacking the tool against his palm. "What to do, what to do?" he asked aloud. Biting his lip and humming, Jackal traced the crowbar and caressed my left side with my own weapon, the chisel end gliding from the small of my back, up to my shoulder, down my left arm, then back up again. It traveled down to my waist, stopping and starting, and I held my breath. Drambooey choked behind him, eyes filled with tears, and I feared he would blurt something out. My eyes bored into him to be quiet and he closed his eyes and nodded slightly.

When my tool reached my waist, it stopped, then gently lifted my shirt. "Goldarn. That explains it," Jackal snorted.

"Explains what, Sir?" Drambooey asked, looking over his shoulder as if to assist.

"Kevlar," he said, then rapped my tool against the vest. "No wonder you weren't picked off. Leatherneck's a sniper. Seen him pick off gophers a hundred yards out. Ginn never told us that. You sneaky devil you."

As he held the crowbar in his left, his right hand was exposed.

"Lower rung," I told him. "That's what Ginn calls you guys."

Jackal blinked. "The fuck you say that for?"

"Guess you suck if you don't have one of these." I showed him my scar on my right hand, trying to lift it high for him to see, spreading my hands apart as much as I could. I was hoping it would reinstall confidence in that Jackal wouldn't harm me. Ginn and I, after all, were connected.

He didn't feign surprise but he tried to fake indifference. My crowbar was then flung into the desert somewhere behind me and landed with a dull thud. "Yeah, well, you're dumber than me. Your soul is eternally damned. Mine? I can ask for forgiveness anytime. Right up until death. So, I'm gonna coast a bit, do the nasty shit we all wanna do, and like the good book says, beg for the almighty to look the other way just before my number is punched." He leaned forward. "So, do I still suck now?"

"You really believe that? You'll be forgiven?" I spat.

"Well, when the time comes, we'll see who takes the elevator up and who takes the elevator down." Jackal stood, then grabbed a hold of Drambooey's arm, forcing him to squirm at the touch.

"What do you want from me?" Drambooey asked, trembling, nearly going limp.

Jackal reprimanded him with a dull slap. "Shut up, Sissy Boy."

"You know why you suck?" I told him. "Ginn couldn't make a deal with you."

That stopped Jackal. "So?"

"So, it means you couldn't offer him anything, shit for brains. Think about it. You don't have a scar. That means you aren't worth squat.

You're just a tool, a minion, a loser. Even Torch knows you're a loser." Jackal seemed to ponder that with a touch of reflection and it was obvious he was not in good graces with the boss. Or maybe Torch for that matter. And then Jackal's demeanor changed and he grew irritated.

"You won't be thinking that in a few minutes," he sneered. "Besides, from what I heard, Torch doesn't have long himself. Maybe you two were cops together."

I ignored the last comment. "Be a real man. Untie me." I dared him.

"Please, good sir," Drambooey said, going back into the act, trying to wriggle loose. "Maybe indulge in another good concoction? I have a specialty hidden, only for the best customers."

Jackal had enough. "Shut your stupid quackery," he said and squeezed the slight man harder. The folds in the poor man's shirt crinkled and wound up under Jackal's fist. Drambooey went light on his feet and shrieked, "What are you going to do?"

"We gonna have ourselves a play date," Jackal answered.

Images flashed in my mind of that fateful day years ago. The horror I felt as a man was about to resume on yet another innocent victim. All because of me. That infuriated me more than seeking revenge and I struggled against the handcuffs, seething through gobs of spit. "Release him!" I shouted at Jackal. "Take me instead, you asshole! You're here for me!"

"Don't worry, Ted, your sweet ass is next. See, I'm a sucker for the skinny type. A two-pump chump so it'll be over quick. But you, you get the marathon," he stated and motioned for Drambooey to move. "Then Ginn can have you all he wants. I finally get to one-up the evil shitbird and he won't even know it."

"You suck!" I cried out. "You follow Ginn and that makes you a wuss! You know it, I know it! You take orders! You're a slave!"

Jackal laughed, deep from his belly. "Yeah, I suppose it is fucked up," he admitted, "But you don't know the power that man has."

"I'll tell him you hurt me!" I shouted.

"Then I'll have to earn that, right?"

They disappeared around the corner. Drambooey was resisting and squealing but Jackal simply laughed it off. He was too powerful for the slight man and the more he fought, the more that turned on the thug. I heard them enter the trailer on the other side and saw the home dip as they stepped into it. I did everything I could to get loose and began to secretly chastise Jock for not coming sooner. My muscles strained and numbness sat in. I was growling like an animal.

Jock rounded the rear corner with my crowbar. "I was squatting behind a boulder. I saw the Jeep come up so I stayed hidden," he said to me in a gentle voice, near a whisper. "I never pulled my pants up so quick."

After he handed my tool over, I wedged it between the cuffs and the rocker arm. It took two heaves, using some of my weight, but the cuffs snapped with a loud crack. Jock and I went immediately still, thinking Jackal must have heard, but the maniac was still whooping it up inside.

"The crowbar landed about twenty feet from me," Jock pointed out.

The rage inside me was tremendous. I avoided eye contact with my partner and never uttered a word. This was not his vengeance and I wanted him no part. Inside the trailer, a slap and a scream could be heard that only infuriated me further.

The bear growled within me. Inside the trailer, the Jackal howled.

Jock asked me, "You're going in there, aren't you?"

I shot Jock a look, repeating most of what I said to Polecat before he died.

"He's going to die badly."

CHAPTER THIRTY-TWO

Jackal was teeing off on Drambooey and every slap and punch carried a sickening thud of bruise-filled trauma. A curtain was drawn across the small hallway, a thin one at that, and even from the kitchen, I could see the two of them behind it in what appeared to be the bedroom at the far end. Drambooey sitting on something, maybe a bed, facing Jackal, his arms flailing, not being a deterrent. Jackal towered over his victim and mocked Drambooey with every strike. The barrage of punches then stopped, and I could see Jackal spin his victim around.

As I crept in, only the recollection of the man being armed with a gun stopped me from completely barging in. Jackal's attacks were loud enough to drown out my approach where I planned to end the one-sided affair but I couldn't lose my shit. Not yet, anyway.

Peeking around the curtain, I saw Drambooey bent forward on the edge of a bed a good six feet away, his chest atop rumpled blankets, his legs spread apart on the floor. While his pants were still fastened around his waist, there was no telling what would come next. Jackal was unbuckling his belt behind him but in front of me. He let his pants drop to the floor. While his gun wasn't visible, I couldn't see his right hand and I assumed he carried his gun there. Jackal became bare-assed in seconds, his dirty cheeks scarred, looking like two pitted moons.

With his left hand, Jackal caressed Drambooey's back, rubbing up and down, groaning in anticipation, his hips bucking, mumbling *ooh* and *fuck yeah*. He then tore at the poor man's pants, yanking at them, pulling them down to knee level, still with his left. His right hand was still nowhere to be seen.

"Yeah, now this is a party," Jackal stated as he shimmied the underpants down.

Drambooey was bare-assed himself now, his own curved and more bulbous, a softer white and more delicate. "Silky smooth! Dang, you have fucking nice skin! You're gonna get tore up!" Jackal shouted.

It was Jackal, though, who suddenly backed up in shock, looking sideways at his prey. "What the fuck is this?" he shouted.

And then, a female voice from the bed. "I'm sorry!" It was Drambooey, turning now and I saw the hair move, sliding to the side. A wig there and under it, dark hair.

Drambooey was a woman.

"You got goldarn lady parts!" Jackal shouted and pointed.

"I'm really a woman!" Drambooey cried. "Sorry, I didn't mean to trick you!"

"But you did!" Jackal cringed. "I can't have that!" He balled up his right fist and was about to strike when I threw open the curtain, ripping it from some of the rings that held it in place. Drambooey saw me and shrieked. Jackal saw her reaction, then jerked his arm outwards and under the blanket without turning around. His gun was there.

My crowbar smashed into his right arm, breaking the forearm instantly. Jackal wailed and fell forward, clutching his right arm with his left hand, partially landing on Drambooey. She quickly scuttled to get out, however, then slid and cowered in the corner of her bed under a blanket. Jackal, face down, moaned into a bedsheet and I saw the indent in his arm where I connected. Next to him was the gun. I snared that with the claw end of the crowbar and hurled it behind me. With my left arm and left knee, I pinned him down, then slammed my homewrecker down on his spine with a loud whump, and he arched, bawling, his head shaking vigorously. Drambooey shrieked herself but remained huddled there, too afraid to move.

"Get out now," I told her, calmly. "You don't want to see this." She locked eyes with me and understood. Seconds later, she was gone, having slid past me in a hurry.

Regaining some of his strength, Jackal lifted his head and turned to the side with a wry smile. "That's a big rod you got there, Crowbar Man," he said, straining. He didn't make a move to rise but just lay there. Sweat was rolling down his face.

"You enjoyin' this faggot?" he asked me. He then began to slowly rotate his hips. "Oh, yeah, you like this, huh? You like to fuck guys, right? Yeah, I can tell. We got us a little party here, don't we?"

Turning his head once more, I caught a glimpse of the man smiling seductively. "Why don't you bury the tip in there, just a little?" he asked through puckered lips.

The bear inside me erupted.

Later, I would recall swinging down hard, smacking his skull, and knocking him out. The rest were festive blurs, jabbing like a pitchfork, my right hand holding the claw end, my left hand on the shaft, aiming the chisel end right between his ass cheeks. Deeper and deeper my weapon went, my hands and tool becoming covered in blood and shit as Jackal's prostate exploded. Every thrust dug deeper into the unknown, opening up a wider slit than the last and I had created a large crevice as if boring into a slab of meat. All I knew was, I was wailing away, relentless with my quest to bury my tool into the rapist as far as it will go, not satisfied until the chisel end breached his mouth. Jackal woke suddenly and began to screech and wail, his hands flailing uselessly, trying to reach back and stop me. Thirteen jabs, maybe fourteen, and Jackal stopped screaming. Tiring, I continued the onslaught and swung like a miner hacking away at rock until I was pulled back by little arms. I sucked in long gulps of air and was led away with my arms at my sides. The last vision I had of the rapist was that of the sick fuck's face down on the bed and the huge crater between his legs. A mixture of red and brown fluid was flowing along my impaled tool to the floor.

"That's enough," the voice told me from behind and I turned to see

Jock standing there with a worried look. I barely heard him as I stumbled outside.

Jock's next words were, "He's been dead for over a minute now."

———————

They were whispering behind me, talking like a concerned family over a patient's medical condition and what the next steps would be. Words like *worried, unbelievable, insane*, and *lost it* surfaced. I was zoning, shirtless, sitting on a boulder behind the camper by myself. My arms and hands were a bloodied mess. None of the redness was mine.

"We need to go," Jock said to her.

"That would be best," Drambooey sighed. "But let me clean him first."

"Please do," Jock replied and I saw him duck back into the trailer.

I suddenly felt a chill and wetness from a damp rag. The water was cold and unnerving. Drambooey was behind me, wiping me down. The scent of lavender told me she was using a bar of soap and it smelled good.

I straightened and arced my back. The desert was quiet around us, only subtle grunts from inside the trailer could be heard. "Are you okay?" she asked me, holding the bloody rag in her hands. She still wore her snake oil salesman get-up, but she had parted with the wig. She had short dark hair and looked distinctly female now. Even her voice has settled into a softer, plainer version than the con man we first encountered.

"I'm fine," I mumbled although neither of us believed it. I had visions of striking at Jackal and I felt like I needed to do more. Drambooey sensed it and placed a firm hand on my shoulder.

"You did enough in there," she said.

I disagreed and contemplated going back inside.

"I still have some more to clean," she said. "But I want to thank you. I thought he was going to kill me."

"Anytime."

"Can I be honest though?" she asked, rinsing out the rag into a bucket. I saw that it was a dirty red with some bits of flesh and hair.

286

She came around and leveled with me. I saw she had light blue eyes, a slight nose, and the clearest complexion I had seen in a very long time.

"As evil as he was, he didn't deserve that," she said with a slight demure.

"Bullshit."

"I knew you would say that," she said. "But there isn't much left of him. He died horribly. I wish it had been quicker."

"Rapists don't deserve life. Any life."

She wrapped up, then fished out Jackal's keys from her pocket, handing them to me. "Not exactly a fun job getting these, but you'll need them to drive out of here. Your other ride doesn't look like it will go far."

I took the keys and studied them. Three of them in various shapes, one meant for the Jeep, but what captured my attention was something else there and I shook my head. The keychain fob; it had an image of a spastic, drooling, naked human-like creature with large teeth and one large middle finger, raised high, with Just Kidding Loser in lettering underneath, the J, K, and L in bold. It reminded me of the cartoonish Tasmanian Devil.

She touched it. "Demonic, I'd say. Who would want that as their fob?"

"JKL," I said and showed her.

"Hmn. I remember seeing that on his wrist."

My crowbar was led out of the trailer at arm's length by Jock as if it was poisonous. "So sick," Jock said with a disgusted face. Drambooey saw Jock struggle to carry it and tossed him a clean, wet rag and he wiped it down immediately.

"I finally got this thing out of him," Jock said to us. "I had to use my feet too as leverage. I think it was jammed between some bones."

"Come on. You're exaggerating," I said.

He gave me a look that could be deciphered as either awestruck or scared. "I got most of the smell out. I think." He then handed it to me. It looked remarkably clean.

"Thanks," I said.

"It looks like a bomb went off between Jackal's legs," Jock added.

Goddamn, right it did.

Drambooey gave him a look and he murmured an apology. "I'll go clean up. Get my things too," she said and walked off.

Jock watched her go then kicked the bucket, spilling the contents that flowed like a red river between grooves in the sand. He said, "We should be going. In case more Rogues show up."

Jock started in on our plan to leave, the direction we should head, and which car we should take if one at all. I barely listened, however, as I cradled my bully breaker and smiled at the vengeance I was able to reap.

The elevator went down.

"Are you listening to me?" Jock whined.

"No one is going to stop us," I said. "No one."

His eyes fell on my crowbar and he nodded.

I kept those babies sharp.

CHAPTER THIRTY-THREE

Stealing Jackal's Jeep boosted morale big time. That meant severing ties with the El Camino, however, but the rickety jalopy, noisy even at idle, would traverse desert terrain much better than a seventies car-truck equipped for asphalt. Plus, it was a boring black color, probably common, and not an eye-popping red. However, the prize was not without faults. Ripped seats, check, cracked windshield, check. Suspicious smells coming from the rear, double-check. All that I cared about was that Jackal's Jeep started and it did, on the first try. The hood rattled nonstop, but the fuel gauge looked generous and the large wheels said adios to roads if need be. That was all that mattered. Humping over the sand once we get closer to the 40 and 10 Freeways could be the best option. I slid the keychain fob off and tossed it before I climbed in. The less that reminded us of Jackal, the better.

Jock noted the Jeep was filthy inside as he climbed into the rear. Jackal didn't look like the type who gave a shit over grime and he certainly wouldn't have disinfectant wipes in the glove box. Blood, fur, bones, and empty moonshine jars rimmed with mold served as floor mats while above, the plastic dashboard was stained, faded, and cracked. From the middle console, Jock pinched a half-empty bottle of lubricating gel with a look of disgust and dropped it out the window, quickly wiping his hand on his pants as if germs would spread immediately. At the rear, two jugs were tied to the back, held by bungee cords, almost full. The Jeep was certainly not the El Camino, which I was sad to leave behind.

Earlier, we had pushed the El Camino behind Drambooey's trailer, hoping to buy some time and keep it from view from the road. It was heavy as hell and there wasn't a lot of cover to properly conceal it. There was no cliff to push off either. Not close, anyway. Maybe the Rogues wouldn't stop there and just drive past.

The sun was dipping in the west. The Jeep should make up for lost time and I was hoping we'd make the Salton Sea by nightfall. That was if nothing stood in our way – which seemed entirely improbable at this point. The mental map in my head suggested I got creative. The Jeep should allow us to do wonders.

My backpack occupied the empty seat behind me, the crowbar back in the quiver, shiny and clean. Jock had left the front seat for Drambooey on purpose, who I spotted outside her trailer, staring at her life gone awry. A life she had been accustomed to, surviving on wits and trickery. Holding her luggage in both hands, she looked like a passenger about to board a train, but her legs wouldn't budge. The ambiguity in the next chapter of her life was discouraging. I knew there would be hardships ahead. When I gently honked the horn, she jolted and snapped out of it, humbly making her way over.

Jackal's body was still in the trailer as I left it and she reluctantly entered it to gather her things, on the condition I didn't go back in myself. She wanted to burn the trailer, but I advised her not to. Torching it would only send Rogues in this direction if they hadn't thought of circling this way by now anyway. We didn't need that attention that fast. If we buried him or left him in the desert, birds would flock to the corpse one way or another, and little old me wasn't about to offer the rapist a decent burial. In addition, it was a mess in there and no one wanted to touch him. We decided to leave Jackal where he died and get a move on. Time was a wasting too. I had a plane to catch.

Gone was the persona of a wacky salesman. Drambooey was all woman now, hair nicely brushed, she dressed in a shirt and jeans. However, she was sad and tired, shoulders slumped as an unknown journey lay ahead. I was guessing what was in her luggage were all the belongings she needed from the heap of a mess I saw inside. She arrived at my side of the Jeep to talk but said nothing.

"You okay?" I asked her.

Shrugging, she sighed at her trailer. "That was my home."

"You had me fooled, Drambooey," I told her. "I dig the dress up and the act."

"My real name is Iris," she confessed sedately, but that quickly turned to shame. "I was raped a few times as a woman. To think, it almost happened again. I thought I was safer pretending to be a man."

The empty front seat was the hint for her to join us but she didn't catch on for some reason. I sensed some reluctance on her part but clearly there was no choice. She wouldn't take the El Camino, even if it started. She wouldn't get far. She swayed in the gentle breeze, contemplating her choices, and I realized she was leaving a legacy she built. I was afraid she didn't really want to leave the joint and roll the dice.

"Hop in, Iris. I can't leave you out here," I told her which almost came across like an order.

"Thank you," she said and smiled. Suddenly, she was much happier.

She'd be dead if the Rogues swung by and I was one hundred percent positive they would, at some point, venture this way. Jackal was sent here to search this road and maybe this fun house outpost. No sign of the slob returning would send a small force along this route soon to be checked out. Man or woman, if Jackal's body was discovered here, no amount of torture and cruelty would be good enough for the hysterics of the Rogue horde finding their comrade dead, missing the entirety of his own ass.

As she planted herself in, dropping her luggage between her legs, she became visibly irked by the mess inside. Compared to what I saw inside her trailer, I thought she'd assume it was home. "I'm normally very clean," she said to me. "I had to think like a man to survive like a man. That's why my home was trash."

Giving her a look, she caught herself and corrected. "I meant, if it had been too clean inside, some people may have taken advantage of me. It was easier to keep dirty."

"Rogues will come looking for their buddy," I said. "They won't be in the mood for spring water."

"The Rogues know who I am," she said. "They won't stop, will they?"

"No, unfortunately not."

"Can we go now?" Jock spoke up from the rear. He shifted side to side as if bugs were crawling around him.

"What's going on back there?" I asked Jock.

"You don't want to know," Jock replied. "Also, there's a lady present."

Popping the clutch, the Jeep jerked in reverse back to the road, and both of my fellow travelers whiplashed, complaining out loud as I braked soon after.

"Sorry," I admitted. "Clutch is a bit sensitive."

We took the road heading in a south east direction. As we rounded a corner, I spied the 40 Freeway in the distance, but we had many more turns ahead of us before we got there. The ride was as firm as the steering was stiff and I wondered how this rust bucket ever rolled off a dealership lot in the first place. I had to slam the gear into second and third was a grinder. Fourth was fine and I gently kept the speed to forty again, hoping not to shift too much. The wheel pulled to the left so I had to use my right and pull opposite. It drove lopsided. What a pile of junk.

"Alignment is off, brakes are shot, the suspension is iffy, and the engine feels weak," I informed the others. "But all in all, it's still a shitty car."

"I noticed," Iris said and surveyed the rest of the vehicle, sticking her tongue out and making a *blech* sound. "My old boyfriend had a Jeep once, he liked to take me off-roading. Taught me how to drive in it too. Boys and their toys." She rolled her eyes and fingered the crack in the dash.

Something was missing. There was no CB radio in the Jeep. Maybe Jackal wasn't in touch with Ginn and the others as much as I thought. That could buy us more time and I settled back thinking maybe I won't have to go heavy footed. Iris glanced out the window, taking in what I believed was a last look at the surroundings of her former life. The familiarity of the hills, streams, wells, and views. She couldn't return and would probably be hunted forever now. A name change took top priority. The Rogues would find Jackal and she'd get some of the blame.

Feeling bad, I gently touched her hand. "I apologize for the fiasco that happened back there. That man was looking for me."

She squeezed my hand back. "Yes, I realize that."

I thumbed behind me. "Jock and I only planned to stop for a quick drink and let the engine cool down. Chachi told me about your place."

"Chachi?" she asked.

Oh, shit. I named the kid that. "Kid back in Kelso."

She searched her mind and slowly shook her head. "I don't know who you're talking about."

"Maybe thirteen, wears a bandana?"

"Sorry."

"Well, you don't want to go there anymore," I said and told her what had happened. She listened and shook her head in disgust when I was done.

Rounding more hills, Jock made fake barf sounds. I got the hint and slowed a little, fighting the steering and easing off the gas.

"Seems kind of remote up here," I pointed out.

"Bad spot for business anyway," she confided. "You were my first customers in over a week. I'll find another spring. I'm quite good at it. If you know where to look, there's water everywhere in the desert. Same with food. Ever had chuckwalla stew?"

Never heard of it. "Chuckwalla? What's that?" I asked.

"Lizard that looks like a gray iguana. Stocky, big old fat things you can find in the rocks up here. No shortage of them. They wedge themselves in the rock and inflate themselves to stay stuck there when threatened. Nothing a sharp stick can't handle. I sauté the meat in honey mesquite, brings out a sweet taste."

"Honey mesquite?" Jock asked from the back.

"Large green bush with yellow bean pods," Iris answered and used her fingers to show the approximate size and shape.

"Is that what those are called?" Jock says. "Huh. I've seen them around."

I piped in with, "I dig rattlesnake."

Iris shook her head and frowned. "Meat's too tough for me. Scary things too. Only when they got too close to my trailer did I kill them with a shovel."

A pothole bounced the Jeep and we all took the hit. She gripped the door and looked over. "Where are you headed? Hope it's not like this the whole way."

"South," I said.

"Where south?"

"I need to get to the Salton Sea but I'm not sure which way to go. I was there a few years ago, but I walked and found it on accident. Never drove."

"Salton Sea?" she perked up. "Why go there?"

I brought her up to date from the last day or so, leaving out the parts of Ginn and his band of fun boys. The wind howled inside the Jeep and I had to nearly shout to her. Iris' hair tossed around and she spent half the time smoothing it off her face as she listened. On the conclusion of me going to the vast salty lake to rendezvous with the plane to meet my family, she turned back to look at Jock.

"Unrelated," I told her and she smiled. Jock didn't hear it over the wind coming in and he was content to look out over the sand. "He's just tagging along."

"Why?" she asked.

"I don't know. Bored I guess."

"I can help you find the Salton Sea," she said. "I grew up in Palm Springs. We used to go there and drink beer when we were teenagers. I can show you where to cut through to the 10 Freeway too."

"Good. Lead the way," I told her, feeling confident, but when I glanced at her, she had gone sullen and quiet all of a sudden.

"What is it?" I asked.

She wouldn't say and I think I caught on. I reminded her that her life was in disarray now and here I was, boasting of finding a plane to take me away from all of this. I wanted to reassure her that the plane could take good people. I was convinced of that, but that might be too much for her. There were too many unknowns for her to grasp, being a woman alone out alone in the desert the direst of them all. Then I realized she was used to bargaining and trading. She was offering help for me and I was only driving her away from all she had known with nothing else to offer up until this point. Cheap on my part. I placated the situation by reaching back and smacking Jock on the leg.

"Backpack," I told him. He clued in right away and handed it up front to me. I slid it to her and she took it. "Take whatever you want," I told her.

Smiling, she unzipped it and poked around inside. "Anything? Are you sure?"

"We'll trade. Directions to the sea for whatever is in there," I said. "I won't need it anyway."

Her hands dove in and shuffled around. She yanked up a can of corn and a can opener. "You can do better than that," I insisted. While food was mostly gone, given away to Song and her boys, and the majority of the precious moonshine left behind with Chachi and the El Camino, I know I still had some crap in my backpack I wouldn't need.

"I'm starving," she said.

"Then let's eat," I replied.

After Jock worked the can opener, we all shared the can with a long spoon. Iris resumed her shuffling in-between bites and plucked out a bag of batteries. "You said anything, right?" she asked. I nodded. I had no use for them anymore. Not where I was going. If they can fly planes, I was sure they were well stocked with Double-A's.

"Can I have these?" she asked. "Really?"

I shrugged. "I'm more of a 9-volt guy."

She bent down and popped her suitcase open. Besides clothes, there was a microphone and karaoke machine inside. She flipped open the lid and tucked in the batteries. Giddy, she closed the lid and switched on the mic. At first, there was a squeal, like interference.

"Testing, testing, one, two, check, check," she spoke into it. Her voice resonated in our car. The road ahead flattened out and we'd left the hills behind us. The 40 Freeway loomed dead ahead.

"Step right up, Ladies and Gentlemen!" she said, the voice loud and clear, broadcasting to us and the desert. "Bear witness to Drambooey's Magical Liniment known to cure all ailments and illness! Snake bites, frost bites, you be the first to bite back!" She then smiled.

Jock and I did as well.

We had been making good tread for some time, traversing an old dirt road and avoiding any major routes covered in asphalt, but not without some headaches. Potholes and rocks swarmed and we jarred with every jolt. The can of corn rattled on the floor, empty, and I wished there was another one. Iris said only a can of asparagus was left and we all made a face. Cold asparagus? Was that any good? Song took all the good stuff I had, but she needed it more than I.

The bumpy ride continued for an hour, open and clear, the course twisting like a rally car track, sometimes precariously so. Small hills surrounded us once we got off Homer Road just before the juncture to the 40 Freeway, staying clear of the underpass which would no doubt have either spotters or drifters there that could have possibly delayed us. She had directed me to cross the freeway about a mile away from there, steering around a large gap of abandoned cars and smashing through a dilapidated wood fence on the other side.

We managed to stay on course in a southerly direction, finding the new passageway that ran parallel to Homer Road on our left. The road had no name, just a side deviation from a paved road that hung close to the freeway. We saw no Rogues thankfully, nor any other running vehicles the entire time we drove. It was as if we owned the desert, the lone inhabitants of a dwindling population, and it was smooth sailing ahead. During the quiet times, when the conversation calmed and the wind hollered, thoughts began to swirl in my head on my impending reunion. I could picture the Cessna parked near the sea, the Doctor checking her watch, patient that I was coming and content to wait. I imagined it fully fueled, door open, she and the Pilot playing cards, maybe gambling a little bit on my arrival time. A pothole snapped me out of it and I immediately checked the rearview mirror and became unhappy with the dust cloud we were creating. Some cause for concern, but the early evening sun was lower in the west and darkness would hide that. I peeked at Jock; thankfully I received no cynical comments from the little guy in the back. He just hung on, one hand gripping the roll bar next to him, the other tight on his seat belt. It was windy for him but he didn't seem to mind. I saw him on more than one occasion closing his eyes, feeling the gust and sun on his face. He peeled back his coyote mask too so it wouldn't flap annoyingly against his head.

Iris knew the area well and informed me the quickest route would be to take Dole Road and head south. Along the way, she fingered old dirt bikes trails as if she was there yesterday. She had an old boyfriend who used to drag her out there with his own Jeep, a model not much older than the ride we were in. They'd ride all day, camp, drink, and fire guns, she admitted. That was before she moved to LA to be an actress. I glanced at her, raised an eyebrow, then nodded. The snake oil salesman routine was Oscar worthy.

"Do I look familiar to you?" she asked me at one point during the ride.

I shrugged. "Not that I know of."

"I was on TV," she confessed. "Soaps, sitcoms, even did some work on the Disney channel."

My boys used to watch the Disney channel but I never paid much attention. She still didn't look familiar. "That helped you play the part of Drambooey I bet," I remarked.

"I was known as a character actor. Lots of small roles, did some commercials too. This one show I did for Disney was about a kid who worked with his Dad at a circus. We did ten shows before it was dropped by the network. I played the part of the mind reader with a crystal ball. The boy would come to me about halfway each show and ask me what was troubling him. I would help him *see* the answer because I was all worldly and all knowing. Truth is, we told him some basic discipline to follow to set a good example for the kids."

"What was it called?" I asked.

"Circus Frank. Like Circus Freak, but the kid's name was Frank." She said that and laughed. "It was my major break besides being recognized for a soap commercial."

"You were on Circus Frank?" Jock asked from the rear. Leaning forward, he turned to look at her closer. Iris lit up, blinking her eyes like a starlet.

"You saw it?" she asked him. No doubt, that was the first time she could talk freely about her past life in a very long time. Her expression flashed a tinge of excitement having played the part of actress, playing pretend in the fairy tale world of television of old, for money and fame. Now, she did it for survival, making do trading water, eking out a living as a man and fooling the crowds that could have turned on her at any moment.

"Oh, hell yeah," Jock admitted. "It was a good show too."

Figures, Jock knew about it. Put him on par with my boys. Between the Star Wars stuff and TV, they could huddle in a room for hours. "Thank you," she responded and turned back, smiling now, proud that she was remembered.

Jock shifted closer. "Why was it canceled?"

"Ratings," she said. "We did good the first show, the pilot, then it dropped off after that. It was fun while it lasted."

"Report," a voice suddenly said, a man's voice, and it came from nowhere. "Jackal, come in. Over."

Like every horror movie, we three all looked at one another in astonishment just before the big reveal. "Where the hell did that come from?" I asked them.

Iris looked stunned while Jock rocketed skyward, grasping the roll bar above his head, peeking and twisting in every direction, checking our surroundings as the wind battered his costume. We all heard the voice, its eerie surprise unexpected and distressing, but where did it come from?

"See anything?" I asked Jock, checking my mirrors myself, seeing only open desert but now the dust clouds billowing behind us was large and massive. I shifted down to third, and we slowed, hoping to lessen the dead giveaway.

"No," he cried out, his voice tinged with alarm, and he dropped down again, now searching the back seats. "I can't figure it out. Do you see a CB radio up there?"

I scanned the interior again, seeing nothing. "No CB, no radio, no old car phones. Beats the heck out of me."

"Why aren't you responding, fuck nuts?" the mysterious voice then asked. It was slightly muffled and tinny. A broadcast of some kind.

"I heard static that time," Iris stated. She opened the glove box and found it full of trash but no radio.

"Check under the dash on your side?" I asked her. "Maybe one that isn't visible?"

From behind, Jock dove under my seat and came up with a walkie-talkie. A red light was on. He handed it to me, his hands shaking. I stared at it and slowed the Jeep to a crawl. It was a walkie-talkie alright, the battery very much alive inside.

"Ted?" the voice asked.

My heart leapt up to my throat and I instantly slammed on the brakes. Jock and I froze instantly. Iris sat there with her mouth open. Laughter erupted on the other end of the walkie-talkie. Deep, profound, guttural laughing. It lasted a good five seconds and then the voice came back.

It was Ginn. Calling me.

"You're good, Ted," Ginn confided. "My bad for sending an idiot to find you."

"How does he know?" Jock asked, worried. He popped his coyote head back on and swiveled, looking for any sign we were being watched or followed.

"Behind us?" I asked Jock out loud.

"No, nothing! The sides are empty too! I don't see anyone!" he cried.

I was about to toss the walkie-talkie out when Ginn suddenly chimed in. "You can't escape me, Ted. I know where you are. Driving south in that Jeep, heading to the Salton Sea. Nice piece of work you did on your old boss, by the way. We found him an hour ago back in Kelso."

Iris looked alarmed. "Ever heard of a dude named Ginn?" I asked her. She didn't reply. I couldn't decide my next step. I felt stuck. Somewhere, Ginn was out there and the asshole was toying with me.

"The scar is a dead giveaway," Ginn said. "Everyone knows it, everyone knows you made a deal with me. I assume you heard my broadcast over the CB in my precious El Camino. If you don't turn yourself in, you will be hunted down. I believe you know all about the pets I carry with me."

"What does he mean? Pets?" she asked silently.

"Boars," Jock squealed from the rear. "Big ones. Scary."

Iris touched my hand. "What will you do, Ted?"

"You remember that fateful night at my hotel, don't you?" Ginn interrupted. "How that scar came to be. We made a deal, Ted, and you know it. I aim to collect."

Anger flooded my thoughts of how close I was to finding my family for the first time in years. And why a madman from my past was hell-bent on finding little old me.

Suddenly, I couldn't make sense of where I was. The dashboard in the Jeep was fuzzy. Waves of heat wafted off the hood outside the windshield. How could this happen? Why was he doing this to me? Why was he trying to stop me? Who sent him?

"There was no deal!" I shouted at the walkie-talkie, gripping it so hard that the plastic began to crack. Ginn hadn't heard me as I had yet to press the talk button but I was tempted. Iris shook my arm trying to get me to let it go. I couldn't hear her but she was talking to me. Finally, she clasped her hand over mine, that being the one that held the walkie-talkie.

"Turn it off," Iris said to me, concerned.

Tilting the walkie-talkie, I opened my palm and saw the scar once again. The skin was lifted, uneven, crisscrossing my palm, the line linking me to my past. A permanent reminder of an oath I never agreed to.

"Throw it away!" Jock shouted from the rear.

"End this madness, Ted," Ginn said softly over the speaker finally. "You owe me. You know it. I demand to collect my share as I should have long ago."

"Just get rid of it!" Jock yelled.

"Please let go, Ted," Iris said to me, calmly. "Whatever he's talking about, it's not worth it. You'll be okay."

I hurled the walkie-talkie like a baseball player, smashing it into a rock next to the Jeep, breaking in two. Jock and Iris breathed sighs of relief. I slunk in my seat, somewhat embarrassed. Ginn was getting to me.

"I didn't think you'd let go," Jock cried. "What the heck is wrong with you?"

"Go easy on him," Iris said to Jock. "We all have our demons."

"Sorry," I managed to say to both as I sat back up. "Can we go now?"

Iris and Jock looked at each other. "Lead the way," Iris said and Jock patted my shoulder. I popped the clutch and we jerked forward, the Jeep's wheels spinning in the dirt. We drove in silence for a few minutes. From the corner of my eyes, I caught the two of them sneaking glances back at me. I didn't blame them, I was a mess. I noticed the road began to fade right and Iris grew concerned, lifting herself in her seat.

"Wait," she said, grabbing my arm, sitting back down. "We have to change course. Find another route."

"Why?" I asked over the loud wind.

"Ginn said he knows you're going to the Salton Sea so he's probably over on Dole Road." She then stood up in her seat, the wind buffeting her hair. She was staring westward, in the direction we were heading. "I think we're heading there the way this road goes. It probably meets up there."

"We don't want Dole Road, do we?" I asked.

She quickly sat down. "He'll ambush you there. He knows you have Jackal's Jeep and that puts us somewhere behind him. I'm sure Ginn is there on Dole Road."

I was at a loss. "Are there other roads?"

"Yes, but they are way out of the way. Let me think."

Remembering from when we came, I suggested, "What about Homer Road? The one we were on earlier? I saw that it headed south."

Iris shook her head. "Too far out of the way now. It also heads off in a south east direction. It would take you way off course and you'd have to circle back."

The fuel gauge looked like it would support such an endeavor. Time would be lost though, yet would still fare better than an ambush.

"Ooh. I have a better idea," she said and pointed. "Turn left up ahead." Her eyes lit up and she practically jumped from her seat. She even did a small fist pump. Around the next hillside, I saw no road yet a bright glare caused me to wince and turn my head.

All I saw was flat and white.

"Salt flats," Iris said. "They won't expect it."

CHAPTER THIRTY-FOUR

Just driving across the salt flat gave me hypertension. It looked as if we were driving across a frozen pond, honeycombed with snow drifts and jagged edges that cracked and buckled as the tires sank through the top layer of crust. Not knowing what was below the top layer, nor knowing how deep it was, was unnerving.

The wind had picked up blowing particles inside the Jeep like light snow. When it landed in your eyes, it stung, so I leaned towards the center of the Jeep to shield myself from the open windows. Iris did the same and managed better than I, she had two hands to cover herself. Jock plugged his nose and kept his head down so his coyote skull stared straight ahead at me, the perpetual smile of the dead animal mocking at our latest venture.

The salt literally smelled awful too, like musty salt in a wet container you might find in the back of a closet. It was like sand only bigger, clumpy, and crunchy.

"Can you eat it?" Jock asked Iris loudly.

She turned around, shielding her face. "What? The salt?"

"Yeah," he nodded. "Is it edible?"

"I don't know. Most of the grains are larger than table salt. I think it needs to be broken down more."

"The Doctor told me they use salt from some salt flats," I said, turning to face Jock. "Wherever they are, they need this."

Jock then asked, "Where does the salt water come from?"

Iris mentioned, "It could be runoff from the Salton Sea. That's full of salt."

I got my hopes up; that meant we were close.

Surprisingly, we sped through the salt flats in good time. Iris' plan was genius; most vehicles could not make the trek as they would bottom out and that probably kept Ginn out. The mud alone under the sand sheets was slippery too, you'd need large wheels to plow through and I don't know if Ginn had any vehicles at his disposal with eighteen-inch rims and good tread. We lucked out with the Jeep.

I kept watch over the hills to our left and the rearview mirror. Iris took front and Jock scanned the hills to the west towards Dole Road where supposedly Ginn would be waiting with unwelcome arms. I doubted whether he'd head off to the Salton Sea straight away. He knew we were behind him by virtue of me in Jackal's ride and only so many roads led there. He didn't know where to go once he got to the Salton Sea.

Jock tapped Iris' shoulder. "Where were you when the gas hit, Iris?"

"Funny you should ask," Iris replied. "I had a small role for a Lifetime movie in Las Vegas. We wrapped up shooting and I was heading back to LA when it hit. I had just managed to escape Vegas too and I was stuck on the 15 Freeway with the rest of the traffic." She then paused. "It was brutal."

I wondered if we crossed paths before. "Where did you go after?" I asked her.

"Here, there, nowhere. Small groups came and went. Found love once, strangely, with a man I met, stranded like the rest of us. He took care of me, but he died of an unknown illness and all I could do was comfort him during his last hours. Decided to be by myself after that. Less chance of getting sick."

"You were lucky you didn't catch it," I offered.

"Yes," she said with resignation. "Lucky me." She bit her lip and looked off. A tear rolled down her cheek and she wiped it.

"The Blue Flame," Jock said aloud, changing the subject. "That

Rocket Car did over six hundred miles per hour over the salt flats. Set a land speed record back in the seventies. But the salt flats were firmer than this stuff."

I wished we were in the Blue Flame.

We exited the Salt Flats much to our relief and found a road carved years ago by campers and RV'ers. A sign we passed had said 'Joshua Tree National Park 10 miles' and the telltale trees reminded me we were closer to my goal.

The Joshua trees themselves were used to getting robbed. *Stick 'em Up* someone must have said to them once long ago and they held that pose, their limbs cocked at angles and facing towards the sky, lest they get shot. Jock aimed his finger like a gun at them as we drove past and squeezed off two rounds.

During the last hour, I had finally opened up to Iris and told her all about the plane and the Doctor and the whole ride up to meeting her. At one point, I hinted that my marriage took an unexpected turn and that I had been set up with bogus photos of me with another woman. That took a lot of out me, I hadn't admitted that to anyone in years, since Matias and Luke. Jock perked up behind me, eavesdropping, probably growing pissed that I hadn't said as much to him. Maybe I needed a woman's perspective.

It was dusk and my concern was traveling at night. The moon wasn't up yet. "I don't know if I should put on the headlights," I told them. "Maybe we should camp for the night."

"We aren't far from the Salton Sea now," Iris said and then touched my hand. "I could take the Jeep and head east, draw them away."

"Take the Jeep east?" I asked, missing something. "Aren't you coming with us?"

"That would be selfish of me," she said.

"Why?"

With a serious and calming tone, she exclaimed, "This is your journey to find your family. I don't know why you weren't with them, but you do. You started this and now you have to end it. More importantly, you have to realize that greed shouldn't dictate who you are."

"Yeah, I messed up. I get it," I sulked and slowed the Jeep to a stop.

She was gentle with her words. "Just because you felt that you had to escape doesn't mean you actually have to follow through with it."

"Are you suggesting I set myself up on purpose?" I asked.

"We all have urges to make better for ourselves and our loved ones and sometimes, they two are confusing. If you put yourself in that bind, you are responsible for your actions."

"I need to make things right," I admitted.

Iris smiled and patted my hand. "Good," she said and then began getting ready. "The moonshine jugs in the rear looked full. There should be enough for me."

I then noticed the fuel gauge. "Oh, right." It was low but from what was still stocked behind us, she could make good tread.

"What's east?" Jock asked her.

Iris tuned around. "I'm actually heading down to Mexico. I'll turn right in an hour and head south to the Sea of Cortez. I heard there's a little town that escaped much of the gas, near the mouth of the Colorado River. I forget the name but I'll find it."

Jock sounded worried. "You haven't been there?"

"No," Iris said. "But I'm told its wonderful. Filled with kind, generous people like me. Call it a pilgrimage."

"That sounds like a great place," Jock offered. "Maybe we should consider that."

Iris had a good plan as Ginn knew we had the Jeep and he'd be searching for it. If she led them away, it could buy us more time. We still had a hike though and it was getting dark. I emptied the two jugs of moonshine into the Jeep's tank for her.

I overheard Jock asking Iris about the town in Mexico and she said, "These men came to my trailer talking of the town. There's food from the sea, water from the river, places to worship, a library, and a clinic. Many people speak English too."

"Sounds too good to be true," Jock said.

"I know. I declined that time but they said I was always welcome.

That was a few months ago," she stated. "Now that my trailer is gone, it's time for me to find out."

"Turn the key," I said to her as I walked up. "How much you got?"

Iris slid into the driver seat and jerked the key. "Tank says three quarters full. Plenty," she noted, pointing at the fuel gauge.

"You sure that's enough?" I asked.

Iris gave a thumbs up. "I can hoof it if need be. Wear my disguise and pretend to be a man again."

"Stay on the dirt roads as much as you can," I replied, then dug into my pocket and handed her Jackal's gun. "And take this."

"You don't need it?" she asked me, nearly holding it as if it was infected.

I turned to Jock and he shook his head for me. The little guy then stepped out of the Jeep, although I felt like he wanted to stay in it.

Iris put the Jeep in gear, blew us a kiss, cranked the wheel, and shot off down a small slope. The dust kicked up and soon, one could only see the top of the Jeep as it blasted through the desert sprawl.

And just like that, she was gone.

CHAPTER THIRTY-FIVE

Squatting in a dry riverbed, with low-lying cover, I couldn't help but think we were definitely up shit creek. We were headed south no matter what, paddle or no paddle, and I wanted to brace Jock that the eventual confrontation was near at hand. He seemed to take it in stride, but I could tell the option to go with Iris was the better choice for him.

The wind picked up and cooled us down. The moon was rising in the west, still full. Leaning on the small sandy bank, sipping brownish water we found just moments ago, I felt vulnerable for the first time being on foot but kept my optimism at a high level. I had used my small shovel to dig in the hard dirt and found some murky water about two feet below the surface and scooped out a few handfuls for our canteens.

Jock, in the meantime, caught a toad. It struggled in his hands, pushing and nudging to get out between his fingers. Webbed feet suddenly flickered from his palms and I saw the thick muscles in its brown legs. Jock said he was going to keep it as a pet but thought better and gently put it back down. The toad quickly hopped behind a rock and crawled under a small opening. I was secretly thinking of barbequed frog's legs and pretended to lick my lips. Jock grew disgusted and waved a no-no finger at me.

I rose from our rest stop and stretched. We could make up some ground at night as the moonlight would provide some good visibility for us.

What a day! We started out at the newly abandoned Playhouse, ran into Chachi and Gruff at Kelso, had the run in with the tatted freak at Drambooey's trailer, crossed some smelly salt flats, and were now trekking on foot with the finish line so close. Iris left us an hour ago and I wondered if she made the right turn towards Mexico okay. I liked to think she did.

We got moving again, following the creek bed as it took lazy turns heading the direction we wanted. The Joshua Tree National Park was to our right, small hills to our left, and flat land ahead. It was like a straight shot to redemption as if the hills parted for us like the Red Sea.

Make your way to the Salton Sea. Find the place of judgement. If you are truly worthy, head north and you'll find redemption, the Doctor said. Redemption. I still hadn't figured that part out.

"We should turn back and follow Iris," Jock suddenly said behind me as we leapt over small rocks. "She seemed happy where she was going."

The Shoeman had come from there as well, I recalled. Something about whales being a good omen. Sighing, it did sound tempting, as was the stay at Coppertown, but I shook those memories free. "The Salton Sea is just head. We're almost there," I reminded him. The air seemed to have shifted and I thought I caught the scent of more salt. I was willing to bet this creek bed and the sea were tied together.

"That place in Mexico sounded awesome though," Jock piped in. "They speak English too."

"They all sound good," I said. "But I can't eat tacos every day."

Jock then declared, "At least there isn't a lunatic waiting for us there."

"Ah, the dude doesn't know where we are," I said. "Even if he did, the sea is huge. No way would he find us."

Jock caught up to me and pulled on my arm. "Tell me about the deal."

"What are you talking about?" Playing stupid should have quelled the upcoming questioning, but he didn't get the hint and I didn't want to divulge.

"You know."

"There was no deal," I said sternly. "Got it?"

"Humor me," Jock then replied. "Tell me the story. I'll decide."

I stopped and faced him. "Fine. You want to know what Ginn did to me? He helped me fuck up my marriage. He helped me get the job I always wanted, made me rich, got me some drugs, and framed me for having an affair. Ginn was simply a concierge at the hotel I always stayed at; he'd call me with cheap offers, free comps, and a suite to die for. But then he screwed me over." Jock listened intently as if studying the scenario, maybe reliving it with me. I ended my preamble with, "And then we shook hands. Supposedly."

Quickly, he demanded, "Tell me about the handshake."

I opened up the palm of my hand. Staring at it this way and that, he then lifted it higher to see in the moonlight. The scar was there, as it always was. I confided with, "His index finger is long and sharp. He slit my palm without me knowing. I was bleeding, so was he."

"Gruff had this on his hand as well," Jock noted, pointing to my scar. "I saw it when we were loading him on the handcar. He must have made a deal too."

"Ginn was a popular guy," I shrugged. "He could get you whatever you wanted."

"So, your deal was, he continues to help you live a richer life in exchange for what? Your soul?" Jock asked, cocking his head as if studying me.

"Soul," I laughed. "Give me a break."

"Well, then, what did he want in return?"

"It was drugs at first. Anti-biotics, vitamins, all for his future army, I finally figured out. But the last half, he didn't say," I said. "He refused any sort of payment."

Jock didn't believe me. "What did he say? Must have been something."

"He said he wanted something precious of mine," I admitted, not looking at him.

"Your soul," Jock repeated.

I continued to walk. "I have no idea. Dude is so out there."

Jock then piped in but not moving. "In some cultures, a handshake is a contract. A blood handshake means even more."

This was a conversation I didn't want. I was in no mood to debate the proper etiquette of a handshake and folksy meaning. "So what if some religious group or traditionalist faction says a handshake is binding? Big effing deal. This was the land of lawlessness now; no court would uphold any law that supported that anymore. There's no judge to bang his gavel. No lawyer to scold me, no police to cuff me, no jail to hold me."

The point was moot as far as I was concerned and my little buddy needn't fret over something so trivial and mundane. It was like arguing with my kids. Stopping then, I realized what he said and raised my voice. "What do you mean a blood handshake means more? Like what?"

"Did Ginn talk about himself? What he was? Who he represents?"

I spelled it out for him. "He is just a guy. A man. That's it."

"How does he spell his name? Ginn?"

Unbelievable. I raised my fingers and outlined letters for him. "G-I-N-N."

Jock looked like he was going to faint. "I should have asked you that earlier," he mumbled. He found a rock and sat down. "This whole time, I thought it was Gin, like the drink. You know, like gin and juice. This is not good." He shook his head as if he was disappointed. "What were you thinking?"

"So he spells his name a wacky way. Am I missing something? So what?"

"Haven't you ever heard of a Djinn? D-J-I-N-N?"

"Yes, years ago, a teacher back in Coppertown gave me the lowdown and I wasn't impressed. Supposedly, another maniac called Bale thought of himself a deity as well and that could be spelled B-A-E-L. So, unless that dude was a good spelunker, we buried him under tons of rock and he hasn't surfaced since. Not so powerful now, are they?"

Jock wouldn't stop. "A Djinn is a supernatural being that can be good, evil, or neutral. They have the power to travel far and are often found in remote areas. They control people."

"You get that from a comic book?" I asked.

Jock got defensive. "Yes. Comic books have a wealth of knowledge, bro. Think of all the legends, fables, myths, and tales they create. There's research, insight, history all included."

"And imagination too," I pointed out.

Jock rambled on about the so-called myth of a Djinn. "They mislead and destroy humanity. They whisper to people's souls and tell them to submit to evil desires. They are full of lies and are treacherous. They work for the devil and will not stop. In Muslim lore, they are one of the five demons that plague the earth."

"He's a con man!"

"This is madness!" Jock cried. "We're heading for doom!"

"Why do you know so much about all this shit? What work did you do?" I asked him straight out. "Besides being in college?"

"Clerk," he said softly. "I was a clerk."

"Where?"

"Comic book store," he stated proudly.

"Of course," I laughed. "I fucking knew it. You were surrounded by fairy tales so much, you started to believe them." I shook my head in disappointment, then turned around and headed into the creek bed.

"Do you have a problem with where I worked?" he asked, following me.

"Yeah, it was make believe," I replied. "Bat suits, web slingers, tall buildings in a single bound, a talking duck."

Jock tried to keep up. "Some are drawn from real life experiences. Some are accounts of what really happened."

I turned on a dime. "So, you're saying I made a deal with the devil?"

Jock mulled that over, unsure. "I hope not."

"Give me a break."

"Are you religious?" he asked.

I didn't answer. I hadn't thought of that in a long time. Wanting this to end was my new agenda and I was tired of the cross examination. This witness wanted to walk, so I did just that and started onward again.

"You're still going?" he asked behind me.

Without stopping, I said aloud, "Look, if you don't want to go, don't. I understand. No one is forcing you to come with me."

"Do you even know what's out there?"

"My family," I replied.

"There's only death," Jock said and ran after me. "You struck a deal with the devil and now he's coming to collect!"

I pointed south. "Salton Sea is that way. I'm going that way. End of story."

An engine rumbled to our left in the distance. It was smaller, like that of a dirt bike and it was making a heck of a lot of noise. Its single headlight appeared from the east and seemed to be headed north of us, jolting and jumping as it crossed rugged terrain. It looked to be about a hundred yards away. The rider was shifting and goosing the throttle as he skirted bushes like a slalom skier. He slowed once he saw the creek bed, dipping the front tire into the shifting sand, spinning a tire that finally caught once it hit the hard, crackly dirt. It gripped and caught, the bike lurching momentarily, and he goosed it to the other side where he hit the bank and jumped the bike a few feet in the air. I thought he was gone, but he circled around as if to do it again.

The dirt bike rider dropped back into the creek bed and circled a small area. Then, he brought out a flashlight, shining it down. Holding the flashlight with his left, he revved the dirt bike and began to follow the creek bed towards us.

Our footprints. The dirt bike rider throttled faster and closed in. There was no sense in running, he'd see where we went. I'd wait until he got close enough. I brought out my crowbar. Just when he got within a few yards, he skidded in the sand and swiveled his light.

It shone on me. Jock appeared next to me.

The rider stared at me, then to Jock. I glared back at him. I tapped the crowbar against my palm. Whap, whap, whap. He looked at it, then up at me again. He dropped his flashlight and tried to turn and flee but he was facing my direction. I took off after him as he spun his bike around in the sand. The bike shot forward about ten yards when I dove, thrusting my crowbar between his front spokes and released it. The crowbar spun in the wheel, jammed into the front forks, and cartwheeled the rider instantly. He slammed hard on his back into the dirt, the bike on top of him, the engine sputtering and then dying. I scrambled back to my feet and lifted my crowbar out of the spokes. It was still intact, barely a scratch. The bike was another matter; the spokes had snapped, the tire rim busted, the forks had bent.

The rider was sandwiched under the bike. His arm looked broken and he had a deep gash in his forehead. I stood over him staring at his face noticing he was of Asian descent. His eyes were closed, lights out. I didn't recognize him.

What to do with the guy. What to do.

"Let's leave him," Jock said, standing next to me. "Even if he gets out from under there, it will be a long time before they find out."

Jock had found the walkie-talkie and handed it to me. I tossed it in the air and smashed it with my crowbar, baseball style. "Chachi would be proud," I said, watching plastic pieces scattered on the ground in the moonlight. The crowbar went back into my quiver and I hiked back to the creek bed. "Time to roll," I said aloud. I had a lot of ground to make up and the sooner we leave the fallen rider, the better.

"You seriously aren't heading there now, are you?" Jock asked, following me. "You're really going to the Salton Sea with them so close?"

"What now?" I said, without stopping. Man, he could get annoying too.

Jock pointed west. "This guy's friends know he is out here. He had a walkie-talkie which means he probably told them where he was. When he doesn't show up, they will come out looking for him and when they find him, they'll know it was us and that we were out here."

"It could have been anyone," I noted.

"What happens when he wakes up?"

"Okay, I'll go back there and bash his brains in. The dead don't talk right?"

"You don't get it," Jock said. "They will know it was you. They will assume we headed towards the Salton Sea after. This is the break we've been looking for. They will follow the creek bed and they'll miss us."

That halted me in my tracks. I turned, wondering what the hell he was getting at. "How? We're headed in that direction."

Placating, he approached as if he was wise beyond his years. "We head east and south to Mexico. There is no redemption, there is no plane, there is no family. Say goodbye to Ginn and his ogres. We won't see them. There is a better life waiting for us in the Sea of Cortez."

I huffed at that notion. "I'm going to the Salton Sea. Nowhere else."

"You're a stupid, confused, stubborn old prick is what you are," Jock replied.

Never before had I actually wanted to squeeze the little runt's neck, but I did so, and roughly. My arm shot out and snatched a handful of coyote and undershirt, then twisting up under his chin. His eyes bulged and I purposely lifted high. Both his hands grasped my arm but there was no way he was going to get me to release. Through gritted teeth, I said, "I am going to the Salton Sea to find my family. I will not stop until I find them. Got it?"

"They want nothing to do with you," he managed.

"Shut up!"

Jock struggled under my grip and I sensed that I had taken it too far. I finally let go and shoved him back, just hard enough to make him stumble and nothing more.

"The woman in white lied to you," Jock stated. "They only told you that so they could escape in the plane."

"You know what your problem is?" I said, leaning down almost face to face. "I have hope! You're jealous that I have a family and I'm going to be with them! You're alone and you want everyone to be just like you! Alone!"

"Then tell me this," Jock sneered. "Why haven't they come looking for you?"

"Get lost," I said. There it was again, that nagging thought and it was a low blow.

Jock manned up and stood tall. "They don't want you back, do they? You know what the lady and the Pilot did? I bet they told your family and warned them."

With both hands, I shoved Jock to the ground and quickly removed my crowbar, leveling it at him. "Go back to your hole or wherever the hell you came from!" I shouted.

"I think you're chasing a dream and hell is waiting to claim you," Jock said.

He wasn't worth it. I put the crowbar back behind me and started walking again. I wanted to put distance between us. I wanted to be alone.

"You made a deal with the devil!" Jock shouted after me. "How foolish are you?"

When I turned around ten minutes later, Jock was nowhere to be seen.

The Bee Gees tape finished up their single, *If I Can't Have You,* and the cassette suddenly stopped. I shook the cassette player, pressed buttons and nothing. I figured dead batteries as I had been playing it for some time. However, I continued to sing the song over and over, especially the chorus. "If I can't have you, I don't want nobody baby, if I can't have you, oh, oh, oh!"

I was in a good mood. The Salton Sea was just ahead and I was alone again. The first words of the song, "Don't know why, I'm surviving every lonely day," stuck in my mind though. I scoffed at it.

I was surviving for this moment. That's why.

I imagined that the place my family was now being a good place. Wherever they were, life returned to normal. I pictured baseball games, barbecues, movies, and parties. I imagined people laughing and sharing, wine, and good times. I dreamed of a society away from the horrors of the wasteland I was in, trying to make anew and succeeding.

Such a place existed. I was convinced of it.

Admittedly, I peeked behind me a few times to see if Jock was following me, and I saw nothing that resembled the little man nor the coyote fur he wore. There was no rumble of engines, no Rogues in hot pursuit either. I was upset with myself for threatening him with the crowbar. Sometimes, my temper got the best of me. The little guy was only trying to protect us from certain harm and detour to a small Mexican town on the coast on the Sea of Cortez where we could lay up on soft beds and drink Coronas. That wasn't going to happen though.

If Jock was smart, he'd be chasing Iris. The mission to the Salton Sea was mine and I don't even know if the plane had an extra seat for him. I don't blame him for leaving. I always traveled alone. Part of me believed I deserved no company.

After I ducked under a barbed wire fence and crested a small hill, a house appeared out of nowhere.

In the middle of nowhere.

CHAPTER THIRTY-SIX

It was a two story, crumbling mess. Windows were shattered, walls chipped, and the sidings faded. Shingles on the roof were missing in patches. An empty clothesline swayed in the wind. A long windy dirt driveway snaked between a set of hills and meandered away from me to some unknown road far off.

Chicken wire surrounded a large shed in the backyard. Portions of it formed separate pens. The shed itself had a fallen wall. Inside, large aquariums lay broken. Strange place to keep fish, I thought. I watched the house for about ten minutes, watching for movement, and saw none. While the house did seem vacant, I was fixated at what was leaning against the rear wall.

A mountain bike.

I was able to watch my step and creep up to the house. I peered into windows and saw no one inside. Only crickets surrounding me made any noise. I made my way to the bike and inspected it. The tires were firm with decent tread. The frame was sturdy and straight. I lifted the rear and used my foot to the slowly move the pedals. The rear tire spun so the chain was fastened well enough. Somewhat perplexed, I hesitated. This was too good a find with no one around to claim it.

As if on cue, from the creek bed, I heard an engine. It sounded like a motorbike and was coming closer. Then, I heard two. I figured it was the mountain bike's owner but I had to make sure it wasn't Rogues. Either way, I needed to move. I had two choices; hide inside the house, which was a dumb move, or try for the open road. Since I came there for the bike, I grabbed it by the handlebars, climbed on, and raced around the other side of the house, using it as cover so I could gain some ground. After hopping on it, I struggled for balance in the sand.

Just when I caught my groove, I jammed the brake levers when I saw pairs of headlights coming down the driveway towards me, causing me to skid sideways. I counted four vehicles at least. Behind me, a pair of ATV's with lights crested the same hill I was once on. I was stuck. I flipped the bike around and headed back to the house. Once there, I leaped off the bike and let it coast on its own until it hit a shrub, bounced over it, and flopped in the sand, the rear tire still spinning. Convinced I hadn't been spotted yet, as there was no war cry or shouts, I planted myself against the wall of the house and contemplated my next move.

Just as I readied myself to head for the open desert, headlights crept towards the side where I was. Looking up, an open window to the house was a foot away. I climbed inside, hoping they hadn't seen my legs as lights followed me in that instant.

Inside, I sidestepped garbage and filth, tiptoeing so I wouldn't trip or make noise. The headlights from the front bathed the entire house and I had to duck to avoid any shadows. I hung by a busted kitchen window facing the front, keeping just out of sight.

The Rogues hadn't entered the house and I was curious for their delay. Instead, they were outside, conversing, their headlights showering the front in white. There were three cars plus a flatbed truck. I counted eight Rogues after they stepped out and mingled. Two in the ATV's around back. That made ten Rogues to deal with. Ginn and Torch were not among them.

The flatbed truck reversed, turned around, and backed in, splitting a pair of their cars. I could see two large cages in the bed of the truck. Two huge masses were in the cages, shuffling and grunting.

The Razorbacks.

The flatbed lowered itself to the ground. When the rear of the cages was opened, every Rogue stepped away. The Razorback on the left shot out too quickly and it looked like the handlers weren't ready. It twisted and bolted down the ramp but was immediately halted when I heard a loud buzz. It squealed and flopped, tossing its humongous head and snout around. One of the handlers held a device and showed it to the others. Around the Razorback's neck, I saw the harness again and assumed it was a big-time shock collar. The handlers pounced, some holding its legs, the others attaching a long, metal pole to the harness as the beast squirmed. Once they got a grip, they held him there and motioned for the next one. The handlers on the second pig were ready this time and they slid their pole inside the cage, latching that to the collar. The cage had horizontal slits that allowed guidance in and out of the cage. They coerced the brother down the ramp and brought the two of them together. The first pig gathered its strength back and fought with his handlers. They struggled to contain it.

A Rogue walked forward and stood out. He was wearing a sweater and I remembered his name from the time he drove Torch's truck; Froggie.

"Time to have some fun," Froggie said and nodded to handlers. Simultaneously, both handlers released their pigs and the beasts got the hint. They tore towards the front of the house and vanished from my view.

"Oh God," I mumbled to myself.

The pigs crashed through the front door. Hooves scraped the floor as they tried to avoid the staircase and both smashed into it. Squealing, they regrouped and charged in different directions, banging and crashing into the walls. I immediately leapt up on to a countertop, trying to stay quiet. One of the boars barged into the room and ripped into the cupboards in the kitchen, battering its tusks just below my feet. The other sounded it like it was thrashing porcelain in a bathroom. They were a pair of four-legged wrecking crews going to work. Just when I thought it hadn't seen me, the pig in my room lifted its thick head and I saw its deep black eyes. The Razorback squealed and rammed the counter again. Drywall pieces began to crumble around me and white dust wafted over us both. Outside, laughter erupted.

The Razorback backed up and charged once more. It crashed through the counter, splitting it in two, knocking me to the floor. The momentum, however, caused the large boar to bury itself under the rubble. I gathered myself and ran from the room, hurdling the staircase, and scampering up the stairs.

A few steps broke under my weight. I caught myself and kept going, finally making it to the top, staying low to avoid being seen. The ATV's were at idle behind the house and I could hear shouting, but again, none of it sounded like I had been spotted. I ran into one room, and saw an opening to the attic from there, but it was due to the ceiling caving in. Most of the attic in that room was exposed, right up to the roof. I chose another room and found the ceiling intact with a small access door to the attic there. Before I went up, I stared down the staircase below.

The Razorback from the kitchen entered the hallway and suddenly zeroed in on a storage room under the staircase. Lowering its head, it charged and crashed into a door, cracking it in two. A human shriek came within and the Razorback didn't let up. The brother boar heard the commotion and joined the fracas. The pigs thrust their tusks and snouts up and down, side to side, trying desperately to get to the prize inside. When the door finally gave way, a baseball bat began to swing. After a few small smacks, which did little to stop the frenzy, the batter wised up and used the knob end and stabbed it at their eyes. One Razorback took a hit and backed up momentarily, but that blocked the other brother from charging. The batter, a slight man, saw his opportunity, rose from his hiding spot, and ran out the front door.

I ran to the window. The batter tried to run past the cars. The Rogues let him by, jumping to the hoods of the cars and I thought for a moment, the man might escape. However, the Razorbacks were in hot pursuit. They caught him just beyond the parked vehicles and tore into him with their tusks as he shrieked.

"Get these things off me!" the Batter wailed. He kicked, slapped, and twisted but the brothers continued to tear and shred both his clothes and skin. One pig clamped down on his ankle and I heard a pop. The Batter screamed and leaned back. Blood was oozing from his legs and stomach. They shredded the man until the cries stopped and he went still. The Razorbacks began to gorge and pull pieces of flesh clear.

"That's enough," Froggie called out and climbed down a car's hood. "Ginn wanted the pets hungry."

The handlers reigned in their panting pets, latching their poles again. Once secured, with blood covering their snouts, Froggie stepped forward. The brothers tried to charge him but he jumped aside as the handlers pulled back. Froggie yelled, "Whoa! Fucking hold them!"

"Is it the man we're after?" someone asked.

"I don't think so," Froggie said and inspected the carnage and said, "Nope. This man is Mexican. We're good. Our guy in still in there. We saw him climb the window."

"Shit," I said to myself.

"Search the upstairs!" a Rogue called out. "Let's get the brothers up there!"

"Can't," Froggie interjected and walked to a car. "Pigs can't climb stairs."

"No shit? So, what do we do?" a Black Rogue asked, flipping his gun in circles. I could see an afro and a moustache on him, straight out of the seventies.

"You want to go up there?" Froggie said, and faced the other man. "Go against the crowbar man yourself, Freebase?"

Still spinning the gun, Freebase responded. "Not after what he did to Jackal. That's some bad juju right there."

So, they found Jackal, or what remained. With this smaller group and the fact some had backtracked to find what was left of Jackal, that told me the Rogue team was splitting up to cover more ground.

Wonderful.

Froggie popped the trunk on one of the cars and hauled out a jug. "Let's make it easy on ourselves. Grab a few jugs. Let's smoke him out."

"Yes, sir," Freebase said, tucked his gun away, and hoisted out two more jugs. The men then separated; Froggie went left, Freebase went right.

"Light them up!" Froggie yelled from his side. It was only a matter of seconds when the glow from climbing flames flickered in the night sky on each side. Smoke seeped through the floor and vents. When I touched the wall to my side, it was warm.

The rear fared no better. A fire was spread there too, making its way up to a second story window. The ATV riders must have joined the party.

The upstairs was growing thick with smoke. All around me, the fire was spreading and beginning to creep inside. Only the middle of the house remained unlit but would be soon consumed by the aggressive flames fueled by years of dried and neglected wood. As the smoke surrounded me, I coughed once and fell to my knees, counting my very limited options.

CHAPTER THIRTY-SEVEN

The attic barely held my weight. I had climbed up the exposed portion in the first bedroom, hoping to slide across to the front room where I just was, not as to hide, but to find an opening to the roof. Flames began to scour the second floor. The heat below me was intense, forcing me to crawl quickly. Smoke engulfed me, causing me to wretch and cough. My eyes stung. A four-foot hole at the base of the attic showed darkness and stars on the other side. There was an opening there.

I climbed outside, balancing on the edge, drawing in cleaner air. The flames were still climbing up the wall below me and gaining in intensity. Smoke was everywhere. It was a two story drop and I contemplated jumping. Thankfully, there were no Rogues below. To my left, at the corner of the house, I saw a gutter attached to the wall that ran to the ground. I decided to slide down it, saving my ankles from a perilous jump, and balanced along the edge to get to it. Once I grabbed on, I swung my body over. The gutter creaked but held.

As I descended, the wall beside me cracked and caved inwards with a loud whump. Sparks and embers floated past me, showering my clothes. I batted some out while others singed. I got to about halfway when the gutter crinkled and snapped, causing me to fall backwards to the ground. I landed hard on my back, the wind knocked out of me. I reached above my head and tried to draw in much needed air. It seemed like I was there forever, not found, and not on fire.

I struggled to my knees. Hands quickly found me, but not of the saving type. These were savage hands and they hauled me away from the flames. "That's him!" Some Rogue shouted. "Kick his ass!" Another replied. At a safe distance from the heat and flames, I took a pounding from numerous strikes and kicks. At one point, I was able to stand. I balled my fist and struck at the closest Rogue. I really connected. His jaw snapped and he fell backwards, tripping over a bush. I received three more hits then, one to the head. Already dazed from the fall, I was seeing stars. I staggered like a drunk until one man foolishly tried to grab me from behind. I whipped my head back and cracked his nose, causing him to scream and fall away.

Froggie parted the crowd and sized me up. Glancing around, I saw the ATV riders behind me, blocking any attempt to run in their direction. In front, there were still more Rogues to deal with. Just as I reached for my crowbar, hands from behind caught mine and we all tumbled to the ground. More punches landed.

Too exhausted to move any longer, I heard handcuffs once again and soon I passed out.

CHAPTER THIRTY-EIGHT

I woke on my back, staring up at a yellow sky. A fire crackled in the distance and I could smell smoke. I tried to sit up but found I could only lift my head. Looking down at my body, I was relieved to see myself fully clothed, but bound by ropes. My arms and legs were extended at forty-five-degree angles, with ropes knotted around my wrists. My ankles were also tied at the same angles and I had seen this configuration before with Cherry and the man in Kelso.

I was staked to the ground.

Shifting my head to my right, I saw the source of the yellow sky. The house I was hiding in was entirely leveled by the flames. Rogues were near it, talking to each other, some drinking from a jug, while others were sitting on their vehicles content to watch. All seemed calm. The truck that held the Razorbacks was parked away from the action. I noticed more vehicles had arrived while I was unconscious. I must have been out for quite a while.

No one seemed to be paying attention to me. I was left alone. I yanked and pulled at the stakes but nothing budged. Using all my limbs, I tried to draw into myself, yet no stake gave way.

"Don't waste your time," someone said above my head. "Those stakes go two feet underground. You won't pull them out."

Torch was above me. Alone, he came around so I could see his face and he held something in his hands. Suddenly liquid began to pour around my mouth. I squirmed and shook with all my might. "Relax, it's water, numbskull," Torch informed me. "I'm not going to piss in your mouth. I am not a fucking barbarian like the others." He came around to face me, dropping into a catcher's stance. "Just drink," he said and showed me a canteen. "You need it."

As much as I wanted to, I turned away. Torch sighed and poured some liquid into his mouth. "Happy now?" Then, he turned the canteen and dumped water into my mouth. I drank until he pulled up. "The boys worked you over pretty good," he continued. "But I see you did some damage yourself. You broke Rimjob's nose and cracked Arab's jaw. They want payback."

I smiled, which was about all I could do.

"I expected more from you. Your first mistake was letting StirFry live. He found your tracks on his bike and it wasn't hard for Vicious and Muskrat to take over and follow them along the creek bed in their ATVs. Of course, StirFry's got a concussion and broken arm from you, so he's useless."

A bottle shattered at the fire. "Vicious and Muskrat, huh? Respectable citizens?" I asked. It was a minor attempt to show my disappointment in the groups he called friends, but what the hell?

"Vicious is the meathead who believes he channels Sid from the Sex Pistols. Muskrat, well, he looks like the rodent itself. They were the ones who held your legs down while Maggie tried to get her ride," he said.

"They're dead," I noted. "They just don't know it yet."

"Your second mistake was to hide in the only house around here for miles. The boys pegged it, give them credit. I thought you were apt to stay to the roads so I was manning a roadblock up on Dole Road."

Torch tested on the rope that bound my left wrist. He said, "You know what this house was called? The Snake House. An old retired couple owned it; they used to breed anacondas, pythons, boas, and all those big snakes. Sell them to pet stores. Some of them fetched up to one hundred bucks per snake and their litters could be as high as thirty at a time. Believe that shit?"

I thought back to the shed in the rear with the aquarium tanks.

"Only thing was, their deadbeat son was a meth dealer. He set up a lab in the rear too. His folks resisted at first, then saw the profits in that and abided. Look around, no neighbors, out in the middle of nowhere, a perfect spot for a drug lab."

I strained my neck and scanned the grounds behind Torch, searching for Jock. Hoping he'd help when an opening presented itself.

"See that tall piece of shit?" Torch asked me. "The one in the lab coat?"

I peeked and saw a tall, gangly man with frizzy hair at the fire in a long coat. He was chugging moonshine and spewing it into the flames. A huge whoosh of flames erupted and the others had to stand back. "The Scientist. Educated, but caught with kiddie porn. Resorted to making meth after he was fired. Knew the son that lived here well. Knew the story of the house too. We found him here two years ago and he figured you'd head for it. He's the man responsible for perfecting the moonshine and other great narcotics back at the camp. Anyway, this house has been ransacked over and over. Some snakes escaped too. The old couple's bodies were rumored to have been fed to their snakes by some unsavory characters. Must have been quite a show."

"I'm not interested in the history of this house or your goons," I said. "Where's your boss, Ginn?"

"Delayed, but he'll be the one to decide what to do with you. It's a good thing I came just after they caught you. Those boys had planned to have some fun."

"You figure out which one knows you were a cop?"

Torch put a finger to his lip. "Quiet now. And no. I haven't had much interaction with them. Since Kelso, we've been spread out."

"What if I was to shout it out? That you were a cop?"

Torch shrugged. "These idiots wouldn't believe you. They think I am an ex-Marine. Truth is, my partner at Rampart Division was and I heard enough stories while out on patrol to assume his identity. I'm not called Torch for my red hair, but because my pyromaniac partner was gung-ho in the Afghanistan battlefields. He'd shout, *let's torch the fuckers!* before they'd swarm the caves. My hair just strengthened the profile."

"Someone could be convinced," I said. "The one who knows."

"That won't help us."

"Us?" I asked.

The Rogues were grouping. Some casting glances back. I caught Torch's unease. His secret was very precious to him. The timing of this wasn't good.

"Ginn wants you bad and I don't know why," the former cop admitted. "Hell, you two could be old fuck buddies for all I care. But when he gets here, your plan to find the plane will be jeopardized. I know Ginn, he will want the plane for himself. He'll torture you until you admit where the plane lands, take you there, and hold you hostage. If your friends have any sense, they will not land, especially if they're a bunch of armed nutjobs below them."

"You got that right," I said.

"He'll be wasting his time only he's too stubborn to admit it."

"I'll never tell him," I confessed.

"Well, you being tied here doesn't suit either one of us very well."

"Us again?"

"I can make a deal with you. Right here and now."

"I don't need you to help me."

Torch nodded to the open desert. "You mean your midget friend? Think he'll come to your rescue?"

I stared hard at him. "No, we don't have him," he continued. "Your little friend is still out there, but he's no match for these guys. His best bet is to remain a ghost."

The Rogues handed a bottle around, taking turns swigging. As much as I'd like them to take out Torch, that meant some bad times for me. I believed him that they wouldn't touch me as long as he was there, but something was amiss with his crew. I could sense the tension in Torch. He was aware of something brewing too as their heads were all facing us.

"Fuck me," Torch whispered. "I don't like this."

"Let me go," I told him.

Torch eyed them as well and I felt the rope loosen. "There's a Gypsy camp about two miles south. They have a horse." From his pocket, he dropped a buck knife and buried it in the sand near my left wrist. "Not much else I can provide in the way of transportation. I can only hold them off for so long."

The Rogues began to walk towards us as a group. There was something up.

"I think you better pay attention to what's coming this way," I said.

Torch reached over to the spike on my left hand. "Make a deal with me right now. I'll let you go but you have to tell me where the plane lands and I meet you there. Get me out of this shithole wasteland. Get me away from Ginn."

"No."

"If I don't help you, you're a dead man. You hear me?"

The Rogues began to form a wide circle. I could feel the tension loosen on my left wrist. Torch gritted his teeth. "Make a deal with me, goddamn it!"

Froggie was the one to step forward. "Torch, can we have a word with you?" he asked, in a calm voice. The others giggled and laughed at that.

"I'm not done, Froggie," Torch answered, staring at me intensely. He knew what was coming and he knew right then who knew the secret.

"Oh, I think you're done. So done, you're roasted. Pig."

Torch got it much worse than me. They plucked him from my side with punches and kicks raining down on him from every angle. "Die pig!" the men chanted.

"Marine! I told you I was a fucking Marine!" Torch wailed.

While he too got some shots in, there were far too many this time to be effective as arms ensnared his limbs and his exposed body was a free-for-all. Men lined up throwing bombs. Torch's head snapped back from a haymaker.

They quickly ripped his clothes off. Torch was nude.

The Rogue whose nose I busted, called Rimjob apparently, carried a flaming stick and seared Torch's backside with it. A pipe was tossed into the crowd and used to bash his head. There, barely conscious, he was thrown down hard as everyone laughed. His body was dragged, by his feet, to a softer spot about twenty feet away. Arab, with the busted jaw, carried four spikes toward the melee. With his chin wrapped in a bandage, he eyed me as he walked by.

"My father was killed by a pig!" a Rogue shouted and spat. "Shot four times during a traffic stop!"

"Fucking Five-Oh busted me all the time," another one said. "How's this feel? I got my police brutality right here!" I heard a slap and Torch grunted.

I squirmed and fought, believing I would be next.

The others were content to harass Torch and leave me be, possibly due to the fact Ginn wanted me unharmed. Or maybe they wanted to take out their jollies on the former police officer first. I heard the spikes driven into the sand by heavy hammers. His limbs were forcibly stretched out. Ginn was nowhere to be seen and I wondered what was in store for Torch and how long he'd last. Cherry was used for sexual means and the Kelso man was killed for his information on my whereabouts. I didn't know what they had planned for Torch but I was betting drowning by piss to be the heavy favorite.

After they tied him firmly, Froggie took over. "It was Spaz who discovered the secret for us! He told Vicious and Muskrat just a few hours ago! Lo and behold, I was just informed minutes ago! No time like the present!"

"Kill the swine!" An older Rogue with gray hair yelled.

"Gramps is right!" Froggie acknowledged. "This man shall be put to death!"

"You have me mixed up with someone else!" Torch cried out. "I was with the 14th Marine Expeditionary Unit! That's why I am the way I am!"

Froggie ignored Torch's cries. "We come to find out Spaz overheard *the man* saying Torch was a cop! And, coincidentally, Spaz and his pals are no longer with us! How convenient, I say! Torch wasted our comrades so they wouldn't speak!"

"That is so fucked up," someone spat.

With everyone else occupied, I used the time to probe the knot with my fingers and try to loosen my wrist. Part of the rope came off, but there were too many Rogues nearby. I didn't want to make it obvious so I chose not to loosen too much more yet.

"You'll pay for this! All of you!" Torch yelled. The men laughed at that and continued to harass and beat him.

Froggie continued. "So, now, here we all are. In the midst of a traitor. I, for one, am shocked. Shocked that this man, a person I called friend, comrade, and fellow Rogue, would deceive us into thinking he was one of us. Which, he clearly wasn't. Instead, he was a cop. And what do we do with cops?"

A skittish, ugly Rogue with fat lips sauntered up and unzipped his fly. "This is what we do to cops!" A steady stream of urine splashed Torch's chest and the men cheered. "Coonchugger has the right idea," Froggie remarked, then studied the crowd. "Who will join him? Form a line behind me!"

Other Rogues jostled for a spot and their turn. The circus was in full swing.

From behind, Gramps seized Torch by his jaws and pried them open. A stick was wedged between his upper and lower teeth. Gramps held Torch's head in place, his gaping mouth a target. Drowning was a horrible way to die and Torch tugged hard on his restraints, grunting and moaning, shaking his head.

Torch gasped and he suddenly relaxed. He actually opened his mouth wider. The group grew excited in that gesture, whooping it up, and readying themselves for their turn.

"Look at that! The cop wants it!" Coonchugger shouted. "And I'm dry!"

Froggie moved into place between Torch's legs and unzipped his pants. "Hold the infidel's mouth wide! I shall be the first to quench his thirst!" I shuddered at what was going to happen next and almost looked away. I glanced up at Froggie's face, wondering how such a man could conduct such a heinous act.

However, I never got to see the man's reaction.

Froggie's face exploded and his body pitched forward. His body landed on Torch, who squirmed and managed to roll the body off him.

An abrupt silence descended on the men. Confused heads turned to see a man standing in Froggie's place.

It was Ginn, gun in hand, smoke drifting from the barrel.

CHAPTER THIRTY-NINE

After the ropes were cut by a shaking Rogue, a weakened Torch was brought to his feet by Ginn who soothed the guy with a calming touch and silent words I couldn't hear. All around them, Rogues looked uncomfortable, shifting on their feet, trying not to make eye contact with the boss or the man they injured. Torch suddenly roared and punched a nearby Rogue, the older one I heard called Gramps. Gramps fell like a timbering Redwood, thumping the ground hard. He didn't get up. As for the rest of the Rogues, Torch pushed by them and stormed to a waiting RV. The other Rogues appeared demur and fidgety, the obvious fact that Ginn's presence suddenly made each one incredibly vulnerable and responsible for an act not approved by the boss.

Torch reasserted his spot at second in command. What that meant for the Rogues that partook in the onslaught, I had no idea, but I doubted he'd let many go unharmed. I also wondered if he'd have second thoughts about the loosened ropes. I still didn't trust the man.

Near the RV, Ginn was appraised by some sullen Rogues of what happened earlier to them finding me in the house. He cast the odd glance my way and I figured he'd make his way over soon enough.

"Leave him there for the time being," Ginn said instead, looking my way. "We have other matters to discuss."

Ginn strolled to the center of the men. They all fell in and listened.

"I don't care if Torch was a cop and neither should any of you," Ginn shouted at all the men. Eyes were cast down, like children getting admonished for unruly behavior. "Torch is a valuable asset to my empire and no one, under any circumstances, is to make any judgement on any comrade without my approval. That will be considered a mutinous act and the penalty for that is for a very slow death. One that will involve the Razorbacks. Is that clear?"

Nods from all around. Even a few murmured apologies. I caught more than one shivering at the nightmarish thought.

"Excellent," Ginn replied and then scanned the crowd. "Where is Coonchugger?"

Coonchugger was shoved forward by the crowd and brought dead center. Torch made his way over, fully dressed then, and adjusted his holster. The Rogues parted for him once more, probably hoping his memory was too fuzzy to pinpoint the ones who worked him over. Torch came face to face with the man who first pissed on his chest.

"I ain't sorry," Coonchugger said, his head bowed. "You're still a fucking pig."

Torch sneered, whisked his own gun from his holster, spun the Rogue around, and fired into the skinny man's spine. Coonchugger fell to his knees, then pitched face forward to the sand. Other Rogues gasped and leapt back. Coonchugger's legs were useless and lay twisted and askew. Torch rolled the man over with his hands, then stood above his fallen victim and unzipped his pants. Seconds later, with a deadpan stare, Torch unleashed a steady stream of urine that splashed Coonchugger's face. When he was done, Torch zipped back up.

"I want this man tossed into the fire!" Torch demanded to the crowd. "Right fucking now!"

Coonchugger was carried away by numerous hands in mere seconds.

CHAPTER FORTY

Later, it was Ginn who came to visit me. Flanked by Freebase carrying a lawn chair, Ginn sauntered over to me with a warm smile, leaving the rest to prep their digs for the night. "I'd like to chat, but I see you're tied up at the moment," he said to me. That was his lame attempt at humor.

Behind him, tents were assembled ready for the night. I doubted many of them got any sleep the night before after their rampage in Kelso. Campfires stayed lit, despite the crumbled house far off to the right, still smoldering. The chatter had dropped off too. Strangely, I was still tied down and that told me we weren't headed back to the camp, which we could have made in a few hours. I realized Ginn wanted to see the Salton Sea and the plane, just as Torch claimed he would.

"What the hell is this?" I asked, hoping I'd distract him from the loosened ropes on my wrist. I even faked pulling hard to show it was still taught and uncomfortable. "Why am I still kept here?"

"It's your bed for the night," he said. "You've been quite uncooperative as of late, so I think this is best for both of us."

"Let me go, Ginn," I said. "This isn't right."

"In due time. We'll see how you behave in the morning."

"How am I supposed to take a piss?"

Ginn turned to the Black Rogue beside him. "Freebase here, he will assist." Freebase didn't look too happy but nodded at the order.

"This isn't winning any favors with me," I noted. "I won't tell you shit."

"Yes, I am afraid you will," Ginn sighed. "Need I remind you of my pets? You shared accommodations with them at my camp, didn't you?"

Freebase giggled. Ginn shot him a look and continued. "The whereabouts of the plane are still a mystery to me. The Salton Sea is huge, after all, and I couldn't be bothered to cover its entirety, nor chase a landing plane from the wrong side. A small plane could land anywhere. I know you have specifics so we'll work together tomorrow on that."

"Your stupid deal was with me to be at your side," I barked. "Not chase some random airplane."

Ginn shook his head. "You're mistaken. While I demanded you be by my side, that was a consolation price. Not what I originally wanted."

"Then what?"

"In time," he said.

"I don't trust you. I saw what you did to Gruff and he had the scar."

"Gruff tried to resist my orders. Tried to prevent me from entering his town. You saw what happened there. It was entirely his fault. He stood up to me and the rest of them paid the price."

"What did you arrange with Gruff anyway?" I asked.

Ginn leaned down to get close to me. "Gruff wanted to be Sheriff, only the old boss man, Stu, wouldn't retire. Stu wanted to stay on for a few years. So, Gruff saw an opportunity for advancement during the Baker to Vegas races."

Freebase interjected. "Baker to Vegas race?"

"Annual marathon in the desert," Ginn stated. "Teams from other police departments from all over the country run relays in the desert from the town of Baker in California, go up to Pahrump, Nevada, then sprint all the way back down to Las Vegas. There's a party in Las Vegas afterwards. Gruff entered his department."

"They did that for fun?" Freebase asked. "That's stupid, man."

Ginn continued. "So, one night, Gruff sees his boss Stu messing with the hookers downtown. Really into the ebony. So Gruff comes to me and asks, if we get one of the hookers over here, you can video it, right?"

I could see where this was going. Film at 11.

"Stu's wife is a religious type. Stu, caught in the act, convincingly retires right away. Gruff gets the job as Sheriff. Last I heard, Stu was living in Palm Springs with a wife who never found out."

"What was Gruff's end of the deal?" I asked.

"Guns, bullets, weapons. He seized them all the time from cars he stopped. Yahoos firing them in the desert. Some he kept in an evidence locker." Ginn stood up and brushed his pant legs. "He was not the only Sheriff on my payroll."

So, men like Gruff helped arm Ginn's army. Still, Gruff was dead and I knew Ginn wouldn't hesitate to waste me either. The ace I held was the location of the plane's landing strip, which was, unfortunately, still a riddle to me. Ginn didn't know that either.

"Freebase will keep you company and assist with any latrine duties you require," Ginn added, then rose to stand. Freebase set up his lawn chair and plopped down into it.

"Rest up. We'll see you in the morning." Ginn remarked, then walked off towards a campfire where he was handed a plate of food by Arab.

"You any good at wiping?" I asked Freebase.

"Nah, man, you go in your drawers," Freebase replied with a look of indifference.

CHAPTER FORTY-ONE

Freebase was yawning. He was already slumped in his chair and his legs were spread out in front. His head bobbed. A plate of food was dangling from his lap. My mouth watered at the half-eaten pork and beans on his plate. Behind him, the other Rogues were drifting off too around campfires. Unlike those bozos, I got the necessary shut-eye last night at the Playhouse. One Rogue fell off his lawn chair and hit the sand. He stayed there, still asleep.

Freebase startled at the fall, looked back, then slowly closed his eyes. Meanwhile, I was slowly unraveling the rope and had managed to free my hand. Not sure if he was out, I asked him, "Hey, why they call you Freebase?"

"What's it to you?" he said with his eyes closed.

"Just want to know."

"Ain't nothin'," he snapped.

"I'm not going to shut up unless you tell me. Why the call you Freebase?"

Freebase opened one eye. "For reals?"

"Tell me and I'll go to sleep."

Freebase groaned and shifted in his chair. "Fuck, dog. You know Richard Pryor?"

"Not personally."

"Some of the dudes think I look like him because I got an afro and the stache, only they don't know any of his movies," Freebase admitted. "So, they think they smart, call me Freebase on account the funny man almost lit his ass on fire when he was shootin' up heroin. That's why."

"That's stupid as hell," I laughed.

"Whatever, man. You try finding a barber who can cut a black man's hair. Even back in the day, next to damn impossible unless you in the hood."

"I would have called you Daddy Rich. From Car Wash."

"Truth," he said and nodded.

I laid my head back and zoned at the stars. It wasn't much later that Freebase began to breathe heavy. I used that time to slowly move my hand away from the spike and search the sand. I found the mound right away and gripped the buck knife Torch planted for me.

Using my left elbow to prop up, I took in the sights of the camp. Snoring was infectious. No one awake, not even the two guards I heard ordered to stay alert. They were slumped in their chairs as well. The RV and other vehicles were quiet too. Only the small crackle of a few fires and the crickets that surrounded made any noise. Freebase had drool coming down his chin. I leaned over and cut the rope that bound my right hand, then quickly sliced the ropes that held my legs. Still, I laid back down just in case anyone saw and none did.

I was tempted to cut Freebase's throat, but that could have caused a commotion. Instead, I rolled a few feet, dodged a cactus, then rose to my feet. I stayed low and walked between a few cars, searching for my backpack and crowbar. Rogues were sleeping in cars, tents, chairs, while the rest were snug in sleeping bags on the sand. I had to sidestep some so I wouldn't trample them. As I rounded the hood of a Mustang, I heard a snort and stopped immediately.

The pigs. They were asleep in their cages in the truck parked nearby. One of them let out a small squeal in its sleep and kicked out with its hooves. The other snorted once more and its large snout blew snot. Figuring I was pushing my luck, I slunk lower to hide and practically crawled out of view. Once I cleared the truck, I saw the RV parked ahead and thought that to be the best bet. That was where the boss was sleeping.

And that was where I found them. My belongings, propped against the RV bumper. I quickly hiked them over my shoulder headed for the house – or what remained of it.

I wound around sets of shrubs. I found the mountain bike and hiked it over my shoulder. Soon, I was gone, the fires behind me small, and I had the open desert to myself once more.

CHAPTER FORTY-TWO

With the Rogues far behind me, I was relieved that no one seemed to notice my absence yet. There were no engines starting up, no shouts, no horns. There was also no Jock. I was alone, peddling through the creek bed but struggling. The sand was soft and I almost crashed twice. The paths were hardly clear, despite the generous moonlight guiding me along and I was burning a lot of energy. I needed a more solid ground to make any progress and decided to junk the bike as I got too tired. I had only made it a mile or two and it was slow going. I could have walked just as fast.

Suddenly, I was hit with a glorious smell. Meat, over a fire. My mouth drooled at the thought of a barbeque ahead somewhere. As if under a spell, I began heading towards a hill where the scent of cooking was strongest.

Ahead of me, there was a footpath between Joshua Trees, mixed with shrub. I was drooling, thinking of a smorgasbord with side dishes and desserts. My survival sense was screaming at me, telling me to turn back, that this was nonsense. A façade. I should continue down the creek bed to the Salton Sea. I was too curious though and fucking hungry. Whoever was grilling was about to have a visitor.

The footpath was slim. I hopped, straddled, and snaked between some egg-shaped rocks going higher and higher with each step. Moments later, I heard the crackle of fire and saw a yellow glare off some rocks. I stooped to duck. Using my hands as a guide, I swam past more rocks until I reached the top of the path and took cover behind a large Joshua tree that had one arm upright, the other lying flat. Around me was a clearing like animals had camped there, with soft sand flattened, vacant of vegetation. Another good vantage point from there. I could see the desert floor behind me and the creek bed I was following.

I concentrated on the actual camp once more. It was in another flat area surrounded by Joshua trees and walls of sand. In the center, a tented wagon was parked, while ropes and pulleys laid in the dirt. A fire pit was before it, with logs arranged for seating out front. An animal was roasting rotisserie style, attached to two poles at opposite ends, but I couldn't tell what the main course was. Clothes hung on a tree to dry.

I braced when I heard a loud snort. To my right, hidden among some trees, a brown horse was tied to one some twenty feet away, probably catching my scent and growing irritated. Facing me, it shook its head up and down, a large harness draped around his neck with reins flipping in the air. I didn't see any people yet but I knew someone must be close by. A horse was a valuable commodity.

The Gypsy camp. That had to be it.

The tent flap suddenly lifted up and a large man with a red shirt, black pants, and shiny boots crawled out on all fours. Hiking one leg over the side, he lowered himself to the ground, his back to me, struggling with his weight. He was obese; a definite rarity those days. I was mesmerized that this man can be that big, uncoordinated, and that successful at getting food. With both feet on the ground, he turned, hiked his belt up, and grunted loudly. The belt itself had a bullwhip attached to it. That was the only weapon I could see so far. When he bent down to the fire, I finally saw his face which was weathered, bulbous, and backed by dark skin. His hair was wild like a bird's nest. He had a thick, wiry black beard that looked like a mop.

The large man spun the dead animal over the pit, cranking what looked like a handle slowly. Words belched from deep within, foreign, and unrecognizable. Clearly not Spanish, which was what one could assume that far south. The juices singed and sizzled in the flames below and that's when I saw it. There was no mistaking the canine-like, slender frame.

A coyote.

My heart skipped for a second but then I came to grips and realized it wasn't Jock getting roasted. It was the real deal however; the front limbs were tied forward, the rear legs fixed towards the tail. It looked as if it was leaping the fire. The brown hide was splayed out, drying on a log.

Using the Joshua tree as leverage, I crept closer and stepped between a set of rocks. Suddenly, the air cracked, I heard a loud whoosh, and my right foot slipped out from under me. I fell forward, slamming my forehead into the ground and unexpectedly, I was jerked and whisked high backwards, my right foot snagged. I was airborne for a moment and hung upside down in an instant. I then found myself staring down at the ground, swinging back and forth like a pendulum. I twirled and grasped at the nothingness of air. My head thumped and pounded. I felt a trickle of blood running down my temple. I was tied somehow from my ankle to a branch on the Joshua tree.

My other foot dangled awkwardly and uselessly, causing me to spin as I flailed my arms. The rope around my ankle was starting to burn into my skin. The branch above me groaned under my weight as I yo-yoed so I tried to heave myself up and down to snap free. That didn't work. I was twirling hopelessly, feeling the circulation cutting off. The world around me was upside down, blood was rushing to my head, and I was bemoaning the fact that this was the second time today I was *tied the fuck up.*

During one of the gnarly spins, I caught sight of the large man lumbering towards me, huffing himself, his left hand on his whip. I searched in vain for my crowbar, patting my backpack, and realized the quiver was empty. I then saw my weapon on the ground, leaning on a rock, just out of reach. I would need to swing my body to reach it but I didn't know how.

"Hello infidel," the large man said to me, reaching the tree, and he patted me on my ass, causing me to spin more. I smelled bad BO and booze on his breath.

"Cut me down!" I told him, the blood starting to flood my face. I reached out to him but he stepped back, just out of reach. That caused me to spin again and I was growing dizzy now too.

"Now Stevo get reward," the man said matter of fact and laughed, a great belly laugh, and he almost fell over a rock doing it. Catching himself with a large paw, he then leaned on one of the egg-shaped rocks.

"I am Stevo," he said, pointing to himself the obvious.

"Nice to meet you," I snapped sarcastically. "How about some scissors?"

"Do you see this, infidel?" he asked me. I was still spinning, slowly then, and even in the moonlight, I could vaguely make it out. He held a whistle in his stubby, dirty fingers. The type referees used at ball games. "Do you know what this is?"

"Doesn't look like scissors," I remarked, and saw the crowbar again.

Stevo blew three times. The noise startled me, it was screechy and piercing, and I cupped my ears. I was sure the entire desert heard it.

"What the hell was that for?" I asked. I hung for a moment, letting my arms drop. I could barely touch the sand. My jaw opened and my eyes were bulging.

"I get reward," Stevo stated proudly. "I get rich." He beat his chest like a gorilla.

"Don't blow that fucking thing again!" I shouted, lifting myself up again, trying once more for the rope around my ankle. It was useless, there was no way that sucker was coming off. I slunk back down, thinking of Plan B. "Reward for what?"

"The Ginn will soon be here," he said.

"Ginn? I don't know who the hell you're talking about. Please get me down." It was getting hard to breathe too. I felt like I was going to pass out.

Stevo started to circle me. "The Ginn broadcast on CB radio. Ask where special man is. I knew I catch you. Stevo is good trapper. Attracted you with smell of meat." He then patted his stomach. "Big belly. Stevo never go hungry."

Arching my back and legs, I began to swing myself instead of just hanging there. Anything to distract him. I created a circular motion, twisting like a desperate fish on a line and soon I could sense I was getting closer to my iron bone cruncher. At one point, my fingers grazed it and Stevo seemed oblivious. I was resilient though and keep at it. I didn't trust Stevo and assumed he'd never stop blowing the damn whistle.

"You...have...the wrong...man," I insisted.

"No," Stevo replied. "Handsome man with tool. You."

"I found...that tool...on a dead man."

Stevo unfurled his whip. "The Ginn is born of smokeless fire. He travel nonstop. Always look for souls to corrupt. He builds an army, you see." He then pointed at me. "You must have been in danger to be damned, my friend."

His whip cracked against my side and I yelped, the sting feeling as if fire crept up my chest to my leg. "He was a hotel concierge! Nothing more! He was just a fucking gopher!" I yelled, grimacing at the pain.

"Ah, but a concierge who can get whatever you desire. And plenty of peoples want plenty of desires," he pointed out, like he was admonishing a bad child.

The whip cracked against my skin again, this time higher across my right knee. I groaned in pain and reached up to rub it, but found I was getting very tired and could only lift myself part of the way. Stretching out, I touched the ground again, gathering sand in my hand this time and I tried to throw it at him but it missed horribly, only showering his feet.

Sidestepping with an awkward gait, he then said, "The biggest mistake you did was not to take the Ginn seriously. He is a demon."

Still twirling, eyes bulging, I yelled, "You're full of shit!"

"No, I am Romani. A Gypsy. Legends follow me," he then said proudly.

I could feel my strength waning. "Cut me down or you'll pay!" I shouted.

"I don't think so," he replied and whistled again. Shrilly, loud, and just plain obnoxious. Who the hell invented those things?

"You heard Ginn," I told him, my voice straining. "He said...not to hurt me or you'll see his fury. I'll tell him...you whipped me."

He considered that, then shrugged it off. "Oh, this is just games and fun." He whistled again, less so this time, as he was expelling a lot of energy doing it. I could tell he was tiring, just from blowing the whistle and talking. Clearly, the fat Gypsy was out of shape. "I will talk on CB radio next."

"Knock that shit off!" I cried out and began twisting. "I'm going to kill you...kill you..." I confessed, curving and bending my back and legs once more. My fingers grazed the crowbar but then the rope toyed with me, pulling me back for another go.

Stevo suddenly stood as if spooked, looking back at his camp. "You have dog?" he asked me, looking down at his camp, then at me.

My body swung back towards the crowbar again. "No...I don't... have a dog!" I stretched harder that time, the rope ready to slice my ankle in two. I grunted, fingers out, just about...

"I see dog. I kill it," Stevo said, gathered his bullwhip, and began to walk towards his camp.

The crowbar was in my grasp.

"This dog walks!" he shouted amazed and his hand suddenly whipped back, the very hand holding the bullwhip which was summarily dropped. He hollered and staggered, backing up towards me, holding a bleeding hand in shock.

I lunged up and I buried the claw end into Stevo's collar as he was slouched. Having snared him, I used the crowbar to pull myself forward, climbing up my tool to reach him. He gagged and tried to resist me, pulling away, my crowbar tearing into the fabric. The rope behind me was strained, resisting mightily, and my leg felt ready to be ripped off.

"Dog must stay...away!" he mumbled, pitching forward.

We had a tug-of-war going on and he was beginning to pull us away. Stevo out front, me almost horizontal, the rope taut. The pain in my right leg was almost unbearable and I groaned out loud. With the rope cinching tighter and tighter, I pulled back with all my might. Finally, behind us all, the branch on the Joshua tree groaned and cracked. The strain got to be too much and the branch snapped in two and sent both of us crashing to the ground.

Stevo face-planted into hard ground, while his back took the brunt of my weight with me landing there. He was on his chest, huffing, out of breath, hands uselessly clutching dirt ahead of him. My head pounded from the ordeal but I could tell the fuzziness and dizziness were thankfully going away. I swore at the fat sonofabitch and slammed him on the side of his right ear with my fist. That caused him to squeal and I drilled him a second time, making him screech again. I then drove my elbow into the back of his head and followed that up by mashing his head into the ground. A muffled yelp sounded and I could tell he was swallowing sand.

"Where's your fucking whistle now, fat boy?" I whispered with a sneer, feeling for the crowbar behind me. Combing through the sand, I found it, then decided to end this fat man's life quickly. I still felt the sting from his whipping.

I reached under his throat with the crowbar, grabbed each end with my hands and began pulling back towards me like I was rowing. Spit flew from him, his legs kicked and his stubby arms tried to grasp the crowbar. He shuddered so violently, I wasn't sure I could hold on so I dug in deep and pulled harder. The big man gargled, his breathing became labored, and his strength waned. With one last mighty pull, something snapped. Stevo went limp and loudly defecated.

I rolled off the fat bastard, onto my back, and laid there, catching my breath. And then I remembered the whistle. The fucking whistle. I snapped out of it. My ankle throbbed as the rope was still tied around it. I used my crowbar to dig between the knot and pry it apart, my ears now in tune with the quiet that surrounded me, listening to any movement. I hoped the sound of the whistle didn't travel far. I needed time to recoup.

After a few anxious digs, the rope came loose and I rubbed my ankle. It was sore and tingly, like it had fallen asleep, but after a while, I could move it again. My head was still ringing and through the fog that inhabited my world, I saw the coyote walking towards me from the camp, although he was not charred or burnt. No, this one was walking on two legs and it carried a familiar, worried look on his face.

Jock. His slingshot drooped in his left hand. Eyeing me with pity, he was suddenly distracted by the body of Stevo. I thought he'd be repulsed, but instead, the little man whisked out his buck knife, bent down and grasped Stevo's hand. Turning it this way and that, he carved out the ball bearing that was imbedded there deep and admired the bloody, round piece of ammo like it was gold.

Still feeling the effects of the hanging, I asked him bitterly, "You couldn't have shot him sooner? Before he whipped me?"

"I needed a better shot,' Jock smiled.

"You did that on purpose."

Ignoring that comment, he then pointed to the camp and held the slingshot out. "There's someone in the tent. I think it's a woman."

Turning, I could see it, but no movement. "How can you tell?"

"I can smell her," Jock said and lifted his nose. "Perfume. It's dope."

"What are you doing here?" I asked as I rose, albeit it slowly. I eased up on my ankle. Damn, that hurt. Dancing lightly, I put my full weight on it and after a few moments, the feeling came back.

Jock glanced at Stevo, then the rope. "You need help, obviously. And Mexico is too far a walk."

With my crowbar in hand, I considered a double-tap on the fat Gypsy, mostly for kicks at that point, but the wagon had me concerned. A new distraction, and whatever I could do to add to Stevo's misery, the better.

Jock said, "I could suggest we keep moving and not find out what's behind door number one. But I know that's not on your mind."

Gripping my crowbar tight, I informed him, "Let's go make a deal."

Jock sighed. "Yet another timely reference."

CHAPTER FORTY-THREE

I circled the wagon, trying to figure the best way in. The bubble top was rustic, slightly weathered, made of thick canvas. The lower half was solid oak, still holding old world craftsmanship and charm. The wagon shifted and creaked as if someone inside had moved. Below the front flap was a bench for riders, big enough for two abreast, with a slanted foot rest. The horse behind us was busy snapping its head up and down, agitated and tugging at his ropes. I didn't know how to calm a horse, so I put my hands out and mouthed "whoa" to no avail. It was worth a shot.

Jock stood behind me, armed with his slingshot. The coyote meat continued to sizzle, causing a bit of a distraction. I climbed up on the bench seat and reached for the flap. Jock climbed up after me on the other side.

"Ready?" I asked him.

"Not really," he said with a gulp but kept his slingshot primed.

I yanked the flap open. With the aid of the fire behind me, I could see a mess inside. Blankets and clothes were strewn about while pots, pans, and utensils lined along the side. Once I opened the flap further, the fire's light streamed in and a waif of a woman cowered in the far corner, shackled there by chain. She was unlike Stevo in both size and color. She was slim, pale white, but disheveled. A prisoner no less and Jock gasped. Why he was surprised was beyond me. Out there in the desert, nothing was a surprise anymore.

"Stay outside," I told him, buttoning the flap so it remained open. "Two of us might frighten her."

He nodded and jumped down. "I'll go up the hill and see if anyone's responding to the whistle."

In a calming gesture, I showed my open hands to her, although the crowbar was still in my grasp as I climbed up and in. With the low roof, I had to crabwalk past a set of beds, moonshine jugs, cigarettes in a carton, and comic books (of all damn things). Although I showed her that I meant no harm, she bought none of it and tried desperately to morph into the wall. Bruises and welts revealed she was an obvious captive and I shook my head, wishing I kept Stevo alive just a bit longer, just so I could hurt him more.

"It's okay, I won't hurt you," I told her and she startled at my voice.

Clasped tight on the chain was a large lock, fit for a key. I tugged at it and she yelped. "Don't worry, I'll get you out. I won't hurt you," I informed her.

Sorrowful blue eyes scrutinized me from behind wisps of long dark hair. She had a small nose, small mouth and nice teeth. I pegged her to be in her forties. Despite her conditions, I could tell she was pretty once but Stevo worked her over pretty good. Grabbing the lock, I searched all around. "Where does he keep the key?"

She nodded outside. That fat bastard probably kept it on him. Motioning her to lean back, I slid the chisel end of the crowbar between the prongs of the lock and jerked the tool upright. She jolted as the metal snapped and the lock crumbled, breaking much easier than I thought. I quickly loosened the chains from her shackles, tossing them aside in a heap. She was free and we stared at each other for a few seconds and then, strangely, she tried to gather the chains again and cover herself. I imagined this was the first time she'd been free for some time and I stopped her, palms out again.

"It's okay, you're free," I told her. "No more bad guy."

Tears streamed down her cheeks. She rolled on her side in relief, almost as if she wanted to sleep. Deep scars from whippings flashed from under her shirt and I had the sudden urge to take *el crowbarino* back to Stevo and see if Gypsy meat would tenderize.

"Who are you? Why did you do that?" she whispered to me, not looking my way. No accent, she was local. American.

"You were held captive," I said. "I can't let you stay like that."

Sitting up, she glared at me. "So, I belong to you now?"

Whoo-boy, that could take a while I thought. I tried to appear trusting but time was not on my side. "No, I'm just trying to help. What's your name?"

"Grace."

"Well, Grace, Stevo won't hurt you anymore."

She seemed to consider that. "Did he whip you too?"

My sides still burned and I flinched so I nodded. "We need to get you out of here," I told her and held my hand out. "I'm here to help. Stevo is dead, that fucker, and I've got a good mind to grab my crowbar, go back there, and ..."

She interrupted me, worried. "What about the other one?"

"Other one what?"

"There are two of those bastards," she told me and at that instant, I heard a rattle behind me that I was all too familiar with. The flap opened up to my left side, at the rear, and a large rattlesnake was tossed inside. The woman shrieked and cowered into her corner again, taking the chains with her as cover. The rattler was a five-footer and it coiled immediately, afraid of the new digs and warm bodies that surrounded. Sensing my movement first, it struck my boot, and quickly withdrew. I quickly scrambled to the side and checked my boot. Thankfully, the fangs didn't penetrate the leather. Another two inches higher, however, I'd be staring at the wrong side of grass.

Moving away from the woman, the rattler's head followed me, the slits in its eyes focusing on the motion, the blackish-purple forked tongue flickering, acquiring my scent. The pits behind its nostrils sensed heat and they use that to pinpoint their next strike. The tail shook vigorously, like a baby's busted rattle, and it struck again but this time, just stabbing air. I was just out of reach and I watched it retract into a coil once more. Across from me, the woman was too afraid to move and only whimpered in her defense.

I slammed my crowbar down hard on the snake's head, crushing it instantly with the claw end. The dead reptile, its body twitching, was then lifted and tossed by me, skidding to the front of the wagon. Even dead, it tried to coil itself. Nerves had a funny way of not letting go.

The woman's eyes widened, staring to my left and she shrieked. A hairy hand then reached through the tent flap behind me. A thick forearm snaked under my neck and I was suddenly hauled out through the rear tent flap.

I was outside, stuck in a choke hold, dragged backwards. The man doing this to me was thinner than Stevo, that much I could tell, but nevertheless, was very strong. Like Stevo, his booze breath was rancid and he had matching BO. I still had my crowbar in my hand and I threw it behind me, over my head, but the man ducked and weaved, avoiding each swing. He tried to squeeze my neck like a python, but the number one rule to outlasting a choke was to breathe, so all I had to do was turn my head and body. Doing that, my windpipe opened wide. Rule number two was go for a major nut tap so I balled my fist and connected squarely, to which the man grunted out loud and released me instantly. As he staggered back though, the momentum carried us in the same direction and I fell to the ground, thumping my head on a log next to the fire.

It stunned me a moment and when I turned over, I was face flush against the flames. The heat from the fire was intense and I rolled away opposite, feeling behind my head where a bump appeared. I struggled to my knees, the pain in my ankle still present from the rope. The other man had fallen too, away from me, and he started to rise, his legs together and he rubbed his privates. Even bent slightly, I could see the man was taller and thinner yet just as hairy as his partner in crime. Another Gypsy, my guess. The two of them reminded me of Laurel and Hardy. He swore in a language native to him, cupping his groin, but then somehow grew a new pair and reached for an axe stuck in a nearby log.

"Well, here's another nice mess you've gotten me into," I told him as I got to my feet. Not my best impression, as Laurel stared at me confusedly, not getting it.

"You kill Stevo. Now I kill you," he mumbled and charged me with the axe held high above his head, chopping down with both hands and missing as I sidestepped it. His axe buried itself into the log I hit my head on and it stuck there. Given recent events, it wasn't difficult to summon the bear. Growling, I smashed my crowbar on the back of his legs and he crumpled to his knees, as if motioning to pray. I sent another blow in the middle of his back and he arched in pain. With his back to me, I snagged the claw end under his chin, like I did with the Wrestler back at the Jupiter Playhouse, but instead of cupping the son of a bitch with a warning, I wrenched with both hands towards me with a quick yank.

A mound of bloody flesh and bone stuck in the claw end. I had ripped his throat out and I tossed the chunk of bone and tissue aside. Clutching his throat with both hands, he gasped and choked loudly until I swung my crowbar down on top of his head. Silently then, he teetered face first into the edge of the fire with a thump that caused sparks to fly. His scraggy hair caught fast like lighter fluid and his head became engulfed in seconds. There was no scream, no sound, his body only twitching like the snake did minutes ago.

Nerves had a funny way of not letting go, I thought again.

CHAPTER FORTY-FOUR

Grace said little since I helped her from the confines of the wagon. We were gobbling shards of overcooked coyote at the fire, casting suspicious glances at one another as we shared the warmth. She needed not fear me, but she didn't know that; the apocalyptic men in her life had been brutal and I was guilty by association. She stood about five-foot-five and was now dressed in a dirty white shirt, dark sweat pants, but remained barefoot. She ate feverishly, tearing and gnawing, food an obvious scarcity she was taking liberty with.

Laurel Gypsy's body continued to burn and occasionally sizzled and popped with a steady stream of smoke wafting upward. His head and upper torso were fully cooking; if you stayed downwind, you'd inhale the nauseous bouquet of human barbeque. I didn't remove him as we wouldn't be staying long and her captor deserved to fry anyway.

We found a bag of rattlesnakes nearby with a cord tightened around the top. Laurel Gypsy must have been hunting when he heard the whistles.

Grace clearly despised both men and kept staring at Laurel and then at Stevo up the hill to make sure they were both dead. Really dead. I assured her they really were and asked her to hurry and eat as fast as she could. We needed to move, like, yesterday, as I feared the Rogues heard the whistle. Jock hadn't notified us of any change yet but it was bound to happen. My disappearing act at the Snake House was sure to get noticed too. Slamming the meat down our throats should provide us with much needed energy until I could figure out what to do next. I couldn't leave her behind, so I was already drawing plans in my head to take her with us.

"Could use some steak sauce," I told her, holding a piece out for emphasis.

Next to me was Stevo's CB radio. I found it when I went to get Grace from the tent. An older model, I turned it on and moved the dial, hearing only static. I found the same channel Ginn had used before and left it on, volume low, the static more like white noise that could drown out any vehicle until it was too late. Good thing I had a sentry posted at the hilltop. One that would never fall asleep. Not under these conditions.

"Where are we?' she asked me out of the blue. "What state?"

I was taken back by that question and answered with a frown. "California. Middle. Southern."

A rattle sounded behind us. "The snakes don't move much when it's cold. Easier to catch," she mumbled, nodding backward. "They know of a pit where they hide when the temperature drops. Usually, there's about ten in there."

"I like snake meat," I confessed.

Grace nodded and bit into a piece we tore from the coyote's back leg. "You aren't alone, are you?" she asked, her eyes still shifting side to side.

"No."

"Woman?"

"No," I told her. "I have a friend and it's just us. He's keeping watch as we speak." I fingered the hill behind her but was not sure which hill he was on. The moon has shifted high above and cast a wide shadow on the camp, part of which was dark.

She considered that and asked, "Is he dangerous?"

"No, but he whines a lot."

Right then, Jock slid down the slope behind the horse, which startled and rose on two legs. Grace shrieked at the sight of Jock running towards us in his coyote get-up.

"It's okay, he's with me. His name is Jock," I reassured her, again placating with my hands. "It's just a costume."

"Headlights in the desert! We need to go!" he shouted to us. Grace stared at him, partially hiding behind me. "Rogues are circling in the distance! A few miles away! They are on the creek bed we took!"

Grace's lips trembled. She said, "Rogues," and slumped as if defeated already.

Lending a hand, I reached out to Grace and stood. "Come with us. I can't leave you here." It was more of a statement than a request. I wasn't going to take no for an answer. Confusion spread wide on the little captor. She couldn't make up her mind about me and now Jock entered the picture so I braced for a possible struggle to get her going.

"Where are you going?" she asked, standing.

"The Salton Sea," I replied, growing anxious. My eyes shifted around the camp, looking for a hidden vehicle of some kind and, of course, saw none. I imagined the horde barreling towards us and we were stalling because of trust issues.

Grace cocked her head, like the others did. "Why would you go there?" she asked.

Trying to hurry her, I kept it short. "It's a long story. I'll fill you in on the way."

Grace stared back at the camp. Just when I thought she'd go with the plan, she said, matter of fact, "I can't leave the horse."

That remark stopped me instantly. "What?"

"The horse," she pointed. "Pandz is a good horse. I won't leave him behind. I worked with horses all my life and I won't let them get him."

"Get the horse then," I told her. "Bring him with us."

As Grace ran off, Jock shot me a look and all I could do was shrug. Grace worked fast, calming the animal with gentle strokes, then untying it from the tree. Jock and I paced nervously and at that moment and I wondered if she'd take off and leave us there. Honestly, that would have been a smart, welcomed move.

"Are you serious?" Jock whined. "*Now*, she wants to rescue her horse?"

"Guess so," I said, shaking my head. "Nothing I can do, that's women for you." In a time of escape, she was more concerned with the damn horse than herself. Grace backed the horse to the wagon with a series of tongue clicks between two pulleys and attached them to the harness. Jock and I watch from afar, astounded she could work so fast despite her shoddy condition. I might have underestimated her, she no longer resembled the terrified, captive creature, and instead, grew headfast and strong willed. Grabbing the reins, she then vaulted to the top of the wagon and dropped into the bench seat. The wagon rolled forward, the wheels squealing, the tent flopping.

"What is she doing?" Jock asked me, as she turned towards us. The horse was drawing a bead on me and I wasn't sure which way to step.

"Hop in the wagon! Hurry!" Grace yelled to us from her perch.

"Looks like Pioneer days," I said, stepping aside the last moment, grasping the side of the wagon and urging a worried Jock to climb on.

CHAPTER FORTY-FIVE

Pandz huffed and snorted as he pulled the wagon over the uneven ground. I rode shotgun next to Grace out front, she in control of the reins, me doing not much else except look concerned. We had been traveling for some time, up a long windy road that separated a large set of mountains. The moon's glow was waning a bit, the bright orb in the sky had shifted to the west even more. She used a gas lamp to help illuminate the way as well.

"Do you know where you're going?" I asked her.

"You wanted to head south, this is south," she replied. "These mountains only have so many places to cross and this is one of them."

I filled that time with some of the details of the plane and Salton Sea. Maybe a bit too much; I confessed again to the situation that led me to be far from my family. Just like Iris, it felt good to talk to a woman and get their point of view. However, unlike Iris, Grace only hemmed some of the details as if the past was the past and hinted that maybe I should move on. A simple shrug would do that.

"Have you seen a plane in the sky?" I asked her.

"No, not at all. Watch the potholes," she said and pointed. "Hold on to the sides." Ahead, the pockmarked road looked treacherous but Pandz tackled it easy enough although I heard Jock grunt behind me.

Occasionally, I glanced down at the wooden wheels to see if they'd fall off or break a spoke since the route we took was harsh. Amazingly, the wagon had some shock absorbers underneath and the ride was not as bumpy as you'd assume. Jock was somewhere in the back staring out the rear flap, keeping watch and silent so far. I figured he'd be the first one to backseat drive yet he didn't utter a peep.

"What kind of name is Pandz for a horse?" I asked her. She had told me the name earlier and how it was spelled.

Shrugging, she said, "It's a Gypsy name is all I know. Them and their wayward customs and freaky fables."

I nudged her knee. "Not a convert, eh?"

She gave me a look. "No, I are educated," she joked.

It was about an hour later when we came across the 10 Freeway. I couldn't contain my excitement. We were closer than ever and I fidgeted like a kid. The freeway itself was virtually free from any sort of activity, thankfully. Only one abandoned car was in sight and no one was living in it, as far as I could tell. We crossed the freeway with no interruptions and continued south towards the goal.

"Probably best if we make our own road," she piped in. "We don't want the Rogues following us and its flat the rest of the way in."

"I agree. Make way."

To pass the time and keep our mind off the pursuers, we got to talking about Gypsy's and their tall tales, including one where I rolled my eyes that involved Ginn.

She started with, "I had seen Ginn once in the past, at another campsite east of here, probably in Arizona. Stevo and Milosh feared the man and went out of their way to cater to him, throwing themselves at his mercy but receiving little in return. They did that for no one else which was strange and often bullied their way into barters and trades along other sects and communities."

"Trading what?"

"Mostly meats, pelts and salt," she said. "Anyway, Ginn was revered by others as well, that his men would follow him blindly, and some would say to their deaths if he so commanded. I figured that such a strict allegiance could only mean one thing; the man was the devil himself. Only when we left Arizona did the brothers breathe. They said Ginn was a demon. He was magical. He had great powers. I figured Ginn was nothing more than a late-night TV infomercial pitchman, but what did I know?" she said.

"He's nothing. Remember that," I mentioned, hoping it would sink in.

"Still, the stories and tall tales of the guy. I didn't know what to believe. But if too many believe the hype, it must be true. Right?"

"The legend of Ginn seems to grow each time I hear it," I replied.

"We had been at the site we just left for about three months or so. We were always on the move, but always close to water. The brothers would set up snares and traps all around watering holes and they were quite successful at it, trading the excess meat and hides to the Rogues. Milosh would take the meat, preserve it with salt from the salt flats, and be gone for days taking Pandz with him. He'd return with moonshine and stories of the whores at the camp he sampled. I dreaded those days. That meant rough, drunken sex with a riled up, jealous Stevo."

A cold shiver rode my spine at just the thought. We ended our quaint, *get to know you* conversation and drifted into silence, thinking of each other's perseverance to get through our new lives.

After some time of riding in silence, she looked down at my foot. "The snake bit you, didn't it? Back at the camp?"

I tugged on the one boot and slid my finger inside, showing no holes. "Just blanks, I guess."

"Your boots are..."

"Mismatched. I know."

She shook her head. "Worn. What are you, size eleven?"

Shrugging, I said, "Yeah, I think so."

Grace handed me the reins. "Hold them tight, but give a little slack. Don't jerk back. Pandz likes to be in control but don't give him too much."

"What? Why? I don't..."

Grace disappeared to the interior of the wagon. "Where are you going?" I asked, gripping the reins, not sure what else to do. Pandz realized someone else was driving and he bucked his head twice. Like a lame-ass, I muttered *it's okay* and *nice horsie*. New boots suddenly appeared next to me on the bench, in near perfect condition. Socks were stuffed in them as well, blue in color.

"You're the same size as Stevo," Grace said and climbed back into the bench.

I patted my stomach. "So much for Pilates."

She laughed. "I meant your feet."

"What's Jock doing back there?" I nodded back.

"He's fine," she said, brushing him off. She clearly enjoyed my company more. "Try on the boots."

They looked newer, hardly worn. A tan brown with dark soles and laces. Much better than the pair I wore. She urged me to try them on. "Stevo hadn't worn these yet. They are good hiking boots. Complements of The Shoeman."

I shifted in my seat and looked at her. "The Shoeman? You knew him?"

Grace nodded and she retook the reins. "He stops by occasionally and trades with the brothers."

"Unfortunately, he's out of business for good," I said but didn't lead on. I removed my boots and instantly got hit with a mighty whiff, a horrid bad egg smell from my feet. Grace held her nose and I meekly apologized. Rolling my old socks off, I tossed them overboard, then quickly slid one sock over my foot that masked some of the stench. It felt good, a perfect fit. Wiggling my toes, there was room and as I stood, holding the roof of the wagon, the contours of the boot made me want to hike right away. I really resented not trading with The Shoeman back when I had the chance.

As I sat back down, Grace started with some history. "I am not a Gypsy, like those pigs. These assholes kidnapped me outside Tucson, where I was from. I was with a small group and went to lead our animals to a nearby river when these two cornered me and took me. How does it feel?"

"What? Oh, the boot" I wriggled my toes again. "Feels good."

"Put the other one on," she said, her nose twitching. "Please."

My other foot slipped into the sock and eased into the boot like butter. Jock muttered something about a weird smell and we laughed.

"These rock," I told her. "Thank you."

"You're welcome."

"So, Tucson," I said, hoping she'd continue. "I heard it wasn't hit?"

"Right. The city wasn't hit at all, but that didn't make us fine, by any means. We relied on other cities for food and other necessities. We suffered in the heat of summer without working AC. The heat wiped out most of the inhabitants. Electricity is such a vital component for human survival. I don't know how they did it back in the old west without it. How did you manage the heat?"

"I avoid the desert in the summer. I wander a lot too."

"We often traveled at night," Grace admitted and tapped the lamp above her head.

"How did you come across the Gypsy clan?"

Sighing loud, she continued. "I was staying at a ranch a few of my friends found refuge in. On the outskirts of the city. We did okay, lost a lot of people to suicide though. They just didn't want to go on, especially another summer. Some people just can't handle it, you know? Trading was a big part of our existence. Stevo and Milosh had wandered by one day, traded some meat for some corn and other veggies we had grown, then took root in a camp not far off. Turns out, they been watching us for days and singled me out. Even though there were a couple younger girls in the ranch, they wanted me as I could cook, clean, and fuck. I think that was a year ago."

"Sorry to hear." The life of women those days was horrific. Unless they were with a group, their lives were treacherous. Even in some groups as well.

"They wanted a woman, a slave," she pointed out.

"I got that."

"You seem like a decent guy. What was your name again?"

"Ted," I said.

"Ted," she said aloud. "It's an older name, isn't it?"

"Actually, its Theodore. Ted for short. Named after my grandfather."

"I like it," she said and nudged herself closer to me. It wasn't until we were touching, arm to arm, that I sensed there was more to her gap closure than just comfort. I found it, however, *uncomfortable*. "Tell me you're a good guy," she purred.

Although dark, I knew my face reddened and all I could offer was a small smile.

She whipped the reins to get Pandz moving faster. "The last good guy I was with was so long ago. My boyfriend just before the gas hit. He was diabetic."

"Awful."

"I avoided men the best I could. Men can be awful. But not all men." Turning her head, she breathed softly against my neck. My mouth went dry and I found it hard to swallow. She stroked my hair. "You'll treat me right, won't you?"

"You don't have to do that," I told her, but she didn't listen. Instead, she brought her face closer to mine and kissed my cheek. I turned my head slightly away and felt a stirring in my groin. Her hand was on my thigh, slowly massaging the inside of my leg, a bit too close to you know what. She kissed me again closer to my lips.

"Don't worry, Stevo hasn't touched me in months," she stated, quietly. "Most times the fat asshole was too drunk to get it up. Or too fat. I don't know. Try getting Viagra these days."

Good one. I tried not to laugh. She told me more. "He'd slap me around, then get winded and pass out."

"Jesus." Those were images I did not want to bring up.

"I used to pee in his drink. Spit in his food. Once, I swatted a scorpion under his leg while he was asleep. It stung him and he vomited for days," she said and giggled.

"Points for effort," was my lame response.

Nodding, she smiled. "Small victories."

We rode a bit longer with her body against mine. I wondered if she took that as a sign to continue. I was battling two fronts; one to save her from embarrassment, and two, to make sure my little head was working in unison with my big head.

She loosened her grip on the reins. "I could stop the wagon if you like."

My mouth was getting dry. My pants were really uncomfortable. I wasn't used to this attention.

She then reached down and touched my crotch. "Someone wants me to me play with them," she cooed.

I was getting aroused and for the first time, thinking that I was entitled too. The Doctor said Tracy found a new lover. Why not me?

"Take me. I want you," she purred.

I felt uneasy. This wasn't what I wanted to do.

"I'm a good cook," she said. "I fuck really well. I could do some whoring to get us by, if that's what you want."

I couldn't believe where this was going. "Stop," I demanded.

"No, I can't and I won't," Grace replied, quite sternly.

I shoved her hand away. "I just rescued you. What's wrong with you?"

"I am alone," she said suddenly turning angry. "Without a man, I'm as good as dead in the desert. I won't survive. I need to belong, do you hear me? I need to be a man's property."

Pandz grew irritated and seemed to want to tag in. I noticed the wagon was slowing a bit and I angrily looked at Grace. Soon, the horse was at a small trot. Too slow for my liking.

"We need to rest Pandz," she noted. "The weight of us and the wagon is too much. He doesn't travel this hard and this far often."

Jock thankfully thrusted himself between us. "Rogues behind us, a couple hundred yards back. Headlights in all directions. I think they are on the 10 Freeway we passed. We need to speed it up."

"Oh, shit," I said, considering ourselves lucky we traveled through there when we did. They must have been trying to cut us off. We were hardly in the clear, though. "What do we do now?"

"We're too heavy for Pandz!" she cried.

Jock disappeared into the wagon and shuffled around. "Grace, do you need a stove?" he called out.

She thought for a moment. "Well, kind of. I don't think so. I don't know."

"Can I toss it out?"

Grace nodded. That was enough for Jock. He opened the rear flap and hurled the old Coleman stove out into the darkness where it smashed on the ground. Jock wasn't done though. "What about this chair?" he asked, gripping it as if he knew what needed to be done.

"Fine," Grace said. Jock tossed that out too. Her possessions probably meant the world to her then. I could sense she was feeling neglected.

"Maybe I should help him," I suggested, placing my hand on her shoulder.

"Just keep the important stuff," she sighed.

I joined Jock in the rear, tossing what I thought were useless junk. We went back and forth like that, some items staying, others tossed out. Pandz picked up the pace as Grace egged him on. When we were done, I returned and stood, peering over the roof of the wagon tent at headlights crisscrossing in the distance. Then, just behind us, I saw a glint of metal shining from the moonlight. That was when it hit me.

"Wait!" I shouted. "Jock, everything you're throwing out, stop!"

"Why?" Jock asked, poking his head out of the flap.

"We're leaving them a trail!"

"Oh shit!" Jock yelled.

However, another mile further, we had made some progress. We were leaving a larger gap between us and them. Just in time too, Pandz slowed again and Grace shot me a look.

"You okay?" I asked.

"We can't go on. Pandz is tiring. We need to stop." Clicking her tongue again, she reined in the horse and we stopped. She dismounted and was at Pandz's side, rubbing his nose. "He can't take the wagon anymore. Isn't that right, boy?"

Pandz seemed to understand her and shook a leg.

Appearing from the tent, Jock looked glum. "I don't think we should stay here. The lights look further out but they'll pick up soon."

Although I had a feeling I knew the answer, I asked anyway. "Can Pandz take all three of us if we get rid of the wagon?"

Grace shook her head. "No. And right now, he needs rest. He's never carried the wagon that far before, especially over this terrain. We had another horse that helped pull before but he died a few months back."

I stood up on the wagon and looked behind us. The moon had dipped further on the horizon, yet I could still see the headlights in the distance. I was guessing the vehicles were having a tough time in the loose sand and shrub; the path we took would be difficult, even for a Jeep. "We need to keep going. It's not too much farther," I said confidently. We still had some time.

Grave sighed. "I don't even know what's out there. For me."

"I told you. The plane."

"This is your journey," she whined. "Not mine."

"You're welcome to come," I said, jumping down and facing her.

"No, not with that man chasing us," she said. "They will kill Pandz too. I can't bring myself to lead him to that."

"Come on," I told her. "There's going to be a safe place out there. I know it."

Stroking Pandz's neck, she added, "And what about Pandz? I just leave him there at the sea as we fly off?"

I blinked at her. "Yes! Your life is worth more..."

She instantly brushed me off. "No, this isn't right."

Jock didn't say anything. He shuffled his feet, then shot me with *what-are-you-gonna-do?* We both knew then she wouldn't join us. Just like the rest of them that we met along the way. None of them came, and none of them followed. It was becoming routine.

"Where will you go?" I asked her.

She shrugged. "No one will want me anyway. I'm as good as dead."

"Don't say that."

"You don't want me, no one will." She began sobbing into her hands. Pandz nudged her with his nose and she leaned on him. "I'm old and ugly."

"Come on," I said. "You're pretty. I am just...committed." Flashing my wedding ring was useless, she wasn't looking at it.

"You're just saying that," she said.

I pulled her in and spoke to her softly. "You are a beautiful person. Remember who you were and be that person again."

"Look at these scars," she said and lifted her shirt. "Those animals destroyed me. Who would want this? I don't blame you for rejecting me."

"Don't let those animals ruin you," I said to her, holding her hands. "It's not your fault they took you, but you will heal. You'll be okay. I see a pretty woman before me and I am glad to have met her."

She pushed away from me and unsnapped Pandz's harness. "I'm just slowing you two down now. You guys need to go." Pandz was soon free from the ropes and Grace walked back to the wagon. "There's not much time."

Jock leaped off the wagon and joined me at my side.

After quickly retrieving a few items from inside, Grace climbed back on her horse holding a bag with some necessities. In her other hand, the axe the brother used. "I'll head home again," Grace said sadly and gathered the reins. "Back to Tucson and see my old group. See if they will take me back."

Nodding confidently, I told her, "I know they'll take you back. I would. Hell, I'm trying to invite you to come with us."

"Thank you," she said and finally smiled. "There's some moonshine in a small jug inside the wagon if you want it."

"No thanks," Jock said.

"Thanks," I replied.

"Oh," she said and snapped her fingers. "Stay clear of the Muddies."

Jock and I looked at each other. Jock then prodded her. "Muddies?"

Frowning, she stated, "Mud people. Down by the Salton Sea. Sinister bunch. They don't treat their women well." There was that term again. Mud People. When I had walked around the sea years before, I wandered up and down the western side and didn't see any mud people.

"Good luck," she said to me, and then to Jock. "Make sure he completes his mission." Grace and her horse trotted east. We watched them crest a hill or two, and soon they vanished.

"At least her tracks will lead away from us," he said. "Think she'll be okay?"

"She has a head start and can cross the desert better than they can with the horse. But they won't follow her as she's heading east. They know we're heading south."

"Yeah, good to know," Jock said, sarcastically. "That they know we're still heading towards the Salton Sea no matter what."

CHAPTER FORTY-SIX

The eggs above me looked soft, pillow white, yet I knew they could potentially be deadly. The eggs in question looked to belong to a black widow, up on the ceiling of the rock ledge we had been sitting under, the two white sacks wedged into a groove, surrounded by wisps of tough webbing. I didn't tell Jock about them, he hadn't looked close enough, and I know that would have freaked him out if he'd seen them. Momma Spider was not around and hopefully, the small fire between us that kept us warm was enough to deter her from coming back. The eggs were too small and irrelevant, of course, but lack of food forces your mind to conjure thoughts of meals that were once readily available. At times, it could drive you nuts.

The rocky ledge we hid under would be our shelter for the night and would shield much of the fire light we desperately needed hidden. We were both tired and needed to rest, hoping the hounding Rogues would tire as well and catch forty winks. We were close to the Salton Sea, not sure by how much, but we didn't have the endurance to reach there any time tonight - that much I was sure about. The skies were quiet, so my guess was, the plane would arrive sometime tomorrow. I could hardly wait.

Seeing as there was no riverbed nearby, I had set up my dew catch earlier, having dug a pair of holes in the dirt, side by side. In the middle of the holes, I placed a pair of cups. Next, I unfolded a sheet of plastic from my backpack, laid it flat across the holes, then used rocks to weigh it down loosely. Using a smaller rock, I placed that in the center, the weight of which made the plastic into a cone shape, aiming down. Dew would collect along the plastic and roll down the cone and drip into the cups. The dig wasn't too strenuous either and I completed the task in no time.

My little buddy had a different method. Jock whipped out a plastic bag from his little backpack, neatly folded it, and stalked a nearby bush. Once he decided it was not poisonous, he then wrapped the bag around a patch of leaves on a branch and secured it with string. The idea was, dew could collect from the leaves and drain into the corner of the bag by morning. He argued that his method was less vigorous than mine and I agreed. Then again, he had to contend with a questionable leafy taste while mine was more like normal, highly coveted rainwater.

I was exhausted, my body aching from the events of the day. Jock flickered with the fire, spreading more twigs we had gathered to assure we had a comfortable flame all night. I was excited for tomorrow as I had no doubt we'd reach the Salton Sea. The air was cold and permeated with salt. Leaning back, I could not find sleep, not due to the eggs hovering above, but the anticipation of seeing my family again. Nor could Jock sleep. His eyes remained open and I could tell he wanted to talk.

Thinking a nightcap could help, I hoisted the small moonshine jug from the wagon Grace left me to my lips and took a swig, causing me to jerk forward and stifle a cough. There was only a little left and I debated drinking it all so I could pass out and actually sleep. Outside our camp, crickets chirped and other insects joined in. We welcomed the chorus because if it stopped, that meant trouble was nearby. So far, they had accepted us and I, too, was glad for nature's foolproof alarm system. The fire crackled little but provided some necessary warmth.

"Helps you sleep?" Jock asked and tapped the jug.

"Dreams," I replied. "I like my dreams. Sometimes, during the daytime, I forget what my wife and kids look like. But in my dreams, I see them and then I remember. Clear as day."

"You don't get nightmares? I do."

"Only when I am awake. That is the nightmare," I admitted.

Jock said, "Tell me about your boys then."

"They're good boys. Smart, funny, rambunctious. Athletes too. They played baseball, soccer, and hockey, but there's so much more I should have done with them."

"Are they like you? Or your wife?"

"Wayne was headstrong like me but cautious. Kevin was more daring but not a planner. I'd say a bit of both. They were stubborn like their mother though."

Jock slightly changed the subject. "What happens if we get to the Salton Sea and there's no plane?"

"I haven't thought about that," I said. "I'm sure I'll make my flight."

"What if you don't make it? To the sea, I mean?"

"I'll die trying."

"What if there's no plane though?"

"I'll hang around. Make the Salton Sea my new home. They will have to land there sometime." I closed my eyes and leaned back. Sleep wasn't coming yet, visions of my family bounced around my head like a tennis ball. Jock stirred next to me and reminisced too.

My own words resonated. *They will have to land there sometime.* Won't they?

Jock then said, "I had plans to go to film school. The comic store was just a part-time job. There are a lot of things I never got to do. You're lucky, you got to experience so much in life. It's a shame you blew it."

I was too tired to argue. From the corner of my eye, I saw Jock reach into his pocket and take out the Queen chess piece. He gently placed it in my pocket. I wondered when he took it from me. I don't recall handing it to him.

"I have too heavy a cross to bear," Jock whispered and shut his eyes.

CHAPTER FORTY-SEVEN

The next morning, the Salton Sea was before us, finally, and I had forgotten just how big it was. I had heard once that it was thirty miles long but within the confines of sand and distant hills, it looked endless. It was early and the sun was up, as was a strong, salty breeze. We could feel it on our faces as we stood on the ledge of a precipice, looking down at the huge pond. There was still a bit of a hike, but it was there, before us, like we were at the five-yard line staring at the end zone after a long, brutal scoring drive. I had no idea we were that close last night where we camped; had we walked another mile, we would have fallen in.

Jock and I hadn't said much in the wee hours, waking immediately as the sun crested a hill in the distance and flashed into our eyes. My dew catcher did its job and one canteen was filled. I would have to replenish it later somehow. Jock tipped whatever he could into his water holder, straining from the leafy refuse that floated in the precious liquid.

Nature called and we both relieved ourselves in opposite, respectful directions, something I hadn't had to do in a very long time. Piss next to someone, that was. Figuring that one of us might have to drop a deuce, I joked about a newspaper and Jock reminded me that he had some comic books if needed. I told him to hold that thought.

We set out but not before checking if the coast was clear. The desert behind us was Rogue-less, allowing me to settle into a less anxious hike. The sky was blue, a few clouds high above, and the temperature cool. This was going to be a good day. Even Jock seemed to smile this morning, possibly realizing the worst was behind us.

My mind centered on the riddle from whence the Doctor spoke. *Make your way to the Salton Sea! Find the place of judgment. If you are truly worthy, head north and you'll find redemption!"*

You'll find redemption. What did that mean? Was there going to be a big sign that said that? Come here to get redeemed? And what was the place of judgment? Was there a town there called Judgement? Maybe another airfield called that? The term had to have a double meaning. I racked my brain thinking of possibilities and none came to mind.

I was betting on an airfield. That had to be it. A landing strip close to the sea, maybe just outside a small town along the shore. That made sense. The plane needed to land, pick me up, then take off. Or, maybe it was some dude watching over the airfield, a guy nicknamed *The Redeemer*? I recalled the statue Christ the Redeemer overlooking the Brazilian city of Rio de Janeiro but I couldn't imagine something similar over the Salton Sea. It was messing with my mind.

I felt at ease for the first time on the trip. The sea looked calm, like a light blue bed sheet spread over a smooth patch of the desert. We were somewhere on the northeastern side, I guessed, almost halfway down and I had thought we'd arrive somewhere closer to the top. On a map, the Salton Sea looks like a stocky rocket ship, narrow up top but wider at the bottom. We would touch the sea, then set south for the main thrusters. I could not see the southern end, the blastoff zone, as a patch of fog lingered there.

"Are we there yet?" Jock asked with a grin.

I smiled at him, then nodded. It was quite a sight. "Oh, yeah."

Jock slurped water from his canteen, then shook it to hear the remaining liquid slosh inside. It sounded half full. I was worried about water myself. While it was still cool, I was hoping it would not get hot.

"I don't suppose there's any fresh water in all that?" Jock asked, pointing with the canteen at the sea. Birds took flight from the banks and soared off over our heads.

"No, it's full of salt," I replied.

"That sucks," was all Jock would admit. Pocketing his canteen somewhere under his coyote skin, Jock looked ready to move. With his hands on his hips, he asked me, "Okay, where do we go?"

I shrugged. "Find the place of judgment. Whatever that means."

"Er, does that mean we go left or right?"

Since most of the sea was to our left, I hedged my bet nodding in that direction. "Let's go that way," I stated like I was certain.

"Ginn is out there, isn't he?" he asked, not moving suddenly.

"Maybe he gave up," I said. "Went on his way. Started a pitchfork business."

"You don't think that," he said with a frown.

"No."

Jock took the first step forward, jumping down from the ledge we were on, sliding down a small, sandy slope, nearly losing his footing. He regained his balance though and kept on as if the slight tweak in his strut was barely noticeable. The coyote's head comically bounced up and down, the soles of his shoes standing out; it was like watching a costumed child trip as they left your doorway on Halloween night.

"Trick or treat," I said, leaping down after him.

And prayed for no more horrors.

Cold, gentle waves lapped the shoreline as I squatted in a layer of thin fish bones and shells, sloshing my hands in some white, foamy froth of the salty sea. Little black flies swooped and fluttered all around me and I uselessly shook my head at them as they bobbed and weaved. Bringing my wet hand to my nose, I got a whiff of rotten eggs and believed the fish that lived in there had it bad.

Bones. They were everywhere, like a carpet, blanketing the shoreline. From a distance, they looked like shells, but the skinny, pointed fragments were dead giveaways. Millions of fish must have died in the sea, floating for days, landing here and decaying, their carcasses left ashore in the tides flowing back and forth.

Behind me, Jock held his nose and looked at me from a bench in what used to be a state park. There were other benches, fire rings, and a rusted swing set behind him. A gate shack at the entrance was drooping, the roof falling apart. The gas didn't erode the state park though, it looked as if it sat here for years, closed, never trying to recover a past glory when families would come here and spend the day. I imagined that it had shuttered decades ago and no one claimed to remedy or tear it down. The Salton Sea was like that, a playground back in the day where scores of Hollywood celebrities like Frank Sinatra came out to play, taking in the easy-floating water, racing boats, sailing, and sipping martinis in the quaint marinas that dotted the shores. However, the increased salinity and subsequent dying off of the local fish population caused a stench that proved so overwhelming that people simply stopped coming. I read that once, in a book about the infamous sea when I came here last.

All around the sea, abandoned structures and buildings, empty parking lots, and decaying boats are all that was left. Only a few homes called the sea home before the gas hit and they probably didn't know any better. Maybe these residents preferred the solitary confines of a once-was, not being bothered anymore. I saw no sign of people anywhere. The sea looked alive yet dead at the same time. Almost as if time stopped. Like the abruptness of Chernobyl. Nothing to be had, nothing to claim. Jock still hadn't moved from the bench. "Are those bones?" he asked.

"Tilapia graveyard methinks," I replied, shuffling some with my new boots.

He scrunched his nose. "Tilapia? Is that a fish?"

"Pan fry with some dill, oil, lemon, and garlic. Good stuff."

"No thanks."

We walked along the shore, hearing a crunch with each step, my feet sinking an inch or two into the soft turf. Jock was next to me but avoided the shore, trudging through the sand a good twenty feet away instead. The sea next to me was calm, just a few gentle waves.

The afternoon sun reflected bright and I had to squint and turn my head.

"This is gross," Jock said. "You are literally walking on dead fish." He bent down, flicking a larger piece of white bone with his shoe. "I see the spine of some animal. I don't know what it is or was."

My focus was what lay ahead, not giving a rat's ass about what I was stepping in. We were quite exposed with little cover and unsure where to go. I looked across the sea, to the other side, and hoped we wouldn't be there, a week from now, still searching for redemption. Thirty miles on foot was a lot of smelly ground to cover.

Ahead, we saw the highway we crossed earlier and decided to stay close to it. Highway 111 hugged the shore about fifty yards off. Roots and weeds had long reclaimed the two-lane stretch, as did the sand and dead brush, blown across by the endless wind.

We walked for hours, stopping to rest on occasion, not seeing a lot of activity anywhere besides birds. During some of the silence, I imagined the plane circling high, banking, then slowly descending from the sky, the wheels touching about a hundred yards out on the highway. The brakes were then applied, the doors flung open in front of me with the propeller still spinning. Knowing the ever-present threat that surrounded us (we weren't out of the woods yet), we would need to climb aboard quickly. I was sure the Pilot would need to take off just as quickly as it landed.

"Highway one eleven is also called Grapefruit Boulevard," Jock said, snapping me out of it. He picked up a rock. I saw the same sign as we crossed it ten minutes or so ago. "You think maybe they named it that if there's a grapefruit tree around?" he asked.

In one quick motion, Jock whipped out his slingshot, aimed, and fired the rock into the sea. It skipped seven or eight times before it splashed in a small wave.

"No idea. I hate grapefruit but I'd settle for one now," I stated. We passed no trees lately and there didn't seem to be any as far as I could see. There was a set of train tracks that hugged the highway and coastline though. "I say we stay between the tracks and the road," I said. "Much safer there. Maybe even a Grapefruit tree."

No sooner had I said that when we saw a strange object atop a pole that was hastily jammed into the ground ahead of us. The object in question turned out to be a human skull, the pole going through the open neck but not piercing the top of it. The lower jaw was open in a perpetual smile, some dried skin still keeping it attached. It was clearly a warning, resting at eye level, that trespassers were not welcome.

The rest of his or her bones were nowhere to be found.

CHAPTER FORTY-EIGHT

The Starfish Shores neighborhood resembled a long-forgotten war zone, like a ghost town that saw the losing end of a major battle a lifetime ago. The sign that once advertised what was once a quaint beachside community was faded, rusted, laying in the dirt. The cartoonish image of the five-legged creature was dead center, each leg protruding from the letter "F." Most of what remained were shattered homes with fallen walls, caved rooftops, tilted fences, and trash everywhere. There didn't seem to be any movement except for blankets and drapes fluttering outside busted windows. No welcome wagon or war party. It appeared deserted and I was just fine with that.

We came across the small town from the road and circled the area moving towards the sea, staying on the outskirts and keeping a wary eye. From our vantage point high on a brick wall near the shore, that seemed like a dyke, we could see a couple roads inside that divided up about fifty homes. A few homes still looked hospitable though, their walls and rooftops still somewhat intact and able to provide shelter.

"What do you think?" I asked Jock. "Beach side property? Interested?"

Jock shot me a grim look. "I think we stay away. It looks like H-E double hockey sticks in there."

"Check out the sign though," I said, pointing to a trailer closest to us. THIS HERE BE JUDGEMENT DAY was spray painted on the side wall. "Someone gave us a hint. I have a feeling redemption is in there."

"Do you even know what redemption is?" he asked me, with a hint of smug, like I was a lost soul just trudging on.

I knocked him on his shoulder and said, "Something to the effect of atonement." Thinking back to my Sunday school classes, I had thought redemption rested on being a good Christian so I gave myself props for that answer.

"Was that a guess?" he asked me.

"You live your life and you're judged accordingly," I shrugged. "What do you think it is, smarty pants?"

"Deliverance from sin."

My hand under my chin as if in deep thought, I nodded like a scholar and said, "I can agree with that. Shall we?"

Jock cast a disapproving glance at me and shook his head. "I don't think you are one to talk..."

I shot a look back at him as if to say, *don't start,* and he wisely went silent. Jock was not privy to my life and had no bounds to critique me. "Don't judge a man until you've walked a mile in his shoes," I grumbled and hopped down. "Until you've been married, don't you dare judge, little dude."

There weren't any other structures beyond this seaside hamlet, only the salty lake to the right and open desert leading to small hills on our left beyond Highway III. "I don't want to walk around this sea again. If you want to stay up there, that's fine, but I'm going in. If redemption is in there, I don't want to pass it up."

"Be my guest," he said and waved me on. "People live in there and they are watching us. I can smell fire. Probably death."

Although there was no smoke to be seen, he was right. Someone had burned something not too long ago, the lingering aroma close to cooked meat. I removed the crowbar from the quiver, held it midway, and set out to play accidental tourist. As I approached the first street, a chain link fence that had seen better days momentarily stopped my advance, until I ducked under a hole to the side. Almost clear, my backpack caught an edge and the fence rattled. I shook violently as I heaved to break free, the fence moving then in a ripple down the line that nearly sounded like it would collapse at that moment. So much for progressing quietly. I was often clumsy like that.

The first mobile home I passed with the ominous message scrawled was a wreck. The salty air had eroded much of the metal and the color of the home was a dull blue. Broken windows showcased empty rooms inside. One wall was pockmarked with bullet holes, while another was oddly shaped like a car smashed into it. Long weeds swayed in the wind while dead, brown grass rested among patches of sand. Someone spray painted WE'RE ALL SCREWED on another wall not visible from where Jock stood. There was no movement inside but the past home owner seemed to be the town crier.

"You're crazy!" Jock yelled to me. He hadn't moved an inch from the perch.

The home across from it was a disaster too. More bullet holes were there, strafed in a zigzag fashion. Graffiti in Spanish was painted on the front door. Car tires littered the yard with some formed in a circle. Dead smack in the center, an old fire pit remained, but that wasn't the source of the ashes we smelled.

Behind me, I peeked and saw Jock still standing tall on the wall. He then leapt down and headed for the shoreline. I guessed I was riding solo.

The road was cracked as if a bunch of earthquakes hit all at once, causing weaving lines in the asphalt as weeds and plants sprout between them. Bees buzzed from flowers that bloomed there and I wondered if there was a hive nearby. Honey sounded good right about then. Further on, a utility pole with saggy electrical wires lay sideways across the road, propped up by a brick wall. I ducked underneath it, noticing a trail that others had taken as well. Glass crunched under my feet. Each home I passed was a shoddy ruin of what it once was although some of them, I suspect, didn't have much curb appeal to begin with.

Tire tracks were in a sand patch in the middle of the road. Recent too, the tread meandered for a few feet then shot off down an empty lane. The wind hadn't covered it up so I guessed *really* recent and that put me on guard. Looking up the road though, I saw no forms of life nor any movement. I hoped whoever it was, they were just passing through. Lack of a tourist information booth could do that.

The next home looked like it had burned in a fire. The roof held charred, blackened beams while the plastic outdoor molding nearly melted from the walls. Directly across the street, the neighbor there had a place in surprisingly decent shape. The walls and doors looked intact, hardly a mark or scratch anywhere, save for the boarded up doors and windows with eye level slits cut into them. A Confederate flag, torn, fluttered on a small pole out front.

After a few more derelict homes, I found myself at a three-way intersection. The road I was on fed back into Highway III, but the road to my right would take me down a main street splitting the middle between old Grapefruit Boulevard and the sea. I opted to hang that right, staring down the long stretch. The seaside town was narrow, I discovered, longer than it was wide.

The top of a camper shell lay in dead grass and with a casual glance, I saw some clothes, pillow, and a sleeping bag inside. No one was there to greet me, however, but it was definitely inhabited at some point. Peeking into another window caused me to jerk when I saw movement. Jock was staring back at me on the other side.

"You need backup. So that's why you came to Tuco," he said and smiled as he popped his head up barely above the camper and wiggled a finger gun at me. His slingshot was out.

"There's five of them," I say playing along, squinting, my best Eastwood impression. The Good, the Bad, and the Ugly was one of my favorite movies.

He eyeballed the road ahead. "No matter. I kill them all!"

So, with my little buddy mysteriously growing a pair suddenly, the two of us swaggered, eyeing the homes and windows just like in the Western we mimicked, looking for gunmen ready to take us out. Yard after yard, just emptiness and quiet which struck me strange. With the exception of a few birds chirping, the Starfish Shores was deserted and I found that hard to believe.

Jock whispered behind me, "He's tall, blonde, smokes a cigar and he's a pig."

"Enough already," I said, shaking my head. More derelict visions crossed our view including a rusted tractor resting on its side, a bird-bath stained with blood, a wheelbarrow crushed under a truck. The more I looked around, we seemed to be the only people there. We stopped and I craned my neck, listening for anything. Only the banging of a screen door swinging in the wind and some ghastly wind chimes filled the air.

Jock kicked a candy wrapper shoved in the mud by a tire tread. "What do you miss the most?" he asked me.

"Miss?"

He picked up the wrapper. Snickers, once. "You know, from the past. What food?" he asked, crinkling the paper, then littering it.

"Hamburgers," I said, thinking I really wanted one.

"From where?"

I figured we were near the center of the town and there was no sign of any redeeming qualities around there. Not that I could see, anyway. No sign, verbiage, no airport for that matter. I don't believe for a second that a plane would land here either. Judgement, redemption, if it was obvious, wasn't simply there. Dejected, I realized the Starfish Resort was a waste of time and we needed to leave. Highway 111 was still the best runway at this point. "I would kill for some In and Out," I said, finally answering Jock's question.

"Now we're talking," Jock nodded. "Double double?"

"With grilled onions."

"Ooh," he said and touched his stomach. "Now I'm hungry."

Nodding to the right, I said, "There's plenty of fish in the sea."

Jock stuck out his tongue and nudged the ground again. He toed a rock and picked it up. "Nice," he said and placed it in the slingshot. He aimed it at a mobile home and asked me, "Target, please."

"Window, top right." There was one there that was actually not busted, a smaller bathroom window under the roofline.

"Too easy," he said. Seconds later, he released. A crash and the window shattered.

"Impressive."

Cocky, he blew the end of the slingshot like it was a smoking barrel. "I once took out a moving squirrel from fifty yards. It was jumping from one branch to another. I caught it mid-air."

"How about you?" I asked him. "What do you miss?"

"Flaming Hot Cheetos," he said quickly, expecting me to ask him.

"Ugh," I said. "My kids liked those too. I tried one once, it was too..."

A crack split the air and suddenly my chest took a wallop, a dull slap that knocked me backwards and I dropped my crowbar. I remained on my feet, however, too stunned to assess what had just happened. Then it hit me, literally. I had been fucking shot again! All I could do was mouth "ow" as I gasped, looking down feebly too, my hands rubbing for blood, and thankfully find none. Glancing up, I searched for Jock and saw him untouched, but gawking at me with his mouth open. My legs wanted to give way for a moment and I fought the urge to sit down. I staggered like a drunk, an obvious sign to whomever fired that their target had been hit. The road was still empty before me, but from the corner of my eye, Jock leapt over a small brick wall to our left. That registered as a damn good idea but I had to collect my crowbar first. Wincing and gripping my vest as I bent down, another shot cracked the air and I heard a whistle near my left ear. I hobbled behind him and timed my hurdle. A third shot rang out and took a chunk off the wall a foot beside me as, instead of leaping over, I clumsily fell over the barrier, landing hard on the other side and on top of my crowbar.

"How bad is it?" he asked me as I lay on my back beside him, my face feeling flushed. His motions were frantic, touching me, glancing back over the fence.

I mumbled, trying to breathe again, rolling off my weapon of choice. "Got my vest again...twenty-two caliber..."

"How the hell can you tell what caliber?" Jock asked peering over the wall.

"Not the first time I've been target practice," I responded, then laughed for some strange reason. Wiggling my Kevlar vest, the squashed slug rolled off and plopped in my hand. It looked like a stout mushroom and I showed him.

"Ta-da!" I said and laughed some more. "Not as bad as the last one."

"How many lives you got left?" he asked glumly.

"For my next trick," I said, then stopped as another shot rang out. It sounded like the same pop, so I guessed one gunman. So far. Propping myself up was a chore and my ribs screamed at me. "It hit me at an angle," I said, rubbing my chest. "I think from across the street."

Jock nodded, peering through a V-shaped hole in the fence. "I see someone in the house on the other side of the street. The blue one. Diagonal."

Closer to me, there was a hole in the brick wall, a twelve-inch opening, and I crawled to it. Like staring down the barrel of a gun, I peered through and saw the blue mobile home across the way. No door, no windows, no movement. "Look left, big window. He's hiding behind some ugly ass drapes," Jock said.

Focusing on the larger window then, the culprit gave himself away as cigarette smoke wafted from behind a set of, indeed, ugly ass drapes. A rifle barrel was poking through it, swiveling side to side, trying to get a bead. It settled on us once more aiming directly then at me.

"Duck," I whispered to Jock. The rifle coughed, and the wall chunked near the opening, spraying brick pieces as I rolled away. "He saw me," I said, stating the obvious.

"We can't stay here," Jock noticed, his voice a small shrill. "We'll be pinned in. There's no telling how many of them are out there."

We were in the yard of a brownish mobile home with a rusted clothes line teetering on collapse. A window was open facing us, as was another, smaller one from the right. The kitchen maybe. Seeing no activity in either, I assumed it was vacant since gunfire usually agitated the neighbors. A screen door hung on its hinges and yielded to a wide opening on the left, the main entrance. As I lifted myself higher, but not breeching the wall itself, I saw cover in a large bush that would give us a chance if we army crawled to it. In all, there was about twenty feet of open space between that and us. "Inside," I told Jock, grabbing his arm and tucking my crowbar back into the quiver. "Nobody's home." We ducked and crawled for it, me half thinking we must have looked pretty silly doing that. Once we rounded the bush, we got back to our feet and sprinted for the door. Thankfully, no more shots greeted us.

Spilling inside, we leapt over fallen drywall and hung a right just as I spoke too soon. A bullet chipped the doorframe inches just from my face. We bypassed the larger living room window and ducked into the kitchen where I took position under the window there, slamming my back into a rotted kitchen counter where old pots and plates rattled. Jock hid behind a ripped couch, its back to us, facing what was once a tiny dining room.

"Do you think they know who we are?" he asked me. That was a good question and very likely, I assumed. As I peered over the sink, staying low but trying to assess the anarchy out front, I noticed a smell of rotting meat and saw animal bones, fat, and fur in the sink. It was someone's dinner and they weren't fussy about cleaning. Taking a risk, I lifted my head higher and saw the home across the way from where the sniper hid. The shadow was gone. The ugly ass drapes were calm. Where did he go?

"Are they Rogues?" he asked, frantic.

"One question at a time, please," I answered.

Jock barely peered over the stained couch. "Do they know who we are?"

"I don't know."

"Are they Rogues?"

"I don't know."

Some points to be considered. If the sniper was alone, he had moved. If he was not alone, they were assembling and they'd try to corner us. I slunk back down and surveyed our new digs. Busted refrigerator, microwave with a missing door, newspaper and wrappers on the floor. Paint chipped, walls scuffed, something a lying realtor would rudely call a quaint fixer-upper.

However, there was a table and two chairs sitting upright. Dirty plates, cups, nude magazines on the table. Looking out over the couch Jock was hiding behind, the living room gave way to see a sleeping bag in the corner, open, and not much else. All the furniture was gone as if someone was stopped mid-move. A pillow with a head indent, dirty socks, a pair of jeans, a plastic water bottle filled with murky liquid told me the house was occupied and we were trespassers.

Also, there were footsteps on the floor caked in mud.

Jock hadn't seen what I had seen, keeping his eyes out front, but he strolled out into the kitchen. "Think they have CB Radio here?" Jock asked. "I'll bet they do."

"First five callers wins a prize," I said grimly.

"First time caller, long time listener," a voice said from the hallway. A giant mud-covered man then entered the room holding a welder's torch, flashing yellow teeth in a vulgar smile, hunched like a praying mantis. I couldn't see much of his face as he wore a pair of thick goggles and behind them, his wispy gray hair was matted with muck. Topping six-four easy, he was shirtless with dried mud caked on his chest and arms, some of it cracked while pieces dropped off him in chunks. Thankfully, he was wearing overalls. Hoses ran over his shoulders to a pair of cylinders on his back.

"Ginn said alive," he pleaded, his dark teeth covered in spit. "I just want an arm. No harm, no foul. Be generous, okay? I ain't eaten in days."

The torch in his hand suddenly erupted in a bright orange flame, jetting out about eight inches. Jock retreated behind the couch shouting the obvious, "Mud People!"

Drooling with anticipation of an upcoming battle, the giant muddy twisted the dial so the flame shrunk but glowed blue and sharp, almost needle-like. His spit drooled on his wrist, just missing the flame.

"You don't want to fuck with the bear," I told him. Paying me no solace, he merely giggled, admiring his sacred toy. Seeing as this was going to end badly for one of us, I conjured up an image of Polecat. Suddenly, Welder Mudball lumbered at me as I tried to level my crowbar in time. The torch was flung wildly, I ducked and bobbed away just in time, but the flame caught my arm as he passed over me, causing me to drop my favorite tool. The pain was intense and I patted my arm quickly, thinking it was on fire. It wasn't, but sure felt like it was.

Mudball realized he missed and slowly turned, having banged into the kitchen sink himself. As I gripped my other hand over the new wound, I saw the crowbar between us.

"I'll cauterize the wound!" he shouted and came at me again, striding over my fallen crowbar as if the tool was redundant. The momentum towards me gave me little room to move, except backwards, into the couch from where Jock hid.

Suddenly, Mudball's left goggle crunched and blood splattered within it, stopping him in his tracks. Some object pierced his left eye. He cried out in pain, dropping the torch which dangled and swung wildly around his legs as the gas propelled like a jet engine. Strangely, he ignored the fluttering flame thrower and cupped his goggles with both hands. Behind me, Jock was loading his slingshot for another round.

Mudball's leg caught fire and a high-pitched shriek erupted from his cracked lips, drool and blood cascading down his chin. As he frantically waved to catch the flailing torch, which had then caught the edge of the couch and caused that to flare up too, I balled my fist and cracked him on the nose with a hard right as flames whooshed behind him. Although I clearly busted his nose, and I guessed he was missing an eyeball as well, the flames riding up his leg took priority. Mudball was in hysterics, flapping and slapping as the blaze was dancing up to his hips. The dried mud stuck there could have stopped the inferno, however, so I took it upon myself to finally end this man's life. Lowering my shoulder, I hit him square in the chest, knocking him over the couch, canisters and all. Landing hard on the other side, he seemed to vanish from sight and I took no time to grab the closest end of the burning furniture piece and heave it on top of him.

Pinned there, Mudball wailed again, thrashing his arms under the blazing couch as if he was a turtle stuck on its back. Intense heat registered from the newly created bonfire, pushing me away. Jock joined me at my side, steadying his weapon but I waved him down. I wanted the sucker to burn. Annoyingly, a smoke detector screeched from the ceiling above that made us both jump, the incessant *beep-beep-beep* drowning out the popping and sizzling of burning fabric and the course moaning from underneath the couch. Mudball's arms sagged, then finally dropped. His right leg twitched out from under the couch and I noticed clean footwear.

"Nice shoes," I said out loud, but they were too big for me.

"Will those canisters explode?" Jock asked, cupping his ears from the smoke detector's screeching.

As I pondered that, a new threat then reminded us we weren't alone again. Outside, an engine started up somewhere. Peering out the kitchen window again, I saw an ATV across the street revving in a carport in the same blue house where the gunfire came from. A man there with a bright green mohawk straddled the four-wheeler. Even from the distance, I recognized that he was the very same Rogue that held my legs down inside the pig pen. The very same Rogue I promised death upon. Torch called him Vicious after the famous, dead punk rocker. Another gunshot rang out just as Vicious popped the clutch and the window frame next to me splintered. Sniper was back behind the drapes. There was at least two more of them now and that was when I realized trekking through this smelly seaside hamlet may not have been the best decision I'd made recently.

Another reality hit me; the Mud People and the Rogues were allied.

The Salton Sea was a large place and of all damn things, we walked right straight down Main Street directly into the spider's web. It was no use in going out the front anymore, I suggested, and we headed out the back as the flames began climbing an adjacent wall. Jock didn't object and followed me close behind.

The backyard was full of rusted appliances and pieces of discarded metal. We juked like fullbacks between dishwashers and ovens as a torrent of bullets suddenly zinged past. With more than one report from a gun, I deduced, real quick, that we were vastly outnumbered. None of the gunfire came from the houses behind us, nor the next block over. They all appeared to come from out the houses out front.

"Where are we going?' Jock shouted behind me.

"I don't know!" I said but hid beside a shed in the rear. The ATV was roaring out front above the gunfire and I then heard a second engine joined the chorus.

Jock joined me and yelled, "There's two of them!"

"I think there's a helluva lot more!" Just as I mentioned that, a bullet struck the wall near Jock and he freaked. He took off for the next yard and I followed, thinking the area back here was Rogue-less.

I spoke too soon. A chain link fence rattled ahead of us. Leaping off it was a teenager, a blonde-surfer dude in board shorts with mud up and down his lean body. A switchblade suddenly whipped out and he flipped it cockily, daring us to approach him. On a dead run, Jock hit him in the head with a ball bearing and the skinny threat went down with an impressive shot dead center in the forehead, the ball bearing imbedded deep within. I leapt over the poor kid, who jerked like he was mid-seizure, and hurdled the fence in two strides. However, in in the adjoining yard, upon landing, I detected I was alone. Glancing back, I saw Jock hovering over the punk, his slingshot drooped at his side, the look of disgust on his face.

"Jock!" I shouted. "Fucking hurry up!"

Clearly tormented, Jock's shoulders sagged as he shuffled my way, ducking under a hole in the fence. "He's just a kid," Jock says, morosely, arriving at my side. "Dude, I feel nauseous." I thought he was going to throw up. A bullet ricocheted off the fence and we both flinched. "Think he'll be okay?" Jock asked me.

"This is no time to feel guilty. It was you or him."

"But…"

I couldn't have been blunter. "He would have carved you up! Let's go!"

CHAPTER FORTY-NINE

The rear door was wide open at the next house, a pink mobile home, so I took a chance and made a beeline for it. Inside, it was full of furniture, some of it wrapped in plastic, with kitschy knickknacks up the wazoo. Amazingly, that house held up the best so far on the block.

However, that oddity was outweighed by a humongous greenish snake in the corner that was mid-meal, with another mudball bound in its coils. The reptile's head was halfway down the body of a smaller man already, its gaping mouth like stretched, melted plastic. It's left eye, closest to us, shifted but even I knew it couldn't do anything to anyone else at this point. We were frozen on the spot, distracted by the scene unfolding before us. That scene actually shocked me.

"Whoa! That's an anaconda!" Jock yelled.

"I guess they eat people," I said, still taken aback.

"They aren't native to this area though. They are from South America," he stated.

"Must be an escapee from the Snake House," I said.

"The what?"

"Never mind."

We weren't alone, either. Another Mudball entered the room from the kitchen and watched in horror as the other man was being devoured. He barely registered us as trespassers and instead, stood as fascinated as we did. The new Muddie was slight, his face covered in mascara, his head shaved. His arms and chest held mud, however, and below his mid-section, he wore a tutu. Beyond that, he held machete at his side. I kept my crowbar gripped tight.

"That's Hortense," Tutu Muddie said to us, referring to the man being swallowed whole. "Asshole. Wasn't kind to the womenfolk. Don't you go rescuing him now. Better this way."

Suddenly, Tutu Muddie swung his machete at me. I brought my crowbar up just in time and both our weapons clanged loud. Tutu Muddie then wound up for a backhand swipe, but I swiveled and struck his cheek with a left jab. He dropped machete instantly and reeled backwards, holding the side of his face.

I then twirled my crowbar in a circle and buried the claw end into his shoulder, breaking his collar bone, the snap loud and obnoxious. He screamed as I plucked it back out, but I needed him to shut the hell up. I flipped the crowbar around, threw the chisel end up, and jabbed his jaw. I was aiming at his throat and missed to the right, so the blow shattered some teeth. Tutu Muddie dropped uselessly to the floor, one hand grabbing at his bleeding mouth, the other cupping his torn shoulder. The squealing from Tutu Muddie didn't stop either, so a swift swipe to the back of his head finally silenced him.

Outside, through an open window, I saw the ATV's stop in front of the house we were in, one of them pointing in my direction. It was time to move. I gathered Jock who was still watching the snake chow down, completely awestruck that a snake could do that to a man. So engrossed was he, I then realized he never saw me and Tutu Mudball battle. A quick slap on the shoulder and he snapped out of it and joined me outside, not wanting to be dessert. Spying the dead Tutu Mudball on the floor on the way out, he then asked, "What happened to the funny dressed Muddie?" I ignored him and shoved the little man through the rear door.

The fence between that house and the next was battered and easy to pass through. Upon reaching the other side of the yard, however, we paused and stared off into a vacant lot filled only with dirt. I guesstimated a good fifty yards to the other end, where a mobile home was present, but it was a very visual gap with zero cover. It was too much with bullets buzzing the air and ATV's circling like sharks from the street. Odds were, one or both of us would be hit crossing that open ground.

"We won't make it," Jock says glumly. I opted to move to the block behind us but when searching for new escape routes there, I spotted movement; Mud People heading towards the original Mudball's house, the Welder Mudball, distracted by the smoke wafting there. The noose was tightening but I didn't tell Jock that. I had to come up with something else.

A thunderous clap suddenly jolted us from behind somewhere. Glancing back, I saw dirt and dust streaming out of open windows a couple houses away. Smoke surged and swelled skyward. Welder Mudball's tanks must have blown inside the home. A nifty little diversion. Hopefully, some would believe we were still in there.

"What do you think of that distraction?" Jock asked.

"Good enough for me," I said and made a run for it. Surprisingly, we covered the vacant lot easily enough as no bullets or ATV's came our way. We ducked under the broken chain link fence and stopped on the other side.

"Where to?" Jock asked. I saw a few Rogues in a couple of yards ahead but they hadn't seen us yet. I ducked and thought about our alternatives.

"Inside," I finally said, nudging Jock towards the house.

"Fine," Jock reluctantly agreed. We crawled through the fence on the other side and ran through the rear yard. As we headed to the rear screen slider, which was intact and closed shut, I lowered my shoulder and barged through it like a running back, knocking down the screen door. I fell in the process and become entangled in the wire mesh. Jock grabbed a portion of the frame and tossed it aside. I managed to kick the rest free, rise up, and head into the living room with Jock close behind me.

Both of us took positions at either side of a large window. Half the glass there was remaining, so we stayed low to avoid being detected. That mobile home was another gem. Holes in the walls, graffiti, stains on shredded carpet which looked blood related. Someone even jokingly drew some chalk on a cement floor to outline a dead body which was, thankfully, not there. The furniture was soiled and dusty, the wood frames of which were torn and ripped out, most likely used for kindling in a fireplace on a far wall where gray ashes were piled up. Kid's toys litter the floor and I silently groaned.

"What was all that about the bear?" Jock asked me out of the blue.

Still staring at the toys, I muttered, "What?" Images of my boys and their toys flipped by like pages in a book. Those were for younger kids though.

"Back with the welder Muddie," Jock mentioned, nodding behind us. "You said no one fucks with the bear. Or something like that. You've said it a few times, bro."

With a serious face, I pointed out, "All creatures make way for the bear."

Confusion crossed the little Dude's face. "Is that, like, some Indian myth?"

"The bear is within all of us. Times like this, we need to awaken the bear to conquer our enemies."

Like the comic book geek that he was, he accepted it. "Nobody fucks with the bear," he stated.

"Now you get it."

"That's so sick," he nodded, then quickly changed his tune as he stared outside. "Oh, no," Jock said with a grim face, glancing back at me. "I see the ATV's. They are one house back, doing doughnuts like maniacs. See anything up your way?"

Facing east, I wanted to say it was clear. "No," I said, an outright lie. More Rogues were streaming out of the mobile homes further down the road but Jock didn't have to know that. Other Muddies were coming out too, but slower and less motivated.

"They stopped and are talking," Jock said, doing the play by play on the ATV's which had since resorted to a low idle. Down my end, I was watching Rogues confidently stroll out front, armed with an assortment of goodies; guns, axes, shovels, pitchforks, baseball bats, even swords. One Rogue had a chainsaw, battery operated, that came to life. Jock jumped at the sound but didn't look back.

"Fingers pointing this way!" Jock shouted. Backing from the

window, I surveyed the new digs thinking this would be our last stand. Our Alamo. "Here they come!" Jock yelled with an urgent tone.

The front door was wide open to our right. As I moved to slam it shut, one of the ATV's gunned it for me, that belonging to Vicious. The door was jammed, however, wedged into the wall itself, and I couldn't force it closed. I whipped out my crowbar just as he barreled through the doorway, slamming it at his neck, clotheslining him, knocking him to his back. His ATV, however, continued on without him, roaring through the home and down an open hallway, crashing into something at the end. Writhing on the floor, Vicious Rogue forgot about me and grabbed at his own neck, gargling for air. His windpipe was crushed by my crowbar.

Outside, the second ATV rider revved and charged for the door too, racing through the opening and colliding into his buddy lying on the floor, going airborne as if he hit a speedbump. Comically, he lodged himself into the wall, his head buried inside the drywall as if mounted there, his feet dangling two feet in the air. Jock cried, out, "Holy shit!" and I laughed inside. His ATV, however, bounced backwards and rolled on top of the first rider, the rear wheels near Vicious' face.

Grasping the brake and the throttle simultaneously, I squeezed the former's handle and rolled the latter. The right rear tire spun, the rubber grinding and chewing, spewing skin and blood that showered the door. After a few seconds, I killed the throttle as I saw that my brake stand did the job nicely. Vicious lost half his face and his whole life, but the second man had since dislodged himself from the wall somehow, holding himself up unsteadily, just a few feet away.

A ball bearing from Jock cracked his helmet and knocked him sideways. Angrily, he removed his helmet and threw it down, bouncing it off the linoleum. It was the Buck Toothed Rogue I saw earlier with Vicious at the camp, he the one holding down my other leg in the pig pen.

Muskrat. It was too perfect.

"I get my reward," he spat, then looked down at his chewed-up partner in shock. "Oh, that's it motherfucker! It's on! Now you're done for!"

With a shit-eating grin, I patted my crowbar against my palm and said, "I hope you got your affairs in order." That caused him to stall momentarily and I could tell second thoughts flooded that wee little brain.

"Fuck it," he said, surprisingly, and lunged, holding a knife in his right hand like he was going to joust. A downward slap from my tool cracked his wrist and he dropping the knife instantly, the blade clanging to the floor next to his helmet. Bone jutted through skin and he stopped, staring at the whiteness in shock. Moving around him quickly, I jammed the claw end under his balls from behind and jerked it up while my other hand gripped his collar. A girlish shriek erupted from his lips and he merely clawed air at that point with his good hand, the broken one remaining limp and useless. Muskrat's bravado had turned meek and fearful in an instant; he was crying, shaking so violently you'd swear he was having a seizure.

"Ginn," I asked him harshly through grit teeth. "Is he here?"

"OHMYGODITFUCKINGHURTSSOBAD!" Rising up on his toes, he tried to avoid the pain from below but it only made me yank up harder.

"Where is he?" I continued and lifted even higher.

"DOWNTHEROADHESCOMINGPLEASEDONT-PULLUPIMSORRY!" I smelled shit now and it was obvious what he'd done. Jerkoff here told me all I needed to know. It was his time to adjust to a new life. One of pain and misery as I would guess he, himself, had thrusted on others.

In one smooth motion, I released him by his collar and gripped the crowbar with two hands, yanking up higher and harder than I ever heaved before, lifting the stupid sod off the ground and hearing the scream no horror movie could ever match.

And that's when the gunfire erupted and our mobile home was peppered with what sounded like a hundred guns firing all at once.

CHAPTER FIFTY

Jock and I took cover below the sink as the bullets obliterated almost everything inside including Muskrat's body. The sap fell, still cupping his bloodied balls. The cupboards above our heads shredded with slivers of wood raining down. The walls became dotted with a hundred holes, the drywall behind them fracturing, creating a sprinkling cloud of white dust. The front door cracked and bent. The refrigerator took a few rounds that sounded like *plonk-plonk-plonk*. Although the slugs were ripping the house apart, the scatter of gunfire suggested that they were all firing blindly.

After the volley of bullets died down and a calmness prevailed, I waved at the swirling dust and peeked out the window. The Rogues were all out front, ditching their guns, resorting to backup weapons such as the knives, bats, machetes, and tire irons I witnessed before.

"I think they ran out of bullets," I said to Jock.

"You think?" he said, sarcastically. "Look at this place!"

"But they are still out there, waiting to move in. They have other weapons. It looks like hand to hand," I informed him. "I can't take them all on. We need to move."

Rogue heads suddenly turned to their right. While I couldn't see what it was they were looking at, I imagined Ginn or Torch walking towards them and the men waiting for the order to raid the house we were in. The Rogues were certainly amped to attack as they danced on the balls of their feet, swinging their weapons, coiled and ready to spring.

Just as I expected, I did see Ginn approach from down the road, only he didn't look happy and held both his old revolvers at his sides.

I recognized the dirt bike rider, Stir Fry, as the closest Rogue to Ginn, holding a butcher knife in one arm. His other arm was in a sling and his head was bandaged.

"We go in. Right, boss?" StirFry asked. Arab, standing next to StirFry and holding a shotgun, nodded his head in agreement, searching his pockets for more shells.

"Leave it to us, mighty Ginn," Arab said. "Just say the word."

Ginn then did something remarkable and completely unpredictable.

Ginn fired at Stir Fry's head, blanketing Arab in mixture of chunky red spray and brain matter. Stir Fry toppled to the ground. Although Arab's mouth was wide with shock, he lowered his own gun, fell to his knees, and offered open hands to Ginn, pleading and begging for his life. "We have not killed the man you seek. Spare us, for we only fired to flush the infidel from his hiding."

Ginn summarily shot Arab in the head.

Gramps wandered out from hiding behind a tree holding a machete. Wide-eyed, he gawked at Ginn and then Arab, but when his gaze returned to Ginn, a bullet entered his chest and blew his lungs out his back.

A Rogue in a cowboy hat tried to run but took a round between his shoulder blades and he fell forward, crashing into a fence.

Freebase took a slug to the face and spun in a circle. Another Rogue emerged from a mobile home with a rifle and a dumb look. Ginn gunned him down on the steps.

The remaining Rogues suddenly got the hint and began fleeing, dropping their weapons and making a run for it. Ginn shot them one by one, calmly reloading in-between, aiming and firing. Muddies also took flight and were also gunned down too. No Rogue or Muddie dared fire on Ginn, however. They all tried to flee. A handful of

Muddies emerged from a mobile home directly across the street. They simultaneously dropped their weapons and awaited their fate. Even as Ginn paused to reload.

"We are powerless against you," one Muddie said. "Have we somehow brought shame to you?"

"We have failed thee," another Muddie answered for him. He turned to Ginn. "Do with us as you wish, Master Ginn."

Ginn obliged them. All shots to the head.

"Filthy mongrels," Ginn said and spat on the dead.

The street was littered with the dead. Torch arrived behind him, shocked as I at the carnage around him. At first, it was just Ginn and Torch standing there, the smell of cordite strong and lingering. Ginn stared at the mobile home we were in but made no move to enter. Neither did he prod Torch to do so.

Then the Scientist arrived behind them as well, mouth agape, arms at his sides. "Hey," he said in a calm voice, "What's going on here?"

Ginn shot him between the eyes.

I could sense Torch's unease. Ginn wasted all the remaining men, except for Torch. It was just the two of them. Without turning, Ginn said to Torch, "If you're going to pull your weapon on me, I suggest you do it now." Contently, Ginn holstered his guns and turned to face Torch. It would be easy at this point, Torch was a fast draw.

"No worries, sir," Torch offered. "Let's get your man. We don't need these idiots to do our job."

"Knock, knock!" Ginn shouted at the home we were in, grinning unexpectedly. "Come out, come out, wherever you are!"

I didn't respond, obviously. Jock was still in awe of what happened. I was both upset and confused as to how Ginn had found us. The Salton Sea was massive. How the hell did he plan this ambush? Of all damn places.

"I know what you're thinking, you predictable silly fool!" Ginn yelled with a smile on his face. "You came to the Salton Sea and merely turned left! You can't escape us! This is the only town for miles!"

I pulled myself from the window and grabbed Jock.

"Let's see how fast these ATV's go."

CHAPTER FIFTY-ONE

The ATV's handlebars were bent and hard to control from the impact it had on the home's wall. I had got us out the back door and into the yard, Jock holding my waist behind me, and steered over glass and long weeds. I had to hold tight to the left so we'd head straight and we narrowly missed a low branch from a tree. The clutch was loose but the gears shifted easily with my foot. It had been a long time since I rode a bike with gears on the feet and I wasn't sure I'd remember. Whatever gear we were in, it was getting us where we needed to go though. What troubled me, however, was not the ATV itself, it was watching Ginn kill his own men.

Why did he do that?

We raced over a small pipe and spun in some gravel. I cranked the handlebars to the right and we managed to veer on to a dirt alley that ran parallel to the main drag. Dust was billowing behind us and we were out in the open though. I shifted the ATV left, heading for patches of dead grass in front of a row of homes hoping the dust will be minimal there.

"What are you doing?" he asked, barely holding on. "We had an open road!"

"Too much dust! We need cover!"

Revving the ATV, I goosed it into a vacant lot. "Duck," I shouted to Jock and I lowered my head and he did the same. We barely cleared a low hanging wire from a telephone pole. A brick wall was at the other end and I aimed towards an opening there, about ten feet wide, wide enough for us to barge through. I just didn't know what was on the other side.

A pile of bricks half-buried in sand caused us to bounce. I lost control, jammed the rear brakes and the ATV went into a sliding skid, slamming us into the fence, my left shoulder taking the brunt of impact. Jock bounced off the wall and fell backwards to the ground. Stunned by the crash, I slowly got my bearings, rubbing my left shoulder, but realized my left leg was pinned against the brick. The ATV's engine stalled and wouldn't start, despite my repeated attempts to wake it up. Smoke began to waft from the engine. I tried to free myself but my left foot was stuck between the pedal and the wall. Pain shot up my ankle and I prayed there was nothing broken. As I stood on the bike, I lifted my leg up, wiggling, and it finally slid free, although my boot was wedged there at the pedal. I leapt off the ride with one boot and grabbed Jock, who lay on his back moaning. A coyote skin strip was next to him in the dirt and I thought, at first, he lost a limb.

"Jock, we got to go," I said to him, scanning from where we came, watching for movement. Thankfully, there was none, but I knew there soon would be. Jock stirred and got to his knees, all limbs working and accounted for. We then heard an engine start in the distance.

That sparked Jock to move again, the adrenaline kicking in and he bolted through the opening we aimed for earlier before I did. Following, I ran awkwardly with one boot only, my left foot clomping in the sand. I thought of going back for the other shoe but the engine sounded like it was getting closer.

A cemented flood channel was in front of us filled with green, smelly sea water that was snaking through massive amounts of brown sludge. It was about twenty feet wide with ten-foot slopes angled about forty-five degrees on each side. Beyond that, it looked like open desert. Maybe Highway III. At the end to our right, in the channel, a large storm drain opening gaped. Wood planks and trash covered the entrance. Between the slits in the wood, I could see darkness inside. I guided Jock towards it. "Where are you going?" he asked me.

"In there," I said, pointing. "That might be our best chance. Maybe he won't look for us in there."

"I'm not going in that!" he protested and stopped.

"If you stay out here, they will find you. We can't go far on foot."

"I'll take my chances, thank you very much."

I slid down into the channel and my feet squished through inches of soft, gooey mud. Lifting them out made a sucking sound and I wished now, more than ever, that I had my other boot as my sock became drenched. A shallower area proved better progress and I sloshed through the weeds and putrid water towards the drain.

"Come on, Jock!" I shouted without looking, reaching the opening, but cautiously slowing. Peering inside, I searched for humans stirring or a sign that the drain was clear and not backed up, nor filled with trash and debris. There was just complete blackness beyond a few feet. The darkness would be perfect.

Jock was up on the slope still but closer to me, having walked along the upper wall, not jumping in like I did.

"Come on," I waved to him and pried open a loose piece of wood. It came free easily, as did another. I urged Jock to jump down.

Jock looked worried. "I can't! I don't like the dark!"

"You have to! It's our only chance!"

"No way, Dude! No way!"

I didn't argue. Jock would have to take his chances out there. After removing enough planks so I could squeeze through, I headed inside holding my breath. A few of the planks fell easy enough and I could make out a small area, about ten by ten square, where the sunlight followed me in.

Surprisingly, the storm drain was clean. The floor was cemented and free from dirt and dust, almost as if a broom had swept up. The walls were about eight feet high and also free from filth and mud. Somehow, all the mud and grime that was outside never made its way inside. After about ten feet in, the outside light faded and it became pitch black. To go any further, one would have to feel with their hands or use a flashlight. There were a lot of sticks and logs on the floor, tidy and organized, as if ready for burning. I saw a child's doll against the far wall but became distracted by the sound of the engine outside. It sounded like a truck.

Backing up, I stuck my hand out to steady myself. I touched something and quickly withdrew. I had touched a human hand in the darkness.

I quickly whisked out my crowbar. I couldn't see what was there but I could swear I felt the bony ridges of knuckles. From the darkness, I heard numerous whimpers. I steadied myself, ready to swing.

I was not alone.

The whimpering sounded odd and I quickly removed my flashlight, keeping my crowbar out front. Dust swirled around me like fireflies, ignited by the sun. Aiming the flashlight, I half expected a shot to ring out and a bullet to blast me in the face as I lit up the place like circling spotlights.

Instead, I found myself staring at sunken eyes of the old and young, frightened, timid, dirty and ashamed. Frail arms and hands, moaning, waving at the foreign light and me, the stranger, who was more wide-eyed than they. There were at least ten of them.

They were not Rogues, nor were they Muddies.

They were women.

CHAPTER FIFTY-TWO

They were frightened, huddling together in chairs, couches, and bunks. A stove, sink, and cupboards filled with cans were propped against the walls. It took me a second to wonder why they'd live there and then I realized they were hiding from men, probably the Muddies, as they were not caked in mud.

"I mean you no harm," I told them. "But you need to be quiet." A couple of them nodded. The air grew fresher as a light wind came from within and it felt cool against my neck and face. There must have been another opening somewhere deep inside as a faint light drifted towards me too.

"Are you people okay?" I asked.

"Are you going to hurt us?" a middle-aged woman asked, her face sullen, her skin weathered, her frame thin.

"No, I am just trying to hide," I replied.

"Don't tell the Muddies we are here," she said. "They are a horrendous lot."

I was flabbergasted as to how they stayed. "How do you all survive?"

"We only come out at night. We raid what we can."

They were haggard in their meager digs, trying to get swallowed up by their furniture. I noticed paintings and drawings on the walls, books and magazines opened. The rest were piled neatly. Blankets and pillows were propped while candles were recently snuffed, because of me, the smoke drifting with the slight, mysterious breeze. Half of these women, despite their forlorn and desolate features, would have been put to whoring if they had been caught by the Rogues outside. I wondered if these women were relatives or family members of the Muddies who were banished and put here to live. Maybe the last survivors of another town overrun? Or just in hiding altogether?

A shaky finger pointed past me by an older lady who stumbled forward. She mumbled, "The devil is outside" to me. She had gray hair and a ripped, stained dress. I made my way to the opening and stared out, trying to gain a sense of what was going on.

I didn't like what I saw.

The flatbed truck that held the pigs was backed up to the channel, the rear of which was facing me. Torch exited the driver's side, then walked to the rear and stood outside the cages. He pushed a lever that lowered the flatbed to the ground. The Razorbacks inside wailed and screeched, lunging at the sides, anxious for an attack. Behind me, the women heard the beasts and tried not to scream.

From the top of the channel, Ginn watched the opening and I could swear he was staring straight at me. Torch leaned back and waited. I could tell he was edgy in dealing with the boars. Ginn sauntered up to him, handing over a flap of coyote skin.

"Well?" Ginn asked, nodding towards the crate. I could hear him even from a distance. "What are we waiting for?"

Torch hesitated. "Are you sure he's in there?" he asked. "I don't think the two of us can put the pigs back in the cages again. This might be a one-shot deal."

Ginn then answered for me to hear, "I know Mr. Ratelle is in there! There is nowhere else to hide!"

"What about the man's boot?" Torch asked. Ginn held a boot and I recognized it as my mine. The one I left back at the fence.

Ginn shrugged and suggested, "Let's see where this goes first." He held the coyote skin strip that came from Jock.

"Here goes nothing," Torch said and walked forward. As he approached, the boar squealed and shuffled in the crate. With the aid of a stick, Torch reached in the cage and stuffed the coyote fur into the boar's snout. The beast bucked and charged, whiffing loudly as the strap dangled for a few moments. Torch pulled the stick back, just as the pig swung its mighty head against the crate door. "He's ready," Torch announced.

"Not quite," Ginn responded.

Suddenly, Ginn was next to Torch, a lit cigarette between his lips. He inhaled like a pro and even blew out a ring. What he did next was so callous, so heinous, that a shiver charged down my spine.

Reaching into the cage from behind, Ginn singed the cigarette on the boar's large testicles. The animal screamed and wailed, bucking and kicking, slamming the sides and front, ready to destroy the pen if need be to escape. Ginn took the cigarette to his mouth, drew in again so the tip burned red hot, and branded the poor beast's other testicle.

"Open the latch," Ginn said as the boar shrieked and bucked beside him.

Torch opened the latch and quickly backed away. The brute shot off like a rocket bashing the door open, the hoofs scrambling in the dirt. It burst forward, not back, along the channel wall but did not drop into the wash. Instead, it tore through a fence opening up in an adjoining yard and disappeared.

"Listen," Ginn said and cupped his ear. More banging's could be heard above and I knew the Razorback was charging through anything it wanted as it sought out the prize it craved; revenge and hunger.

And then I heard a scream.

Ginn ran off to the fence and peered over it at the exact same spot the boar charged through. After a few moments, with some rustling still happening somewhere just beyond, a sight bewildered the man and he backed away, shaking his head.

"Destiny," was all he said as he sauntered back, flicking the cigarette to the ground. He strolled to Torch and they conversed in whispers for a few moments.

Torch, at one point, looked surprised and said, "Serves him right."

Ginn descended the slope, not minding the muck when he reached the bottom, but he stopped twenty feet from the opening. He eyed the storm drain like it was a minor inconvenience, even putting his hands on his hips to show his annoyance. "Get down here," Ginn ordered Torch, turning his head back.

Torch arrived at his side, disgusted with the scenario.

"It doesn't have to be this way, Ted," Ginn said to me in the hole.

I didn't respond.

"Come out of there!" Ginn demanded.

"Do you want me to fire a warning shot?" Torch asked and cradled the butt of his gun. Up and high above somewhere, the Razorback was grunting and squealing, an unsettling noise if there ever was one.

"The wood needs to be cleared," Ginn said to Torch and nodded at the opening. "The Razorback will take too long trying to enter. Might as well go in yourself. Make yourself useful."

"Fuck that," Torch stated. "I'm not going in there."

Ginn un-holstered his gun and aimed at Torch's privates. "Shall we make you a eunuch for the rest of your miserable life?" He then lifted the barrel higher to Torch's chest. "Or should I send you to Hell right now?"

Seeing no other resolve, Torch sighed and proceeded to walk forward.

"No," Ginn said, holding his arm, pulling him back. "Hand me the gun."

Torch looked at him disbelievingly and said, "He's armed. We know what he can do with that fucking crowbar. I can't go in empty handed."

"I prefer him alive," Ginn stated.

"Prefer?"

Ginn thought a moment, then looked up at the fence where the Razorback charged through. There was some thrashing going on, as if the pig was tearing the yard apart. Ginn heard enough and then reconciled with a smile. "Do what you will then."

That caught Torch by surprise and he looked up at the fence as well. "Change of heart?" he asked.

"I have everything I require to move forward now."

As Torch trudged forward, the Razorback high above suddenly squealed and that distracted Ginn for a moment. "Wait," Ginn said and Torch stopped. "Why don't you take this?" He flipped a small flashlight to him and Torch caught it before it sailed into the filth.

"You were a cop once," Ginn smiled. "Act like you're about to arrest a perp."

Watching Torch approach, I gripped my crowbar and dropped my backpack. I expected the remaining Razorback to bust through the wood but Ginn was ordering Torch to come inside himself. I wondered what became of the first Razorback. Where did it go? I had heard a human wail, followed by frenzied squeals and I thought of Jock.

Oh, no...

"Hide," I whispered to the women. "This won't be pretty." They whimpered and scampered further inside the storm drain. They huddled together and left me alone near the entrance. I scanned my surroundings, my battleground, my boxing ring, and frowned at the limited space to defend myself. My last stand. Only one way in or out at the moment. The couch was half in, half out of the light. I decided to use it and placed my flashlight in the crook of a couch and aimed it at the hole where light met dark. The light was off, however.

I crouched in the darkness beside the couch figuring Torch would enter with a gun and aim it chest high. Although I was still strapped with my vest, I wasn't dumb enough to take another hit. With the women frightened, my exit blocked, my friend possibly dead, I began to grow irate. It couldn't go down that way, not cornered like a rat. I couldn't allow more innocent to die. I'd come too far to lose and I'd be damned if I allowed the Rogues to win. Peeking over my shoulder, the women eyed me with sheer fright and I felt a huge pang of guilt. Their eyes seemed to say it all; *what did you do? Why did you bring him here?*

They were right. I fucked up again.

Images of Polecat flooded my mind and I instantly became furious. The bear was awakening. Tensing with all my might, I leaned forward on my haunches, ready to spring. I growled and the women screeched. Outside the opening, a shadow bent down, then righted itself.

A plank of wood was removed. Then another. Soon, the entrance became engulfed in light and that forced me to retreat more into the shadows.

"It's me," Torch said, not entering yet. "Don't so anything stupid, Ted. Ginn doesn't care if you live or die anymore, but you and I, we can still make a deal."

I couldn't see his face yet, but his shadow cast an image on the floor. In his hand was a gun.

"Ted, we know you're in here. You left footprints," he said. "Let's talk."

"Talk about what?" I answered.

Torch hesitated. His shadow showed his head turning back behind himself, then returning. "We can defeat Ginn," he said softly. "I don't trust him and neither should you. You saw what he did to his own men. He killed them all. There's no reason why he won't do the same to you and me."

"He doesn't know where the plane lands. He'll keep me alive."

"I wouldn't be so sure of that. He's got your friend."

I glanced to my right. The women were praying. "No deal," I told him.

"Come on, Ted. No more fucking around. You and me, we take the plane together. I can get Ginn off your hands but I need your help."

"What's taking so long, officer?" Ginn shouted behind him.

Torch's shadow lifted an arm with an index finger pointed up.

"Hurry then," Ginn yelled. "I've not time for buffoonery."

"What do you suggest we do?" I asked him. I wanted to hear him out but in no way was I going to give him any deal. I didn't trust the guy at all.

"We draw him in there. I'll tell him I got you handcuffed and need his help. Then we take him. It'll be just you and me. No more Rogues. I'm assuming it's dark inside?"

"Forget it."

"I'm coming in now," Torch said. "Believe me, you want me coming in here and not the Razorback."

I knew his ploy. He was trying to get me to lower my guard. What he didn't know was, I was doing the same to him.

I flicked the flashlight on just as he entered and hit him with the light. Torch came at the source with his hands raised in a typical cop stance. "Damnit!" he shouted and instantly fired from a gun. The boom echoed loudly, my ears jolted, the wall above my head chipped, the women screamed. A second bullet plunked into the couch, striking no one but tufts of cushion exploding. Before he could adjust and fire again, I leapt from the darkness and slammed my crowbar down on his wrist, missed, but clipped the gun, knocking it out of his hands. The force of metal on metal reverberated with a loud *ping!* I went to swing again, but he was fast and tackled me. We crashed into the couch, the crowbar between us, he on top.

Outside, Ginn was shouting something we couldn't hear.

Torch hit me flush on the cheek with a hard punch and that stunned me, but I shifted before he could recoil and his next strike grazed the side of my head. I palmed his chin with my right and his jaw slammed shut. Blood trickled from his mouth as he scowled. My blow caused him to bite his tongue. Hovering over me, he sneered and tried to grab my hair. A quick jab at his ribs made him wince, yet he had a handful of my hair at that point and countered by yanking hard, some roots ripping from my skull. I clenched my teeth at the pain. We traded blows after that, me swinging up, he bashing down. Both of us were tiring quickly, our faces flush from the blows. I finally twisted hard, shoving him off where he landed on the floor in view of the flashlight. I scrambled to my feet, dazed by the punches, struggling to find balance. Torch wobbled too but rose into a fighter's stance.

Torch came at me with a lunging right punch. I quickly shuffled left, hit him once in the cheek, then followed in close with my right elbow into his temple. I managed a short jab with my left that smacked his nose. The women were frantically screaming behind us.

"What's going on in there, damnit?" Ginn yelled from outside.

Blood flowed from his nostrils and the former cop tried a desperation swing with his left. I ducked but it grazed my ear and stung. Head down, Torch charged me again like a bull and we collided, banging into a wall. I grabbed his collar and yanked him down, so much so that I pulled his shirt over his head. Unable to see, I began wailing on him, hockey style, my right fist acting like a piston, and continued to pound him until he slumped and fell to the floor. He lay still for a few seconds and then coughed. I was too tired to move.

The women stopped shrieking and went completely silent.

Torch rolled to his back and slowly yanked the shirt back over his head. His face was a pulpy mess. "What's that, five minutes for fighting?" he asked with a soft laugh.

The wall supported me and I wanted to sit down. My fist hurt like a mother. "Game misconduct," I told him.

Suddenly, I was airborne, my feet coming up front, Torch having swung his leg as he swept me. I hit my head when I landed and immediately started seeing stars. I also landed on my crowbar as sharp pains racked up and down my spine and that jolted me off it like it was on fire. As I rolled, Torch prodded his ankle while on his knees and somehow came up with a new gun and I figured ankle holster, of all damn things. He quickly lifted his arm and turned, but I had twisted left at that time, my right arm arching sideways with the crowbar as his new gun fired.

And missed. The bullet chipped the wall behind me and ricocheted wide.

My crowbar found purchase, however, the claw end having embedded into the man's stomach. Blood pooled down the length of the shaft and Torch dropped his gun, cradling the tool with both hands while it was still inside him. Stunned was too general a term to describe the look on his face, I would think horrified fit the bill better.

Propping my legs against his knees like a rower, I gripped the crowbar with two hands. He knew what I was going to do next.

"Wait!" he pleaded. "Don't pull. Hear me out."

"Wait what?"

"We can beat him," he said, in-between spitting and wincing, holding the claw end gingerly. "You and I. See, Ginn, he's not...so destructible. He's only...human." He blinked hard. "This hurts so bad."

"I don't care about Ginn nor you."

"Take me to the plane then. You...owe me."

I straightened my legs. "You tried to kill me. That means Ginn wants me dead too. Why the sudden change of heart? What do you know?"

His eyes opened and closed. "Your friend."

"What about him?"

"We have him. Ginn will kill him if you don't come out."

I figured that for a lie and he was stalling. If they had Jock, they'd have pieces of him. The first Razorback wouldn't hold back his attack. This was a ruse to get me to come out, but Torch changed tactics.

"We can join up, run this...fucking desert. Kill Ginn." Then, Torch pointed to his wound. "I can fix this. We have...Doctors...at the camp. The Administer. He's good."

"Not interested."

"We take out Ginn, and we're even then. Okay?" He started to moan. "If I can't have the plane, give me Ginn," he suggested.

"That would mean you take over as leader. You and I would be at war again in the future," I informed him. "The only good Rogue is a dead Rogue." As he shook his head to disagree, I pulled with all my might, sideways, and tore him open. He started to scream as he spilled out all over the floor, my crowbar creating a good foot-long trench. The women gasped at the sight, and I heard one collapse because the others shrieked at that.

"That was for the Shoeman and all your other innocent victims," I said to Torch. The blood from his gut was cascading across the floor and nearly touching my new boots. He was mumbling incoherently as he tried to gather his insides.

"I must assume you've defeated my Torch. You leave me no other choice, Ted!" Ginn shouted from outside.

After I swiped Torch's gun aside, I got to my feet and walked to the opening with my bloodied crowbar. I peered out, ready and eager to greet my foe. Instead, I saw Ginn hovering near one of the boar cages with what looked like a boot. My boot. The one I left outside when I crashed the ATV. Rounding the cage, he shoved the boot in the beast's snout with a small pole.

My scent. I knew what he'd do next and he did. Ginn lit another cigarette.

"Get up on the bunks! He's going to release his pig!" I shouted to the women as I stood quickly, leaping over Torch who was still whimpering and spilling over the ground. They made themselves to the top quickly, scampering and climbing like monkeys. The old woman was slow to climb and I pushed up behind her. With all the women safely atop all bunks, a finger from someone else pointed into the darkness and said, "There is another exit. Straight ahead."

I figured as much. I could vaguely see a small light, but it was far away.

Behind me, Torch groaned and began to slide towards the opening on his back, crawling, leaving parts of himself on the ground. He made it to the opening, half in, half out, before he became wedged and stuck. Maybe the Razorback would stop at him for an easy meal.

At my feet was his smaller gun. I couldn't find the other one. I placed the small revolver in the hands of a younger woman just as the boar outside erupted with a horrendous squeal.

"If Ginn enters, shoot the bastard," I said.

"Impossible," someone said. "He cannot die!"

"What of the pig?" someone noted. A younger child yelped.

"It has my scent. It will come after me," I answered and a chill ran down my spine. Strange to know an animal waited to hunt me down. "Just, you know, don't get in its way. Aim for the head if it gets any other ideas."

Grabbing my flashlight and backpack, I turned to face the tunnel putting behind me the weeping of the innocent, the screams of a murderer, the squeals of a ravenous beast, and the laughter of a madman controlling us all.

The dark corridor seemed to go on forever but there was light at the end of the tunnel and I ran toward it. There was a lot of junk on the ground and I had to maneuver like I was on an obstacle course. The aid of my flashlight helped guide my way although it was still tough going.

The women wailed suddenly and I realized the boar had probably entered the opening. Not a moment later, I heard huffing and scraping as the swine's hooves charged across the cement. It had left them alone and was zeroing in on me.

The end of the line drew near and I spotted an exit. It was a circular tunnel exit but was dammed up with tree branches and sludge. Pockets of light shone through the entanglement of roots and twigs and the breeze entering was stronger the closer I got. I tore at the opening but little gave way except for soft mud trickling down. Peering out, I spied a ten-foot drop into a canal of rushing water that ran perpendicular. I lowered my shoulder, backed up a few paces, and tried to smash through. More junk gave way, but not enough. I couldn't clear it in time. The boar was closing in what sounded like a gallop but it, too, was smashing into objects along the way, but that merely slowed the inevitable. I lowered my flashlight, placed it on the ground, and aimed it toward the direction of the savage arrival. I then leveled my crowbar with the chisel end facing out. The boar would charge head first with its sharp tusks and my mind scrambled to figure out how to stop an oncoming train.

I shrunk to my knees as the boar got closer, the hairy fiend still not slowing, the pounding of the hooves on the cement clacking louder and louder. I squeezed inside the dam fortress and wiggled my way behind some larger branches, hoping to slow the stampede, at least for a moment. With the light shining down the corridor, I finally saw the Razorback and he grew in size, zeroing in on me like a missile, a frenzied cry from its jaws as it had sighted its prey as well. At twenty feet I saw its tusks shining white, jutting up from its jaws like a pair of daggers. At ten feet, the mouth drew open, a bright red tongue surrounded by two smaller chompers coming to view. With two hands on my crowbar, I aimed my chisel end at the red tongue inside its gaping mouth.

Just as I speared, the damn beast lowered its head at the moment of impact and smacked into me like a fullback. It was a jarring blow and the pile behind me gave way as we were knocked through, tumbling out the other side, the two of us rolling down a small hill, trash and rubbish plummeting with us. I splashed into the water canal, sinking below the surface and thumping to the other side. Surprisingly, the water was almost clear except for the random chunks of brown mud and dirt churning around me. The current instantly took me and the pile of debris to the right and I somersaulted, end over end, underwater. A deep redness covered me and I frantically examined myself up and down for an injury, thinking it was my blood, believing one of the tusks pierced me somewhere. From behind, something large bumped me. It was the boar, its frantic hooves clawing as it swirled uncontrollably as I did. Black eyes glared at me as streams of blood clouded the water from its neck, my crowbar embedded behind its ear and below its mane. I yanked on my tool and bubbles erupted from its mouth. The boar's head swiveled side to side, trying to slash at me with its tusks and I switched tactics and attempted to drown it, holding it down. The beast then panicked, the hooves ripping at me, but time was not on my side either. My lungs were about to burst and I breached the surface, finally yanking the tool out from the pig's hide. The pig surfaced as well and I subsequently jabbed at the animal's head, aiming for the eyes as we floated downriver. My crowbar sank deep into its flesh around its neck a couple of times yet I kept hammering away. I didn't stop until more blood filled the water and the hooves stopped moving. Tired, I shoved the damn thing off and saw its lifeless body float away.

Sucking in air, I scanned the canal surroundings, the current taking me downstream to an unknown destination. I twisted in the rushing water and glanced back at the storm drain expecting Ginn to appear there. He didn't, and I was a far stretch down the canal at that point anyway. With a bit of relief, I turned back around and began concentrating on what lay ahead as I had no idea where the current was going. I floated for a long time, like a wild lazy river, treading water, watching the upper slopes for movement. The pig ahead of me floated on its side and we rode together for a while. My clothes were heavy and weighing me down so I had to tread water harder to stay afloat.

At one point, the current began to slow and I swam for the sides, thinking I had cleared enough distance to climb out before I got too waterlogged and lost. Up on the bank, I rested for a minute and removed my one boot to allow the water to pour out. When it was empty, I gathered my wits, then stood up to get my bearings. Starfish Shores was about a quarter mile away.

I heard an engine roar off.

Ginn. It had to be.

I began to hike back to Starfish Shores hoping for good news.

The coyote's skin was ripped, torn, and bloody. I held what used to be Jock's disguise in my hands, seeing one of his shoes nearby. I was under a tree where hoof marks showed scuffs in the dirt in crisscross slashes like an epic battle had just occurred. Poor Jock had probably been trying to reach the high branches before the first boar got to him. All around me, there was death, bodies bloating in the sun, some pecked by the birds of prey. The damn birds. Following me apparently had its merits.

The Muddies and the Rogues met a dismal end, all shot, some from behind. A few looked like they tried to run. Ginn was a true marksman, yet another skill I never knew he possessed. Except for the birds feeding on the dead, the Starfish Shores were quiet.

The remaining Rogue cars had parked behind a small house at the end of the town. Tires were punctured on all of them. I let them be.

I thought of the women and made my way back to the storm drain, afraid of what I might find. Ginn was gone. The flatbed truck was still there, its wheels punctured too. Ginn had left with some unknown vehicle. I found my boot and then saw movement at the opening. The old woman peered out at me and waved. She and two others were dragging Torch's dead body free from their domain. I hoped the women would reclaim what was up here. The seaside community could use a women's touch. They obviously deserved better than a storm drain.

With nothing for me there, I headed towards the sea in zombie-mode. Deathly tired, each step was heavy, and the temptation to enter a mobile home and find sleep hard to resist. I caused another life to end, because of my actions alone, and it was someone I cared about. Jock did well by me and saved me on more than one occasion and I never had the chance to repay him. Instead, I selfishly darted inside a dark storm drain earlier, and let the poor guy suffer outside at the hands of a devilish fiend and his swine from hell. We should have run off together. Again, I was not privy to what makes a person vulnerable and I only thought of myself.

Redemption wasn't clear to me and I was alone again.

The sea was supposed to bring me resolution. It was supposed to be where I'd meet the white plane and soar into the sunset. Instead, I had disrupted many lives along the way and caused many deaths. All because I searched, blindly, and in vain, to find my family, based on hearsay and lies. I was then, more than ever, convinced this was a wild goose chase as the air became calm, the skies clear, and nothingness set in. I was a sucker for believing and a chump for following. The group that left me at the airfield saw me as a liability, one that was destined to thrive among the vermin in the wasteland, and they were safe in their haven, free from the Rogues and the filth that wandered forever. Who was I kidding? I was no better than the Rogues that chased me. I deserved to be one of them.

As for the Salton Sea?

The sea could go fuck itself.

CHAPTER FIFTY-THREE

The ghostly image of a sailboat was naturally coming toward me and I laughed at the absurdity of it. A sailboat now? Why the hell not?

I sat at the edge on a rickety chair, watching the waves of the Salton Sea tap my toes, then retreat. Over and over, they never grew nor faded; they were just the same. I had found the chair on my way out of the town perched on a balcony. Again, finders' keepers. I didn't know what else to do but hoist the old thing on my shoulder and carry it, propping it into the bone/shell beach to sit. I was numb from the shock of losing my buddy and I completely zoned out, sharpening the ends of my crowbar over and over with the stone and watching the waves come and go. At one point, in mid-salivation (is that a word?), I contemplated going back to town to search for the pig, thinking bacon sounded pretty good right about then. Taking on the beast that ate my friend would prove divine and I assumed Jock would want that. It would be the least I could do. However, when I saw the image of the boat approaching, I decided I was too tired to move, and would let this one play out.

"It's not a good sea to be swimming in. Too much salinity my good friend. It will sting the eyes," I heard a voice say offshore. That was odd.

"I wasn't going to swim in it," I said, barely looking up. "Duh."

An old man with gray balding hair and a frizzy beard steadied himself in the boat as it floated to me with the stern coming around. He was wearing a thin white shirt, baggy pants with a rope belt, and sandals. Salty dog came to mind.

Two sails looked to be in good condition on the sailboat, but a tarp served as a third. It was twenty feet or so in length, white, with a large metal wheel. He grabbed an oar and rowed towards me until he found the bottom of the sea and nudged forward. Strangely, there was no name on the side. I thought all boats were named.

"Ride young man?" he asked.

"Ride where?" I asked.

"Wherever you require."

"Sure," I said, picking up my backpack and wading in for the boat. "I'll have pork chops later. The beast can't be too far and he'll gorge on the remains of the dead."

"Sir?"

"The pig that ate my friend," I said and hiked my thumb behind me. "He's back in town somewhere."

The old man gave me a worried look, but then he reached out to me with a weathered, blotchy, but hardened hand. A fisherman's hand. Hoisted topside, the old man was surprisingly stronger than I thought as I fell into a seat quite easily, despite my wet clothes. Leaning back, I felt my head heavy and I lolled it like a drunk. Fish were in a bucket next to me. A fishing rod dangled off the side.

"Name's Oliver," he said. I told him mine.

"Just wrapped up a good day of fishing when I heard the firecrackers," he said. "That's a rare occurrence."

"Firecrackers?" I asked, then thought a bit. "You mean bullets?"

"No, firecrackers," he said with a sneer. "That's what I call the filth that visited there. The only ones with guns. The Muddies certainly didn't have any."

"The Muddies. Who were they?"

Oliver nodded behind him. "A group of slackers and druggies that lived in a campground not far from here. When the gas hit, they attacked the folks at nearby Starfish Shores to take in better facilities. They killed off the men, drove the women out."

"Why did they cover themselves in mud?"

"Show devotion and humility to one another," Oliver said. "Others say it's to mourn their loved ones who passed. Most of their brains were fried already. They sampled a lot of peyote and other drugs from the plant life out there."

The rocking motion was about to put me to sleep. My body ached in places I never knew could ache and I felt sleep coming on. A well-used barbeque lay nearby with pots and plates. All the makings for a man who claimed the boat home.

Oliver asked, "Was that you the vermin were quarreling with?"

I nodded behind me. "There's one still chasing me."

"Well, you must have some good in you then. That or luck. You're safe for now. Where to?" he asked. A strong wind picked up. It felt good on my face.

"Just get me out of here," I mumbled. I slowly removed my crowbar, just in case, and placed it at my side.

He frowned. "While I ask for trades, I have no use for that."

I waved at him. "Please, just go. I won't hurt you."

Oliver refused to move. "And what will you trade?"

I rolled my eyes and unhooked my backpack. I was fighting sleep and the old bastard wanted to trade. Unzipping, I searched inside and realized I had nothing, except for the Walkman. "I have some old tunes."

He gazed at my feet. "I like your boots."

"You can't have my boots," I snarled.

"The jacket looks mighty keen."

"Deal." I don't know why I said it, I needed the damn thing for the chilly nights. I took in more of the man's boat looking into the galley down below. Books lined the shelves inside and above them, a photo of Buddha. "How about I pay you when we get to the other side, ferryman?" I asked, thinking of Captain and DuPont at the last ferry.

Oliver laughed and continued to steer. "So be it. Where are you headed?" he asked, grabbing a rope that flipped a sail. It caught right away and the sailboat began to skim over the surface.

Hesitating, I said, "It's a riddle."

That perked his interest. "Tell, tell."

I recited the quote from the Doctor about judgement and being redeemed and he understood right away. "Right. I can take you part of the way. Mind your head, please." He then flipped the other sail around. It caught the wind and cracked. The boat began to move faster. I knew nothing of boats and sailing, but he seemed seaworthy and I began to trust him.

"You know where to go?" I asked him. My eyes and body felt heavy. Too wiped out to act surprised as we glided over small, choppy waves.

He jutted out a bony finger. "Redemption lies just ahead," he remarked and pointed what looked like south. "We'll be there in a jiffy. You go ahead and rest up."

The boat swung around and we headed more out to sea. The shore was behind us, getting smaller and smaller. I thought of the sight of the sails and wondered if the Rogues had boats. "Are we safe out here? Do the Rogue's have a navy?"

"The firecrackers don't have boats," Oliver corrected. "Most of them are on the roads. I'll go out far enough so they won't see us."

Laying back, I stared up at the sky and saw a few dark clouds, somewhat unusual because I hadn't noticed any up until now. We seemed to have picked up speed and I thought good riddance. I need to get away from this area pronto, the farther the better. My head and eyes drooped as I felt myself giving into sleep. My nightmare continued but at least I still had my dreams.

"Storm approaching," Oliver said.

"Of course, it is," I replied and shut my eyes.

CHAPTER FIFTY-FOUR

Fittingly, I dreamt my family and I were in a row boat, floating gently down the stream, just like the song, except my oldest son ended aloud with, "Throw your father overboard, listen to him scream." I was incensed that he added that lyric and thought it funny, earning a smile from my youngest in the process. My wife didn't react to it as she was more concerned with the sea itself. "It's rising," she said to me. "Can't you do something?" I told her not to worry, we were in a boat obviously. The water was indeed rising and beginning to crest over the sides, splashing my feet and soaking my new boots. The three of them sat there then, facing me, waiting for me to do something, their feet becoming waterlogged too. Reaching for the oars that lay by my side, I stared in horror as they melted in my hands like spaghetti, drooping uselessly into the water. Glancing around, I saw no land in sight and began to panic. Soon, the water filled our boat and my family watched helplessly. "Fitting," my wife said as the level of water reached her waist and soon the sea swallowed us all.

Jolting awake, I must have freaked because I flipped myself around quick, gripped the sides of the boat instantly, thinking they had sunk to the dark depths below. Somehow, I remained topside with the boat still floating and dry. Although I realized soon enough that it was a just a dream, I saw myself in the sea, a torrid reflection staring back up. I cringed and turned slowly back around.

Oliver was manning the sails as I left him and the old man had barely moved. My elbows started to hurt propping myself, old aches and pains returning and throbbing. Dreamtime was certainly over and I was back with the living. Oliver was watching me somberly, a pitiful glare like a disappointed parent to a child. I decided I had had enough sleep and made a mental note; not all dreams were good ones.

"That was quite a nap," Oliver said.

"I'll sleep when I'm dead," I answered.

The rocky motion of a boat caused me to be queasy and my stomach churned. While I was never one to feel seasick, I had not been on a boat in a very long time and the motion felt foreign. I was on an empty stomach too. Feeling a small urge to yak, I leaned over the side to my right and I saw we were approaching the coastline. There were no docks, no structures or buildings of any kind. No Ginn either. Just a small, empty beach.

Oliver smiled. "You were mumbling," he pointed out.

"What did I say?" I asked and turned back around.

"Mostly nonsense. Sounded like a nursery rhyme."

I didn't respond to that. I rubbed my eyes and tried to gather myself. I was never a good napper.

Oliver cocked his head, "Redemption. Why do you seek it?"

"I'm going to find my family," I admitted. "They're alive."

"Is that so?" he asked.

"I wasn't with them when all this happened. The gas."

He crossed his arms in front of his chest and asked, almost accusingly, "Then where were you?"

"Mojave Desert. Heading home."

He cocked an eyebrow. "Why were you in the desert?"

"Business," I said flatly.

Oliver heard my tone and then interjected, "The desert was a good place to be. I, myself, was out here and thankfully, we never felt the gas. It was just a normal day for us, except the power went out and a day later, hundreds of people descended from the north searching for food and water."

He flipped his wheel and we seemed to change course a bit.

"My life hasn't changed all that much since the gas struck," Oliver continued. "I lived on this boat back then and still do. You know how I knew something was really bad? Airplanes crisscross overhead heading to and from LAX and John Wayne Airport. I noticed no air traffic after that, no roar of engines, no jet streams. Just a dark sky filled with millions of stars."

That hit me. "You haven't seen a plane land here recently?"

Oliver gave me a look that went from amazed to sympathetic. "Can't say that I have but at times, there are some strange sounds. Could be a plane, could be a boat. Sorry, I am out on the water often. The sea is enormous, thirty-five miles long."

I ignored that and continued, "I should have been with my family. I wish I could go back in time. I know that now. I know when I would stop."

"Stop for what?" Oliver asked, taking down a sail.

"Stop time to make things better with my wife."

"And when would that be?"

"When I stopped smiling."

Oliver thought about that a moment. "Perhaps one day, you'll realize how perfect things were," he said, then looked up with his hands stretched out. "Tilt your head back and laugh at the sky." Closing his eyes, he brought his head back down. "The grass is always greener on the other side. Many, many fools have fallen for that."

"You got me there."

"You cannot travel the path until you have become the path itself," he commented. "Your first mission is to forgo regret. Take the time to think of some positives. Every bad decision can be rectified. Don't give up."

With my hands out, I pleaded, "I tried telling her that."

"For a good relationship to work, you are bound to be courteous, supportive, faithful, sharing, and offering. Marriage does not make people happy, happy people are happy to begin with. Just live by all your heart and not your head," he suggested.

We slowed to a crawl and the shore loomed directly behind me. "End of the line," Oliver said and lowered the last sail. He then dropped the oars in and paddled with a smooth technique. The boat glided effortlessly, almost as if on ice. Looking down, I could see the bottom of the sea, a mere four feet down.

"Head west two miles down Beach Road. Go up to Highway 86, then head north. You'll find the place of judgement and then after, redemption. You can't miss it."

The boat stopped in the shells after some grinding underneath. A major whiff of the dead fish smell hit me again. "I believe services were rendered," Oliver said to me, not minding the stench.

Standing in the boat as it rocked side to side, I removed my jacket and handed it over. Oliver put it on, scanning the horizon at the same time. "Be careful," he said.

"Beach Road to Highway 86, then head north?" I asked, not quite sure it sounded right. "Right?"

Oliver grinned. "Only a few miles. Don't go any farther north. Some unruly firecrackers in the Salton Sea City. Nor south. Same thing with the folks down there. Stay in-between and you'll be alright. No point going to either anyway if Redemption is what you seek."

There wasn't much to see from where I stood. It looked like fields once grew just beyond. Large, square plots. That seemed hopeful, like leftover fruits maybe.

"Nice and warm," he smiles, zipping up. "I like this jacket."

"This all you do?" I asked him. "Go back and forth, offering rides?"

"Serves a purpose," he stated, his chin up.

Stepping out of the boat, I dipped my boot into a foot of cold, salty water. The frigid temperature reminded me that the desert can get cold and I began wondering how I can get another jacket myself. Oliver asked me to help shove him off as he dug his paddle into the sand. I obliged, the sailboat came free, and then I sloshed back to beach. Oliver was already rowing offshore, safe from the hazards that plagued the shores. Firecrackers, he called the Rogues. Safe at sea, he was. I thought of Jock doing Yoda and smiled.

"What can I expect?" I shouted to him.

Oliver looks skyward. Dark clouds getting darker.

"Rain," he said and swung his sailboat around. Soon, he was heading towards the middle of the sea again and never once did he look back. Before long, he was a small blot on the horizon. Minutes later, with an oncoming fog, he vanished from sight.

I took a much-needed rest on a fence after a brisk, but waterlogged, half hour stroll through low lying weeds, small ponds of foul, darkened water, and lumpy dirt that resembled a marsh. The water was swirling with small insects and fish. While I had been surrounded by fenced fields, they were no longer green or full and plush with vegetation of the eating kind. Still, I was excited. I got some shut-eye on the boat which sort of rejuvenated me, save for the drowning dream. After I left Oliver's boat, I began to think more about my marriage than ever before. Oliver said I could right things again, but I wasn't so sure. My wife could be stubborn and I had allegedly messed up.

She had taken another lover.

That's what the Doctor told me in the bunker. That one sentence caused me a lot of pain.

Rain started to fall, lightly at first, and that was my cue to move faster. While I'd welcome the instant water replenishment as my canteens were nearly drained, the lack of a jacket could make for a cold walk. It would be dark soon too. I lost my flashlight in the tunnel where the boar crashed into me so that was no help either. Shelter was a priority and I really resented handing over my jacket to Oliver.

The Doctor said I would find redemption out there somewhere and that was backed up by Oliver. I could see nothing that remotely looked inhabited ahead of me as I looked west. Only small mountains and more sand.

The rain fell harder and it felt good on my skin, cleansing me of the salt coating on my body from the Salton Sea. Thankfully, I smelled none of it on my hands as I cupped the liquid from the skies and drank, finding it invigorating and refreshing. However, I found myself shivering as I sipped, so I had to seek shelter.

A car, an old Chevy sedan, was half buried in the sand along the shoulder ahead of me. The trunk door was missing but a patch of fur and ears were sticking up from inside, that much I could see despite the shrinking light.

Jock? Buddy! He found me!

Nope. It was a real coyote; the long, slender body leaping out, fixated on me, holding its ground. It growled and gnashed its teeth, its paws slinking in the mud. Little barks and yips came from within and Momma Coyote was simply guarding her young. Just in case, I unfurled my crowbar and growled back, walking past it by about ten yards, and continued to do so, then backwards, showing no fear. She followed me for a few moments, shaking off the rain. Feeling sore for the carnage I brought him, I asked, "You're still coming with me, right Jock? The plane?"

The coyote tilted its head when I spoke. "Come on," I continued. "You can tell me some corny Star Wars stuff. We'll rate the Aliens movies. *Something.*" Hardly amused, the coyote tired of me and headed back to the car where she hopped into the trunk and vanished. While she and her pups had shelter in the old car, they were one up on me as I was nearly naked and drowning in the elements.

Later, with my arms crisscrossed in front of me, I laughed at the snipe hunt to which I'd fallen victim, walking an endless desert road as if any of it was ever true. The checkered flag was supposed to be here with the Cessna ready for boarding, but it wasn't. The entire trip here was filled with gore, violence, and a desperate husband hanging on to a facade. "You got me!" I shouted out loud, shaking my head at the injustice. "I deserve this shit! All of it!" This was nonsense. All of it a farce. Just as I was facing the fact that I had gone officially bonkers, a lightning strike high above cast a bright light and I saw it, almost too good to be true.

A shack in a dirt field just ahead. Two standing walls that I could see, with a door half open. Large enough for me and my crazy thoughts.

With my crowbar out, I slowly approached the small structure, searching for movement. The only sound was the pelting of the rain on the roof and the rivers of water cascading down to the soft mud below. Once at the door, I jabbed the chisel end and threw it open. Nothing jumped out, not even dust. I waited for another lightning strike to see inside, and when another bolt lit up seconds later, only empty seed bags and potato sacks greeted me from a corner. Surprisingly, the shed was empty, although water dripped in places, forming small pools as I treaded in, squishing under my feet. It was no Hilton and I was dead tired, so I decided to check in for the night. Besides, no plane would land in this weather and my guess was, they would attempt to land tomorrow.

If there was such a plane. Back and forth I went with that. Either way, I promised myself not to sleep in and miss my flight, just in case.

I gathered the dirty sacks and bags and draped them around me, providing me with some comfort and warmth as I crashed in the corner. Sleep would be hard to come by with the incessant lightning and thunder, which was growing in severity. Between flashes, I saw a scythe hanging on the opposite wall. I was rooming with Death apparently, he out and about on his own mission, only the moron forgot his favorite tool and there will be hell to pay when the lives of the dearly departed hadn't been crossed off yet. And then I wondered if that overlook was meant for me, that Death gave me a sign that he was coming back for one more name.

CHAPTER FIFTY-FIVE

I awoke, early, the sun piercing through the slits in the wood, the bright yellow rays shining directly in my eyes. Having slept sideways on the cold floor with the seed and potato sacks spread out around me, new aches greeted me along my side. My left arm felt deservedly numb.

My canteen overflowed from last night's downfall. I had planted it upright just outside the shack hours earlier as the rain still dumped and I drank half of it, anticipating a long walk ahead. My morning whizz was one of the longest I could remember, last night's rare desert rain provided me with a body-flushing, twenty second flow. I should know, I counted. Feeling hydrated and rejuvenated, I was ready and amped for the day's hike although my grumbling stomach said otherwise. I would have to make do with whatever I encountered along the way, most likely edible and boring plant life. Smirking at Death's scythe still propped on the wall, I rubbed it in by performing my usual stretches and exercises in plain view. Not only was I not dead, but very much alive. I had a plane to catch.

Upon leaving the shack, I discovered that I was actually surrounded by fog. However, the area where I stood seemed to be the only place where the sun broke free, as if the fog parted for just yours truly. I took that as a good sign, as if God said, *yes, you're the star for the day and now get a move on.* So, I did, continuing down Beach Road, giving props to the big man upstairs. Through the heavy mist, I discovered a canal that seemingly ran into the Salton Sea. It was fresh, however, and I scooped and filled the rest of my canteen. It was not hot out yet, so I thought I could make good tread.

Humming *Staying Alive*, I stumbled across Highway 86 at an intersection, nearly tripping over an old street sign lying in the dirt. Another sign for the town of Salton Sea City pointed north was next to it, the metal peppered with bullet holes. There were a few structures there but they looked like more sheds than anything else, similar to the one I slept in. Old fruit stands came to view as well, offering only brush and weeds and sadly not filled with nature's goodies. Salton Sea City would have more buildings I was sure, but I wasn't headed all the way there. Oliver wisely advised me to avoid it. The less people I ran into, the better. If they were allied with the Rogues in some capacity, my luck could run out and my old nemesis, The Grim Reaper, may have his ah-ha moment after all.

Fog had thickened as I walked north on the sturdy asphalt, as per Oliver's insistence. My steps quickened and the mist felt good on my face. I couldn't see too far anymore, and when I looked back, it was as if I was walking in a calming haze. Maybe I was dead, floating in the clouds, my earthly body resting forever in the shack. That could have been quite convincing a thought and I could have welcomed it, save for the judgement part, but tire tracks were present over wind-swept sand at my feet, somewhat new too, deep grooves a telltale sign that traffic had driven by. That stopped me cold. Suddenly, I felt vulnerable and very much alive.

Still, I kept on. I was determined to find redemption and I hoped the fog wouldn't prevent me from seeing it. Planes usually won't land in the fog, so I would probably be early for my flight. That gave me some solace, until a familiar sight stopped me in my tracks and I'd have to face the music once more.

Normally a two-way speaking device, the Call Box receiver was bitterly one sided and the other end was deathly quiet. The reason? My wife wouldn't answer me; she was giving me the silent treatment. I killed myself walking this far, the least she could do was respond. So far, my questions had been met with zero response. At least in the past, there was some bitterness, some smarminess, sometimes some relief and sadness.

Apparently, my wife had different plans.

"Why won't you talk to me?' I asked in a calm voice, fingering etched graffiti on the box itself. "Have I been that bad?"

Silence. She hadn't said a word the entire damn time.

"I'm almost there," I told her. "You know, Redemption? I am worthy, right?"

An insect buzzed nearby. The only other sounds besides the whine in my voice.

"I am really sorry about the whole thing. Please forgive me," I said into the empty receiver. "I'm coming home." I dropped the receiver, vowing to never speak into a Call Box again as I strolled back on the road.

Two miles later, a structure appeared on the highway with a large canopy that stretched across a set of lanes. It was an old Border Patrol Station where drivers were directed to slow and eventually stop next to a small booth. I imagined the citizenship queries were conducted right there. To the right of the canopy, a one-story building lay in ruin. While it looked abandoned, I cautiously approached and studied the surroundings. Strange that a border control crossing would be there, the map in my head suggested that Mexico was about an hour south. We were way inland on the US side.

I contemplated not entering the building but curiosity got the better of me. I peered inside the station through a door and saw heaps of trash and blankets. Strangely, most of the decor was gone. No desks, jail cells, no handcuffs of any kind. Just a wide, empty space. I noticed the faint odor of death and saw a skeleton of a man nestled underneath some blankets at the rear, some of the skin still present but weltering. Death came not so long ago. He looked older, a drifter who happened across this shelter and perished for reasons I didn't care to know. The rest of the interior contained the basics like chairs, busted tables, shelves, all of it covered in a fine layer of dust.

The Border Patrol Station. *Find the place of judgement.* The agents stationed here judged people, didn't they? That had to be it. Oliver said I'd find it and it would be obvious. Derelict cars painted white with a green stripe in the rear parking lot showed a lot of wear and sand-beaten damage.

Seeing nothing else for me, I traipsed on the right, weary and tired. For a few miles, all I passed was sand and shrub. The scent of salt remained strong and somewhere, off to my right, the Salton Sea stayed with me although it was hidden by fog. Eventually, I did pass a sign that said, Salton Sea City 1 mile, so I knew I was headed in the right direction. Oliver told me not to head that far north and yet there was nothing where I was. I grew despondent, thinking I had missed something and wasn't in favor of turning back.

Then, I saw it. A sign. Literally.

Redemption Road.

It was a small, windswept road that led away from the sea. The fog was still present and I could only see about thirty feet ahead. I jogged along the road hoping for evidence that an airfield was nearby. The corner of barbed wire fence appeared before me on my left with one length running south, the other west. Further, to my left, flattened land where no shrub grew. It had to be part of the runway. The further I ran, I was confident that I had made it. Pieces of discarded metal that looked like part of a wing rested against a fence. In the distance, I saw a single brown building inside the gated perimeter. It didn't look like a control tower but I took it to be a hangar.

The gate was open. I strolled inside. A sign said, SALTON SEA AIRPORT.

I made it! The airport! That was where they would pick me up!

I stumbled around the building, searching for signs that a plane had been there recently. Tracks, engine parts, oil, anything. The more I searched, however, I saw no planes nor any proof that a plane had landed there, ever. There was just a building, a fence, dirt, and a whole lot of fog. I was frustrated and confused.

Make your way to the Salton Sea. Find the place of judgement. If you are truly worthy, head north and you'll find redemption.

I thought back to the last moments before the plane took off. They had supplies. The wounded truck driver. She was worried about the Rogues attacking. The Pilot was concerned with the weight and the fuel. That's why they couldn't take me.

Weight and fuel. Fuel. Enough to get there.

"We need enough to land in the sky, remember," the Pilot had said to the Doctor.

"Land in the sky?" I asked myself. "Why would he say...?" And then I realized what he meant.

Land in the sky.

I knew where my family was!

A bright pair of lights suddenly glowed, putting me under a spotlight. I waved at the shocking brilliance, too stunned and too late for me to move as the glare held me in place, like a deer in headlights.

Headlights. I guessed right. I assumed it was the plane and that it had already landed. I moved closer, believing the Pilot would wave me in. Man, did I have a story to tell he and the Doctor! Strangely, I heard no propeller, nor shouts or commands. Just a calm serenity that only the desert can provide.

I saw a pair of boots, legs, and then a human form between the streams of light. The lights seemed low to me, too low for an airplane. It was then when I shuddered as I realized the glare belonged to a classic muscle car, a familiar vehicle I possessed not too long ago.

The El Camino.

Ginn was there, waiting for me, as if he always had.

CHAPTER FIFTY-SIX

"Quite the journey," Ginn said to me, breaking the ice. "I'm surprised you made it this far." His hair was a dark brown now and he was strangely shabbily dressed more like me. He must have pilfered the get up from one of his dead cronies back at the Starfish Shores Resort.

His guns were in his holsters and I had no doubt they were loaded, despite his shelling of his own men. He regarded me as the type who came fully prepared no matter what and eliminating his army single-handedly probably worked into his warped plan. I'd have to bluff my way through or have him come closer for any success to get by him. Anything else, he'd cut me down in a hail of bullets.

He strutted ahead slowly, shaking his head. "But you know what's really bugging me at this moment?" he asked me, shaking his head, and then stepping aside. "What the hell did you do to my fucking car?" He nodded towards the El Camino with his hands at his hips.

Yep, the kit work Song's teenagers did on his car stifled the resale value, that was for sure. I smiled at that but kept it short-lived. I needed to move past this guy and removed my crowbar from my quiver to show I meant business. "Let me catch my plane and I'll let you live," I said, confident, knowing it was intimidating to others in the past. My legend spoke for itself and he had heard it. That much he admitted himself before I lit him up with 50,000 volts back at his camp, thanks to the taser.

Frowning, Ginn chided me with, "Stop the charade. You know you won't get past me with that." He tapped his holsters for emphasis. "Although, I must admit, that was a nasty job you did on Torch."

I merely shrugged at that. "You have no business stopping me," I told him and tapped the crowbar to show I was willing to carve someone else. "Do what you want with this shit wasteland. I am leaving it and you will not see me anymore."

"I'm disappointed in you, Ted," Ginn replied. "You don't strike me as one to believe in fairy tales."

"This is no fairy tale. This is the real deal."

"I know it is," he stated. "I know it's real. It's very real. The damned plane has been haunting me for about a year. Taunting me. You're not alone in that, you know."

Good luck with that, pal. "That plane ride is reserved for me only," I insisted.

"And that's the fairy tale. You had your family, your perfect little wife, kids, white picket fence. And you gave it all away. I have no idea why you want it all back so badly, you tossed them off with barely a thought. I should know. I helped."

"That's a lie," I said. "I made a mistake and I was going to make amends."

"You made your choice."

"And I regretted it ever since."

"Did you now?" he asked and slowly rounded his bumper, walking backwards to his passenger door, his eyes never leaving me. "I saved someone for you," he said and popped the door open. Inside, an outline of someone there that I couldn't quite make out. I then noticed one of the pig cages in the bed of the El Camino, the top of which visible over the roof of the car.

The Razorback cages. I knew one was dead, but the other?

Ginn still kept an eye on me and fiddled in the inside of his car. Ginn came around escorting someone forward.

Maggie.

She looked stunning. She had makeup on and wore a curvy, white dress. Her dark hair flowed like it was just washed and styled. "Hello, stranger," she said to me. Ginn held her arm and the two of them stood there facing me.

"What the hell is this?" I asked them.

Ginn smiled and said, "A blast from the past."

"Maggie. Sorry you got dragged into this," I said.

"That's okay. I wanted to come," she replied but her face flashed some anxiety.

"She's been a good trooper, hidden in my RV up until a few hours ago," Ginn informed me. He then turned to Maggie and said, "Wait here, sweetheart."

"Of course," she replied but kept her eyes on me.

"I have another surprise for you, Ted," Ginn said and floated back to his car, reaching into the passenger seat once more. A smaller figure was there, having been in the middle. Ginn then came back with someone else I knew.

Jock. Missing his coyote cover-up but still wearing clothes. His hands were tied behind his back though. Ginn hauled him out and threw my friend to the ground where he landed nearly face first. He huffed and rolled over, moaning. Staring at my little buddy was disconcerting. Blood streaks and bruise marks cover his frail, pale body.

"My little piggie treed the poor bugger," Ginn admitted. "After countless head rams to a weak tree, your man here fell from his perch and was summarily torn and shredded. However, the little man is quite the outstanding shot with the sling and blew out one of the eyes on my prized pet. That bought him time to scale the tree once more. Since I lost you in the storm drain, suddenly your wounded ally's status was elevated."

Dipping into his pocket, he brought out clenched fist. Opening it, a white substance fell out, like sand. He said, "From the salt flats. Potent stuff. Just a wee bit of salt on the wounds and any man will talk. And the little man did, further explaining the rest of the secret."

Shaking, I could barely contain myself. I wanted to attack Ginn so very badly, more than anyone else I had encountered these last five years.

"Redemption," Ginn said with a smile. "He confessed. And here we are. All of us. I must admit, it was actually quite easy if you knew the area."

At first, I was in disbelief, but then I became confused, shocked, and finally cheated. Ginn could read my face, and he knew the power he had over me once more.

"I want you gone now, Ted. Take your Maggie and your friend too. Unlike the casinos in old Las Vegas, this is a sure thing."

"No."

"Why? So, you can find your family? You gave up on them. You don't know where they are and you certainly don't care. Otherwise, you would have been with them. Am I right?

"Shut up," I muttered, weakly.

"This is all your fault, Teddy. You left them to rot. You didn't care. You did this to yourself."

"That is none of your business."

"You left them," Ginn ranted. "You had the perfect family and you disgraced them. But then that's been your answer to everything, hasn't it? Instead of facing the issue, you run. You run because you're a coward. Deep down, you're too afraid to confront your feelings and you learn to hide and hate, assert blame, and cast aside. You want to find something new. You're looking for resurrection, a new life, freedom from the things that held you down and you hid from them. You made good money, you demanded more, and you deserved more, didn't you? But what about the others? Did they not earn your love and support? You didn't ask for all the shit that came with it, did you? Kids, work, the struggle. Where were you?"

"That's not true," I mumbled. "I cared for them. I always did."

"Forget them, they're gone. They don't want you back."

"That's not true," I replied, although it came out weak.

"Come on, man!" he shouted and nodded behind me. "They clearly don't want you. Why else haven't they tried to find you?"

"Because they thought I was dead!"

"Or, did they know you were alive and were fine with you out here?"

"Go to hell," I answered. "No one would push this life on anyone."

The keys to the El Camino were tossed to my feet. "Take it," Ginn said. "I know you loved my car. It's yours. You, Maggie and Jock. You're free to leave."

Maggie stood awkwardly, unsure of what to do next. She cast me a small smile.

Ginn the added, "But you leave now. You turn around and go. You give up on finding the plane. Right now, that's the best odds in your incredible survival story."

Maggie took a step closer to me and said, "Ted, I want you. I always have. I saved myself for you. We can make this work. We can be happy." She smoothed her hands over her hips and pouted. "Don't you want that?" she asked. "I'm all yours, baby."

"You two would make an amazing couple," Ginn noted with a smile, then pointed like a salesman. "Ain't she somethin'?"

I shook my head in disgust. "Sorry, Maggie, but you shouldn't have come. I am going to make that plane."

Her smile disappeared. She eyed me like I made a mistake.

I glanced over her shoulder at Ginn.

"Get out of the way, Ginn," I snarled.

Ginn's eyes narrowed. His face scrunched and his mouth formed a slit. He brought up a gun and without looking, fired a single shot at Maggie's back. Her body dropped and fell sideways into the dirt dead. She never saw it coming.

The last thing she ever saw was me.

"Why did you do that, Ginn?" I leaped forward but Ginn aimed his gun and stopped me on the spot. "What did you ever want from me?!?"

This was his moment and he swayed as if he had practiced it. Switching hands, he opened his palm and traced his scar with the barrel of his gun.

"What? My soul?" I asked, incredulously. I stared at Maggie, watching blood drain from her lifeless body. A large hole was in her back. I felt sorry for her.

Ginn smiled, took a deep breath, and let it all out. "She calls me one day. She's upset. She finds the phone number on a cell phone among other numbers. This one, she says to me, is called often. She asks me who I am and why I am there. I tell her that I am a hotel concierge and she doesn't believe me. She flies out and visits me at the hotel. I convince her. She sees what I do. She sees who I am. She cries and I comfort her. We talk for a long time and she begins to understand. She wants to know more."

I stared at Maggie. "Why are you telling me this? Isn't enough you killed her?"

"I remember the first time we met," Ginn continued and he closed his eyes. "She was amazingly beautiful. Soft blue green eyes, dark hair, a lovely smile. Even upset, she was dazzling. She wanted to know why I did what I did and I confessed to her, it's just part of my job. I give people what they want. And I deliver too, but I always ask for something in return."

I could barely stand to listen to the guy. I scanned the area, looking for a sign that the plane would land. Maybe cause a distraction.

Ginn went on. "She's says things have changed and not for the better. It's almost hard for her. And it's unfair that she be the only victim. She wants to inflict pain too."

He was wavering now like he's in a dream. Ginn was about ten feet away and he's preoccupied with his story.

"I suggested to her that we meet in San Diego," he said.

That stopped me. "What?"

"She says he has changed. She suspects something is wrong. She says she wants to leave him but not until there's proof."

My head began to swirl. "Leave who?"

"She is already out the door when I send her the photos. She's got the kids. She knew, Ted. She already knew."

I gripped my crowbar tight and took a stepped forward. He didn't seem to notice. "Who are you fucking talking about? Answer me!"

"Do you recall that time she said she traveled to San Diego? With her girlfriend Paula? Just before the gas?"

I did. My mind was scrambling, relaying information back and forth.

"You never bothered to check, did you? Surely not her. Your wife would never lie, right? Well, guess what. She never went to San Diego. She drove to Las Vegas to see me and we had a very good time."

"Shut up."

She had taken another lover, the Doctor said.

"She planned it all along," Ginn pointed out.

"No fucking way. Not her."

"She wanted you hurt. I told her something bad was going to happen and that she needed to leave. I admitted that I had you in a bad spot. She was fine with it."

"No!" I yelled, clenching my fists. "We were a family!"

"She sought solace in me and she found it."

"Stop talking!"

"This life in the desert. She wanted you to roam it forever."

"Shut the hell up!"

"I told you I wanted something precious from you. Did you finally figure it out? What that something precious was?"

"Go to hell."

"I want your wife," Ginn said. "That's what I demand in return."

He was lying. "You said you wanted me! My leadership!"

"No, Randall said that. But when you were returned to me at my camp just a few days ago, well, I had to collect something at the time. You were still indebted, but it was your wife I always wanted. And still do."

There was no fucking way that would happen. My wife would never meet up with a guy like this. She was too good for him; she would see right through him. "You can't have her," I said, but it doesn't sound convincing and suddenly, I was riddled with doubt.

"I'm going to have her and that little slice of paradise, wherever it is. It's abundant in refined gasoline. It has to be, to fly a plane. And an army that is fueled, cannot be stopped. Once I have control of that, along with the love of a good woman, I can have everything."

"She would never make a deal with you!" I blurted out and took another step. Eight feet away, I could reach him.

"The deal was for you. I keep you away, out here, dead or alive. Hell hath no fury like a woman scorned."

"Except I never cheated."

"You cheated on your family!" he yelled.

"If you made a deal with her, why don't you know where she is?"

That caused him to pause. His mouth shook. He tried to smile but his lips quivered. I hit a sore spot and he knew it.

"You lied to her! You knew Maggie and I were never together!" I screamed.

The sputter of plane engine startled me. High above, somewhere on top of the fog, a plane was throttling, coming in from the west. Ginn searched the sky and followed the sound, like it both irritated and captivated him at the same time.

"I'm going to catch that plane," he informed me.

I slowly shook my head. "They've come for me."

"They'll take me there, one way or another." He juggled his gun for emphasis. "I'll even fly it if I have to."

I took a step forward and raised the crowbar above my head. "You're not getting on that plane!" I lunged forward...

Aiming, he shouted, "I will not be empty!"

My chest sucked inward as if I was hit by a truck and the blast from his gun barely registered. I was blown backwards, falling hard, landing on my backpack, slamming my head on the ground in a whiplash. Winded and stunned, I coughed and tried to breathe but my chest felt like it was collapsing within. Unlike the previous shots I took to the vest, that was a new pain. My finger probed the area where the bullet punctured the vest and when I lifted it up to my face, it was covered in blood.

"No, no, no," I said wearily.

Lifting my head, I saw Ginn with his gun pointing down at me, smoke wafting from his barrel. "Kevlar doesn't stop all bullets, you idiot," he quipped.

My mouth worked but no words came out.

Cocking the hammer back, he offered one last smile. I placed my hands out front to ward off the next bullet. "I'll say hi to her for you," he said. "And don't worry, I'll raise your kids right."

I waited for the gunshot but it never came. Instead, Ginn reached down and ripped off part of my shirt. He then stormed back to the El Camino and hauled out a large metal plate, lowering it like a ramp. He then tinkered with Razorback's cage. The beast inside was going berserk, slamming into the cage, trying to free itself. I sat up, with some difficulty, and looked to Jock knowing what Ginn planned to do.

"Run," I whispered. "Jock, buddy, you got to go."

Jock didn't move. He lay still, but I could see his chest rise and fall. I became worried for him, knowing he'd be an easy target and probably enemy number one for taking out the boar's eye. Then I realized Ginn used part of my shirt, my scent, and the Razorback was going to come after me.

From the rear of the El Camino, a gray blur barged towards me. A snort erupted there, loud and obtrusive. Hooves came at full gallop and the bright white tusks were swiping up and down. The boar charged at me, like his brother did, and I only had seconds to react.

Those were seconds I used to snatch my crowbar. I planted the claw end under my foot and lowered the chisel end towards my grunting opponent. I had all my weight behind it. With its head lowered, the boar launched its attack with a squeal, its head cocked at an angle so it's one good eye could zero in on me. I aimed the crowbar for its gaping mouth, right between the flashing tusks. The beast crashed into me and knocked me back. It barged forward though, the momentum carrying it past me. It skidded to a stop, stomped its hooves, and emitted a terrible, ear-piercing screech as the crowbar was embedded into its throat. The weight of my body allowed the chisel-end to dig deep as the pig rammed into me. I seized the moment to crawl to the boar and wrestle the crowbar from its jaws, which was covered in blood. I had assumed I'd needed to stab it one more time but the Razorback eyed me with its one good eye, the black orb flinching in obvious pain. It suddenly coughed up a pool of its own blood and then the large swine dropped dead in a cloud of dust.

"Look at you, big game hunter!" Ginn shouted as I lay on my back once more.

Jock suddenly bolted and ran off, his small body vanishing into the fog. Ginn swiveled and leveled his gun in that direction, laughing.

"Like target practice. Always a fan of small game," Ginn said and fired, the smack of the bullet echoing off Jock's body. The ghostly image of my friend fell in a heap into some shrubs near the building, tumbling face first into a patch of fog as his hands remained tied behind his back.

Just then, an engine could be heard coming in from the right, growing louder and louder. They were landing! Ginn noticed it too and swiveled to meet them. We both searched the fog like it was some dream. Patches began to swirl and I suddenly noticed a clearing to the right. It wasn't there before. The fog, it seemed, was lifting.

The plane bounced on the hard ground, then roared by us, the wind buffeting us both. I could barely see the Pilot in the window. Ginn waved at it eagerly, as if it were me, and the plane veered into another thin fog bank on the other side. I saw the Pilot give Ginn a thumbs up as it passed.

The dark hair. The clothes. Ginn was pretending to be me and it was working.

The plane slowed, revving its engines louder and we could see it, only slightly, almost vanishing at the end of the runway. Ginn marveled at its sight, clapping his hands. "It's beautiful!" he shouted. Soon, the plane would turn around and come back.

I rose to my knees and stood slowly with some difficulty. My chest felt hollow yet the pain resonated, and I was tempted to fall backwards and rest some more. I trudged forward with one step, then two. Ginn was preoccupied by the arrival of the plane and didn't see me coming. The Cessna was making its turn. I managed to creep up to Ginn, with his back turned, as the plane's engine kept me quiet.

Ginn hoisted a gun from his right holster and placed it behind his back. The coat he wore conveniently covered the holsters so whomever was out front wouldn't see them until it was too late. Ginn had no plans of taking a ride with the occupants. I was convinced he was going to steal the plane after killing those inside.

First, he would force them to confess the secret location prior to their deaths. Ginn would have it all then; a plane at his disposal, the location of a safe haven, the resources to build yet another army or even strengthen the one he already had, and my family to torture at will. Despite being a foreigner, Ginn, the former concierge, the man who could get what you wanted, would no doubt succeed in taking over the new place with his charm and resilience. There was nothing the man couldn't do.

I slammed my crowbar down on his head, but Ginn must have sensed me coming and sidestepped at the last second. I missed his body but smacked the gun from his hand as he whirled and tried to bring it around to match me. I stumbled forward and nearly fell. The Cessna's engines revved and I guessed it was throttling forward towards us.

"Come on then," Ginn teased me, raising his fists. "Let's see what you got!"

Ginn stood in a fighter's stance and once again, that surprised me. He bounced lightly on his feet, enticing me to come forward with his fingers. "Drop it, crowbar man! Fight like a man! Let's give the newcomers a show!"

I did no such thing. Conjuring up the image of Polecat once more, I rushed at him, swinging sideways and clipped his chin with my tool. Ginn staggered from the blow and I saw a slice of red appear and I thought the irony. Ginn would have a scar because of me!

Hardly fazed, however, Ginn moved like a cat and kicked out at me, catching me on the left thigh. It felt like a hammer and my leg stiffened to the point where I couldn't move it. And then Ginn was on me, flailing away with his fists, hitting me at will. My chest still hurt from the gunshot, my leg was throbbing in pain, and I could hardly keep my arms and hands up to defend myself.

I imagined Polecat's ugly face in front of me in place of Ginn's and I growled. I swung upwards and caught his chin again with an upper-cut, using my legs as leverage, and his head snapped back. With my right leg, I arced a side kick and caught him behind his left knee. The man hobbled on the spot with his mouth bleeding. Soon, he spat out a piece of his tongue with blood drooling down his chin.

Ginn suddenly rushed me and barreled into me. We rolled in the dirt, trading blows. I grabbed a handful of dirt, smushed it into his face, and then hit him in the ear with a right cross. He squealed and then responded by kneeing me in the stomach. I doubled over as the blow was close to my chest. I coughed in pain and rolled over. Ginn smashed me in the chest with his elbow. I yelled out in pain but bounced back, balled up my fist and socked him in the face, bloodying his nose. Ginn fell to the ground.

Behind us, the Cessna was slowing, the doors opening. I could hear my name being called out.

Ginn suddenly produced his other gun with his left hand. He

twisted towards me and fired but not before I shuffled at the last moment. The slug ripped into my shoulder, causing me to fall to my back again. The pain was searing, like I had been burned. Ginn went to shoot once more but his gun clicked empty.

Frustrated, he tossed his empty gun aside and crawled to the one I smacked from his hand that was lying about ten feet away. With blood from his nose leaving a trail, I watched him make his way to his other weapon helplessly. There was no way I could beat him to it. The man was laughing as he crawled; a sadistic, devilish cackle.

Within seconds, Ginn was on his feet, his back to me. I spotted the Pilot and Doctor cautiously emerge from the fog. The Pilot had his gun out while the Doctor carried a bag. I could see them through the fog but they were only facing Ginn. They hadn't looked my way and I was still on the ground. I tried to yell, but only managed a cough that was drowned out by the engine.

"Ted?" the Doctor asked, waving at the fog remnants. "Is that you?"

"Hands where I can see them!' the Pilot yelled. "Keep them up!"

"Yes, it's me," Ginn stated, trying to right himself. His gun was suddenly not in his grasp. "So glad you guys made it. Man, that was a hell of a trip!" He tried to mimic my voice and was doing a great job.

"Show yourself," the Pilot demanded and kept his gun trained on him. "What was the gunshot for? Are you alone?"

The Doctor suddenly looked to the right. "Why is that car here?" she asked suddenly asked, her voice filled with concern. "Who's with you?"

"Nobody," Ginn said. "Nobody at all."

Ginn lowered his arms. His revolver slid from his sleeve. Neither the Doctor nor the Pilot noticed the gun in Ginn's hand. It was too late. Ginn was going to win.

My blood boiled and I tensed, gripping the crowbar with both hands. Using all my might, I sat up fast as if doing a sit-up and hurled the tool overhand at Ginn like I was throwing an axe.

The crowbar sunk deep into his back, the claw end curved up and out. The force of my throw knocked him forwards to the ground, in front of the Pilot's feet. While on his stomach, Ginn threw his gun aside and frantically waved his arms uselessly behind him, trying to grab a hold of the object impaling him in his back. Then, after a screech, inhuman and piercing, his hands fell to his sides. From my sitting position, I knew for a fact he was a dead man. I smiled before I felt my eyes grow heavy.

I kept those babies sharp, asshole.

CHAPTER FIFTY-SEVEN

"I've been shot," was all I could say but it came out weak. The Doctor's face came into view directly over me as she checked me over. She had a stethoscope and a small bag with her.

"I can see that. Let's get this thing off you," she said, undoing the Velcro and lifting the Kevlar vest from me and tossing it aside. I then felt the cold metal of the stethoscope on my bare and bleeding chest. From the corner of my eye, I could see the Pilot looking away and frantically scanning the area.

"Moves lie," I stated. "Getting shot hurts like fucking hell!" The pain in both my chest and shoulder wouldn't fade. Both were agonizing and achingly tortuous.

"Well, you have holes in you. What did you expect?" she said and whipped out a needle. Without asking, she plunged it into my arm and said, "This will help you."

Within seconds, the pain began to fade and I felt blissful. Relaxed, like all my muscles went slack. How was that possible? Was I dying?

"I killed the devil," I informed her.

Her face grew grim. "Let's get him in the plane quickly," she said to the Pilot. "We need a compress on the wound."

"Roger that," the Pilot responded. He was anxious to leave.

"Can you stand?" she asked me. I sat up slowly. She took my arms and lifted me to stand. The Pilot grabbed my other side. Soon, my feet were under me and I swayed. "Steady," she said and both of them guided me to the plane as I wobbled like an old man. They led me under a wing to an open door of the plane.

"The fog was so thick, we almost didn't land," she confessed.

"We need to move fast!" The Pilot shouted. "Some folks headed this way!" He nodded south. "They saw the plane circling. The fog is low level."

Bad people, from Salton Sea City maybe. Who Oliver warned me about. Headed towards us. Many of them, whoever they were.

"Wait..." I said and held my hand on the door. "We need to get my friend."

She planted her feet inside the plane. "Hurry up now." The Pilot was behind me, steadying, making sure I entered the cabin.

I grasped the door. "But he's the one who got me here!"

The Doctor had her hands out to me. "Please, there's no time!" she shouted and slid into a rear seat. The Pilot shoved me forward and I managed to sit. He then shut the door and the Doctor was on me, immediately, cleaning the blood from my wound. She then began taping a thick bandage on my chest.

The plane was cramped. Two seats in front, two in back. All the supplies were gone and there was plenty of room. That made me mad. They clearly had enough room last time!

"My friend! We need to find him!" I shouted.

She pointed to the front. "Look in the passenger seat!"

Jock was there. Somehow, they got him in before they got to me. Unconscious, but he had his head turned towards me, strapped into his seat. His face was cleaned and bandages were on his head, neck, and shoulder. He was shirtless and his left leg showed rips in his pants. I wondered if the Razorback did those.

"We got your friend out first," the Doctor said to me. "You kept passing out and quite frankly, he was easier to lift."

The Cessna pivoted, then turned west. The Pilot gunned the throttle like he did the day they left me and the cabin filled with a tremendous roar and I felt it in my stomach. "Is Jock okay?" I asked and tried to touch my friend but her hand dragged me back.

She shook her head. "He's been shot too, so we're trying to get the two of you out of here. Now, can you please relax and sit still?"

As I slunk back into my seat, I felt seat belts strapping me in. The Pilot suddenly shouted, "Enemy behind us!" The Pilot turned to us. "Are we all strapped in?"

"Roger!" the Doctor answered. I nodded but he didn't see me.

"Then I'm getting us airborne!"

Jock hadn't moved the entire time, his eyes remained shut. "Jock, you made it buddy! I couldn't have done it without you!" The Cessna grew even louder.

The scenery sped past me. Shrub, a fence, cacti, sand and shrub, they all zoomed by like I was watching a movie. The Cessna bounced once, twice, and then my stomach clenched as we went up, as if all my weight sank back down. The plane rocked slightly, the wings dipped, but then it began to climb. It had been years since I was in a plane and that was with a commercial jet. I also remembered the last time I was in a plane this small. We were heading to the same place we were going now, a splurge on a short trip that I always wanted to do. I found myself smiling, looking down, not missing the earth and desert below me. My home away from home. To hell with that fucking place. I had enough of the desert.

Ginn's body was lying in the dirt with my crowbar still in his back. That was my last image of him.

The Doctor had settled in some herself and she sat back. Looking at her then, she appeared to look younger than when I first met her at the airfield.

"Who was the woman?" she asked me. "She was dressed nicely."

"Her name was Maggie."

"She was deceased. We left her there. Sorry."

I didn't know how to respond to that. Instead, I asked, "So, was I worthy?"

She laughed. "You found it, didn't you?"

"Damn right I did," I said and turned to her. "No one was going to stop me. You hear me? No one."

"I believe you. So, who shot you though?" she asked me, rechecking bandage. "Was it Ginn?"

"Yeah, but I got him good. He's wearing my crowbar. I keep those babies sharp."

The Pilot turned around. He and the Doctor exchanged looks.

"Do you know him?" I asked.

"We were aware of him," the Doctor replied. "Not a nice man."

"What do you mean?"

The Doctor pressed her hand down on my bandage. "He was well known in the desert." She wouldn't elaborate then said, "So, you made it to Salton Sea and we're glad you did. That's the most important thing."

"Why did you choose that place and not something closer?" I asked her. "I had to travel through a ton of shit to get there."

"It's an easy landmark to get to. There isn't much in the Mojave to send you to and, quite frankly, it's closer to us. Fuel is a concern. The Salton Sea is huge and we use it to get our bearings. When we fly by moonlight, we can see the light reflecting from it and that was our clue to head north east to the airstrip. But telling you to meet at the sea itself if too cumbersome. It's simply too big." She paused and asked, "How did you solve the riddle, by the way?"

"An old man in a boat. He told me where to go. He knew right away."

"You found the Border Patrol Station, I take it."

"The place of judgement," I noted.

"It is, isn't it? Sorry, thought of it on a whim. I thought it as clever though." The Doctor paused and said, "You know, today was the first day coming here. You made it in good time. We were going to try one more day and then that was it. We were going to assume you ran into problems if you never showed."

"Rogues you mean."

"You were surrounded at the airfield. That couldn't have been an easy escape."

"Nothing I couldn't handle."

"We figured five or six days by foot, half that if you got creative," she said. "The Pilot had faith in you. He said if you were desperate enough to cross a minefield, you would try anything to get to the Salton Sea."

The Pilot gave me a thumbs-up and said, "I won the bet."

"I didn't know the mines were real though," I admitted.

"I assumed we'd find you a week from now camped out at the Salton Sea Airport," she confided. "I'm just glad you're here though."

"I stole the El Camino from Ginn."

The Doctor thought a moment, then said, "My Uncle had one once, I thought it was hideous. Was it supposed to be a car or a truck?"

"We can't decide," I said. "What was the bet?"

"Loser has to take the other's spot cooking for the others for a week."

Jock spasmed suddenly. "Is my friend going to be okay?" I asked her.

She shrugged. "We'll get him, and you, to our hospital right away."

"Twenty minutes," The Pilot said, right on cue.

She looked at me. "That was some journey you had."

My heart started to race and suddenly I grew excited. Twenty minutes away from seeing my family! In my excitement, I recounted all that happened since I last saw her. I felt lightheaded and wanted to talk.

"There are some good folks down there," I told her. "Song, a pregnant woman with three teenagers. She says she'll be safe but I don't know. A smart ass kid named Chachi lives in Kelso. You know, the town with no TV? Ha, he's got a temper. Watch out for him. Oh, Iris, she's a snake oil salesman, but the good kind. She's heading for Mexico. Grace, she's on horseback. She's upset but she's better now, on her way back to Tucson. And don't forget Oliver. That poor bastard just goes back and forth across the sea. He's content to do it too. Can you believe it?"

"Sounds like you had a lot of friends."

"They're good people. We can go back and get them."

"We have good people too."

I snapped my fingers, almost ashamed at what I hadn't mentioned yet. "Don't forget the folks at Coppertown. It's a small community in a rock quarry. On the other side of the Colorado River. Arizona side.

Great people. Daisy needs a chance, so do the others. Not much hope for Luke though. That's her father. He might have cancer. And then there's Sara..." I almost choked up.

"Sara?"

I fell silent. The Doctor smiled at me and patted my arm. She stared at me in silence, motherly, a bit concerned. I broke the ice.

"We're going to Catalina Island, aren't we?" I said.

She raised her eyebrows. "How did you know?"

"It makes sense. An island off the mainland with structure in place. My mother-in-law rented a house there once."

"That's a good guess," she said, nodding.

"Also, the Pilot said to you back at the airfield that he had to *land in the sky*."

"Ah." She glanced back at the Pilot.

"I've landed there too," I stated. "Catalina Island's airport is nicknamed *Airport in the Sky*. It's on the top of a mountain. I flew my family there once on a small plane."

The Pilot seemed to catch her look and turned around. "I said that? Huh."

Proud, I remarked, "Yep, you gave it away but it took me a while to figure it out."

The Doctor said, "We'll need to be more careful next time."

"How were you able to survive there on the island that day the gas attacks occurred?" I asked.

"Winds were strong that day, blowing east. None of the gas came west to us."

"It was a very coordinated effort," the Pilot said. "Mass confusion, mass hysteria. It killed quickly. Those of us on the island barely knew what happened."

"The power going out was our only clue," she said. "And then we got reports from boaters that the mainland was hit and it was awful. Some died just going near to shore. It was like a cloud that prevented us from going in. We waited for days for any sign of normalcy or rescue. Any type of rebuild. There was none. All signs of communication stopped and then there was only silence."

The Pilot continued. "Left alone, the infrastructure on the mainland caused mass destruction. No one there to monitor or maintain."

"We barely held on as a group," she confided.

"Is there anyone else left? Worldwide?"

"A military ship entered Avalon last year from New Zealand. They said they combed the entire west coast of North America and said most life is gone. Just pockets of people here and there. Most of it is unruly. As far north as Vancouver down to here. They were heading south to Central and South America next and then returning home but they reported seeing much of the same."

Avalon was the small harbor city on Catalina Island.

The Pilot chimed in. "America was hit the worst, but other countries suffered too. China, Japan, and most of Europe. Only smaller countries survived, places in Africa and the Middle East. Parts of India. Australia was hit too but New Zealand was spared."

"Why did no one come to help us?" I asked, incredulously.

The Doctor continued. "They needed to help themselves first. When the big countries stopped cold turkey, that meant food and water resources stopped as well. Think about it, when the first world stops making food, it's up to the little countries to feed themselves. They can't and won't have the resources to spread the wealth. They had to take care of their own first and hardly anyone wanted to branch out. There is a lot of incivility going on. Pirates, border attacks, you name it."

"What about our military? Where were they?"

"They've tried. There's a navy base south of Catalina at San Clemente Island. They helped set us up with supplies and fuel, but they also ventured off to help the mainland. Two ships sailed the first year it happened, sailed through Panama, and tried to locate Washington and New York. They reported all was lost and managed to coordinate with other US naval ships as to where to call port and set up rescue efforts. Problem is, there's hardly anyone left alive in this country. Not just from the gas, but the ensuing years. Whether it was a lack of medicine, prescriptions, hunger, or sheer brutality, the population that remains is tiny compared to what it once was. And that's true for the rest of the world."

The pain returned in my chest. Stabbing pain. My eyes watered. "Am I going to see my family soon?"

The Doctor scanned my face. "Hurry," she told the Pilot.

My eyelids drooped and I must have fallen asleep. I dreamt we were flying over our old neighborhood, the home still there, the neighbors clamoring for a barbeque. I dreamed that my boys were out front, playing hockey and kicking a soccer ball around. I dreamed that my wife was waiting there, at the front door, a smile on her face, happy, and content. Like when we were younger.

I jolted awake. The plane thumped hard on the landing, the Pilot now applying the brakes. We all pitched forward. Out the window, I could see the blue Pacific Ocean far down below, waves crashing into the rugged cliffs. Avalon was alive with many boats in the harbor. The Cessna then came to a sudden stop. The Pilot killed the engine, got out, and opened my door.

Throngs of smiling people were there waiting. They started clapping. I smiled at them, looking them over. An ambulance was parked nearby.

In the center, two boys walked forward, one bigger than the other. I recognized them right away. They had grown! Wayne, my oldest, looked almost as tall as me. His hair was long, like a surfer. Kevin, my youngest, had his hair cut short. He was growing up too. They were no longer the little boys I once knew.

They came to me and hugged me. My eyes welled up and I babbled my love for them. I held them hard, I didn't want to let go. My family was the sole reason I stayed alive for the last five years. I should have been with them.

They finally broke my grip but stayed close. I noticed they were both crying too.

A pair of paramedics ran over to Jock's door and opened it. One held a stretcher. Before they whisked him away, he reached back to me and shook my hand.

"Thank you," I said to Jock. He nodded and allowed them to take him away.

The group stopped clapping. An older lady moved slightly and a woman appeared there from behind her, holding a rose. The old lady was my mother-in-law and she looked grayer, a bit frailer than I remember.

The woman was my wife. She was still gorgeous, thinner, her hair darker than before. She looked a bit uncertain and reluctant. There were tears in her eyes and she tried to smile. Her Mother was gently pushing her forward but she resisted, almost shy. I wanted to run to her and swallow her up in my arms. Tell her I was sorry. Tell her I came back for her, for them, and start anew. Hoping she forgot the past, ready to move on. I felt weak and I struggled to walk. It was as if weights held me down.

She wouldn't walk any closer either. Why wouldn't she approach me? Was she remorseful? Not ready to forgive? Still angry, even after all these years? Hadn't she known what I had been through? The gap disturbed me and I tried to reason why.

She then waved to me.

I noticed her open hand.

A scar.

CHAPTER FIFTY-EIGHT

On the first day in the new place, I woke to a new bandage over my chest where the bullet had entered, and told I almost died on the operating table. I had lost a lot of blood and was lucky my blood type was very common. The bullet thankfully hit no vital organs and planted itself midway into my chest. Thankfully, that and a few fragments of the vest they were able to remove.

The rest of the days that followed were mostly a blur. I recall a hospital room, machines, lights, and IVs, all powered by generators and solar energy. Sights and sounds I thought I'd never see nor think I'd hear again. I slept, ate, talked, and zoned, the process repeating itself like a constant loop. Mostly I slept and carried with me nightmares from the last five years. They were vivid and relentless, enveloping me in nightly sweats. Half the time, I imagined myself still wandering, watching over my shoulder, scanning the desert floor for food or threats. I'd wake, trembling, thrashing about. Other nightmares included fights and skirmishes. Nurses shook me to calm me and one time and I struck out, gripping the wrist of a poor nurse and almost snapping it. The worst experience was the bed. It was too soft and lying there felt as if I was drowning in a sea. I wished they'd place me on the floor, but they denied that request, saying something about infections and safety.

My kids came to visit on occasion and we tried to catch up the best we could, but I had a hard time following. Exhaustion, I was told. Rest was needed. There simply was so much to discuss and the nurses shooed them away after just thirty minutes or so each time. I treasured those moments though and longed for my kids' return. I avoided speaking much of what happened to me out in the desert saying my life had generally sucked without them and that I wandered and stayed with groups of people. I spoke very little of the violence and the mayhem I encountered. I was more interested in what they had to say and how they had grown.

The boys' lives were far more innocent and cultured. They attended school and learned to sail, hunt, and fish. My oldest was training to become part of the security force, or cadet, for the island. My youngest wanted to be a fisherman and regularly went out to sea on various sailboats that circled the fish-laden island. Each islander now had a duty and all men and women were required to train for a skillset that enriched life on Catalina Island.

I was ashamed and sickened from what my life had done in retrospect and I often found myself gripping the rails on my bed in absolute fury when they left. I could have been here with them, I thought. I should have been here.

Sadly, my wife never came around. The boys offered little as to why. My youngest admitted she was confused and that was the most I could get from them. We last left each other on the airport runway, she at a distance, me getting hustled into an ambulance. The nurses here, at first, watched me with disdain, no doubt hearing how bad a husband I had been to one of their own. Then, strangely, days later, they would retreat quickly, seeming to fear me as if I were a monster in their midst. I wondered if Jock had opened his mouth.

Jock had been laid up in another bed down the hall. His condition was more serious and there was talk of him losing a kidney. He had been in and out of consciousness but was coming around. I never saw him at the facility.

When they decided there was nothing more for me to do but heal,

I was released with a new set of clothes that fit remarkably well. Upon leaving, I discovered I was not in a hospital, but a medical center located high up a mountain road near the island's only golf course. Tender and sore, I was carted off, literally, by golf cart, to a small bungalow near Avalon's harbor. The driver was a young man dressed in scrubs, whose name I already forgot once we got moving. Along the way, I passed curious onlookers who paused to gawk as if I was a celebrity or foe, I couldn't tell which.

When we arrived at the bungalow, I was told it belonged to an older man, a retired doctor from the mainland, who promised to watch my healing. It was a typical Catalina country home that was small, had a large porch, and was colored blue on the outside. When I asked about the location of my family's residence, I was met with an indifferent shrug by the young man in scrubs. I could have strangled him.

The doctor, called Dick, came out to greet me with a warm smile and firm handshake. Dick was shorter than me, had neatly styled gray hair, a small face, and a thin frame. He wore a Tommy Bahama shirt and shorts. He ordered me not to leave the premises until he gave permission. Breaking that rule meant banishment. Dick was serious about that term too; banishment. I wondered then what rules replaced the old on Catalina Island.

The bungalow had sweeping views of Avalon and its harbor from its rooftop patio. From there, I could see boats moored off the shore, fisherman casting lines off the large dock, and people walking and milling about the sidewalks. There was no fighting, no ruckus, no gunfire, or screams. There were no Rogues on the island. That, I was sure about.

I mostly sat on the rooftop for the next few days, taking in both the warming sun and visits with my sons. Each day, they pestered me with questions about my life abroad. Some I wouldn't to answer, those which had to do with violence. One day, Kevin refused to come up to meet me, watching me from behind a pillar on the staircase. Wayne came to me then, by himself, admitting they talked to Jock.

Jock informed them of what I had done those last five years on what little he knew. The man with the crowbar. The legend. At first, they didn't believe the little man, but he was quite convincing, Wayne said. I asked how much was told, and Wayne said enough.

The boys left me that day, promising to visit again. The next day, they never showed. A tear rolled down my cheek and I felt I lost them again. That night, a knock at the door jolted me when Dick announced I had a visitor.

It was my wife.

Dick's living room décor was tacky nautical. Boats, rudders, oars, and ropes lined the walls. Trinkets of drunken sailors and sea life sat atop wood cabinets. After an awkward hug and kiss on the cheek, Tracy and I sat opposite in the living room; she on a dark blue couch, me on a stiff, wooden chair. Dick wisely left us alone, retreating to his room with a good book (his words). Tracy stared at me and shook her head in disbelief. She still looked much of the same but I figured myself to be a ragged mess. She was still beautiful with long hair that fell over her shoulders. Her body looked thin and toned. Her eyes darted uneasily and she began to fidget.

"It's good to finally see you," I said, breaking the ice.

She looked up at me. "I can't believe you are here."

"Neither can I."

"You're probably wondering why I didn't come to see you at the hospital. Well, I needed time to process all of this and they told me not to rush things for you. They thought you might get riled up."

"You work there, don't you?"

"Yes," she said. "I worked the other wing while you were there. I did check up on you once but you didn't know it. You were out of it. You didn't look good. I mean, with all the tubes, bruises and blood."

"Just another day in paradise," I replied.

"They told me you were wandering in the desert. That you came across the airfield. That you were alive. They were so shocked to have found you."

"Pure luck," I nodded. "My friend, Jock, told me of the place and we went to see it for ourselves. It's not often you see an airplane out there."

She cocked her head. "Jock? The other man that came with you?"

"Deadly with a slingshot," I stated.

She considered that and continued. "Anyway, imagine my surprise. The boys and I, we thought, all this time…"

"I was dead?"

She nodded. "Like everyone else."

She struck me as being uncomfortable, even in the presence of the man she spent nearly twenty years married to, counting current time. Yet, inexplicably, I felt the same, as if we were strangers and that kept me planted in my chair. She held her arms, legs, and hands inwards.

"Was it true?" she finally asked. "What you did?"

I wasn't sure how to respond. "You mean the supposed affair?"

"No," she answered. "You killing people."

"Oh. It was called survival. And I only killed bad guys."

She nodded, then smoothed out her pants with her hands. "I can't imagine what life was like out there. We heard…stories." She then shook her head. "I mean, how did you learn that stuff?"

I smirked. "Like I wasn't capable before?"

"Yes," she admitted, too quickly for my sake. "I didn't know you had it in you."

I sat back and told her what happened, glossing over the early weeks and struggle after the gas. The last phone call we shared, the subsequent car crash, wandering from town to town, searching for her and the boys. Then meeting Matias. How he trained me, how he helped me become a fighter. The story of the bear, the crowbar, the Hellion I fought, Bale the warlord, it all spewed out like I was describing a movie, with intermittent parts hardly in order. She grew confused, stopping me on occasion, asking this and that, trying to follow, then becoming exhausted. And that was only year one.

"You need to tell Kathryn that Reggie passed away," I informed her. "About six months after the gas. I went to visit them, in Pinecrest, thinking you were there too."

She didn't look sad. "Did he die from dementia?" she asked.

"Hanging," I said. "Warlords attacked Pinecrest and he, well, it wasn't good." I then spoke of the meeting of Sara and Darcy, two SkyBlue jet employees who helped me find the missing plane, although Kathryn, her mother, wasn't aboard that flight. The subsequent attack on Coppertown and the good people there. Meeting her brother Johnny who admitted that my family was still alive, but that he wouldn't tell me where and simply cast me out like garbage.

She blushed at that. "Johnny takes a sailboat and comes down a few times a year. He never told me you came to visit him."

I gritted my teeth. "That little prick."

I glossed over the next four years and my travels around the southwest, always ending up at Matias' camp and Coppertown. Never finding my family. Battles for food and survival, too many to repeat. Most of it a blur.

"There's too much," she said, stopping me. "What about the woman? Did she die?"

I first thought she meant Sara, but then I realized Sara's mention was in passing. "Who, Maggie?" I asked. "The woman in the photos?"

"Yes."

"I don't know," I lied. "I never saw her again." I didn't want Tracy to know that Ginn offered Maggie up, right up to the last minute. Five years after the supposed affair.

She didn't seem to believe me. I knew that look from her. Deep thought, scrunching her lips.

"I was framed by Ginn and I think you know that now," I said. I got up and sat down next to her on the couch.

"I don't know what to think," she said.

"He framed me all along. He admitted it to me."

"I haven't spoken to him in years."

"If it wasn't for you and the boys being alive, I would have died a long time ago," I admitted. Tracy smiled at that and patted my leg. I caught her arm and twisted her palm. She tried to pull away. There was no hiding it. She had the scar, as did I.

"Your turn," I told her. "Tell me about the scar."

A clock chimed at that instant, reminding me of the cuckoo clock Ginn bashed in not too long ago inside his plush tent. She was searching for words, and I assumed a lie was coming.

"Brenda and Stan told me you dealt with him," she said.

Who was Brenda and Stan? "The Doctor and the Pilot, you mean?"

Tracy nodded. "I've worked with Brenda over the years at the medical center. Stan is one of the few Pilots that were here on the island when the big event happened. He had army training as a medic too."

"How is Don? The driver of the water truck?"

Tracy's face grew grim. "Unfortunately, he didn't make it."

"Sorry to hear."

"Anyway, they said...you killed Ginn."

"With my crowbar. Fuck yeah, I did."

That caught her by surprise. "A crowbar?"

"You'd be surprised at what that damn tool can do."

She leaned her head back and stared at the ceiling. "Did we even own one? In our garage at home?"

"I stuck it in your boyfriend," I said, then pointed back towards the ocean. "It's still there, matter of fact. Go look."

That didn't faze her. "He was hardly my boyfriend. He was just... someone to talk to. I felt lonely. Suspicious of you too. You had changed. Your boss Randall was known to have affairs and I figured you were doing the same."

"Ginn had a different opinion of your relationship," I replied, snidely.

She agreed. "I know he did. That's why I didn't trust him. That's why I didn't meet up with him. After the gas, like he wanted."

"Your scar. Want to tell me what you traded for?"

Tracy stood and walked to the door. I thought she would leave. She then turned to me and said, "What would you have done in my shoes?"

"You mean if I found out you were having an affair?" I asked.

She nodded. I thought hard and came up with the same result. Wish hateful shit on her. Crossing her arms, she then said, "I didn't really believe him at first, about the world ending. I thought it was just bullshit so I didn't even tell anyone, except my mother. She said she was coming out to Catalina anyway and that I should join her. Reggie was making her crazy and she needed to get away so she rented a house here. The same one we visited before. Mother knew something was wrong about us anyway and she flew out a day earlier. But the fact Ginn was going to produce evidence of you screwing around, which I demanded first, was enough to send me into a panic and get the hell out of Orange County and far away from you. Period."

"So, your scar was to make the remainder of my life a living hell?"

She jumped on it. "I didn't know you would be scouring the desert for the rest of your life! I hoped the guilt would eat at you when you came home to an empty house! That's what I wanted you to see! How empty your life could become without us! That would be your hell!"

"Orange County was wiped out!"

"I didn't know it would be! And besides, I didn't know he would fucking cut me! Look at this!" She flashed her palm at me. "You never saw this monstrosity because you left for Vegas before the gas! That was when he did this to me! This goes to show how much attention you pay to me. None."

I calmly let the following words sink in. "Ginn cut me because he helped me, helped us, become rich. His deal with me was vague. I didn't know I would be cut either, it happened so fast. Anyway, some people thought of him as the devil, and that Ginn wanted my soul in return."

"You should have told me about the scar," she quipped.

I hit her with, "Goes to show you how much attention you paid to me."

She paused. "Still, I would have listened."

"I didn't believe it at the time. I thought the scar as a childish prank. I was giving him drugs from work for the secrets he was giving me. I could have gotten into trouble. Lots of insider stuff. Probable jail time if caught. Anyway, little did I know he used the drugs to keep himself and his men relatively healthy and disease free after the gas."

She interjected. "When I was in Las Vegas that weekend before the gas, I stayed at a different hotel from the one he worked at. We were saying goodbye and I only offered a hug. That's it. Then he cut me, proclaiming his love and swearing to hurt you like no other. I pushed him away. Called him a lunatic and told him to get away from me. The cut was very painful. But when I left, he was yelling at me, professing his undying love. I drove straight home, regardless of what you think, but lied about San Diego and shopping on the way home. I needed time to think, so I parked at a rest stop and cried. That's what took me so long. He was very convincing that you were cheating on me."

"What did you get out of the deal?" I asked. This was what I was waiting for.

"Just that you'd suffer as I had. Feel the pain about being deceived."

I said, "Ginn tried to keep me in Las Vegas. He wanted me at his side, probably be part of his crew. He called me a partner. He knew the gas was coming."

"I have no idea what his intentions were then."

"And you were fine with that?"

She raised her voice. "Have you not thought about what you did? You fucking cheated on me! How was I supposed to react?"

"You know the truth! I never cheated on you! Ever! Still to this day!"

"Now I do!" she wailed. "Not back then! Did you see the photos? I mean, how did you put yourself in that position even?"

She was right about that. "It was just some drinks and I got drugged. But you and Ginn, there had to be more."

"All we did was talk! Talk about you!"

"Sure. Yeah, right," I said, rolling my eyes. "He went on and on about you two living a perfect life, white picket fence..."

"He was delusional! Couldn't you tell?"

I stood up fast and approached her. "So, there was no sex, no kissing? None of that?" She cowered as I spoke. There was fear in her eyes. I then realized I came on too strong, in attack mode, and slowly backed away.

Tracy shook her head. "No, there was none. He wanted it, but I told him I needed more time."

"When did you first meet him?" I asked.

"I don't know. Maybe a couple of months before the gas," she replied.

I paced around the room. Just like her, the information was coming in too fast. It was hard to decipher what was true and what wasn't. I missed something all along, the timing of it all. Ginn was vague with his demand of mine. It wasn't what I thought.

"So, when he said he wanted something precious of mine, he meant you all along," I declared. "It was only you he was after. The entire time."

Matias would be laughing right about now. I had it coming. I recalled his story about Johann's Violin that he told me once, about the amateur violin player who summoned help from a Gypsy musician, despite their language differences. The Gypsy agreed to teach the amateur but wanted something in return when the lessons ended and that was the student's own prized violin. The amateur never clearly understood what was bargained and he lost.

"You two already knew each other when he cut me," I reasoned.

"I suppose so."

Tracy then pulled on the doorknob and opened the door. I quickly slammed it shut and she jumped. "The Doctor said you had another lover!" I barked. "Back in the bunker! Out there!" I pointed, meaning the desert.

She stood firm. "You really want to go there?"

"Yes, I do!"

"After your affair? After five years of thinking and believing you were dead, you dare fucking ask me if I had another lover?"

"Hell, yeah!"

She confronted me, face to face. "What? Did you think you'd come all the way over here and reconnect with me? Work on our marriage? Forgive and forget?"

I calmed down a moment. "That's what I spent the last five years trying to do."

"He's a cop on the island," she muttered. "I'm sorry, but I thought you were deceitful and dead."

That felt like a punch to the gut. I wanted to throw up.

Tracy said, "Look, when the plane came back, they asked me if I wanted you back. If it wasn't for the boys..."

"You would have said no," I finished for her.

"I don't know. I truly don't. I've learned to hate you for the last five years. The boys answered and they went to get you."

I made my way to the couch and flopped down. "I'm sorry. For all of this."

"I am too. It's very confusing."

Tracy sat down next to me. "This is your chance to make up lost ground with the boys. Be with them. Learn with them. Life is much different now. They need their father."

"I missed them so much. And you, too."

Tears welled in her eyes. She got up and walked to the door. "We live at 324 Journey, bottom level. Please let me know before you just show up. Kevin is a bit freaked out by you."

"Freaked out? Why?"

"The stories he heard about you were very graphic," she sighed, wiping her cheek. "I think Wayne is in awe of you, however. He is amazed that the legendary crowbar man was his own father and he never knew."

That struck me as unbelievable. "You guys heard the stories all the way out here?"

"Yes," she sighed. "Don, the truck driver, knew people along the Colorado River. He used to spread these tales he heard. They made for good campfire stories on the beach."

Being humble, I said, "I bet most of it is untrue."

"If I were you, I'd keep the stories PG-rated."

I laughed. "Got it."

With her hands on her hips, she took me in and smoothed her hair to the side. "It's so surreal, you know? You being alive. Finding you out there. You being this hardcore, fighting machine. It's like a fairytale."

"I guess there's a lot you don't know about me," I replied.

"It doesn't matter anymore, does it?"

"No, I guess not."

She made a move to the door and stopped once more. "Oh, the mayor wants to see you. He wants you to recount your life to paper. What you did out there. People want to know. I just hope, for our sake, you don't mention, any, you know, infidelities."

"I was celibate the entire time. I told you that."

"Maybe you shouldn't have been," she said and walked out the door.

CHAPTER FIFTY-NINE

The next day, I contemplated paying my family a visit and showing up there unannounced. I stood on the rooftop in a robe, feeling a cool breeze, watching the calm sea when I heard the doorbell downstairs. Not a minute later, Jock made his way to the top and he stopped when he saw me.

"Nice view," he said, taking it in. "But mine's better."

"Hey, buddy," I answered. I was glad to see him. Surprisingly, he was dressed normally in a surfer t-shirt and shorts. On his feet, he wore flip-flops. He definitely settled into island life already. Jock walked to me and we hugged. I missed the coyote getup.

"I'm a few houses down, staying with a family," he said. "Four-bedroom house. Their kid has a mad collection of comic books too."

"They told me you may lose a kidney," I said.

Jock waved it off. "Ah, they said that days ago. I'm fine, bro. I'm on antibiotics now. Should do the trick. Ginn's bullet nicked a few things but didn't do much damage."

"Can I get you anything?" I asked. "They seem to have a lot of shit here. Yesterday, I had a Coke and fries. Believe that?"

Jock brushed it off. "Nah, I'm good. I chowed down on some taco's this morning, even had some ice water." He shook his head in disbelief, then whipped out a stick of gum. "Spearmint. Who knew I'd miss that?" He offered some to me and I declined.

"I met your boys," he continued with a smile, stuffing the gum into his mouth. "You did well raising them, Ted."

"Thanks," I replied.

He nodded as if he already knew. "Met your wife too."

"Oh?"

"You're an idiot, Ted."

I let him have that but said, "Well, someone else has her now."

He seemed genuinely stunned. "I didn't know."

"The doctor who lives here told me they've gone to the mainland to survey and inspect what was left," I said, changing the subject. "There's a lot of damage and ruins, but there are signs of life. Stray cats and dogs, rats, birds, and people."

"People," Jock said and shuddered. "How'd they manage that?"

"They look like cavemen. Covered in hair, animal skins, and lesions. Apparently, they forage for food among the remaining houses and buildings. Some of them are fat. Some have missing limbs. Their language is a mix of English, Spanish, and grunts."

Jock thought a moment. "We're safe out here, right? I mean, look around. We're on an island. No one can attack us. Right?"

I nodded towards the harbor. "There's lots of water between us and them. The Rogues will never get to us."

"Sharks too."

I thought about that, then studied the cliffs that overlook the harbor. "I guess we'd have to put cannons up there, won't we?" I noted, half-serious.

"Pirates, you think?"

"I don't think these Islanders know what awful men can do. They've had it too good for too long," I said with a deep sigh.

"The desert," Jock said as if it was a question.

"What about it?"

He turned to me. "Do you think about the people we left behind?"

I glanced across the harbor and could barely make out the Orange County shoreline some twenty miles east, just beyond the marine layer settling in. I thought of Matias, the folks at Coppertown, Daisy, and her father Luke. Sara. Then, the others we met along the way before we found the Salton Sea. I wondered if Ginn's body was still out there, with my crowbar cemented in his body.

"All the time," I finally answered.

I then thought back to the Rogue camp, wondering what kind of disarray they must be in without their dear leader. A new warlord would emerge and assume control though. Moonshine showed them promise and someone else would take up the reigns to lead them. They would branch out like ants, finding new nests, and overtaking others. I feared that was just the natural order of life now.

Jock said, "They're talking of rebuilding out there. In the desert. They had a good thing going and now they want to try again. Same place, only this time, make it heavily guarded. I heard them discuss it when I was in bed. The Doctor lady said they still lack essentials only the desert can provide and that's their only hope."

"You're joking, right?"

"Wish I was," he said. "But the fact is, Catalina is starting to suffer. They are running out of medicine and water. One of the aquifers that provides water to the island had a buildup of algae and it's made some people sick. They don't have the resources to clean it anymore. And while they have some fuel left, they know that will run out too, so their window to explore is running out."

I was in total disbelief. They were thinking of going to a place I called hell and were desperate to leave what was a safe haven. "I can't believe what I'm hearing."

"They plan to go in and hunker down with an armed force, dude. Create a second settlement. One near the Colorado River. They said that the river has the best source of clean water around and they plan to occupy it."

Great. That sounded like an invasion force. "There's no way I'm going back," I said, sternly. "That's crazy talk. I'm retired. I have my family again."

Jock looked down. "Your oldest son signed up to train for it."

That was a low blow and my gut churned. I knew my son was head-strong, but not stupid. When he said he was training to be a cop, I thought he meant to protect and serve on the island. Did my brother-in-law, the former cop, have something to do with this?

"They're idiots," I said, tightening my robe, ready to walk to the house where my family was staying. "The fact they'll be flying back and forth across this strait? If there are survivors with boats, they'll see that. They'll probably try to come over. And dealing with the Rogues in the desert? Are they crazy?" I began to stomp around the rooftop, yelling, "They're killers and rapists! Has no one thought this through?"

"Maybe they need an insider's perspective," he noted. "Experience."

I was at a loss. "Who do we talk to?"

"Dude, they've already decided. It's a go. The family I'm staying with said some people here have island fever. Many Islanders have gone nuts. They only lived here part-time and some were just visiting on vacation. Isolation gave them the heebie-jeebies. Twice they had riots. They need to branch out, find other resources, and establish contact with others. Find peaceful solutions."

Island fever? Riots? This whole time, I thought Catalina had it good. As I stared at Jock, I then realized he seemed to know quite a bit and shuffled his eyes like he had a secret to tell. Then, the obvious hit me. "Were you sent here to recruit me?"

At first, he didn't know how to respond. Then, he glanced away, out to the ocean. "I know you've only had a week to recover," Jock said to me, then asked a question only the truly insane would ever dare ponder. He asked it as if it was a necessity and one he'd rather avoid.

"You ready to come out of retirement, crowbar man?" he asked.

"Hell no."

He patted me on the shoulder and handed me a piece of paper. "They found this letter addressed to you shoved at the bottom of your backpack. I didn't read it, but the nurses said it was personal. It is still sealed."

With that, he left.

I opened the letter and read it. It was from Sara.

Ted, I've missed you terribly all these years and have always wanted to open up to you. It has taken me some time to get over my sickness but Manson says I've been getting better and stronger as time goes by. I don't blame you for what happened to me. In fact, I feel relieved that you were able to help me escape and that I was able to share some nice moments with you. The most important aspect is survival and I've been able to do that, thanks to you. I hope you do find your family and find them well. If you don't or run into problems there, know that I love you and always will.

I am ready if you are.

Love, Sara.

When did she put this into my backpack? I recalled the time I was leaving Coppertown last time. Just before I slipped through the metal opening in the camp.

"You didn't find it yet, did you?" she asked.

"Find what?"

"Never mind."

She must have meant this letter. I tucked it into my pocket and stared out over the ocean. I did miss Sara and often wondered if we were meant to be together. Maybe Tracy and I drifted too far apart. Too far to resolve anything. Maybe I realized that long ago and put myself into that strange predicament with Maggie and allowed myself to be vulnerable because I wanted out. I wasn't sure what I really felt about my wife anymore.

Maybe this was her end of the deal with Ginn all along. To make me suffer as she did. To be with someone else.

I felt some closure knowing my family was well though. Like I had done my duty. Nagging thoughts began to swirl in my mind, however.

The desert. The Rogues. Sara.

I shook my head knowing damn well I was going back.

to be continued...

ABOUT THE AUTHOR

The author is a Canadian transplant (and naturalized US citizen as well) and has lived in South Orange County, California, for many years.

His first book, *The Doomsday Drifter*, can be found on Amazon and other outlets through his publisher, Draft2Digital. It is a dark thriller and the first of a trilogy. The second book is titled *Wrecking Man* while the third and final book is called *Sekret Agent*. A new book, just released on May 1st, 2023, is a time-travel thriller called *The Reincarnist*. It is only available on Amazon through Kindle and Kindle Unlimited.

His other works include *The Lost Safari*, a book for the young adult genre and is available on Amazon and Kindle Unlimited. Another young adult book, *A Tricked Life*, is available as well.

He is a college graduate in accounting (blech), married to a Valley Girl, father to two awesome boys, owner of the world's most likable dog, and lover of all red wines. Cheers!

Feel free to check out his site for other books, updates, and free script reads:

www.markdasilvawriter.com